Mackenzie —
Stars

HARVEST

and

OF

Shadows...

SIGHS

SIERRA SIMONE

Cover Design: Hang Le
Cover Image: Vania Stoyanova
Cover Models: Shacori Valentine, Keira Leilani

Editing: Erica Russikoff of Erica Edits
Proofing: Nancy Smay of Evident Ink, Michele Ficht
Interior Layout: Caitlin Greer

Content Warning

The prologue of this book contains a depiction of suicide by poison in the nineteenth century. This section can be skipped and its events inferred from later chapters.

This book also has a character who experienced sexual violence once; this violence happens off page, before the events of the story, but it is referenced throughout.

There was three kings into the east,

Three kings both great and high,

And they hae sworn a solemn oath

John Barleycorn should die.

—"John Barleycorn"
Robert Burns

Part One

Prologue

1874

Estamond

Obviously, Estamond Kernstow Guest's final wish was that her husband would fuck the nursemaid.

An hour before she wished this, Estamond gave her sleeping husband a fond kiss on the cheek and an equally fond pat on his cock, which even at rest, was considerable—and on its own, testament to why her breasts were full of milk for their fifth child. But of course she loved all the parts of him, not just his wonderful organ. She loved his big, careful hands and his mighty heart, which thumped so steadily inside his chest. She loved his expression when she made him laugh, which was an expression of stunned wonderment. As if the first forty years of his life had been so friendless and lonely that he'd never learned to laugh, and doing it now was like discovering whisky for the very first time.

She loved his eyes, green and brown like the woods of the valley, and she loved how they were always soft with love for her. She loved how wild and beautiful they became when he made love.

She loved him, and she hated to leave him. She knew if he were in her shoes, he wouldn't be able to do his duty by the land, because it would mean leaving *her*. And there was much Estamond hadn't been able to learn in her thirty-three years on this Earth, but she did know one thing as well as she knew her own name: Randolph Guest loved her more than he loved anything else.

She sighed as she lit a lamp and trimmed it down so it wouldn't wake her husband. Perhaps if he loved her less, she wouldn't have to go to the thorn chapel tonight.

Perhaps if he loved her less, this would be easier.

Perhaps she wouldn't mind leaving. Perhaps then she wouldn't worry if he'd survive her having to go.

After pushing herself off the warm bed—still slightly rumpled from their earlier fuck—Estamond dressed herself. No need for a corset, no need for petticoats or jewelry or any of the other things she normally wore. She buttoned and laced herself into a simple white gown with deep pockets, braided her dark hair, and tucked a note and a small bottle into her dress. She grabbed a pair of sturdy boots, which she didn't put on. Not yet.

Every time she bent down, she bit back a sigh of discomfort. Truth be told, it had been a bit too early to welcome Randolph back inside her body after little Samuel's birth. The babe was only three weeks old, and though her bleeding was well over, she still felt the soreness of his entrance into the world. But she hated going without sex—had hated it ever since she learned what sex was as a girl up on the moors—and no man could be gentler and sweeter than her Randolph. And besides, she couldn't go into the thorn chapel tonight without feeling him inside her one last time. So if there was soreness, she welcomed it. It would be like he was still with her even as she laid herself down on the altar.

The way it should be on Lammas night, she thought, a touch unhappily. Estamond didn't usually feel unhappiness—she could no more be unhappy than a fox or a cat could be unhappy—but today was a day for exceptions.

Normally, Lammas day was a good day, a day for hot bread and sweat-slick sins in the chapel. It was her favorite feast day, if she was honest. Everyone assumed that she loved the more dangerous revels, Beltane with its carnality or Samhain with its stark, heady power, but Estamond was a Kernstow. She'd grown up in a waste of gorse high above the welcoming shelter of the valley. She'd grown up hunting mistletoe and singing to the moon.

She'd had enough wild magic for lifetimes.

And so the homey, domestic harvest of Lammas—all grain and bread and dolls for children and country charms and courting—*that* she loved, *that* she longed for.

Just as a tame person might crave the thrill of Samhain or Beltane, so a wild girl craved the ripe warmth of Lammas.

Until tonight, that was.

Tonight, Estamond craved nothing. Tonight, she mourned.

But true to form, the mournfulness did not last. Even as she murmured farewell to her husband, her sometimes wild god. Even as she went into the nursery and kissed each sleeping child gently on the forehead.

The babe, Samuel, stirred the tiniest bit in his wet nurse's arms but did not wake.

"I'm going outside," Estamond told the sleepy-eyed nurse, who was a girl of just twenty. Estamond had never hired a nurse before—bucking convention, she'd breastfed all her children herself. But after her mother's message last week, Estamond had known she would go to the thorn chapel tonight, and she couldn't leave her newborn unprovided for. And so she found Janie from the next village over, whose sweetheart had died of a cough when she'd been swollen with their child. She was unmarried and plump and pretty, and when she first came to Thornchapel and met Randolph, she'd blushed all the way from her cheeks to the tops of her milk-swollen breasts. That was enough for Estamond. Any girl who could see how handsome Randolph was under all his shy quiet was a girl worth having around, especially given Estamond's task this Lammas. Estamond hired her on the spot and had Janie bring her own babe to Thornchapel to raise alongside the Guest children.

Janie nodded dozily at Estamond and said nothing. Everyone in the Thorne Valley knew what happened in the thorn chapel on feast days. And even though the Guests had put out that they wouldn't attend the village festival or host their own Lammas feast due to Samuel's birth, it still wouldn't seem unusual for one of them to go out to the woods alone.

After all, some things were necessary.

Yes, some things were.

Estamond had one last stop before making her way to the maze, and that was her beloved library. She took what she needed, drank in the moon-bright room one last time, and then left Thornchapel as silent as a cat, unmarked by anyone, not even the nurse who'd already fallen back asleep or the husband whose bed she just left.

She was alone.

If you don't do it at Lammastide, then it will be done at Samhain.

It will be one of us.

I'll do it in the hills.

The light from her single lantern was weak, as Estamond well knew it would be, but the maze's path was as familiar to her as the taste of Randolph's lips or the whorls of her children's hair, and she didn't falter, she didn't hesitate or trip. She even gave Adonis's foot a pat as she slipped down between the doomed lovers and the fountain and into the tunnel.

And then to the woods.

After a girlhood of scrambling over bleak hills and through punishing heather, the verdant woods of Thornchapel bothered Estamond not at all. In fact, she found her step slowing as she walked, she found herself savoring the warm summer night. She listened to the charming rustle of hedgehogs and watched the occasional flap of a bat through the glow of her lantern. Owls called out their territorial cautions, and more than once, Estamond's light caught the reddish flash of fox eyes before the creature darted back into the trees. The moors had always felt half dead to Estamond, scoured as they were by wind and rain, but the woods of Thornchapel—those were *alive*.

And on Lammas night, they were more alive than usual.

Drums beat faintly as she approached the clearing in the woods, and she could hear the soft strains of the Other-music suffusing the air. Air now gone electric and stirring, as if merely to breathe it was to become intoxicated. Any other Lammas, any other feast, and Estamond would have reveled in the intoxication, she would have drenched herself with it.

She had grown up with the wild god carved onto her very hearth, holding his opposing spirals in each hand as his antlers caught flares of firelight and shadow. She'd grown up knowing the feasts and what they meant. She'd grown up knowing a secret that only the country folk still knew.

The spirals don't just mean life and death, her mother had told her. *The wild god holds more than life and death in balance.*

What could be more important than life and death? Estamond had asked.

Here and there, daughter. The wild god keeps in his body the boundary between here and there. And I will tell you another secret.

What is that? Estamond had asked.

Here and there, and life and death...are very nearly the same thing.

The Kernstows kept the knowledge, they lived by it. And the country folk still knew it too, deep in their hearts, for at every feast they still celebrated summer and winter, the green and the brown. They still told stories of *there*, of the cruel, merry things that lived there, and they still honored and feared them.

Gods and saints, Estamond's mother had replied when Estamond asked what lived there. *Saints and gods.*

In the house with the carving of the wild god, there'd been a Bible also, and a small crucifix by the door. The Kernstows reverenced both. After all, St. Brigid was with them on Imbolc, was she not? And the Virgin on May Day? And didn't the parishioners bring their first loaves to the church on Lammas?

Didn't the holy dead demand prayers and adoration on All Saints' Day?

But for the first time in her life, Estamond wondered what the God of the Bible would say to her now as she passes through the menhirs and follows the stone rows to the thorn chapel. After all, there had been a church here once, a church built after Wessex had washed against the rocky crags of Dartmoor. Because Wessex had brought the Guests, and the Guests had brought their brooding death god from across the sea.

And the god brought his church, with his own cakes and ale, his own holy words and rites.

It was always God's place, her mother had said once about the thorn chapel.

Which god? Estamond had asked.

It was always God's place, her mother had repeated. Pointedly.

Then she'd added, *before the Guests, before the Romans, before the druids. When the thorn chapel was alone and the door was nothing but a shimmer in the air. It was God's before all that.*

And that was as much an answer as Estamond was ever going to get about which god reigned among the thorns.

The Other-drums throbbed and thumped through the clearing, loud and louder as Estamond entered the chapel itself. She could hear the voices now, the singing and the chanting that seemed to come from the air itself. Her lantern-light flickered over stretches of tumbling roses, which were blown wide open and trembling in the breeze, quivering like a woman waiting for a lover's touch. The moon shone down on the grassy hillock where the altar once stood—or rather, still stood today, just under a blanket of thick, emerald grass.

It could be any other Lammas in the chapel. Any other rose-scented night with drums and voices calling. Any other warm, moonlit feast.

It could be.

It would be.

Except for the door.

Estamond walked around the altar with the lantern raised high, even though the moon on its own illuminated the door well enough. The first time she'd seen it two years ago, it had been merely a glimpse, a flash of wood and old iron out of the corner of her eye. And then it became more—it stabilized or solidified or pushed its way through whatever thick magic normally kept it hidden—and every feast night, she saw it plain as anything, as if it had been built there yesterday.

Or as if it had always been there.

And then every feast night turned into every new moon, and then every new moon turned into every night. Until it stood there even in the broad daylight. Until even Randolph could see it.

She hadn't told her mother, of course she hadn't.

Because while, yes, her mother was the only one who approved of Estamond marrying Randolph—who had in fact foretold it using copper spoons and blood cut from the tender inside of one of Estamond's thighs—it was also her mother who'd warned Estamond not to fall in love with Randolph Guest.

It will be that much harder if the door opens and the Thorn King must do his duty by the land, her mother had said. *It will be that much harder for you to do your part.*

She knew what part her mother meant. She meant Estamond should kill him if he would not go willingly.

At the memory, Estamond's hand went to her pocket. She could no more kill Randolph than she could kill her own children, than she could kill her own parents, or her twin brother. It was simply impossible. She hadn't known it was impossible then, when she married a Guest, but she knew it now.

So she hadn't told her mother about the door. But her mother knew anyway.

If you don't do it at Lammastide, then it will be done at Samhain.

It will be one of us.

I'll do it in the hills.

That's what her mother's note said—and nothing more. Not that it needed to say more, Estamond could read the meaning loud and clear. If she did not kill the Thorn King on Lammas, then her mother would kill Estamond's father or her brother—or maybe even herself—on Samhain night. And that was the best possible scenario, because there was one other at the Kernstow farmstead her mother could kill, and if she did that, then Estamond would set the moors afire with her despair.

And her mother wouldn't do it in the thorn chapel, where Estamond could try to stop her. No, she'd do it up in the hills, where there'd be no way to find her. No way to predict her movements or protect her family.

No, if Estamond didn't close the door, her mother would. And her mother would close it at such a cost that they might as well already be dead.

The day after she'd received the note, Estamond had dragged her tender postpartum body to the farm to beg her mother to change her mind, but she was gone on one of her mysterious errands and her father was up with a flock near Reavy Hill. Only her twin brother had been there, which was dangerous for a number of reasons.

"Esau," she'd said in surprise as he ducked out of the farmhouse door to welcome her. The house looked as it always looked—damp stone and dark windows—fuchsia foxgloves peeking around the low stone walls surrounding the house, and the hills blushing purple with blooming heather.

And Esau looked as he always looked: tall and lean and broad-shouldered, his hair the same dark brown as hers, his eyes the same glittering emerald. As children, they roamed and romped all over the moors, hiding and darting far away from the drudgery of the farm, pretending to gather herbs and plants for their mother. They matched in more than looks—they matched in wildness, in anger and in thrill—and so perhaps it wasn't a surprise what happened between them later, on the same moors where they used to play so innocently.

At least, their mother hadn't been surprised. After she'd midwifed the child, she'd used the birth blood in the spoons and smiled to herself at what she saw. The boy—Esra, they named him—grew up utterly doted on and pampered by his Nanna and Poppa, as well as by his mother and father. And if his mother and father had the same parents, if they looked alike, if he must not tell certain people who his mother was—well, that all seemed normal enough to Esra. Every farmstead tucked into the moors had its own strangenesses and peculiarities, after all, and anyway, people already expected the Kernstows to be strange.

"Is he here?" Estamond had asked, her heart twisting. Esau and Esra had been the sacrifice she'd had to make in order to marry a Guest—a necessary sacrifice in her mother's eyes, but a sin in Esau's. It was a sin he would never forgive her for, she knew, and yet, she couldn't quite bring herself to regret it. Esra was safe and happy, and she'd never begrudge Esau finding another woman to vent all his feral passions at, and so he could also be happy if he chose. She'd gained the thorn chapel in return for leaving her brother and her son behind, she'd gained the stones and the altar and the door and the place that belonged to her family by ancient right. She'd gained five more children for the one she left to her parents, she'd gained a sweet, devoted husband in place of her twin brother. A brother whose love was like the moors themselves—howling and desolate.

And yet, she still missed them, missed them like she missed the rain on her face or the mist in her hair.

"He's started at the village school," Esau had told her, stepping close enough to seize her in his arms, which he did. "Now, why are you here?"

"Mother," she'd gasped. "Mother sent me a note. She wants me to kill the Thorn King at Lammastide."

"Or it will be one of us," Esau said. "I know."

"Not Esra," she begged. "Please."

Esau had growled then, hauling her even tighter to his chest. "If you would do your duty, then no one would have to die at all."

"No one here, you mean," she hissed, struggling. "You want me to choose between my husband and you."

"I want you to choose between the Guests and the Kernstows," Esau said, scowling. "They stole the thorn chapel from us. Why should you cry over a dead Guest now?"

"They stole it *thirteen hundred years ago*," Estamond said, still struggling in his arms. "When will we forgive them for it? Does a man really deserve to die for what his forefathers did that long ago?"

"He deserves to die because he is the Thorn King," Esau pronounced, his voice as firm as his hold on her. "It's his fate. If I were born to be the Thorn King, then it would be my fate as well."

With some private shame, Estamond had to admit that Esau was much better suited to the role of wild god than her quiet Randolph. If some quirk of fate had meant that Esau had been born a Guest, if he'd been given the torc and asked to wed himself to the land, then what a king he would have become. Uncanny and wicked and wild. Not just a Thorn King, but a king of thorns.

"But if he will not kneel to his fate, then one of us must become the thorn king in his place," Esau continued. "The door must be closed, even if it has to be with a substitute. Here and there, king and door."

King and door. They were words she'd grown up with, words as unmovable and unchangeable as the wild god carved onto their hearth. Part of a song so old that no one knew when it had first been sung.

Here and there, king and door,

Cup and spear, corn and war.

She stopped struggling now as she realized it was pointless to fight this.

To fight the Kernstow legacy. To somehow stave off the hungry heart of the valley.

"Even after our inheritance has been denied us, it's always fallen to the Kernstows to make sure the Guests abide by the rules of the land," said Esau. "And it's up to us to close the door if they won't."

Estamond's head fell forward against his chest. He smelled like heather and rain and home. "Just not Esra," she whispered. "Not him. Please."

Esau was still furious, but she could hear the truth of his next words in his voice. "I would never let it be him, Essie. And for what it's worth, you know Mother wouldn't either. She's seen something for him in the spoons— something about his descendants. He's the future of the Kernstows now. He's all we have left."

It was unwise to tell him what she told him next, but Estamond had never been wise. "You should marry, Esau. Find a wife or even a sweetheart. Get babes on her."

His hands tightened so hard around her arms that she let out a squeak, and then those hands were on her back and in her hair, pressing her so tightly to him that she could feel every tensed muscle and every inch of his erection. "There's no one but you," he vowed. "There will never be anyone but you. And you will be mine again, my own, and you'll never leave me again."

"Esau…"

His mouth and nose were in her hair. His hands shaped to the curves of her hips and bottom through her dress. "You don't need him," he rumbled. "If you simply do what needs to be done, then you'll have won the thorn chapel back for our family, and we'll be together again."

Turbulent longing tangled and pulled with horror; she would never do it, never, never—but oh, how she'd missed this. How she'd sometimes ached for this, ached for Esau's fury and possession. His greedy hands and animal growls. Randolph was sweet and kind and true, but Esau was her very own heart, her very own soul. Their hearts were made out of each other's. So were their bodies and minds.

Even the wild god himself would struggle to compete with that.

Estamond's body didn't hide the truth from her brother—it never could—and before long, Esau's mouth was hot and urgent on hers. He handled her like a doll—not a precious china doll with silk clothes and curls made of real hair, but like a rag doll. Like she was his thing to drag over the hills and clutch in the dark, and even though her tender core twinged and her milk-full breasts ached, she relished every second of it.

Esau was taller than her, stronger than her, angrier than her. With very little trouble or effort, he had her inside the house and on his wool-blanketed bed, his teeth on her throat and his hand up her skirts. With a hot, wet flush, her milk let down, hard enough to soak through her nursing corset and dress.

Esau's eyes narrowed. "Is that for him? For one of his brats?"

Estamond narrowed her eyes right back, and she was tempted to hiss at him like a cat. "For one of *my* brats, yes."

"The child should be mine," he breathed against her skin. "All of your children should be mine."

"I was always supposed to be the May Queen, Esau. I was always supposed to be his."

Esau grunted low in his throat, his hand dropping to his trouser buttons. It was inevitable between them, once again. Two bodies that should have never separated to begin with.

"I only just stopped bleeding," she told him as he moved between her legs. "I still hurt."

"I won't go in," he said. "But I have—to—touch—"

The moment his bare organ pressed against her slick opening and then rode up to grind against her, Estamond forgot nearly everything. Her mother's note, the impending Lammas feast, and very nearly the tiny babe still sleeping in a maid's arms in the cozy Guest carriage waiting for them on the road.

True to his word, he didn't penetrate her, but it was still fucking, there was no denying that. She came hard and keening, and Esau followed her, liquid heat surging out of his tip and onto her intimate skin, and then he collapsed over her, still rutting gently as he slid his arms tight around her. She was his rag doll once again.

"I hate that Mother made you marry him," he murmured.

"No one made me do anything," she said. "I love him."

"Yet you're underneath me."

"You've never understood," she said impatiently. "You've never understood how there could be both at once."

She and Randolph had welcomed others into their bed as visitors— although he only fucked another if Estamond was there too, while Estamond, with his permission and complete knowledge, sometimes sought pleasure without him. The only lover she'd ever hidden from him was Esau, for understandable reasons. Even if Randolph was the wild god a handful of nights throughout the year, in between he was just a quiet country gentleman, whose most outrageous crime was being a Catholic. He'd love her no matter what, she knew; he'd struggle with it for a few days and then overcome it, because there was nothing that could dim his love for her, not even what she'd done with Esau up in the hills. But she wanted to spare him the struggle and the pain of knowing. He deserved to be free of it.

"I've only understood one thing in my life," Esau said, "and it's that I need you. If you ever left for good, I—"

She was surprised at the pain in his voice, but he wouldn't let her see his face.

"Maybe the door will accept a substitute," he said. "But I can't. Come back to me."

She knew she never would, but it still hurt to know it. It was one of life's strange cruelties that she could be married to a man she loved, that this man would let her fuck anyone she pleased, and yet the one person she truly yearned for was still outside her reach. Maybe this was why she let Esau hold her far longer than was wise, until the afternoon shadows began to gather in corners and they needed each other once again.

Later, as Estamond sat gingerly in the carriage while it bumped back to Thornchapel and the maid and the baby both slept, she realized she had an answer. She didn't like the answer, she didn't like the answer at all in fact, but it was nevertheless the answer she'd been looking for when she came to Kernstow Farm.

According to the old ways, the Thorn King had to die. But nowhere did it say that the Thorn King needed to be the same Thorn King who presided over the feasts.

And nowhere did it say that the Thorn King needed to be a man.

Estamond set the lantern down on the grass altar and set about what she came to do. Out came the golden torc, out came the small leaf-shaped knife made of copper—both taken from their glass cases in the library. The knife she set on the altar next to the lantern, and the torc she pried open just enough to slip onto her neck. Once upon a time, she'd crowned Randolph with this. She'd shown him the stories about the thorn chapel were real, and she'd brought the old ways—forgotten by the last few generations of Guests—back to Thornchapel.

She'd put the torc around his neck and then played the part of his bride, his saint, his May Queen. His priestess. She'd sung with him and bled with him, she'd bound herself with thorns to him, she'd guided him.

There was no one to guide her tonight. No one to bleed with her or sing with her. She was a wild god without a consort, a Thorn King without a queen.

She was alone.

I am the Thorn King tonight and that's what matters, she reminded herself. She was keeping everyone she loved safe all at once. She would close the door, and then there'd be no chance of her mother going up into the hills. Esau and Esra would be safe. So would Randolph. It was the only way.

With the torc heavy and cool on her skin, Estamond turned and surveyed the door once more.

It was tall, but not much taller than Thornchapel's own doors, rising perhaps eight feet into the air. The fittings were made of dark iron, and the door itself was made from a wood so weathered and gray that it seemed as old as the chapel itself. It was set into the half-crumbled chapel wall, the stonework rising into a lancet arch around the top, all of it covered in climbing roses.

Elsewhere in the chapel, the roses blushed pink and sweet; here, around the door, the roses were so red they were almost black. In fact, in the shadows and slivers of moonlight, they *were* black.

The torc suddenly felt too heavy, too tight, and Estamond found that she was scared. Terrified, like she hadn't been since she was a girl. It wasn't that the roses were black. It wasn't even that the door was there at all, when there should only be the bramble-gnawed remains of a chapel wall.

It was that the door was open and she could see through to the other side.

She stepped forward once, twice, close enough to press a hand against the pitted stone of the doorway. Through it, there was an expanse of flower-studded grass and then the woods—the same thing she would see if the door weren't here. The same thing she *should* see, if everything was as it was supposed to be. But somehow she knew it was not the same. It was not the same grass, not the same trees. The forest would not be her forest and the valley beyond would not be her Thorne Valley.

Here and there, king and door.

How did the rest of the song go? It was hard to remember with her entire body trembling like this, hard to remember the words that made sense of a door to nowhere and everywhere all at once.

The breeze ruffled through the trees behind her and tugged gently at Estamond's dress, but through the doorway, all remained still. No breeze moved through the leaves or disturbed the grass, no wind stirred the branches there. It was a world as still as cut glass.

Estamond lifted her other hand, thinking maybe she'd reach through the door to feel the air on the other side of it, but right as she did, something flickered across the unmoving grass of the other place. Like a lantern or a torch being carried just out of sight, close enough to send light playing over the ground and faintly into the trees, but not so close that she could see the source of the light itself.

But then came a shadow.

It fell across the path of the light, stopping so that only the silhouette of a man's upper body could be seen. Lean but still powerful.

Estamond dropped her hand, took a step back.

The shadow didn't move. It waited, patiently, almost like a gentleman waiting to hand a lady through a carriage door. But the light on the other side continued to move, flickering and flaring and making the shadow waver at the edges. Estamond realized the drums were slightly louder here, and so were the chants. Through the raised voices, she could discern a lone, wailing cry—a single note of lament amidst the estival joy—and the sound of it sent hairs rising on Estamond's arms.

It was a sound of anguish. A sound of sacrifice.

Still the shadow waited.

All the stories she heard, all the things her mother had told her—they seemed like such mockeries now. Clumsy half-ideas sketched out by the ignorant and proclaimed as the truth, because how could any story convey the reverent, wonderful terror of *this*? The open door with something waiting behind it? And Estamond wondered—a little wildly, a little heretically—what would happen if she just left it open.

Or what would happen if she simply…walked through.

The voice keened louder now, plangent and strange. It was a wail both unearthly and not, both disquieting and oddly familiar. Estamond had the uncomfortable sense that it was for *her*, somehow, that the voice was lamenting *her*.

Or if not her, then the Thorn King come to die at the door tonight.

She took another step back, and then another, until she stumbled back against the grassy hump of the ancient earth-covered altar. She felt more terror than wonder now, more horror than awe, because inside of that lamenting voice was her fate, and her fate was a forlorn and lonely death, and she didn't want it, she didn't want any of it. She wanted Randolph and her children, she wanted Esau and Esra. She wanted more harvests, more Lammas revels when her biggest fear was making sure there was enough mead and ale for the feasters. She wanted sticky summer nights and snow-heaped winter days, she wanted the hills and the mist and the bright chatter of the River Thorne.

She wanted to live, and yet living was impossible so long as her mother drew breath. Living meant death to someone she loved, and she was incapable of allowing that.

This, and more, the mournful voice seemed to know. Without understanding the words, Estamond understood the meaning.

Life was beautiful and bursting and ripe, and sometimes it had to be given up or given back. Sometimes it had to be sown back into the earth from where it came.

It was a lesson Estamond had always associated with Samhain, the feast of the final harvest, but she supposed it worked for Lammas too. Tonight instead of weaving dolls out of barley or crowns out of meadowsweet, she would be cut down like the first of the grain.

Everything in its time, her mother would say.

John Barleycorn must die, she would say too.

But what if I just left? What if I didn't close the door?

What was the worst that could happen?

As if hearing her thoughts, the shadow moved. Just a step, just enough so that she could see where its hips tapered to long thighs. And then it lifted its hand, and then she saw the hand itself—a man's hand like any other man's hand, except it was glistening with something dark and wet and—

Estamond screamed.

The chanting and singing stopped, so did the drums. The only thing that remained was the piercing voice of sorrow, singing its ageless song. Singing as Estamond stared at the bloody hand, and prayed and prayed she wouldn't see any more of the man who waited on the other side.

"I'll do it," she called out in a trembling voice. "Please, don't—I shall do it myself."

The hand lowered but the shadow remained.

Here and there, life and death …

Nearly the same thing.

Estamond felt the weight of the words as surely as she felt the weight of the torc on her neck and the weight of the bottle in her dress pocket. She understood then, why the door must close, why the veil could flutter but not part. Or at least she thought she did, because as terrifying as that shadow was, as maddening as the singing lament became as it urged her on to her own grim fate, she had to admit she was still drawn to the world beyond the door, she was still enlivened by it, even as she unstoppered the bottle that would smother the life right out of her. The world beyond the door was just like here, but *more*. Both more wonderful and more strange. More sweet and more dangerous.

Perhaps she could've lived near the open door, but many others would not wish to. Perhaps even most others.

The brew was bitter, and Estamond wished she'd brought some whisky or sherry to wash out the taste. With a regretful sigh and a careful eye on the door and the shadow behind it, she took the small knife and drew it across her palm.

It hurt.

It hurt and she hated it and her whole body seemed to light up with bone-thrumming pain as she held out her hand and let the blood drip from her fingers to the grass at the door's threshold. An offering, a prelude to the offering to come.

The shadow didn't move, but the chanting began again, loud and urgent and wild. There was no malevolence to it, but no benevolence either—just pure, unfettered energy that could be harnessed to any purpose. *Like life itself,* Estamond thought, and then felt the thought recede with a slowness that mimicked being drunk.

That would be the brew, then. Leaching through her blood like rot through grain.

Blood given to the threshold, Estamond arranged herself on the grass-covered altar. Her hand hurt and she tucked it up against her chest as she fought the urge to throw up. Dizziness came and receded and came again, and it wouldn't be long, she was certain, it would only be a matter of minutes before she fell asleep. She was very afraid and she didn't want to do this anymore and her hand hurt so much that she had to scream, but when she opened her mouth to scream, nothing came out, nothing but strangled breath.

Being the Thorn King is the worst fate possible, she thought, feeling almost angry about it. Why did death demand that life be fed to it at all? Why must there be a door here? And why did anyone ever, *ever,* decide the door was worth being near? Why didn't they run away from it the moment they realized what it was? Why wasn't the entire valley marked as unsafe, unholy, taboo?

The shadow in the doorway moved, and again Estamond tried to scream, and again nothing came out. Her vision was twinned and blurred, and so the shadow itself remained nothing but a tallish and strongish smudge until it was leaning right over her.

Would it kill her? Would it drag her back through the door?

Would it cry for her? Sing for her? Hold her gently as she died?

Was it a saint or a god?

But no, she knew the truth as she heard its pained, anguished roar—it wasn't the shadow of the door at all, but Randolph, her own wild god, her own lord of the manor.

Randolph who was no longer the Thorn King and who would be safe because she chose to be the king in his stead.

He cradled her in his arms and it made everything worse—the nausea and the dizziness and the infernal pain in her hand—but it felt so good to have him here that she couldn't complain. Not that she had the breath for it anyway.

"Why?" he gasped, his gasp so wounded and desperate that Estamond felt the pain of it even on top of the pain of dying. "My God, Estamond— *why?*"

She pressed her bleeding hand weakly to his face. Damn, but she loved him. She loved him enough that she knew she would make the same choice again. If it came down to her or this shy, tender man, she would wear the torc in his place, every time.

"I hired the nurse for you," she managed to wheeze out.

He shook his head, tears falling fast from bright hazel eyes. "I don't— Estamond—I don't understand—"

"Make sure the children know how much I loved them," she forced out. "And I mean it—about Janie—for you—"

She couldn't breathe, and the agony of not breathing was beyond pain, beyond fear, and then suddenly, like the tumble of a ripe apple from a tree or the slice of a scythe through wheat, the pain was over. There was only the distant warmth of Randolph's arms and the song of lament pouring through the doorway. There was only the weight of the torc around her neck.

And then?

Then there was nothing at all.

Seven miles away and nearly a century and a half later, Esau and Estamond's many-times great granddaughter woke up in a car with a thrashing scream. Alarmed, her lover pulled the car to the side of a moor-topping B-road and parked it, coming around to the side and pulling her out of the car before she could manage to scream again.

He sank down to the ground with her in his arms, cradling her against his chest and rocking her gently back and forth as she sobbed into his shirt.

"Shhh," the sole heir of the Guest family murmured, stroking her hair as he held her close. "It was just a dream, little bride."

She cried even harder, shaking her head, as if unable to put words to what she'd just seen.

He kissed her hair and held her tighter against him. He loved her more than he'd ever loved anything, and he would sit with her on the side of the road and hold her all day if that's how long it took for her to feel safe again.

"It was just a dream," he repeated, even though he had no idea what kind of awful dream would have her like this, shaking and inconsolable. "I've got you now. I've got you with me. It was just a dream."

I

Present day

Rebecca

It was an accident, the day I saw the gardens of Versailles.

In the hotel, my mother and father had argued—bitterly. To this day I don't know what they argued about, but I do know that they fought incessantly in those years, the kind of fights that would end in slammed doors and my mother's sobs. Back then, sometimes I'd catch my father crying too, yelling, shouting, matching my mother rage for rage and grief for grief, the pain written on his face for anyone to read.

She would move back to Accra from London two years after that day, but I didn't know that then. I didn't even know enough to see the fighting as a portent of a dying marriage. It was upsetting, but in the same way thunder was upsetting—it came, it went, it was a part of life.

And so while they'd fought, I'd sat in the window seat and played with the Barbie dolls Daddy had brought back from New York a few days ago. One came with a little tea set—plastic, incomplete to my eyes, because there were only two cups and two saucers and a teapot—but I made do. I pretended that my doll had a complete tea set at one point, but she'd taken in some of the items to get valued. Or perhaps they'd been chipped by a careless guest, and she was currently having them repaired by an expert in antique tea set repairs.

The other doll came wearing a striking red dress with a silk stole. Her hair was pulled up in a high bun on top of her head, exposing her throat and her shoulders. She had stars hanging from her ears, and I thought she was the most beautiful thing I'd ever seen, so beautiful I hardly touched her, for fear of ruining her. Instead, she sat remote and barely interested on the windowsill while Incomplete Tea Set Barbie made her cup after cup of tea. Tea Set Barbie would tell her over and over again how beautiful she was, how pretty her red dress was, how she hoped they would be best friends forever. Sometimes Tea Set Barbie would kiss Red Dress Barbie because Red Dress Barbie was so perfect. Sometimes Tea Set Barbie would lay her head in the other doll's lap and simply savor her untouchable beauty and cherish every second that she got to be near it. Every once in a while, Red Dress Barbie would pat Tea Set Barbie on the head, acknowledging her reverence and affection, and those were the moments Tea Set Barbie lived for.

"The only two black Barbies I could find, and they're both in dresses," my father had complained to my mother when he'd met us here in Paris. He'd been at a landscape architecture conference in New York, and now there was one here. There were times he lived conference to conference, one city to another, only coming home for short jaunts to sleep and repack.

"Why shouldn't they have dresses?" my mother had said. "Girls like dolls with dresses. Anyway, the white Barbies have pretty dresses too."

"The white Barbies are also paratroopers, presidents, and surgeons," Samson Quartey had replied, but he'd dropped the subject, probably wary of another fight.

I was playing with the dolls when my mother shut herself in the bedroom that morning, tearfully telling Daddy that he'd given her a migraine, that he'd known she got them while traveling and then he'd callously gone and argued with her anyway and now her head hurt so badly she couldn't even stand up. It was proof he'd never loved her, she said, proof that he wanted her to be unhappy.

My father stood outside the bedroom door for a few minutes after that diatribe, a single hand braced against the wood, as if he wanted to reach through it to touch her. As if he wanted to see through every opaque and brittle thing in the world to the truth behind it.

When he finally came to my window seat, the wet tracks on his cheeks glittered in the sun.

"I was going to leave you with your mother, but I think…I think you should come with me," he said. His voice was thick. I didn't understand all the ways he was unhappy then, and I certainly didn't understand the small, irremediable ways that two people could sow unhappiness in each other. But I did know my daddy needed a hug, and I'd slid off the window seat to wrap my arms around his legs.

"Sweet girl," my father said. He was crying again. "We should get your shoes on."

And then I'd asked the only question I cared about. "Can I bring my Barbies?"

I was six, and so I had only the shakiest idea of what my father did for a living. He told me it had to do with flowers and soil, but all I ever saw at home were rolls of paper and neatly sharpened pencils. Computer screens with flat, colorless drawings.

I didn't know then that not every father propped his daughter on his shoulder and made her find the horizon. Made her identify which was bigger, this tree here or that tree there. Made her identify which was closer, which was planted to hide something, which would blossom in the spring and which would be a collection of stark branches in the winter. And in Accra: which leaves were taro and which were caladium? And there, that tulip tree crowned with blossoms so orange and so red they looked like blossoms made of fire? Was that an invasive species? Wasn't it true that sometimes the most beautiful things in life were the most destructive, the most grasping?

It didn't seem remarkable to me that my father wanted me to understand proportion, unity, form. Repetition, color, and texture. When one is a child, one only knows the tiny perimeters of their own world, and so I must have assumed this was how every child was raised. I couldn't know then that my father's appointment with the head gardener at Versailles was an unusual privilege, something not every father got to do.

But there was a moment, there must have been a moment, when I started to see. When I stood at the head of all that majestic symmetry, and I finally understood what my father was trying to explain to me about balance and about vision. About horizons, about light and dark, about transitions. About harmonies. Before me was not just an imprint of a design—tidy, ordered, controlled—but an assertion of human will over nature.

I did not know yet that Versailles had required villages to be moved, earth to be leveled, rich wetlands drained. I did not know then that there was a cost to correcting irregularities, to valuing geometry over tumult, that flattening and diverting and carving and scraping could give one something less than the sum of its parts.

I only saw the wide, curlicued parterres, the Grand Canal stretching into the distance. The marches of orange and oleander trees. The four seasonal fountains—Flora, Ceres, Bacchus, and Neptune. The straight paths of fine gravel, and the regimented oaks, and the mathematical little yews, clipped into cubes and cones and spheres.

I only saw perfection.

I turned to the keeper of the gardens and asked in my halting French if he had built the gardens.

"Non, chouchou," the gardener had said, eyes crinkling with an amused smile. "Il a été construit par un homme nommé Le Nôtre."

Le Nôtre.

I was silent the rest of the day, thinking of this man. Thinking of what he must have felt to have built this place. He must have felt like a god.

By the time Incomplete Tea Set Barbie and Red Dress Barbie were dust-covered relics on a shelf, I'd become the foremost pre-adolescent biographer of André Le Nôtre. I had a poster of Versailles on my wall—a reprint of an antique map—and stacks of books about the man himself and jardins à la française. But then my father took me with him on a trip to Italy, and there we saw the statue-lined parterres of Villa Farnese, its lush enclosures and mossy staircases with splashing streams running down the middle of the steps themselves. There we went to the Sacro Bosco, following in the footsteps of Salvador Dalí himself to peer at moss-covered monsters made of stone, at elephants and grottos and crooked houses and Greek Furies and virgin temples.

Thus came my Mannerist phase, which coincided nicely with the quirks and sulks of puberty, and after that came my Baroque stage. At some point I put up a poster of Capability Brown; The 1993 adaptation of *The Secret Garden* was background noise for years of schoolwork. One Christmas in Accra I was so bored that I built an Archimedes screw from plastic bottles and a dowel I harvested from a clothes hanger, and then I arranged all the potted plants into a facsimile of the Hanging Gardens of Babylon. Once I made a Zen garden in my room with a baking tray and aquarium sand, and had a gritty floor for years after, no matter how many times I swept.

I went through a potager phase, a ferme ornée phase, some time each obsessed with arboretums, alpinums, and palmetums. When I was a teenager, I truly believed I was the first person ever to appreciate the ecological sense of a bog garden, the mystery of a hedge maze, or the dark seduction of a poison garden.

I became something of a garden hipster; some of my schoolmates drew *Twilight* fan art, instead I sketched out what I imagined King Solomon's ecclesiastical garden of despair would have looked like. I asked people if they'd even heard of Assyrian hunting parks or Egyptian funeral gardens. I asked them if they knew the word *paradise* came from Old Persian for "walled garden." Had they heard of Sennacherib? Olmstead? Gertrude Jekyll? Did they understand how different Giverny was from other gardens? Like *really* understand? Did they even understand the difference between a garden and a park? Between a park and a landscape? Did they even look at the spaces they moved through? Were they oblivious? Heartless? Dull?

The year I went to uni, Daddy took me with him to Istanbul for a conference. He had a birthday present for me after, and I spent the entire conference guessing what it was. Would we go home to Ghana after the conference and see Ma? Would I come home to a car of my own? Perhaps he was finally going to offer me a job at Quartey Workshop—something I'd been craving for the last three years—even if it was only getting coffee and manning the plotter printer?

But it was none of these things.

Instead, after the conference ended, we boarded a plane that took us to a city called Urfa. It was the ancient home of Job and King Nimrod, and also home to the oldest life-sized statue of a human ever found, but we didn't stay in the city long enough to explore any of its history. We took a taxi through it until we were thoroughly in the countryside. And there we found Göbekli Tepe.

Rings of concentric standing stones were scattered around the site. They were carved in the shapes of vultures, scorpions, lions; there were human and animal remains found all over the hill it was perched on and yet no houses. No one had ever lived here. No one had even tried.

The entire site was a strange honeycomb of stone. It was built six thousand years before the invention of writing, it predates the agricultural revolution, it predates metal tools and even pottery. Wheat was domesticated near here. Some might even say the idea of a temple itself was born here, the idea of a holy place built by human hands.

Carved right out of the living rock, the limestone pillars were planted like trees in a sacred grove, the butchered bones from humans and gazelles sown into the earth like seeds. It had been built to be open to the wind and the stars—a garden for gods and men to walk through together, and yet, at some point, it had been buried. The spaces between the stones filled with rubble and dirt and broken tools, never to be gardened again.

My father and I circled the site in silence. All around us was a landscape of olive and umber; the sun was relentless, the breeze was sparing. It felt impossible to believe that this was counted as part of the Fertile Crescent. After growing up in England, a place so damp and green that things just *grew* whether one wanted them to or not, this place seemed almost barren. Which made the temple all the more striking.

Why here?

Why this place?

"I feel God here," my father said finally. The excavated site had been roofed and ringed with a walkway, and by this point we were leaning on the railings, staring down to where the pillars rested in their mess of stones and dirt.

I looked around then, at the stark, sloping hills and the dry valley below. It seemed like a godless place—and yet, strangely I could feel the thread of divinity as well. It was thin and distant, it was as dusty and unused as the buried temple structures themselves, but it was there.

A lone note from a forgotten song. A footprint baked into the earth.

"I think I feel it too," I said, a bit eagerly, and then my father had smiled at me.

He had never become cold, my father, even after my mother finally made good on her ultimatums and moved back to Ghana, and even after our summer at Thornchapel, when I would sometimes find him dialing a number on his cell phone only to hang up before the call could connect. But even though he wasn't *cold*, he was undoubtedly cool. He had begun to hold himself back, bit by bit, more and more each and every year, until he was a man of walls, a man of locked doors and drawn curtains. I no longer saw him angry or sad—when we went to visit Ma in Accra, he was unfailingly polite, he was kind, he would even be affectionate in a perfunctory sort of way. But I also no longer saw him happy; his happiness faded into pastel-tinted childhood memories, and the reality of living with him—of bringing my marks home to him, airing my petty grievances, bandaging my scraped knees, and later mumbling my requests for money to buy feminine hygiene products—was a reality shaped by his dispassion and reserve.

So to have seen him smile then...it felt like more of a birthday present than seeing the oldest known designed landscape in the world.

It wasn't until later—much later, actually—as I was back home in England and preparing for uni, that I realized I'd felt that thin thread of the divine only one other place in my life. There was another place that was hidden and strange and holy.

I'd lived there for a summer.

It belonged to my best friend.

It practically called out for a gardener, a keeper, someone who would patiently unravel all its secrets, not as archeologists do, not through digging and scraping. But through tending. Through planting. Through growth.

And I knew then, as I know now, that I was always meant to come back to Thornchapel. Not because it was meant for me.

But because I was meant for it.

Rebecca

I wake with a kitten tucked into my side.

Outside, the sky is the kind of sweet blue that comes only a handful of times in an English spring, and inside my room, everything is orderly and quiet and in its place. Except for the kitten. She's very much out of place—sleeping with a leg thrown over mine and her face nestled into my shoulder. Her hair is everywhere, and she's snoring softly, sweet little breaths that puff warmly against my skin. At some point, she's twisted her fingers into the silk of my nightgown, as if to keep me from leaving.

From this angle, I can only make out the dark fans of her eyelashes and the pert snub of her nose and the coral-colored bow of her upper lip. She's like a doll, like the perfect doll Sara Crewe is given in *A Little Princess*, except Delphine is also a doll I get to pet and kiss. A doll I get to pose and lick and fuck.

Her hair really is fucking everywhere. Shining gold and silky, spilling over my chest and shoulder and stomach. It's long enough that wisps of it tickle the exposed skin of my thighs. Just a few years ago, this would have irritated me beyond measure, but today the only irritation I feel is frustration that I can't play with it too much without waking her. I have to settle for stroking it away from her face, for sifting it through my fingers and then letting it fall back to my stomach again.

When she's awake though, I'll pull it. I'll tug on it until she whimpers; I'll use it to guide her mouth between my legs. I'll wrap it around my fist, and then I'll let it go again so I can watch the light play over its aureate waves as she eats me.

My cunt gives a kick at the thought, and then a second kick as I realize I can feel *her* cunt against my thigh. Even unconscious, she's got it pressed needily against me—as if she fell asleep seeking some kind of friction or relief. I let myself indulge in a fantasy: rolling Delphine onto her back and sliding my fingers into her before she's all the way awake. Letting her wake up with me kneeling over her, already getting her halfway to an orgasm by the time she flutters those honey eyes open.

A hungry ache settles just behind my clit, and a matching ache curls low in my belly. I want to fuck her like she belongs to me...but she doesn't belong to me. Not yet.

As much as we've fooled around here at Thornchapel, as many small, beginner-level scenes as we've done in this room, I haven't truly made her mine. I haven't asked her to be my submissive for real. I haven't invited her to my flat or invited myself to hers. I haven't asked to meet her parents as her girlfriend, and I haven't ever even hinted that she should meet mine as the same. I haven't taken her to the club.

I haven't told her she makes me feel like my lungs have shrunk and my heart has grown into a quavering, defenseless, easily bruisable thing.

No, I've fucked her here at Thornchapel, as if Thornchapel is its own club, its own world, with no consequences or connection to my life in London. I'd say I used her, except I'm not entirely sure she's not using me right back, and sometimes I'm not entirely sure I'm the only reason we haven't become something more. I can never forget that we used to hate each other—I can never forget that up until three years ago, I thought Delphine the worst kind of brat, the worst kind of spoiled rich girl. And after that fateful week at my flat, I still thought her a brat, but a brat I jerked off thinking about more times than I'd like to admit.

Brats need to be broken and tamed, a little voice tempts.

If you made her yours…

As if sensing the direction of my thoughts, Delphine stirs, rubbing her face into my breast and arching in a big, toe-pointing stretch like a pampered kitten in a sunbeam.

"What time is it?" she mumbles, not opening her eyes.

"Near noon," I say, feeling a little guilty. I rarely sleep past six, even on weekends, and even though last night was Beltane and we were awake until near dawn, I still have the unpleasant suspicion that I've wasted time. I should have been working—I should have been catching up on emails or finishing the Severn riverfront proposal or planning a site visit to that boarding school in Wiltshire. I could have even gone down to the maze and made sure everything was ready for the hedge removal tomorrow. But I didn't.

Work is a privilege. Work is a gift. My father has told me that almost every day of my life; it's one of the unwritten rules of being a Quartey. We work. We will be the best.

And yet even the best is still not enough.

"Mmm," Delphine murmurs, still rubbing her nose and jaw into me. She stops stretching and slides her leg over mine again, making more contented purring noises. She's naked, and so I feel the brush of her intimate curls against my thigh as she snuggles close. I can feel the soft curve of her breast, and the plush give of her belly against my hip. Her mouth is so close to my nipple now that I can feel the warmth of her breath through my silk nightgown. "Let's go back to sleep."

"I have a better idea," I growl, finally doing what I wanted to do earlier and rolling her back so I can climb between her legs and push her thighs as far apart as I want them. They're soft and sweet and pinchable, and her cunt is a little heaven made just for me—a bewitching furrow that opens up to reveal a blushing hole the color of sweetness. It already glistens for me, and I'm reminded of being a child in a sweet shop, reaching for the shiniest, pinkest lolly I could find.

I fight off a shudder of delight the minute I feel her against my fingertips, tender and so very, absolutely wet.

Delphine hasn't wanted penetration, so I keep my fingers outside, petting her and stroking her until she's writhing below me, a flush crawling up her chest.

"I would have thought after last night, you would have had enough," I tease, finally pressing against her swollen clit and enjoying the whine I get in return. "You're turning into an insatiable little slut, aren't you? My own little whore."

God, even saying it feels so *right*. How much more right would it feel to have her with me always? To take her to the club and show her off? To be the woman whose task it was to keep her so flush in orgasms that she could barely walk without remembering what her Mistress was capable of?

I've been holding back, I know that. I've been keeping this at a distance, because the moment I let myself think about it—the moment I let myself recognize that this spoiled kitten is actually Delphine Elizabeth Dansey, who has millions of Instagram followers and a trust fund the size of a small nation's GDP—the moment I acknowledge she's somehow become my friend and I care about her and the idea of being without her someday makes me want to scratch and kick and scream—panic swells like a balloon, squeezing everything inside of me until I can't breathe.

Girls like Delphine aren't for people like me. They're for people like Auden or Becket, for minor celebrities or business tycoons. They're for lovers who are as famous or wealthy or pedigreed. Not for emotionless landscape architects.

And anyway, even if an emotionless landscape architect could be suitable for an heiress-turned-internet-star, Delphine is all wrong for *me*. She's flighty and vain and so very, very coquettish and contradictory and dryly witty and secretly brilliant—and *shit*.

She's dangerous.

God, so dangerous. She could break my heart. If I stopped being strong, if I unbricked walls just for her that took years to brick up…If I let her into a place where no other person has ever, ever been, then she will step on my huge, quavering heart and she will leave bloody designer-shoe footprints on the floor as she walks away.

I will get hurt. She will hurt me.

But what if she doesn't? the voice tempts again. *What if you take her as a submissive, what if you trust her and then you're happy?*

That's the thing they don't tell you about strength, about guarding your heart and keeping yourself safe from being hurt: it's fucking exhausting. I don't want to be exhausted anymore.

I just don't want to be hurt either.

What if this is a gift?

"Delph," I say, still rubbing the juncture at the top of her thighs. "I want you to be mine." The words come out so easily, so clearly, that I suddenly feel foolish for waiting so long to say them.

I hate feeling foolish.

Her gathering climax has her voice breathless when she answers. "Aren't I already?"

"We've been playing," I tell her, "but I want you to be *mine*. My submissive. I want to take you to my club. I want to do everything I want to you, wherever I want and whenever I want."

She shudders at my last sentence, biting her lip and staring at me with huge eyes. "What would we have to do?" she asks.

"You'd stay with me when we were in London. You'd come to the club with me. We'd go on dates and anything else you wanted. We'd decide what rules we wanted to share, and we'd decide what our limits were. And then I'd fuck you constantly. Everywhere I could. Anytime I wanted."

Her already-parted mouth parts a little bit more. "Oh," she breathes. "*Oh.*"

She comes suddenly, and I press a hand on her thigh and clamp it tight to the mattress so she can't hide my favorite bonbon-pink toy from me.

I watch her finish, and then I'm kneeling over her face, flicking her jaw impatiently until she opens her mouth and gives me her tongue to use on my clit. But it turns out I'm too impatient to let her flutter and lick me there—after a minute, I slide my hands into those Goldilocks tresses and hold her right where I need her.

"Suck," I say, and she obeys, sucking me until the orgasm detonates in my belly, until I cry out and buck against her mouth, trying to chase every last dirty second of this, determined to feel more, more, more.

But I'm not—I'm not chasing, I'm not determined, I'm none of that because I'm everything else. I'm smiling and near-laughing and surprised at *how good* it feels, and I'm relaxed, and I want more in the exciting, delicious way of knowing that I will get more anytime I like.

I'm *happy*. I'm giddy, a little girl surrounded by bright, gleaming sweets once again.

I wish I could say all my orgasms are like this, but no, no, it's Delphine. Goddammit, why did it have to be Delphine?

It could be good.

It could be so good.

What if this is a gift?

I move down to the mattress again, and then roll us both so that I'm cradling Delphine from behind. Her bottom is round and inviting against my hips, and I let myself fantasize about fucking her like this, with my fingers and then maybe with a cock.

I'd get a pink one to match her pretty pink cunt. I'd make her come so hard with it.

"What do you think, pet?" I whisper into her hair. "Would you be mine?"

My post-orgasm high slowly twists into real nervousness. Real fear. What if she says no? What if she laughs in my face?

What if I've spent the last six weeks thinking the only barrier between me and Delphine was my own fearful reluctance—when really it's that she doesn't want me? Doesn't want to be mine?

What if she hurts me right now, right here in this bed, before I even have the chance to make the hurting worth it?

It's on the tip of my tongue to take it all back, to tell her I didn't mean it, I was joking or teasing or lying—even though I rarely joke or tease or lie. In fact, I've already pulled in a breath and loosened my arms around her, and I'm just about to say, *forget it, Delph, I was only having a laugh,* when Delphine says, "Yes."

Yes.

"Yes?" I am so surprised I can't think of any other words. "Really? You want…to?"

Delphine squeezes my hand and brings it to her mouth, giving it a kiss. "I've only been waiting for you to ask."

She doesn't sound recriminating at all; her voice is still the cheerful, elegant drawl of a girl who grew up with horses and a second family home in the Cotswolds. But that's almost worse, because I sometimes worry that as spoiled and privileged as Delphine is—and even with as patiently and warmly as Auden loved her—she still doesn't seem to expect enough from the people around her. I've been acting like a boy at uni, showing up for a shag and then ducking away before she can ask for anything else, and she would have been well within her rights to call me out on it. She would've had every right to ask me why I'd fuck her here but not in London—and then every right to be utterly unimpressed when I told her that I was terrified of being hurt.

It's an unimpressive reason. *I'm* not even impressed by it.

Delphine moves so that she's on her back and I prop up on an elbow to look down at her as she traces the line of my collarbone. I've swatted other lovers on the arse for less, but somehow when she does it, the only thing I want to do is smile. I let her keep doing it, which is probably worrisome. The risk of being an indulgent Domme with her is very great, because who could scold a sweet little sub for doing this? For touching me so reverently but also with such confident affection, as if she has every right to do so?

But as soon as I'm warm all over from this small affection of Delphine's, I'm resisting again. I want to hide my face or roll out of bed or act like the things she does don't have the power to excite or terrify me.

Should I tell her? Should I crawl over her and bury my face in her neck and confess? Explain that I don't trust my own feelings and I never have, and yet at the same time, I've become such an apostle of fear that even something as simple as having a girlfriend feels impossibly brave? Worse than brave? Stupid? Because it is stupid, from a logical standpoint. I would be better off alone, better off not letting Delphine inside my heart where she could rake her manicured nails along the tender insides of its chambers. I would be safer without her, safer without the complication of having a sub-girlfriend-kitten who was also objectively beautiful and glamorous and dripping with old and new money both. Safer without maybe…accidentally…*possibly*…catching feelings for a girl I've spent so many years hating.

But as Delphine smiles up at me—such a shy, happy, *open* smile—I know there's no way I can sour the moment with all of that. It would be dumping my own shitty problems onto her lap, and it wouldn't be fair to her. It wouldn't be fair to this perfect moment, when I asked her to be mine and she said yes.

The reward for being strong isn't just for *me*. It's for everyone else around me too.

"Let's get you something to eat," I say instead, kissing her mouth and then rolling off the bed. My feelings I tuck back away where they belong, and instead I allow myself the small and safe satisfaction of knowing I'll get to take Delphine home with me this week, I'll get to show her off to the world. I'll get to fall asleep with her hair all over me and her fingers fisted in my nightgown—and if the feelings come back, well…then at least they'll come back when I can soothe myself with her body.

After I take down my hair and dress, I go to the guest room where she's been staying and bring her back some clothes. Delight wavers through me as I pluck out knickers and a bra and shorts so tight I know I'll be able to easily trace the V of her cunt while she's wearing them. I get to dress her now, if I want. I get to feed her and wash her and then make her sit at my feet while I work.

Just like the first night we fucked, it feels a little bit like playing house, but I don't care anymore. I want it. Even if it's a trick, I still want it.

When I return, Delphine takes the clothes with a pout, because she still wants to cuddle in bed. I do too, I'm shocked to find, but after the night we had of drinking way too much and fucking like insatiable teenagers, I know she needs to eat something nourishing and drink plenty of water.

"Abby's not in today, so I'll make you something," I tell her. I don't cook often, but I very rarely am bad at something once I decide to learn how to do it, and so I'm a dab hand in the kitchen. Cooking is chemistry after all, and I'm very, very good at chemistry.

Delphine just yawns a kitten-like yawn and steps into the knickers. I valiantly resist the urge to go over and cup her simply for the pleasure of cupping something that is now officially mine.

"I wonder if Saint wants something to eat too," I say, trying to distract myself from Delphine's body long enough to focus on the rest of the day.

"I think he left." She yawns again. "I heard his car going off outside the window this morning, you know that *rattle rattle* noise it makes when you first get it going? A couple hours ago."

St. Sebastian is definitely an outside cat. He comes and goes according to his own whims, on his own timetable, a solitary, wary boy who's somehow all the more lovely and interesting for how solitary and wary he is. I don't doubt that he left without telling Delphine and me. "Maybe he followed Poe and Auden to Exeter?"

"They went to Exeter?" Delphine asks, baffled. "*Why?*"

"To get levonorgestrel for Poe."

Delphine just blinks at me.

"The morning-after pill," I clarify.

"Oh," Delphine says. Then, "*Oh.*"

I look at her, wondering what she's thinking. What she's feeling. It's only been three months since she ended her engagement with Auden, and the thing that's sprung up between him, Poe, and St. Sebastian in the last few months is…palpably intense. Even I feel a little jealous and I don't have romantic feelings for any of them—nor have I ever. But if one of them was my ex-fiancé, even if I was the one who broke it off, I don't know if I would be quite as calm as Delphine is being right now. I make a mental note to keep an eye on it, and then fight off the urge to smile because Delphine Dansey is mine to keep an eye on. And no matter how much it seems like a trick, no matter how scared or chary I am of it, I can't lie to myself. I want to keep her, and now that I get to keep her, I want to keep her for a very, very long time.

3

Proserpina

"Are you sure you're okay?" Auden asks, glancing over at me. He has his glasses on today, and there's the faint shadow of a beard coming up on his jaw, and it's one of those moments when I see once again just how beautiful he is. Even unshaven and tousle-haired, even with smudges under his eyes from a night of drinking, fucking, and staring at a door that shouldn't exist, he's gorgeous in the way that Thornchapel is gorgeous. Like he's walked right out of fairyland. Right out of the door behind the altar.

The door. I remember my nightmare again and shiver.

Auden notices. "I can pull over again," he says.

I shake my head—a reflex. "I'm fine," I say, which is not true, I'm not fine at all, but his perceptiveness and kindness are somehow more upsetting than if he were ignoring me altogether.

But when Auden looks over at me, there's no irritation or pity in his face. He looks like he wants to pull me onto his lap and bury his face in my hair—which, honestly, is how he's been looking at me all day anyway.

"I'm *going* to be fine," I amend. "It was just so…it was so real."

"And you said it was about Estamond?"

I look out the window of the car. My head aches a little bit—something the pharmacist says is normal after taking Levonelle—and I'm still so tired, even after the nap I took on the way back. With the narcolepsy, it doesn't take much to knock me sideways. Allergy medicine or a string of early mornings or a stressful week at work—any of those on their own will do it. So Beltane night plus the effects of the morning-after pill? I feel like I could sleep for the next ten years and still wake up tired.

"It was," I reply, and then I turn to him. "Do you think dreams can be true?"

"Certainly," he states, steering his Land Rover as easily as a golf cart through a twisting village road with a narrow bridge at the end. "So much else has been true. Real. The drums. The door."

"Do you think I could dream something that already happened?"

He glances over at me. "Do you think that's what you did?"

I chew on the inside of my cheek. I didn't tell anyone about the dream I had on the equinox, the one where I dreamed the future. It seemed so silly and small at the time—no one can dream the future, but if they *could*, what's the use in dreaming a conversation that happens fifteen minutes from the present? But this dream, with Estamond and Esau and the shadow, it not only felt real but important.

It felt like a warning.

"I read that Estamond died in childbirth," I say, "somewhere in the library. But in the dream, she—" I pause, searching for the right words, because suicide isn't right, but neither is murder, even though Estamond's mother was the reason Estamond had to die. "She sacrificed herself," I explain. "In the thorn chapel. For the door."

Auden frowns but doesn't take his eyes off the road. Above us, branches lush with late spring make a tunnel of green and brown.

"The door—in my dream. It was there and it was open, and it had to be closed."

"Why?"

Why. It's the same thing I've been wondering since Auden calmed me down on the side of the road.

Why does the door have to be closed?

Why does it need a life to close it?

Why is there a door at all?

But then, why anything? Why is Thorncombe hung with garlands for May Day? Why did I have sex with five people in the light of the Beltane fire last night? Why did the man sitting next to me—the one with the Cambridge degree and swish job in London—chase another man through the woods and fuck him like a rutting stag? Wearing antlers the entire time? There's something about the Thorne Valley that makes *why* the most necessary and also the most irrelevant question of all, because why do we do any of it?

"I don't know why," I finally say. "I don't think Estamond really knew either, except she was—" I close my eyes for a minute, recalling the way the lantern light flickered over the midnight-colored roses around the door. Recalling the shadow. "She was scared of what was inside. She was terrified."

Auden drums his fingers on the wheel, still frowning a little. "I suppose it's possible that she didn't really die in childbirth. It wouldn't have been difficult for someone with influence or money to change the reported cause of death, especially if the actual cause were self-slaughter. That would've been shocking enough that a doctor would've helped Randolph keep the truth as quiet as possible."

I think of Randolph in the dream—miserable and horrified by what Estamond had done—weeping and roaring as he gathered her to his chest. "She wouldn't let him be the Thorn King," I murmur. "She couldn't let him die when she could take his place."

"The Thorn King?" Auden asks. "Do I want to know?"

"I don't think you do."

"Tell me anyway."

We're in Thorncombe now, only a few minutes away from Thornchapel, so I tell him as quickly as I can about the rest of the dream. About the Thorn King and the torc and the song and the door and the Kernstows keeping watch over it all from their outpost in the hills. By the time we pull into the driveway, Auden looks so upset that I wish I hadn't said anything about it.

I put my hand over his where it still rests on the shifter. "The Thorn King is an old story, Auden. Too old to touch us."

He looks at me, something haunted in his green-brown eyes. "People could say Thornchapel is too old to touch us too, but we both know that's not true." He sighs as he turns off the car. "Sometimes the oldest stories are the most dangerous ones of all."

When we get up to the bedroom, St. Sebastian is nowhere to be found. I check my phone to see if he texted us or the group thread, and there's nothing. Both Auden and I shoot off quick messages to him, but there's no immediate response.

Auden stands in the middle of the room, looking puzzled. "I wonder where he went. He didn't have to work today."

"Maybe his uncle called him in for something," I say, sitting on the bed and then curling up on my side. Which is a mistake, because the moment I do, I feel my eyelids grow heavier, like I'm one of those baby dolls whose eyes close when you lay them flat.

"Maybe. Or maybe he went to get things from his place?" Auden asks. Then he nods, as if just speaking it aloud has made it so. "I'm sure he'll be back soon."

"Mmhmm," I say, my eyes all the way closed now.

The bed dips as Auden sits next to me. He kisses my cheek. "You look good in my bed."

I manage a sleepy smile at that. "I know."

"You should sleep, Proserpina. The chemist said you might want to rest."

"Mmm."

"And when you wake up, St. Sebastian will be here and we'll all be together." Auden sounds a little uncertain though, and without opening my eyes, I find his thigh and squeeze.

"Go find him," I mumble. "You won't be happy until you do."

He sighs. "You're right. I've managed to wait eight years, but suddenly I can't stand wasting another second. You'll be okay here? I don't want to leave if you might have another bad dream."

I wave him off, already nestling into a pillow. "Go find your boy-toy and let me nap in peace."

I hear him laugh a little to himself, and then I'm folded into soft, expensive blankets. A final kiss on my temple and then he's walking away. "Sleep well, little bride," he tells me, and his voice is so full of possessive affection that I'm smiling as I fall asleep.

I don't sleep long.

I'm jolted awake by my phone ringing, and I fumble for it in that just awakened *what the fuck is happening and why is everything so loud* panic as I sit up. Sir James Frazer is a dog croissant at the edge of the bed, and the only response he gives is a single rotated ear, which he rotates back to its usual spot the moment I slide the accept button on the phone and the ringing stops.

"Hello?"

"Proserpina. It's Dad. Is this a bad time?"

"No, Dad, it's not, I just—"

Was napping because I just took the British equivalent to Plan B?

Am tired because I spent the night having sex with five different people in the one place you never want me to be in?

"I had a heavy lunch and needed a nap," I lie instead.

"Are you taking your medicine?" he asks. "Every day? And you know you have to follow a schedule; sleep hygiene is the most important—"

"Yeah, Dad, I know," I grumble, feeling like a teenager again. Nothing irritates me more than him trying to help me manage my own fucking brain. And then I try to remember that he loves me and that's why he worries. I soften my voice. "What's up?"

The pause before he answers my question should have told me, but I'm still sliced open when he says, "The detective sergeant working on your mother's case called. They've…finished. Whatever it was they needed to do, they're done now."

"Done?"

"They didn't find enough evidence in Ralph's things to say with real certainty it was him, although the detective believes it was, as I do. But with him also being dead, there's not much more they can do. So. It's over."

"Oh," I say. And then that's it, I can't say anything more, because even though I should've expected this, even though I *did* expect it, I didn't realize that the investigation ending would feel so strange. Finalizing somehow. Closure without being closure at all.

"They're sending her home," Dad says quietly. "In two weeks. The funeral will be late June; I wanted sooner, but the headstone won't be ready until then, and I thought since it's already been so long, it wouldn't matter if it was a bit longer and she could be laid to rest with her name over her grave."

His voice thickens the slightest bit, like he's holding back a deep misery. "She spent so many years in unmarked ground, you know? I couldn't bear to put her back into the earth that way. I couldn't do it."

"Dad, it's okay," I whisper. "You don't have to explain it to me. I understand why."

He lets out a heavy breath. "I know, I just—I don't want you to think that I'm stalling or that I don't care. I care about it more than anything, and that's why I need it to be right. I failed her so badly, Poe, more badly than you'll ever know, and I'll never have a chance to fix it. The only thing I can do is give her back the dignity Ralph took from her when he buried her in that cursed fucking place to begin with."

4

St. Sebastian

The light has shifted in my mother's office, casting a framed picture of Richard Davey into shadow and throwing warm squares of sunlight onto the paper-covered floor. I kick away a metal box that I always trip over in here and then slide onto the floor, sifting idly through nearby papers with unseeing eyes.

My mind is full of Auden. Of the sun gleaming along his bare chest and the tines of his antlers as he chased me through the forest. Of him pinning me to the soft, bluebell-covered earth and kissing me until I couldn't breathe.

Anything I want from you is mine.

He knew. Even then he knew, which of course he did. He was desperate afterwards, wild with something that wasn't the forest, but was all Auden instead.

Nothing tears us apart again.

Never again, because I won't survive it.

Swear it to me.

And I did. I did swear, because what would ever compare to belonging to Auden Guest? What force of history or nature could ever match the force of *him*? The tousled-haired, asymmetrical-smiled, public-schooled, artsy, cruel, elegant magic that was Auden Guest?

Nothing would or could, and so I swore never to leave him, but how could I have known? How could I have guessed *this*, of all things? And now I'm alone in my dead mother's office, too numb to be as furious with her as she deserves, too shocked to start fixing the things I need to fix. There's nothing but this crushing weight on my chest. Nothing but the acute knowledge that nothing will ever be good again.

That I can never be Auden's again.

I feel—I feel *wrong*. I feel dizzy and floaty and infected with something that's so much worse than loneliness that I don't even know the name for it.

From my mother's office down the hall, I hear the front door click and swing open. No knock. No calling through the mail slot. No hesitation.

Truth be told, I only have five friends in this world, and only two of them wouldn't bother to knock. But before I can wonder if it's Proserpina or Auden, Auden's voice fills the house like a low, silver mist of clipped consonants and relaxed vowels. I hate it, I hate that voice right now, and for once it's not because it's a reminder of a way I'll never be, but because it's so horribly, heartbreakingly *happy*.

Auden sounds happy.

"I thought I'd help you come pack your things—if that is what you're doing here; Poe thought maybe Augie called you in." Footsteps move through the hall, a graceful but powerful-sounding gait. Without my permission, my mind conjures up images of Auden's thighs: the way they reveal themselves in the occasional pull and stretch of his tailored trousers; how they look naked—long and athletic and dusted with brown hair, the kind of hair that feels rough on your cheek when you rub your face against it.

"Also my firm is having a party in two weeks, and I'm bringing you and Poe as my dates," Auden goes on. He's coming closer to the door to the office and I should stand up, but I can't. I can't. I want to touch my brother's naked thighs, and the memory of rubbing my face against them has desire twisting hot and knotty in my belly, and I can't stand up.

"Don't worry about the tuxedo either," he says, very close now, almost walking past the office without seeing me because there're no lights on and it's silent and I'm on the floor. "I'm having one done up for you, and I'm quite serious about you being a date, I'm keen to show you off, you know—"

His sentence breaks off as he catches sight of me sitting on the floor. His brow furrows with worry as he steps inside the office. "St. Sebastian?" he asks. "Is everything okay?"

I look up at his face, cast in the glowing light of a May afternoon. Wind blows through the tree next to the window, sending a pattern of leaf-shaped shadows dancing over his high cheekbones and sculpted jaw. He looks like magic now; he looks like a wild god even in tailored trousers and the brogues he considers his *casual* brogues—as if there's any discernible difference between any of his fancy leather shoes.

His glasses are tucked in the collar of his long-sleeved henley—a shirt I'm sure is one of those deceptively ordinary bits of clothing that actually cost hundreds of pounds—and they hang there with just enough weight to pull down the collar and reveal the full glory of his throat, which is a throat I could spend forever kissing. It could be the throat in an anatomy textbook, in an art reference book, that's how perfectly molded and shaped it is, and when he swallows—as he's doing now, looking down at me—I can see the elegant strength of its inner workings, this confluence of air and blood moving inside him.

I drop my eyes.

I can't look at his magic face or his artful throat. They're no longer mine to look at. *He's* no longer mine to look at, because he's no longer mine at all.

He is nothing to me but forbidden now, he can never be anything more than one of the deepest and oldest sins.

And he lied to me.

He lied to me.

To get what he wanted, because God forbid Auden Guest not get what he wants.

He squats down, trousers perfectly hugging every part of his hips and ass and thighs, a gorgeous watch on his gorgeous wrist, and he has everything I never had, money and grace and a world-class education, he has Thornchapel and the easy confidence that comes with knowing exactly who you are and where you're from.

"St. Sebastian," he repeats, reaching out to tug at my lip piercing with his thumb. And I hate him so much right now. Not because he lied to me—although I hate him for that too—but because his eyes are so open, so honest and so clear. And his voice, that cool patrician voice, is warm. Warm for me.

A thought comes, as horrible as it is penetratingly possible:

What if this is a lie too?

What if the warmth, the honesty, the way he kissed me and held me last night—what if it's all some kind of awful trick, the biggest deception of all? What if he only wanted me as a prerequisite to having Poe? What if he blames me for Ralph's sins, for being living proof that his father was a shitty and disloyal man? What if I was always, always right, and there was never a world where Auden Guest could love a poor, sullen boy like me?

I push his hand away from my mouth, even though my lip twinges a little at the loss, and I scramble to my feet, feeling an ugly, sick twisting everywhere in my body. Everywhere that isn't pulled tight with yearning, that is.

And in my belly, the two mingle together until I can't pick them apart.

He straightens up too, pressing his hands to the wall on either side of my shoulders so fast that I can't dodge away, and he crowds into me, his brogues trapping my boots inside them. His perfect mouth hovers just over mine.

"If you ever slap my hand away from your godforsaken mouth again," he says slowly, "I'll shove you to your knees and fuck that mouth until you cry. Am I understood?"

I hate how my body reacts to that; I hate how my body kicks to life at his cruelty.

"Fuck you," I say.

Confusion filters through his forest-colored eyes at that, and for a moment he looks baffled and very, very young. But then of course, because he's Auden, he decides that everything must be the way he wants it, and the confusion is replaced by hubris once more.

"Oh, is this the game we're playing right now?" Auden asks, a smile tugging at the corner of his mouth. He moves his nose along the line of my jaw, breathing me in. "I'll play, St. Sebastian. I'll play any game you like."

I manage to wedge a hand between us and trap it against his chest. I mean to shove him away, but I can feel the beat of his heart under my palm and the smooth, warm curve of bone and muscle that protects it. I can smell the woody, floral smell of him, and I can feel his interest pushing insistently into my pelvis.

Auden presses into me even more, his erection grinding unerringly against my own, and the bite of zippers and buttons and seams in between only makes it better. I can't help but shudder.

"You want me to fight you for it?" murmurs Auden, licking a warm trail down my neck. He gives me a quick, sharp bite, and I give him back a reluctant groan.

"You want me to chase you again? Because I'll do it, you know I will. And when I catch you, we can play another game."

"Like rich boy, poor boy?"

I don't know why I say it, I don't know why I'm provoking him when I should push him away, but here I am, digging at our old wounds as if we don't have a brand new one that can never, ever heal. Maybe I'm trying to remind myself that Auden was always a spoiled prince, that beneath that noble face was always an ignoble rapaciousness, and we have too much between us ever to overcome. Betrayal and money and blood.

He gives a low snarl against my throat, and his hands come up to find my wrists, gripping them so tightly that I can feel the imprint of every single finger. "I've already told you that you'd regret playing that particular game with me," he says, and he ducks down to bite my collarbone through my shirt—hard enough that I make an embarrassing squeak that's half pain, half delight.

How can he do this to me? He shouldn't be able to do this to me.

He shouldn't be able to make me hard and desperate and so bitterly enamored—he's a liar and he's selfish and it's so, so wrong now. In fact, it's always been wrong. From the very beginning, it's been wrong. That kiss in the thorn chapel when we were children, the grinding, fumbling embraces of that one teenage summer…yesterday, in the woods, with crushed bluebells damp under my back as the wild god claimed me as his own…

From the moment we met, we were a wickedness. A sin and a tragedy.

Auden lifts his face from where he's bitten me, and I get a glimpse of cheekbones and long lashes before his mouth is full and lush on mine, demanding everything he's ever demanded from me: my soul, my body, my future, and my past.

Everything. He's demanding everything, and right now he's kissing me like even everything won't be enough.

"We can play so many other games, St. Sebastian," he says as he pants into my mouth. "We can play enemies again if you want. Lovers. Sluts. Husbands."

Husbands.

The word sinks through me like a stone through water, its meanings rippling out with cold, rhythmic pain.

We can only ever play husbands. Because we can never be husbands.

Siblings can't marry.

And he knows that.

Fury fills me, and shame, infecting me everywhere. "What about brothers?" I say against his lips. "Do you know that game, Auden?"

Auden goes completely still against me, his lips still molded over mine, his exhales becoming my inhales as we stay there panting and rigid. It's as if I've stopped time, as if I've turned the amber-colored light in the room into amber itself and we're both suspended in it. Choking on it.

I feel him take a deep breath. The shuddering, slow kind. "St. Sebastian," he says.

I try to yank my wrists free, but he doesn't let me, and he doesn't pull away. Our mouths are still touching and so are our clothed cocks. I can feel the heave of his tight stomach against mine.

I finally manage to turn my head to the side, rolling it against the wall and hating how much I miss the feel of his kiss.

"St. Sebastian," he says again. A bit wildly.

"How long did you know, Auden? I know it must have been before Beltane, but how much longer before? Before Imbolc? Before Proserpina came? Before Christmas even?"

"No," he says quickly, "no, not then, not before Imbloc, nothing like that."

"But you did know before Beltane." *Before you caught me and claimed me. Before you made me swear never to leave you.*

He takes a minute to answer.

Finally: "Yes."

I struggle to get free again. "Let me go, you fucking wanker."

"No," he replies, as easily as anything. "Not unless you use the right words."

I turn my face back to his, stunned. He's leaned back so he can study my face, but my hips are still pinned by his and my wrists are still trapped high against my chest.

"Are you kidding me?" I ask. "That's over. All of the kink, all of our...well, whatever we had—that's *over* now. That's done."

"*Whatever we had*?" Auden repeats with narrowed eyes. "You can say it, St. Sebastian. In fact you better say it to me, because if you call it anything else, I'll tie you to my bed and write it all over your skin so you don't forget. It's love, and it's not over. It's not done."

"Are you insane?" I demand, my voice breaking over my anger and my shock and the secret rush of warmth I still feel at hearing Auden tell me he loves me. "Are you *mad?* This isn't normal for siblings. *We* aren't normal! We can't—I won't...Damn you, Auden, let me go."

"Use your safeword, and I will."

I open my mouth.

I can't make the words come out.

May I, I think. *May I, May I, May I.* But still my tongue won't move; the sounds won't push past my lips.

Auden's mouth curls up at the corner. "That's what I thought."

"Fuck you," I retort.

"No," Auden says heatedly, his hands tightening on my wrists, "fuck *you*. Just yesterday you promised—you *promised* me that you were mine, you promised me forever together. You *swore*. And now you're running away again? You couldn't even keep your promise for twenty-four hours?"

I sputter, tripping over the words as they tumble out of my mouth. "There is no promise, Auden! Things have changed! We are—we're brothers—*brothers*—we're related, we share blood, we share DNA, we share a fucking *father*, for God's sake—"

"Half-brothers, and we didn't grow up together, and it doesn't—"

"—and you lied about it! Jesus fucking Christ, Auden, you *lied* about it."

"I didn't lie."

"You didn't tell me."

He sniffs. "That's not lying."

I glare at him. He glares right back at me. "That's a juvenile justification and you know it," I say.

"I was going to tell you."

"When? After you'd fucked me again? Or after Lammas? Or maybe ten years from now when I finally worked up the courage to ask you to marry me?"

Auden's glare softens into something boyish and vulnerable. He blinks long-lashed eyes at me. "You want to marry me?"

"Oh my God, Auden, that's not the point," I groan. "The point is we can never get married, and we can't be together, and we can never be together again, and you knew and you didn't tell me. You let me—you let us—yesterday, we—"

I can barely get the words out. He and I have done something unthinkably bad, something so wrong that even the word *wrong* isn't heavy enough. We were more wrong than wrong—we were corrupt and unholy. Immoral and depraved.

"I know what we did yesterday," Auden says, his voice as gentle as the grip on my wrists is firm. "I don't see the problem, and I don't see why you can't keep your promise to me."

I stare at him a moment, totally confounded. "Auden…am I talking at thin air right now? Am I not making sense? Is it my accent? Should I switch to yours?" I say the last part in my best *I wear a regatta blazer to actual regattas* voice, and he makes a face.

"Don't do that, you're terrible at it," he says. "Listen, it's not like—this isn't like you're thinking. I didn't wait to tell you because I was trying to trick you, I waited because I wanted to find the right way to explain it all. Say it the right way so that you wouldn't run away from me when I told you, so that you wouldn't sever your heart from mine. I didn't want this to be the end of us. And why should it be? Why shouldn't you belong to me?" he finishes with a wild urgency.

I search his face. His stupid, handsome face, where even now I see glimmers of yesterday's revels. A small bruise in the shape of Rebecca's bite on his jaw, visible even under the shadow of his day-old beard, a small scratch disappearing into his cinnamon-colored hair from his run through the trees. The vibrant flicker of those hazel eyes—the eyes of the forest.

Never in a thousand years did I think God would be this sadistic or this pitiless, to put me in a position where I have to refuse this man.

"You know why I can't," I say finally. "We can't. We just—it can't be, Auden. You know this."

His eyes stay stark and raw on mine as he says, "But I want you."

"You can't."

"But I want *it*," he says, and with his eyes like that and his voice so low, there's no mistaking what *it* is.

"You can't want it," I whisper, and his grip tightens on my wrists as he pushes them out to the sides until my arms are spread on either side of me and my wrists are pinned to the wall. It's like I'm about to be crucified, like I'm already on the cross, but without the nails and the thorns, because Auden himself is all the nails and thorns I'll ever need.

"Oh, can't I?" he says. "Because I do, St. Sebastian, I do want it. I need it. I don't care what that makes me, I don't care what that means for my immortal soul. I've known you were mine since I kissed you in the thorn chapel, and I've known that you wanted to be mine since you let me bite your lip until it bled." His eyes drop to my lip piercing now, and I can *feel* how much he wants to pull on it and kiss it. I can feel how much he wants that labret running along his shaft, how much he'd love to see it gleaming in the dark while he fucks me. "You can run away all you want, but it's too late. You already swore to me. I've already known what it was like to have your heart in my hands, and it's simply too late."

He ducks his head enough to move his lips over mine—something both more and less than a kiss—something like a promise made with touch instead of words.

And fuck me if I don't want to promise something right back.

"It can't be too late," I whisper. "Even if you did wait to tell me until you got what you wanted."

Auden doesn't lift his mouth from mine, and I feel his words as much as I hear them. "And what did I get, my little martyr? What do you think I wanted?"

I wish *so much* I weren't still hard as I answer him. "You wanted to fuck me."

"No," he says, tugging on my lip piercing with his teeth. "I wanted what I still want." He kisses me again. "I want forever, stubborn boy. Only that."

I let him kiss me. I let him kiss me as he fucks against me, clothed and slow, and I let him kiss me as he keeps my wrists pinned to the wall like a sacrifice. I let him because letting him makes me feel like myself in the best possible way. I let him because letting him feels like living, even when it also feels like dying.

Maybe I am a little martyr. And he's my Diocletian, my emperor and my persecutor both. I'd let him martyr me as many times as he wanted; he'll never stop wanting.

He murmurs the words again, in between slow, silken strokes of his tongue. *Little Martyr.*

It was meant to be, I think dizzily, kissing him back and earning myself one of those low groans I love so much. Auden was born to torment me, and how can I resist such a thing? Such a tormenter? Even if he is tied to me by blood as well as desire?

My mother named me for a tormented man, after all.

My mother.

The memory of her sears through me like fire. Her words that summer. *Tell this boy you have to stay home, and then don't see him again.*

Suddenly I can't think, I can't breathe. I can't even *be.*

Panic and shame thud through me.

Mamá.

She would be so horrified to see us right now. Crushed and queasy and despairing.

I rip away from Auden's kisses, gasping for breath. "May I," I choke out, hating myself and hating Auden and hating Ralph and hating everyone and everything in the entire world, everything *everything*. Hating the words because the words sound wrong, just like they sounded wrong coming out of Auden's mouth all those years ago. And yet they have to be said, they *have* to, because if they're not said, if I let Auden keep kissing me and fake-crucifying me, I'll never let him stop. I'll let my own brother do hellish things to me and I'll love every second of it—and every second of it will infect me, until all my memories of my mother are flecked with spots of rot and shame. Until I can't look at myself in the mirror for fear of what she'd see if she were alive to look at me.

"*May I*," I murmur again, and Auden's still so close, close enough that he could easily recapture my mouth, and part of me wants him to. But the other part of me is noticing with some alarm that Auden hasn't let me go yet, he hasn't backed away. He hasn't even lifted his lips from where they hover near my cheek. And his hips…

Even now we are pressed together so tightly that I can feel every thick inch of him. Hard and wanting.

Everything I know about kink, everything I've ever read or heard, dictates that when a submissive says a safeword, the Dominant should spring back like a vampire leaping away from the sun. Or a tempting virgin.

But Auden doesn't do that.

Instead, he closes his eyes and takes in a shuddering breath, agony sketched all over his face. His entire frame is shivering against me, like the effort it's taking to keep from devouring me whole is more than he can bear, and for a moment, I think he's going to give in. I think he's going to take me, safeword or not, and I hate that it thrills me a little that he might do it.

"Please," I whisper, my voice breaking over the word. "Please."

He sucks in another quivering breath—one that ends on something sounding like a sob—and then he abruptly shoves himself away, wheeling around to face the window as he runs a hand through his hair. The fabric of his henley clings to his shoulders and sides, and I can see the heave and quiver of each rapid breath as he drags it in.

"Auden," I start, but he gives a sharp jerk of his head, still facing away from me.

"Give me a minute," he bites out, his fingers tightening in his hair as his other hand flexes dangerously at his side. "If you don't want me to touch you, then I need a fucking minute."

Ignoring the quickening in my blood at the realization that he's about to snap—fuck, why is it so sexy to see him about to snap?—I point out, a little petulantly, "This is supposed to be about giving *me* a minute, not you. Or don't you know the rules?"

"When," says Auden, "have we ever done anything by the rules?"

And he's right. But then of course, so am I.

"I never wanted to say it," I say to his back. "You know I didn't."

His voice is tired when he replies. "I know, St. Sebastian. I remember that summer too."

"You begged me to stop you if you went too far. And last night—you said the same thing last night too."

Auden turns enough that I can see his face in profile; he looks profoundly sad, although the jumping pulse at the side of his throat tells me he's aching to pin me against the wall again. "And is this too far?" he asks quietly. "Am I too far for you now?"

My mouth is dry. My body is a living contradiction of shame and angry arousal. "I can't unknow it, Auden. And I can't forgive that you hid it from me."

Auden nods, once. Not in agreement or concession, but in mere acknowledgement.

"Tell me how you found out," he says. It's a command I'm not sure I obey because I want to, or because it feels good to obey him with something, anything at all, now that there's this impossible gulf between us.

"Your journal," I admit. "I found it in your journal."

"Spying on me?" he asks, but he doesn't sound angry. It's hard to tell with him turned, but it sounds like there would be a fond tilt to the corner of his mouth if I could see it.

I'm honest now, too honest for my own good. "I just wanted more of you," I mumble. "I wanted to touch the things you touch and see the things you see. I wanted to feel closer to you."

My confession has him turning all the way around, his hands dropping by his sides to flex and flex and flex, and his erection still swelling unapologetically between his hips. His eyes are like the forest again—alive and hungry.

"This isn't over, St. Sebastian," he promises in a low voice. "I hope you know that."

"It has to be over. Stop being such a bad fucking Dominant and accept it."

The edges of his mouth tug down, and it's not fair for any man to look so good in his displeasure. "I think you've forgotten last night. The thorn chapel."

"Owning Thornchapel doesn't mean you get to make up whatever rules you want."

He ignores this because of course he does. He's Auden Guest, lord of the manor, and his family has done whatever they've liked in this valley for fifteen hundred years. "What about Proserpina?" he asks. "What about the three of us?"

I think of Proserpina clenching her fist between us, pumping it like a shared heartbeat. The shared heart that somehow beats for all three of us.

My chest is tight. "I don't know."

"Well, I know," he says with that impossible arrogance. "I know that both of you are mine, and I also know that Poe is as much yours as you are hers. I'd rather you not hurt her while you and I—" he makes an impatient gesture "—figure this out."

I lean my head against the wall and close my eyes. "There's nothing for us to figure out."

I hear Auden step closer.

"You're right about that," he vows.

I open my eyes to see him avid and beautiful in front of me. For a long moment, we just look at each other. I can't call it a standoff, because I know there's no way Auden will stay frozen for long.

And I'm right.

"This isn't over," he repeats silkily, and then he starts for the door.

"Auden," I half warn, half beg.

He turns the full force of his gaze on me once again. "You're still mine, St. Sebastian Martinez. And you're still going to my fucking gala."

And then he leaves.

5

Proserpina

I sleep all day, and most of the night, only waking up when Auden slides into bed and silently tugs me into his chest. The sheer pleasure of being held by him, of rubbing my cheek against his bare chest, is enough to have me back asleep within mere moments, and I don't wake up enough to ask why St. Sebastian isn't in bed with us.

I wake up again as I feel Auden's lips against my temple and then him gently disentangling himself from me. I blink against the faint morning light, fussing a little as Auden leaves the bed and takes all his nice-smelling warmth with him.

"Sleep, little bride," he says, tucking the blankets in around me. I'm conscious enough to recognize that his voice is sad, but before I can ask him why, he kisses me. "Rebecca's team will be here to start tearing apart the maze in earnest, so you may as well sleep while it's still quiet."

I want to sleep—I still feel wrung out from Beltane and vaguely queasy from the Levonelle—so I don't protest. "Did Saint have to leave for work?" I ask on a yawn, my eyes already closing.

Auden's voice is careful when he says, "He does have work today."

"Okay," I mumble, and then I'm unaware once more.

I dream of Estamond.

She and Randolph sit on a red blanket between the standing stones at the edge of Thornchapel's property. A summer breeze toys with their clothes as they pick at the remains of a picnic.

A lone bee has found its way to the half-eaten strawberries; it buzzes indecisively around the plate, hovering at the edges like a nervous guest who won't sit down.

They have their shoes and jackets off, and Randolph is stroking Estamond's bare foot. His hand is trembling and his lips are parted. His stare is pinned to where his large male fingers touch the dainty curve of her ankle. He looks like a man who is being very, very brave; he looks like he can hardly believe his own daring.

There are no rings on either of their fingers. They're not married yet.

"Tell me more about it," he says to her, and I know they've been talking, continuing some conversation started several days ago.

"It's better to act than to speak," Estamond murmurs, putting her hand over his. She pushes his hand up to her knee. Without stockings, her skin is warm and supple, and his fingers twitch underneath hers. "Wouldn't you agree?"

Randolph can barely speak. He knows he should pull away, he knows he should angle his body so she can't see the shameful response he's having to touching her under her skirts.

"I like to learn." His voice is quiet, but gruffly so. A man's shyness, not a boy's.

Estamond parts her legs, savoring the small grunt that leaves his lips as he watches. "One question, then."

"Only one?"

"How else will I lure you out for more picnics?" she teases, and he meets her eyes with a look so tender and helpless that Estamond's chest hurts. He doesn't need to say it; they both know.

He doesn't need to be lured or fed. He's hers and has been since he first saw her on the village green as Thorncombe's May Queen.

"Proceed with your question," Estamond says, reaching out to finger the small curl behind his ear. His hair is a light, pleasant brown—Wessex mixed with Dumnonia—but near his temples and behind his ears, there're a few strands of silver. She knows he is embarrassed by it, embarrassed by his age—he thinks it unseemly for a man of nearly four decades to desire a girl of not even two—but she likes it. She likes how big he is, how powerful his hands are, how thick hair dusts his forearms and the tops of his feet. She likes how it feels to be soft and new against his hard muscles, she likes all that power and experience giving way under the gentlest of her touches and the smallest of her smiles.

Randolph's hand stays near her knee, but she can feel the quivering in his touch—he wants to pull away, he wants to push higher. A thick column of arousal is pressing against the front of his trousers. His voice is distracted when he asks, "Who is John Barleycorn?"

I know—with sudden dream-certainty—that they've been talking about the old ways. About the thorn chapel.

I also know, with the same certainty, that Estamond hasn't said that name to him. Intentionally so. I know that when he says it—the innocent *John*, the haunting *Barleycorn*—fear tickles through her belly like the dry awns of a barley spike.

"Why do you ask?" she says.

Randolph stretches a little, ursine and contented, although Estamond notes with some fondness that the hand on her knee stretches too. Her bear's not fully contented just yet. "The villagers were talking about when to go up and start scything the bracken in the hills—which means the barley in the lowlands won't be far behind. Then one of them mentioned the name— they'd pour out their ale for John Barleycorn before they started."

Estamond hates the name in Randolph's mouth. She hates thinking of what that name means while the sun is shining on her silver-templed bear, a bear still too shy to reach for the freely offered honey beneath her skirt. Suddenly, she's had enough.

"John Barleycorn is a memory, that's all," she says abruptly. "He is nothing to us." And to keep Randolph from asking anything more—or wondering at her sharp tone of voice—she takes his hand and leads it up her skirts until she hears another bearlike grunt, and then there's no more talk of John Barleycorn.

By the time I force myself out of bed, it's late morning and the hedge removal in the maze is well underway. I peer out the bedroom window to see digging machines and backhoes and a veritable swarm of people in bright vests tearing the maze apart bite by bite. Chewing through one hundred and fifty years of beauty like it had no right to be there in the first place.

Carrion birds, ripping the flesh from Thornchapel's bones.

The memory of my mother's bones flashes through my mind, and I close my eyes, thinking of the white arch of her eye socket, of the dark mud St. Sebastian had scraped away from it. I think of him desperately murmuring a prayer in my ear, I think of Becket's confession about that Samhain and what he saw. It should feel cathartic, maybe, to see something so quintessentially Thornchapel torn up beneath those machines, to see the land punished for the crime of hiding my mother from me, but it's not cathartic in the least. It's miserable, and I wish Auden would have stayed its sentence and let it be for another hundred and fifty years. Undoing the maze won't undo Ralph's sins any more than it will bring my mother back to life.

I'm full of contradictory thoughts and feelings by the time I'm down in the library with a cup of coffee and Sir James curled by the scanning station in easy reach for the idle foot-pets I like to give him while I'm working.

How can I love this place when it's the place that killed my mother?

How can I feel so protective of it when I'm basically a stranger to it, and its own golden scion seems intent on scrubbing it down to the bedrock?

Estamond was protective of it too, I remember, and then look at the stack of books I'm supposed to be working on. They're "scientific" agricultural treatises from the late eighteenth century, and I decide I'll get back to the ruminations on the best soil conditions for barley in Devonshire in a minute. I set my coffee down, and much to the disgruntlement of the German shepherd already rolled onto his side for tummy rubs, I start hunting through the stacks, climbing up one of the steep wooden staircases to access a far upper corner of the second level that I know holds some Guest family history. I want to see if I can find more about Estamond, or even just the time period when the Guests moved in and took the land from the Kernstows.

The day is one of intermittent drizzle and clouds, and so I'm listening to the rain patter softly at the glass and to the slide of leather and cloth as I tug at books to look at the covers when I hear footsteps. Expecting a lost construction worker or maybe Delphine wandering in from wherever she's been curled up with her phone, I step over to the wooden railing that rings the upper story of the library and then beam when I see it's my favorite priest.

"Proserpina," he calls up, and before I can come down the stairs, he's climbing up them, taking the steep risers two at a time with his long legs until he's up here with me, pulling me into his arms for a solid embrace. I catch the woody, spicy notes of incense; I breathe them in, reminded of that day in his church when he trapped me against a wall and fucked me with a hand shoved down my panties.

As if knowing where my thoughts have gone, Becket asks in a low voice, "Can I kiss you?"

"Yes," I say eagerly—then remember Beltane night and the promises Auden, Saint, and I made to each other. I'm a claimed submissive now, and I belong to someone. "Wait—I should ask Auden," I whisper into Becket's shirt. "I'm his now."

"Oh, I know," Becket says, and I'm not sure if I'm correctly reading the tone of his voice, so I lift my face to look up at him. He's smiling in that priestly way of his—like happiness is the serious business of God—but there was something in his voice that seemed more serious still. Before I can ask him about it, he's pulled his phone from his pocket and is showing me the screen. "Which is why I've already asked him."

I glance down, and then I laugh a little. Leave it to the boys who've grown up with Latin lessons and horses to turn something like this into a mannerly, gracious exchange.

May I kiss Poe?

You may do whatever you like with her, Auden had replied. **Provided she agrees and she's returned to me happy.**

"Well, then," I say, still laughing when Becket's mouth captures mine. His phone clatters to the floor as he grabs for my waist to haul me close.

You may do whatever you like with her.

I shouldn't be so turned on by that, right? But hell. Every stroke of Becket's tongue, every squeeze of his warm hands—it's at Auden's pleasure, it's at Auden's will. *Auden* is letting this happen, and so even though it's Becket's mouth against mine and even though it's Becket's long body crowding me up against the bookshelves, it's like Auden himself is kissing me. It's like Auden himself is slowly lighting my body on fire.

"You like this," Becket whispers between kisses. "You like him loaning you out."

Even the word *loan* makes my toes curl, and I'm searching for something to rock my hips against until Becket pushes a hard thigh between my legs as graciously and calmly as he would offer his shoulder for a parishioner to cry on. The pressure is so good, it makes me wild, and I paw shamelessly at the hard shoulders underneath Becket's tab-collar shirt. A loaned toy already whining for more.

My voice is breathless when I finally answer. "I do like it. So much."

"Auden knows you very well." Becket's hands move to my hips, helping me move against his thigh, as he kisses me again. "Even after such a short time."

It *has* been a short time—it's been less than six months since I returned to Thornchapel. And yet, it feels like so much longer, and I'm not sure why. I'm not sure if it's because we knew each other as children, or if doing sacred things together out in the woods means you know someone much more intimately than normal, but whatever it is, it makes me feel like I've been bound together with Auden and Saint for much longer than a few months.

I wish Auden were here right now, so much. And St. Sebastian too.

"You taste so sweet," Becket says, bending down to kiss my neck. "You taste like everything good."

My wandering fingers find the collar of Becket's shirt and run along the edges. He's taken his priest collar off, and so the notch in the shirt reveals the base of his throat: strong and warm and vulnerable. I trace circles there as he tastes my mouth. "Is this okay?" I ask him as we break apart for a breath. "Are you sure?"

His eyes glow down at me, a deep blue made even bluer by the pale light pouring in from the north-facing windows. He gives me another serious kind of smile. "I am more sure about you than I am about anything apart from God himself," he murmurs, and then he brushes his lips against my forehead—a kiss that could be priestly if not for the thigh pressing so perfectly against my cunt.

I don't take my eyes from his face. He looks so wholesome and handsome and holy, and even though I've carved out my own lush and forgiving version of Catholicism, I know that's not everyone's Catholicism. I know that Becket will face internal and external consequences for what he's done because of me and Thornchapel, and I'm torn between trusting him and wanting to take care of him.

"I don't want you to regret this," I say. "Just because we've done things before—just because we were together for Beltane—doesn't mean we have to do it again."

"Are you telling me," Becket asks with a crooked smile, "that it's never too late to repent?"

I don't answer him because I don't really *know* what I'm trying to tell him. I think it's presumptuous for one person to try to be another's conscience; I also think being a good friend means you feel concern for someone's future as well as their present. I keep searching those flame-blue eyes, and finally say, "I want to be good for you."

His smile fades into a sigh, but it's a tender sigh rather than an impatient one. "I don't believe you could be anything else. Do you love me?"

"Of course."

"Do you love me like you love Auden? Or St. Sebastian?" Before I can answer, he's shaking his head, eyes closing as if he's ashamed. "I'm sorry. I shouldn't have asked that."

I chew on my lip. "Do you want me to?" I ask. "Love you like I love them?"

The priest drops his forehead to mine.

"Yes," he admits, voice troubled. "I do."

He sounds so miserable that I ache for him. I cradle his wonderful face in my hands and lift my lips to his, giving him all the love with my body that I can't give with my heart. "Please don't be in love with me," I beg in between kisses. "Don't hurt for me. Please."

"It's too late," he whispers back. "But I'll never ask you for what you can't give. I just need you to know what these kisses are for me, because they're not a sin. For me, they are a sacrament."

And what can I say to that? What *should* I say to that? As much as I love knowing things, I wish I could unknow this, I wish I could unlearn that

Father Becket Hess…loves me. Not in the way a friend loves a friend, not in the way an occasional paramour loves a lover, but *love*-loves. And I want to give him all the love he deserves, I want to love him back with every molecule of my being, but it won't be what he wants from me, it won't be the same.

He pulls up and studies my face. "I mean it, Proserpina," he says gently, correctly interpreting my worry. "Just this—what it is, what you can give me—is something I cherish beyond measure. The last thing I want is for you to feel like I'm waiting for you to give me more or change how you feel."

"Becket…"

"And I'm sorry I said anything at all," he tells me, running a thumb along my lip and then trailing it down my jaw to my throat. "It's ridiculous, wanting more when I already have so much. When I've already been so greedy…"

His thumb moves farther down, his whole hand, and then he's palming a breast as he gives me another sweet kiss.

I decide something then and there. "You can always say it," I tell him, meaning it with everything I am. "You can always tell me and show me. You can always let me feel it."

I find the hand not currently cupping my breast and guide it under my skirt. As per Auden's earlier request, I'm wearing nothing underneath it, and so the moment I tilt away from his thigh, he encounters me bare and wet and hot.

"Proserpina," he groans.

"Let me feel," I tell him, letting go of his hand so that mine are free to slide through his hair. "Let me feel every bit of it."

The next kiss he gives me is not so sweet. It's ardent and harsh, and it feels like he's unleashing weeks and months of longing into me. His lips mold over my own, his tongue strokes against mine. One hand squeezes at my breast as the hand under my skirt searches me relentlessly. From the firm bud at the top to the tightly pleated button in the back, Becket refuses to let any part of me go unexplored. Unprobed. And soon the same fingers I'm pressing against are charting the hidden well inside my folds, pushing inside and sending me to my toes.

"I was here," Becket murmurs. "Just a couple nights ago, I was right here."

I part my legs as much as I can while still standing, and he groans again, the hand on my breast now falling to his belt. It's the work of seconds for him to have his belt undone and his pants opened, and then his hands are under my skirt again, shoving it up to my waist so that there's nothing but cool library air brushing against me. But he doesn't push his way inside me. Instead he kisses me again, gripping my thigh to hold it against his hip as he explores my mouth.

The emptiness against my cunt is excruciating.

"Please," I beg. "Please, Becket—" and the rest is swallowed by another avid kiss—wet and hot and hard.

He breaks the kiss to suck at the pulse pounding in my throat, saying roughly against my neck, "It hurts, doesn't it? It hurts to want something so much."

I'm wild by now, trying to climb him, but he won't help me, he won't do anything to fix the need I have for him. I twine my arms around his neck; I bite his lips as much as I kiss them—and still he won't relent.

Made brazen by the ache between my legs, I slide my hands down his chest until I find the hanging ends of his belt, and then I pull at the stiff fabric of his shirt until I feel bare skin. His lower belly is firm and flat, but not ostentatiously sculpted, and there's a fine trail of hair leading down into his pants. I know without looking that it's as golden as the hair on his head—I remember seeing flashes of it on Beltane night, made ruddy and copperlike by the flaring firelight, or made silver and pale whenever a wandering flashlight caught it in its beam.

"Touch me," I whisper, going farther down until I feel the heat of his erection against my fingertips. Until I can fill my hands with his cock and tug gently upwards.

He stiffens but he doesn't relent. In fact, he barely reacts at all—just a small tensing of his stomach and a little hitch in his breathing.

"You're made of stone," I accuse.

He smiles against my mouth and pulls back enough that we can look each other in the eyes. "No. Not stone."

Becket's hands find mine, and he moves me like I'm a doll, cinching my skirt and curling my fingers around it and then placing my other hand against his heart. "This heart," he murmurs, pressing me back into the shelves, "beats and pounds every minute of the day so that I can exist to love. I was created to love. And I know no other way to love than with my entire body." His hips are against mine, and I can feel the dangling ends of his belt against my thighs. "I know no other way to love other than to be consumed by it, to throw my entire body on the altar of it. I want the blood in my veins to be burning with worship. I—" and here he drops his lips to my ear "—want—" and he finally pushes against me like *that,* sending the taut curve of his maleness pushing into my cunt "—*ecstasy.*"

I shudder as he pushes against me again—expertly, not penetrating me but teasing me, the tempting pressure of his erection sending me writhing against it. But every time I chase him, he moves with me, keeping us just at the edge of joining.

"I want nothing between me and what I love," Becket whispers into my mouth. "Between you and me. Between me and God. Ecstasy always."

I moan. "Becket, *please—*"

"But we can't live day to day consumed by love," Becket says, as if I hadn't spoken. He cups my breast and slides his other hand into my hair. "So I have to keep my love at bay. I have to deny myself the full force of it." His cock pushes against me, but still he refuses to let me impale myself on him, even though I'm wet enough that he's slid past my inner folds right to my very entrance. All it would take is one nudge. One tilt.

"Denial," Becket murmurs to me, closing his eyes, "is the imprint love leaves on the world. It is love's fossil. Its sign. Sacrifice is the heart of love."

It's the same voice that exhorts a flock to return their hearts to their god, and it seems to fill the cavernous library, all the way up to the plasterwork arching above us and all the way down to the gloomiest leather-scented corners.

Sacrifice is the heart of love, I repeat to myself, the words thrumming through me. I think of Estamond's torc and the black roses covering the door. She who became the Thorn King so that the men she loved wouldn't have to. Because she couldn't think of any other way to keep them safe.

"Sacrifice," I say, and rock myself against him, "sounds like a lot of work."

"Sometimes," Becket agrees, "it's far too much." And then he pierces me fully with his broken denial, driving me right to my toes.

My head falls back as he thrusts inside, and even at this angle, there's a stretch and fullness that has me gasping. He has my bottom filling his hands as he lifts me higher and can finally stroke in all the way to his thick, golden base.

"Oh," I mumble, feeling Becket's invasion now, and the Beltane sex a couple of nights before along with it. Becket is too gentle for real sadism, so the lingering soreness is all the roughness I'll get. I hold on to it, I savor it. Use it to remind myself that I'm Auden's May Queen, his and Saint's little bride to be wedded by the Beltane fire. I don't need pain to come—just kink, and being loaned out to a desperate priest is kinky enough—but I'd be lying if I didn't say the reminders of Auden and Saint's rough use of me don't help me get there. And fast.

"Becket," I say, and then I forget what I was going to say because Becket pins me against the side of the shelf again and gives me a taste of that mysterious expertise of his, stroking in and out of me until I can barely breathe for the climax building in my belly.

"You're magnificent," he says, his face so close to mine. "You're heaven. You feel—so—good—" The smooth strokes of his hips grow jerky and abrupt, and I swear I feel him swell inside of me, bigger and harder than ever.

He's going to come.

A small firecracker of panic flares and pops in my mind. I just started taking birth control pills yesterday, and I'm supposed to use a back-up method of contraception for seven days after starting to be on the safe side. Shit, shit, shit.

"I'm not—don't come inside me," I say, hoping it's not too late, hoping he won't be mad. "I should have said something earlier, I'm sorry, but—"

I forget that he's a priest; I forget that he's *my* priest, and the look he gives me as his hips go still is as patient and understanding as any shepherd's. "Don't apologize," he murmurs. "I should have asked. Are you close?"

I nod.

"Do you want me to stay inside you while I make you come? There might still be some risk even then, but I'll keep myself from coming."

"You can do that?"

"Yes."

I'm too horny to be a hundred percent safe right now. *Mostly safe* sounds good enough to my pussy. "Yes, I want you to stay inside."

He needs no other encouragement, fingertips digging into my ass as he starts working me against him—not with short thrusts, but with deep, grinding rolls—strokes for me, not for him. Almost immediately, the earlier panic is replaced by pure, urgent pleasure.

"Is this okay?" I pant in his ear. "Will you be okay?"

"Do you mean," Becket asks, his voice near-guttural with need, "will I be able to keep myself from pumping my release inside you once you go over the edge? Or will I just give in and give you everything I've been feeling all these weeks?"

I can't answer him, because his obscene words—and in *that* voice, like he's seconds away from throwing me on the floor and rutting into me however he wants—send me careening into bliss. The burst below my navel is bright and sweet and wonderful, and I ride it easily, my eyes open and my fingers clutched tight in his hair.

"Sweet saint," he murmurs lovingly. "I'd give up everything for this, for you."

Even in the haze of my orgasm, I know that's not true. Even if I'd allow him to give up anything at all—which I wouldn't—I know he could never give up serving God. *Should* never. Being a priest is too deeply rooted in him to weed out now; those roots are threaded through his nerves and veins and bones.

Becket pulls out of me, leaving me squeezing around nothing, and sets me back on my feet. There's no time for words, for him explaining what he needs, and so he spins me around to face the shelves and uses a foot to kick my legs together. Before I realize what he's up to, he's sliding his slick cock between my thighs from behind, fucking my pressed-together thighs like he would a mouth or pussy.

Every surge sends the dusky tip of him emerging from the front of my legs, and on every stroke, the top of his shaft glides along my wet seam, making everything slicker and slicker. It peeks out a final time—huge and taut and near-painful-looking with how swollen he is—and with a moan that's deep and rich and musical, he erupts. Thick jets of seed spatter against the shelves and run down my thighs; his hands—suddenly more forceful than they've been all day—press into my soft thighs and yank me back, over and over and over, so he can fuck every last drop right out of himself.

Semen runs down the front of my leg, and his breath is warm and fast on my neck as the last few shudders rack his frame.

He gradually goes still.

"Are you okay?" he asks.

His hands become gentle and careful on my legs, stroking up once or twice before he smooths my skirt down over them. He pulls back as he slides free from my thighs, and it isn't until he makes a low noise in his throat that I realize it's because he wants to watch. Both the act of him pulling through my flesh and also the inevitable ruffle of my skirt back over my exposed bottom, which is no doubt bearing the fast-fading reddish marks of his hands.

"I'm okay," I reassure him, and turn to give him a hug. He's warm—so warm—even through his shirt, and his heart is still beating fast. "Are you?"

I want to say something more—maybe about how he should try to stop loving me or about how I could attempt to love him like he wants me to—but both of those things would be wrong, and so all I can do is repeat what I said earlier. "Anytime you need me—anytime you need to show me how you feel…"

His lips find my hair.

"I know," he says quietly. "I know."

6

Proserpina

After Becket leaves, I can't concentrate. I decide to leave my work for later and go find Auden before he drives to London.

I stop at a window on the way up to his office and watch the bustle and swarm of the maze's destruction. Workers crawl over its carcass, and emerging from the mud and stubble of removed hedges is the statueless plinth next to the fountain. There're a few people standing next to it, waving in a small crane-looking thing, which I assume is to remove the heavy masonry of the fountain. For the first time in a hundred and fifty years, the secret stairs will be exposed.

I wonder how Estamond would feel about that.

Rebecca is there too, in a camel-colored trench coat with her iPad tucked into the crook of her elbow, a slender, still fixture in the midst of all the chaos. Occasionally workers come up to her and she bends her head to listen—one time she pulls up something on her iPad to show them and then points to where the thing shall be done—but otherwise she doesn't move. She is the axis the work rotates on; she is the order, the intelligence, the will that reshapes the earth. But as I finally step away from the window, I see her turn and glance back at the house.

She's looking at her bedroom window, where even now from down the hall and up the stairs, I can hear Delphine talking about backlinks and follower benchmarks to someone on the phone.

Outside, Rebecca twists her head away, as if irritated with herself—but I notice she looks at the house one more time before she shakes her head and then strides determinedly to the other side of the maze.

Auden's new studio and office takes up a huge swath of the renovated third floor. Like in the bedrooms, he's kept the old beams and he's floored the entire story with planks of pale, buttery wood. Windows are everywhere—windows which had been removed, taken apart, cleaned, repaired or replaced as needed, and then releaded and reinstalled. I know it must have been an enormous expense, but for all his en-suiting and rewiring, Auden has kept the parts of the house with the most flair and the best history, and the leaded windows were some of those parts. And now even on a cloudy day, the studio glows with light, the latticed shapes of it tracing back and forth over the floor like a grid.

On the far end of the massive room—past the rows and rows of bookshelves and the two drafting tables and the sprawling model table already covered with tiny shrubs and piles of baby-sized bricks and neat stacks of balsa wood—Auden sits at a desk with his head thrown back against his chair and one arm dangling by his side. That hand flexes now and again, and once or twice it balls in some powerful emotion, but the rest of him is utterly still—a study of *Brideshead Revisited*-esque tweed and mussed hair.

I suddenly have the awful premonition that he's angry with me—one that's not eased when he says, in a flat, emotionless voice, "Come here, Proserpina."

Is he upset about Becket? Or maybe that I didn't come up the very moment Becket left the house? Is he upset that I didn't refuse Becket or personally ask permission to play?

Come to think of it…am *I* upset about these things? Should I be?

I get to Auden and I don't wait for him to turn around, I don't wait for him to speak. I just drop to my knees next to his chair and press my face against his leg.

"How was your time with Becket?" he asks, his dangling hand coming up to toy with my hair.

I don't know how to answer that, other than honestly. "Good," I say. "And also…not."

"Why was that?"

I want to bury my face against Auden's thigh forever. "He feels very strongly about me."

"Ah," says Auden. He tugs at my hair so that I have to look up at him. His eyes are soft.

"So you know then," he says. Gently.

It takes a second for his words and their unspoken meaning to sink in. "You knew Becket loved me." I try not to sound accusatory, I really do, but it's hard. "You know how he felt."

"Loves and feels," Auden corrects, and then with an effortlessness that belies the strength of his lean frame, he hauls me easily onto his lap and pushes an impatient hand up my skirt. "It's very much a present emotion for him, I believe."

I try to look at him, but it's impossible from this angle. "You're not jealous—*ohhh, oh, oh*—" Auden's clever fingers have found the heart of me, and they delve easily inside. I'm still wet and open from Becket, and there's nothing stopping Auden from adding a second finger after a moment, and then a third.

I twist and groan on his lap, the stretch almost too much and still not enough, and so I try to fuck myself on his fingers, bracing my hands on the armrests for leverage. I know it must look beyond undignified, me with my legs splayed and my dress up to my waist and my mouth dropped into an *O* of surprised, submissive pleasure, but I don't care. And given the hard male arousal underneath me, I don't think Auden cares either.

"Of course I'm jealous," Auden says, nipping at my earlobe as he fucks me with his hand. "Some days, I want to lock you away like fine china. I want you on a leash so I can keep you curled at my feet wherever I go, and I want you kept in a faraway tower where only I can have you. Because I'm selfish and mean, and I want your bright eyes and sweet body just for me. But I don't really need to be jealous, do I?"

"You—you don't?" I manage to say.

I can feel his smile curving against my neck. I know this smile. It's probably the same smile his ancestors wore when they began ranging and ravaging their way into Dumnonia. "It's my fingers you're currently screwing this curvy little body down onto, and this weekend, it will be my bruises you wear. It's me who claimed you by the fire, and it's me you love. You're mine, little bride, and you have been since you were a girl."

His words are like his fingers—pressing and probing into secret parts of me. My head drops back onto his shoulder. "I have been yours since then," I whisper. "Saint's too."

For just the briefest second—too brief for me to react—Auden's breath catches behind me. And then he's back to exploring my pussy, and when he speaks again, he doesn't mention Saint.

"You're wet," he says. His voice is low and dark and cool. "You're wet from Becket."

"Yes," I say. "Are you—are you very angry with me?"

"Am I angry that my little slut acted like a little slut when I wanted her to?" The hand not working me open slides up my thigh and brushes over a streak of dried semen. "He didn't come inside you?"

He sounds disappointed, like he'd loaned out a prized sports car to a friend and they came back having driven under the speed limit the entire time.

"I only just started the birth control," I say. "I'm supposed to be extra careful the first week, and—"

He gives me a little nuzzle—nothing but gentle affection, as if he doesn't have three fingers jammed inside me and didn't just call me a slut. "I forgot about that. I'm glad you were safe then."

My heart swells until I think it might pop like an overblown balloon. I knew before Thornchapel that I needed love like this, that I needed it rough and tender and mean and sweet, all jumbled together like a wild garden. But now...now I know it like I know nothing else. I need Auden, I need Saint, and I need love to be like this.

I don't know why.

I was the little girl who tied ropes to her wrists just to feel the scratches and itches of it while she played. Maybe I was made for a raw, scratchy love from the very beginning. Or maybe I grew into it the same way that certain flowers push through the brambles to bloom.

Who can say?

"Becket took it on the chin," I add.

Auden traces a fingertip up my thigh. "By the looks of it, I'd say he took it between your legs."

I laugh, which sends me clenching around his fingers—and we both make noises at the same time, mine a gasp of surprised pleasure and his a hoarse kind of growl.

"I need to fuck you," he says on an exhale, pulling free of my body and banding an arm around my waist. He lifts me up just enough to reach into his pocket to retrieve a condom and unbutton his pants, and then I'm perched on his knees while he prepares himself. I can't resist sneaking a look over my shoulder, catching a glimpse of expensive fabric rucked up the firm planes of his stomach and the taut, swollen head of him already glistening with latex.

"Come here," he growls, even though I'm arguably already *here*, and then I'm hauled squealing and laughing to where he wants me. And once I'm facing him and straddling him, he uses his fist to angle his organ upward and then orders me to sink down.

"Slowly," he cautions. He fists my skirt in one of his elegant artist's hands, lifting it to my hip so that everything below my waist is exposed to him. "I want to watch."

I obey his will and lower myself onto his sheathed cock as he leans back and studies the sight like he's going to paint it one day. It nearly kills me to go slow—it turns out my orgasm with Becket has done nothing but made me hornier, and I'm craving the rough bite that a fast ride would give me—but I know disregarding a direct request from Auden will have me ass up over his lap and spanked until I can't breathe. And *then* he'll punish me for real and refuse to let me come. Which will kill me at this point. So slow it is.

Auden watches me work with a composed expression, his gaze unreadable and distant. Only the trembling of his hands where they grab my hips gives away his eagerness—at least until I'm fully seated against him, my clit flush against the abdominal muscle right above his cock and his desire spreading me wide, wide open.

Then the trembling is all over—his thighs and his belly and his breathing, and his eyelids flutter, as if he wants to close them but can't stop looking at the place we're joined.

"I'd give up everything I own for this cunt," he says. And then a wicked smile cuts across his face. "If it weren't already mine, that is."

His words are more effective than a thumb on my clit; I drop my chin to my chest and remind myself to breathe as my belly hollows at his coolly obscene observations. It's so close to what Becket said earlier—*I'd give up everything for this, for you*—but it might as well be miles apart in meaning.

Becket wants to belong to me. But I already belong to the filthy architect-prince with the lazy smile and the forest-colored eyes.

And when Auden flicks those eyes up to me, I see the full force of his shameless want, of his crude hunger—all of it underpinned by another hunger—the same I saw twelve years ago when he kissed me for the first time. A hunger for my very heart.

And oh, how I want it to be eaten.

I feel a small flush of guilt that I can't match the same surge of desire for Becket's unselfish decency as I can for the person currently leaning forward to bite at my breasts through my dress. Although I don't think it has anything to do with Becket or decency, and everything to do with Auden. And with Saint.

If Becket were all I knew, he would be the most mesmerizing light I'd ever seen. But he's not all I know. I'd met two bitter and beautiful boys in this house and tumbled into a new life. A life that was all stars and shadows, glimmers and gloom. And I was done for.

"Make yourself come on me," Auden says. "While I listen to every single thing Becket did to you."

So I tell him. I tell him about the kisses and the hard thigh between my legs for me to rock against. I tell him how Becket teased me with his cock until I begged for it, and how I came after he talked about coming inside me, even though we both knew he wouldn't do it, not after I asked him not to. I tell him how Becket ended up finishing and making a mess on the bookshelf.

"The wooden part," I clarify, my breathing coming in short bursts. "I never would have let him—on the books—biological debris—"

"Good. Biological debris on the books was my chief concern," he says in a grave tone.

I almost think he's serious until I see the faint dip of a suppressed dimple, a quivering crenel that he tries and fails to hide, and then he's grinning up at me. I swat at him, and he catches my hand, laughing.

"You're a good librarian, Proserpina, even if you do need to be fucked twice a day to keep you happy enough to work."

His voice is teasing, happy, but his words give life to one of my real fears, now blown to full life since everything that happened on Beltane. "Auden," I say, hips slowing. "I mean, *sir*. Maybe…maybe I should look for another job. I don't know that I should be your employee now that we're actually together; I don't want you to feel obligated—"

Auden claps his hand over my mouth, eyes narrowed. "No," he says firmly. "You can quit because you're bored or because another position sounds more fulfilling or because you don't want to be here anymore. You quit because you can't stand the sight of me or my house. But you don't quit because you think I feel obligated to pay you. I pay you because you're good at what you do, because you came personally recommended, and because in the four months you've been here, you've done incredible work. I'll write anything into a contract you'd like, but you don't get to leave just because you think you *should*."

I try to speak against Auden's palm, and he sighs but loosens it anyway so the words can come out. "I feel like I'm taking advantage of you. I've spent the day sleeping and playing instead of working."

"I know you have narcolepsy. And I *wanted* you to play. Do you really think," he asks, pushing his hips up so I feel him deep, deep in my belly, "I'd rather you be scanning books than doing this?"

"But—"

"My god, you are stubborn," he replies. Another sigh. "Can't you just pretend that we're opening a very twee and painfully overpriced shop on a high street somewhere? Or an apple orchard where we charge schoolchildren to come and visit? People in love own businesses and work together all the time."

"But we're not working together," I say, unable to let this go. "I'm working *for* you."

"Okay, we're going back to the hand," Auden says. And sure enough, the hand comes up to cover my mouth again. "You're not in my library right now, you're on my lap, and that means different rules, so *shhhh*. I love you and you belong to me, and once I'm finished using you, we will slide back into real life and make sure the terms of your employment make you comfortable. But in the meantime, please understand this: I. Trust. You. Inherently, explicitly, completely. I trust you with my house, with my old books, with my money, and now with my St. Sebastian. I trust you with everything, and I inflexibly and pertinaciously believe that our respective work is made better by us being kinky and playful and in love. Now, you still haven't come, and that was the only command I gave you, which means I'm very close to bending you over my desk and fucking you that way so I can spank you as I do it. Can we be very done with this now?"

"Yes, sir," I say, ducking and burying my face into his wonderful-smelling neck. The shift in angles rubs me both inside and outside in just the right way, and the next words come out husky. "Thank you."

"Thank me by doing as you're told," he says, just as huskily, but he turns his head enough to kiss my cheek. Lingering and warm. "I haven't got all day, little one. I've got to get to London at some point, you know."

"I know," I say, sitting up so I can properly fuck him some more. And also so he can see my little pout—which is mostly to be cute, but it's also a genuine thing, because when he's gone, the whole house feels like it's made of yearning. Even the trees outside seem restless when Auden is away.

"Little brides miss their lords when they're gone, hmm?" Auden says, leaning back again and hiking up my skirt so he can watch as I fuck him.

"Everyone misses you," I whisper, watching his face as he watches my cunt. His eyes are hooded, a faint flush on his cheeks, and every now and again he pulls his lower lip between his teeth, as if he's biting me in his mind. "Thornchapel misses you."

Four months ago, he would have scoffed or spat at that. He would've had some bitter, careless response, made some obscure or tenebrous pronouncements about Thornchapel's future or his own, and then changed the subject. But not today. Not after Beltane.

Maybe not even after Imbolc.

Instead, he merely lifts his eyes to mine and nods, like it was something he already knew. And it's as he's nodding, as he's tacitly admitting that the thing which started as a game between bored friends has now become something vividly and frighteningly real—it's then that I reach my peak, lost in his eyes and the whisper of the waiting forest outside, waiting and rippling with cricket-green leaves for its king.

I move against him harder, faster, urging my climax on and on and on, and it's so much *deeper* and *stronger* and *meaner* and *longer*—it's the kind of orgasm that possesses me, like everything below my belly button is no longer my own, it belongs to the wild world outside, it belongs to the wild god I'm riding. And I forget, I always forget, how much the pure rush of dominance gets him off, how watching someone else obey him is heady delirium, because the moment I finally come, he lets out a soft, tattered sigh. His cock swells big, so big, that last impossible bigness before the end, and then he releases into the condom with long pulses that make his stomach and thighs flex and tense against me.

He only watches at first, chest heaving as he thickens and starts spending, but after the first few surges, he crushes me to his chest and holds me tight as he fucks his way through the last of it—hard, hammering thrusts that shouldn't be as powerful as they are given his position, and yet he does it, lifting his hips and me with every single one.

I cry out against his throat, my climax still stuttering on, and he is relentless with me, fucking until we're both panting and sweaty and until he's made sure that I've milked him of every last second of pleasure.

When he stops, I stay slumped against his chest a moment, listening to the pounding of his heart beneath his sweater, sighing through all those sweet aftershocks. He cradles me close and kisses my hair, and after a few minutes, he pulls carefully free and perches me on the edge of his desk while he takes care of the condom and sets his clothing to rights. Then he tugs me back into his lap, and I curl up there, feeling small and content.

Auden begins stroking along my back, soothing, possessive strokes, and I close my eyes. "What should I do about Becket?" I murmur.

"Do you love him?" inquires Auden. His voice is neutral, but there is a stillness to him as he asks the question. I have the distinct sense that while Auden didn't mind loaning me out for pleasure, he'd feel a lot differently loaning me out for love.

"No," I say honestly. "I don't."

My Dominant loosens a little beneath me, his voice more open when he says, "Good. I can share a lot, Proserpina, but I'm not able to—well, the problem is, I'm fundamentally possessive when it comes to you."

"And Saint," I add for him.

Auden draws in a breath. He lets it out very carefully. "And St. Sebastian," he says finally.

"Should I have known? About Becket?"

"I think it's been growing slowly over time—slowly enough it would have been easy to miss."

"But you knew."

"Yes."

"Yes?"

Auden sighs. "Becket told me once after Imbolc that he dreams of you—those strange God-dreams of his, you know. He dreams of you in the middle of everything, you in the very heart of the thorn chapel. After that, I began noticing the signs. Long looks. Prolonged quiets after you would kiss him hello on the cheek. I don't resent him for it, even if I'd fight him bloody and bleeding if he tried to take you away." He holds me tighter, in what seems like an unconscious reflex.

"The thought of you two playing together—it's quite sexy to me," he says, "and more pertinently, I think it is very sexy to *you*, and nothing gets me off like getting you off. He is one of my closest friends, and I trust him implicitly to cherish and adore you. But I cannot stomach the idea of you being in love with anyone other than me and St. Sebastian. If it happens—if you love someone else—you must tell me. Please. I'll accept it, but it will gut me, and I deserve to die on my feet. I—"

It's my turn to clap a hand over his mouth. I squirm in his lap until we're facing each other, and then I tell him the truth. "You and Saint have ruined me," I whisper. "More and more, I think it was that day when we were children. There was never any hope after that. It could only ever have been you two."

Auden blinks, looking bewildered and haughty and relieved all at once, in that way only rich boys are able to pull off, and I remove my hand.

"And I know St. Sebastian feels the same way," I reassure him. "He'll never stop loving you."

"Oh," Auden says, softly, as if I've hit him. "I don't know about that."

A story—pages and pages of it—moves through his eyes, the shadows of a hundred hundred thoughts, the sparks of a thousand thousand unanswered prayers, and I am suddenly, acutely aware of how evasive he's been about St. Sebastian all day. Acutely aware of our silent text thread, of my dark phone, of our missing lover.

"Tell me," I demand. "Tell me right now."

Auden closes his conflicted eyes and swallows. And when he starts to speak, his voice is threaded with so much pain it hurts to hear it.

"Twenty-four years ago, my father had another son. Six weeks ago, I learned his name."

7

Delphine

I was wearing Cherry Tree when it happened.

Sometimes I think about that night—I think about sitting in front of the mirror in my tiny room at the Grange. I think of all the other lip colors I could have chosen instead. The ones that would have been ironic—999 by Dior, maybe, or Tom Ford's Bruised Plum; the ones with talismanic names, like MAC's Angel or Heroine; the ones that would have been restrained and sweet: Jolly Molly or Georgie Girl or Christian Dior's Grege 1947.

I have a therapist, and I know what she would say about my fixation on lipsticks, I know, I know. And it's not like I think of Cherry Tree in the *what was she wearing, did she smile at him, how much did she have to drink* kind of way. It's not like I needed to be wearing a peachy-nude lipstick to prove to myself and everyone else that I didn't deserve to be raped.

It's more like—well—just—one never knows when the worst moment of one's life is going to happen and so one never knows what tiny details are going to be etched into one's memories forever. And sometimes it's hard not to feel like everything would be so much easier if one could only go back and make this one tiny thing different. Because maybe I would have forgotten Angel or Georgie Girl. Maybe I would be able to think of the night with a wryly sophisticated distance if I'd been wearing 999.

But I wasn't able to forget Cherry Tree, and now sometimes I have to send back drinks if they have cherries in them. Once two years ago, I burst into tears at a dinner party with my parents, right there at the table, just because the dessert was cherries jubilee. Someone once gave me a cherry blossom scent, and then spritzed me with it without asking, and I spent the rest of the evening being ill in my cousin's lavatory.

At Girton, there was another girl living in the Grange whose favorite pair of knickers—delicate, silk, practically doll-sized—were embroidered with cherries, and she'd drape them over the radiator to dry after she washed them in the bathroom sink, because they were too fragile for the washing machine or the dryer. Which meant there was a solid year where I had to pretend the radiator didn't exist, just in case I accidentally looked and saw cherries there inside of bare metal and had to think *cherry — Cherry Tree — that night in Audra's garden.*

Sometimes, even just the word *cherry* gives me that feeling of—of inside rain, like it's raining inside my body as my stomach falls to my feet and my thoughts go a little dizzy-fuzzy and my skin is tingly, but in, like, *big* tingles, not little needly ones—like there's more than one Delphine inside me, there're lots of Delphines crowding inside my skin, and they're tapping and kicking trying to find a way out. And I just keep thinking—no way would I be like this if I'd worn Grege 1947 that night. No way would it be this hard. No way would I be like Florence's embroidered knickers, and be too fragile for ordinary life. Ready to unravel at the slightest touch.

I'm wearing Pirate by Chanel as I follow Rebecca into her stylish Peckham flat. We set our bags on the floor, and she turns and looks at me.

"Are you ready?" she asks. Behind her is a wall of windows, and behind those is a cloudy, purply twilight, with low cloud bellies underlit with every lamp, sign, and glowing window in London. She's still in her trench coat—a sort of sand-colored thing, narrow and belted at the waist—and her braids are pulled up into a high bun. She looks like she just strode in from a chic London office—and I have a terrible moment where I think: *this isn't real, this isn't real, this is all a joke, this is an elaborate lie.* Rebecca is too disciplined, she's too good, her cheekbones are too high, and her IQ is even higher—why is she wasting her time with *me*?

Who could want me? asks the Greek chorus chanting behind these thoughts. *Who?*

I swallow. I swallow the thoughts down like they're knives and hope they don't slice me open. I don't want these knife-thoughts at all, but I especially don't want them right now, when I'm finally here, when I'm finally Rebecca's. I don't want my new Domme to know that inside her chirpy submissive is a girl who questions her own worth and sometimes flinches at cherries.

It's the literal last thing I want.

"I'm ready," I whisper.

Rebecca smiles, but it's a small smile, and there's something in it I don't entirely understand. Almost like disquiet, but that can't be right, because Rebecca is never uneasy about anything, ever. I've watched her stand inches away from landscaping machines that would liquefy her bones if they rolled over her foot; I've seen her sit composed and eyebrow-archy through chats about orgies and human sacrifice.

No, she's not anxious. She can't be. It's *Rebecca.*

She doesn't ask me to kneel yet; she doesn't even take off her coat. Instead, she crosses her arms and walks over to one of the large windows, peering down onto the damp street below. "Do you remember the first time you came here?" she asks, not looking at me.

I don't know if we're in a scene or not, and so I stay standing where I am. But I do let my eyes rove around the box of glass and brick, thinking back. Skylights puncture the ceiling at intervals, letting in views of the lavender haze above, and I have a faint memory of watching rain fall like silver pearls on those skylights. Pinging like beads from a broken necklace and then sliding off to the side, jittery as mercury.

"Yes," I answer. "I remember."

"The flat was brand new," Rebecca murmurs. "I'd only just moved in."

I almost wish she didn't remember that week, that undeniable proof that I am not a living sunbeam made of long eyelashes and inspirational captions. And I wish I remembered more of it, just so I could know how embarrassed to feel right now.

"You helped me," I say, because that's what I remember for sure. "Even though you hated me."

She looks over her shoulder, but not at me. Her stare is pinned to the floor, her lower lip caught in her teeth for a brief instant. "I wonder," she says softly, as if to herself, "I wonder if maybe...I didn't hate you like I thought I did."

"Didn't you?"

She doesn't answer, and I think it's because she has no more answer to that than I do. Instead, she raises her gaze to mine, and she's beautiful, she's so beautiful, she's all liquid eyes and delicate jawline. And my heart is crashing against my ribs because I want her, I am parched for anything from her, any drop of affection and attention, and suddenly it's no longer a choice. I can feel her across the room, I can feel every inch and foot between us, and the distance is pulling me apart like a cheap sweater, row by row by row, until I'm just a pile of limp, grotty yarn, and the only way to make it stop is to kneel.

The moment my knees touch the floor, everything stills. The fears, the gnawing insecurities with their vicious little teeth. Because nothing has ever made more sense than kneeling in front of Rebecca.

For a moment, there is nothing. Nothing but the sounds of the street below—the clang and whirr of the mechanic's shop, the obnoxious din of an art gallery party full of guests who are clearly very proud of themselves for being at an art gallery next to a mechanic's. I stare at the floor, an old knotty wood that's been refinished in such a way that one can still see the ghosts of old nails and paint, and hope I haven't done wrong by kneeling when I'm not supposed to. And maybe hope a little that I have done wrong, and Rebecca will punish me for it.

And then she walks to me, a deliberate pace that sends shivers chasing up and down my spine. She wore flats for the trip from Devon, but she might as well be in stilettos for how devastating and dramatic her footsteps are, and when she comes before me, all I want to do is press my face to her ankles and tell her I adore her, I worship her, I love her.

I love her?

I think about this as I stare at her feet in front of me. Her flats are sensible and ethical wool things that are comfortable and quality, but a little bit ugly, and I have the fleeting thought that if she'd just let me, if she'd splurge just a little, I could find shoes that were equally comfortable and ethical, but that actually deserved to be on her gorgeous feet.

The hem of her coat sways a bit as she stands in front of me and I deduce that she's taking it off. Even though I know she's fully clothed underneath it, that small disrobing has heat simmering along my skin.

But can I love her?

Could I really? Already? After years of thinking she was so full of herself just because she was a certifiable genius, after years of assuming I'd marry Auden—because, honestly, who wouldn't marry Auden?

The coat disappears; I hear it drop onto the footstool behind me.

"You look so good, pet," she says, her voice almost a purr, it's that low and breathy. "Whenever I needed to come, I'd think about this. About how you'd look on your knees for me."

I don't say anything, even though I have loads of words bubbling and popping on my tongue. Like popping candy, but made of bad ideas instead of sugar.

What if I love her?

I think I might love her.

Rebecca strides over to a low sofa—elegant, unfussy, modern, exactly her style—and sits. Even with my eyes on the artfully battered hardwoods, I can sense the perfection of her, the slow grace in which she lowers herself and slants her legs to the side instead of crossing them.

"Come to me," she says, still in the wonderful, breathless voice. "Hands and knees."

I'm still in my own jacket, I'm in heels and a suede skirt so short that it pulls up around my bottom when I lean forward to crawl. Nothing about what I'm wearing is comfortable to crawl in, and nothing about it is explicitly sexy—except it is actually *very* sexy to be forced to crawl mere moments after walking through a door, to know I look this slutty and debauched with my skirt up around my hips and my Saint Laurent heels sliding across the floor as I slouch toward the sofa.

Maybe I should be asking, *why this*? Why is this such a fucking turn-on? Why is my cunt already wet and aching to be touched when all I've done is crawl? But it feels like the answer is right in front of me, parting her legs and digging her fingers into my hair. I nuzzle the inside of her knee—silky and warm—and risk a glance up at her face. Her eyes are hooded, liquid and hot under her sinfully long lashes, and her mouth is pressed together in a way that's lush and stern all at once.

"I didn't say you could touch me yet, did I?" she says, tugging on my hair.

"No, Mistress."

"Hmm."

I dare another nuzzle, and those eyes hood even more.

"Delphine," Rebecca warns.

I can't help but smile at that, so I press my face into her knee to hide it. She's wearing a short romper today, the kind with an immaculately fitted bodice and skirt-like shorts underneath, and the fabric has slid down her thighs enough to expose a sleek expanse of leg. Her skin is so soft-looking, so smooth. The way the light falls in the flat, I can see where the muscles under her skin curve and pull, making a subtle path right to the heat between her legs. I can't help myself, I lick that path, just to feel it under my tongue, just to taste her and maybe show her where else my tongue could be if only she'd spread her legs a little farther apart.

Rebecca doesn't react to my naughty tongue, no gasp or jump or tensing or anything, it's like licking a living statue. And when I look up at her, I realize I've made a very, very big mistake. Those eyes are hot with more than ordinary lust now—there's now irritation and excitement and a simmering cruelty that I just *know* is about to boil over.

I'm smiling so big now that there's no point in hiding it.

"You're so much trouble," she breathes. Her fingers tighten in my hair. "So much *fucking trouble.*"

It's what she said in the car on the way here. That I was a brat, that I was spoiled, that she'd have her hands full with me. But then, just like now, the way she said those words—*brat, spoiled, trouble*—made it sound like I was a Christmas gift all wrapped up for her, like I was the kind of thing she'd bite her pillow thinking about at night, and then we'd both grinned at each other, like we'd just learned the most marvelous secret.

We talked about a thousand other things—safewords and boundaries and limits—but that was what I kept coming back to: I'm a brat. And Rebecca likes it.

She likes me. And I think I love her.

When she says I'm trouble, I nip at her wrist and dimple at her, and then giggle as she yanks on my hair in reprimand.

"Oh you think it's funny, do you?" she says, but there's a twist at the edges of her mouth, like someone about to take a bite of a dessert they claimed just seconds ago they didn't want.

"I think a lesson might be in order," she says, regaining some of her sternness with a struggle. "But first…"

She finally does what I've been yearning for her to do since I got to my knees, and uses her slender fingers to draw aside the fabric between her legs. She's wearing narrow lace knickers—so narrow that they barely cover her sex—and from this angle, I can see her secret places. Bare, soft, and already wet.

"Why you wear cheeky knickers when no one can see them, and then the ugliest shoes that everyone else has to look at, is beyond me," I say, which earns my upper arm a sharp pinch.

"I wear these knickers so that I can put little subs with impudent mouths to use at a moment's notice," Rebecca says, and with a sharp tug of my hair, my mouth is pressed against her lace-covered sweetness. "Do your work, little pet. And I'll think about what needs to be done about all this misbehavior of yours."

My work. God. We talked about this too before we came here, about what me moving in would mean, about how we would be here in Rebecca's flat and in the club and out in the world. Where I would serve her, where I would kneel, and where we would just be a regular couple. The places where there might be a little of both—certain dates, maybe, certain evenings at work when she was alone in her office and needed to fuck.

Here—here though, it will be absolute between us. She will be mistress, and I will be her pet—and although it will sometimes be informal, because we are also people with jobs and Netflix shows to watch and face masks to use (in my case anyway)—my first priority will be her. My work will be to please her however she wants, whether that is offering up my mouth for her use, or offering up my body for punishment.

I remember the night I watched Rebecca and Auden spank Poe in the library. I remember how I felt Rebecca's commands to Poe like fingertips on the nape of my neck, even though I wasn't even the one being commanded. Later, I'd found Poe and asked her about the spanking, about the pain, about kink and what it meant. *What about the parts that aren't about the pain?* I'd finally asked. *The parts that are about doing what someone says?*

It's like being loved, Poe had answered. *Like loving.*

And she was right. Because with Rebecca's hands twisted in my hair, and my lips pressed against that wonderful part of her, I know that all my doubts earlier were not doubts at all, but tiny, rippling awakenings. Like coming awake next to the ocean and realizing that I'd been dreaming the roar of the waves for hours without even knowing it.

I was falling in love long before now.

The realization is so exciting, and to have it like this, with my tongue flickering over lace and warm skin and with assertive hands fisted in my hair, is heaven.

Before I can think better of it, I murmur the truth. "I love you."

It's like I speak the words into her very skin, like they coil up through her belly and chest as hungry, grasping vines, because suddenly her body is tensed and flexing and trembling. She's not breathing, and for a moment— oh, for a stupid, ditzy moment—I think it's because she's happy. I think it's because she's about to say it back.

And then the silence bores on, chewing a hole through me, and I simply know. I have a problem with being blurty and blunt, and I should have *thought*, I should have shut up, because now I've poisoned this.

I thought I was being so careful hiding how needy and uncertain I am, but now I've just gone and proved it by saying something unsophisticated and unwelcome.

Rebecca relaxes the tiniest bit against me, and even though this time I'm not brave enough to look up at her, I know she's relaxed because she's figured out what to say. I've given her a complicated maths problem and now she's solved for *x*. She's solved for *Delphine Can't Be An Adult About Kinky Sex*. It's in her voice when she answers, gently and knowledgeably: "That's common to feel in a scene, Delph, it's very natural."

She sounds like someone assuring a teenager about getting an erection in P.E.—*I know this is embarrassing for both of us, but don't worry, it's normal, you'll get control over it one day.*

I close my eyes, my mouth unmoving against her, although I can still taste her on my tongue, I can still smell her. She is sweet and the littlest bit tart and something else that's all her. Perfect. She is perfect and I love her and she doesn't love me.

"I'm going to take you to the club as soon as I can," she's saying, and now she's stroking my hair, like I'm a pet in truth, "and you'll meet lots of other submissives there. You'll get to see so many other people playing, so many scenes, and then you'll see. You'll see that it's a perfectly natural reaction to have."

What can I say to that? What can I do other than nod against her? *Yes, you're right, Mistress, it is just the scene, it's just hormones.*

It isn't the way you frown so adorably at elevations and ecological impact studies. It isn't the way you suck your teeth at certain soil reports, like you've just found out soil has been subtweeting you for weeks.

It isn't the way you know obscure plants that medieval monks grew and it's not the way you never come back inside the house without a wildflower for me—a different kind each time, as if you're worried I'll get bored if you keep bringing me the same species.

It isn't the way you smile when you come, it isn't the way you hold me when you think I'm asleep. It isn't how the light itself changes around you, like you are a living filter and your mere presence makes everything bright, saturated, alive.

No, I can't say these things. I don't think she'd want me to.

"Delph," Rebecca whispers, and her voice is strange, and if she hadn't just told me in so many words that my feelings weren't reciprocated, I'd think maybe she felt conflicted? But I know inside her firm exterior lies a perceptive and kind person, so she's probably worried about me. Worried that I'm upset.

I don't want to worry her, I know that much. I don't want to be anything other than someone who makes her happy. I want to be easy for her, so easy that she'll never tell me to go away.

I open my eyes when she cups my chin and lifts my face to hers.

"Delph," she says, and then swallows. "Are you—are you okay? We can stop if you need time to process. I should have waded into this. We should have started slow and built our way up, and that's my fault that we didn't. I'm sorry, pet, I'm so sorry." She does look sorry, and each and every word is like a slap, a burn, a cut. Each word of her apologizing for *my* hasty declaration. Each word undoing my own feelings and reshaping them into a byproduct of bad dominance. Even though they're not a byproduct. And she's not a bad Dominant.

"I don't need to stop," I tell her. "You didn't do anything wrong, please. Rebecca. Mistress. It's fine. Just the scene, like you said."

She doesn't let me lower my face for a long minute, keeping me tilted up to her gaze. Her eyes flick dark and concerned over my face, and I just want to die, I'm so embarrassed. "Please," I say again. "Let's please forget about it."

She releases my face, but she looks like she wants to say something else, like she's not finished trying to smooth over my gawky blunder, and I can't stand it, I can't stand it a second longer, and so I bury my mouth between her legs once again, running a slow lick up her core.

I feel her relent; I feel the moment she chooses to let it go. Her breath stutters out, a long exhale, and then she spreads her legs even more, pushing her hips against my kiss. I respond eagerly, using the tip of my tongue to make wet promises through the lace, and then sighing in contentment when she finally pulls her knickers to the side and lets me service her bare skin.

With her legs parted like this, the tight well at her center is exposed, and so is the dark berry of her clit. I lave and lick at both the way I know she likes, following her sighs and the tugs in my hair. I feast on her until she starts arching and pushing even harder against my mouth.

"Almost, pet," she says. "Just a moment longer."

But before she finishes, there's a creak and a slam—the door downstairs—and then footsteps on the staircase, shoes thudding on solid, new wood. Instinct seizes me, and I start to jerk away, but Rebecca holds me close.

"Shh, shh," she soothes. "I know who it is."

I lift my eyes to hers, and she strokes my hair back from my face. "Only one other person has a key," she assures me. "And when we're at the club, lots of people will be watching us. Think of this as…practice."

Practice. Yes. I will be watched and shared—I *want* to be watched and shared. We agreed on all this.

"What's your safeword, pet?" she asks, her hands still stroking at my hair.

I take a breath before I say it, and my breath is full of her—the woman I love who doesn't love me. I force the knife-thoughts down, away, and try to remember who I am. The sunny, happy girl who's left red lipstick on her Mistress's cunt.

I answer.

"Grege 1947."

8

Rebecca

"We can stop whenever we need," I tell her. And we will if she needs to, but I'd be lying if I said I wasn't relieved someone was coming up. And while yes, this is actually good practice for a baby sub—a little bit of Thornchapel in London, a little bit of our magic world to get her ready for the prying voyeurism of the club—truthfully, that's not why I'm relieved.

I'm relieved because I'm a coward.

Delphine's mouth is hot and searching against me when I push her face back to her work, and I try desperately to lose myself in the slick pleasure of her kiss before our visitor makes it up the stairs. I want every feeling I've had since Delphine uttered those terrible words to disappear, to shift into what they should be, which is satisfaction and pleasure and pride in my new submissive.

I'm almost there when Auden emerges from the stairwell, looking miserable and morose, the spattered rain on his shoulders matching the sudden plinking and plonking on the skylights above. He pauses when he sees us, Delphine on all fours and me with my hands in her hair and my legs stretched out as insouciantly as any man's.

"Rain outside?" I say lightly, as if there isn't a tongue in my pussy. As if he's just popped in for a chat and interrupted nothing more important than me responding to emails.

Auden meets my eyes and I nod at him, answering his unspoken questions. It's a sign of our friendship that he doesn't ask the questions aloud—or maybe it's just a testament to whatever it is that has him looking so pathetic.

He finally answers, his voice filling the space as Delphine stiffens in front of me. "It's only spitting," he says. "Nothing bad. May I come in?"

"Certainly," I say graciously, untangling my fingers from Delphine's hair to smooth a hand along her back. "Have a seat. I'm almost through here."

Auden shrugs out of his jacket and tosses it over a low bench by the windows before taking a seat next to me. I'm a little surprised he doesn't want to sit where he can see Delphine's heart-shaped bottom—that's where I'd prefer to sit, if I wasn't exactly where I was—but when he sits down and tucks a bit of stray blond hair behind Delphine's ear, I think I know why.

She flicks those honey-brown eyes over to him and he gives her an almost-smile.

"Hi, Pickles," he says softly. And I feel her lips curve up against me as her body relaxes.

"Hi, Auden," she replies. I *tsk* at her, and she corrects, "Sir."

"May I watch?" he asks her, voice still soft. "I'd like to."

She nods and closes her eyes, leaning her cheek against my thigh for a moment before she starts licking me again.

Yes, I know why Auden chose this spot. He sat here so he could set her at ease, and it worked. He's a good Dominant. He has the things that can't be taught, the instincts, the right amount of cruelty and the right amount of compassion, and he knows how to oscillate between the two. Knots can be explained, flogging can be learned, all of that can be tutored into a willing student. But balancing arrogance with care? Being fully capable of both? That's a rare thing.

"She's good at this," Auden remarks, leaning forward to brush more hair off her face.

"She is," I agree as I tilt my hips up. She follows my lead and kisses me lower once again, her delicate, rich girl tongue stroking into my center. Delph and I have only been properly fucking for the last six weeks, and she's still more eagerness than skill—but the eagerness is incredible, it's fervent and wholehearted, and when she's trying to please me, no matter what it is—kissing, tonguing, crawling, enduring—she does it with her entire self. Her body and her heart and her mind—every part of her is present and artless. Totally honest.

She's like clear water, like a tropical ocean, where one thinks the brightly colored bottom is only a few inches beneath the surface, but truly it's so far down that one could drown trying to touch it. All of her is here, all of her is visible, and yet she's the opposite of accessible, the opposite of easy.

I think I could spend years diving down to touch the reality of her.

"Give me your fingers, pet," I whisper to her, and she obeys, glancing at Auden from underneath her lashes. It is a little bit like Thornchapel right now, the three of us here with a cool summer rain pattering at the glass, and I look over at my oldest friend, to where he's shifting restlessly next to me. An erection swells against the front of his gray tweed trousers, and he impatiently presses the heel of his palm against it, as if it's being impolite.

I arch against Delphine's fingers and against her clever tongue. "Getting close," I say. My voice is hitching, and I can feel an orgasm coiled around her fingers inside me, gathering underneath her wet little kiss. Auden's eyes on us are sultry and interested, and the hand on his erection has stopped trying to make it go away. He's rubbing himself through his trousers now, slow strokes, and I reach over and pluck at the button holding his trousers closed.

His eyelids flutter as my fingers brush over something thick and rigid.

"Make yourself at home, Sir Guest," I say.

"I just—before I came here, Poe and I—" He shakes his head, even as his hips lift to chase my touch. "I shouldn't need to again."

We are all of us consumed by whatever we woke up in the thorn chapel—we are all of us so full of appetite that we are snarling with it. *Shouldn't* seems so far away, like a rule meant for children in the schoolyard, for beginners and initiates, for people who haven't kissed and bled in the woods.

"Who cares if you shouldn't need to? It's only us here."

"You're a bad influence," he says, but he pops his button open and slides a hand inside. Immediately his head falls backward against the sofa. "*Fuck.*"

I almost don't know where to look as I crest over the edge—whether to look at Auden's hand moving inside his trousers or the gorgeous submissive between my legs, or even at the reflection of the three of us in the window, all splayed legs and arching throats.

But Delphine looks up at me just as the climax hits, and it's her eyes I see as I come. It's her honest gaze shimmering like clear water all the way to the honey-sweet bottom. It's her faith and trust and—and fuck, love—*fuck*—

My hips twist and push as the first wave shudders through my cunt and up my belly, and Delphine responds in kind, more fingers, sucking harder, eyes warm and eager as she makes me come and come and come. Next to me, Auden's freed his cock, which is pulsing in his grip and releasing onto his jumper with long jets of seed. Together, we are lost, lost, arching and pushing through the pleasure, and it feels like I've been coming forever, like there's only ever been these waves, each one more deliciously harsh than the last, like there's only ever going to be more; I'm set adrift on a sea of seizing, rippling sensation and I never have to leave, I never have to work or compete or shield myself ever again.

Here is a small swath of vivid, vital heaven.

Delphine's eyes—those pretty, too-revealing eyes—keep me anchored to her as the climax gradually abates and I'm Rebecca in real life once again. Although I'm a much happier Rebecca now, after an orgasm from a beautiful submissive. *My* beautiful submissive.

We'll be able to do this every night—this and so much more.

She's mine now.

"Well done," I whisper to her, brushing her hair away from her face. At my touch, she sighs and leans her head against my thigh, closing her eyes. "Such a good girl. Such a good girl."

She practically purrs.

Next to me, Auden is a rumpled ode to indecency, his sex exposed and pushing between the placket of his trousers. His charcoal jumper is spattered with his pleasure, and his long legs are still stretched out in front of him. He's an immodest sprawl of muscled limbs and silk and wool—and the cock jutting up from it all only adds to the impression that he's some kind of insatiable, deviant aristocrat. But he looks very forlorn for a boy who just came all over himself, and I remember how unhappy he looked when he came upstairs, as wet and sad as a puppy caught in the rain.

"Would you like to change?" I ask Delphine. She's still in her jacket and heels, and as much as I love seeing her with her skirt hiked up and her blouse gaping down to expose the swells of her tits, she'll be more comfortable in cozy clothes.

And she'll be less tempting. Because if she's on all fours in those shoes and that skirt for another minute...

Delphine is already nodding against my thigh, and she gives it a quick kiss—and my cunt, which is a liberty she gets her hair pulled for—and then rises up to her knees and then to her feet. Auden and I are treated to the view of her soft thighs and her lavender silk covered cunt before she manages to tug her skirt back down. Auden's cock gives a lazy stir at the sight of it, and her first instinct is to look over to me, as if to make sure it's okay that he's aroused by her.

I'm not jealous of the history between the two of them—and I'm more than comfortable sharing her with Auden for sex—but I can't lie to myself. That little flick of her eyes to me, that checking to make sure her Mistress approves…it's deeply pleasing. She's mine.

She said she loves you.

Panic spikes through my ribs with the memory of it. Panic and shame and—no. I refuse to acknowledge any other feelings. They are not invited. They are not welcome. And they don't mean anything anyway—they're just the chemical signatures of a limbic system that doesn't know any better.

"Dress quickly and come back," I tell her, my voice a little more steely than I'd like. I try to soften it. "Lean down a second, pet."

She obeys, her hair swinging down like a veil and hiding her face from everything in the world but me. I use a thumb to wipe at a small smear of lipstick at the corner of her mouth. She's all smudgy and disheveled from having her mouth thoroughly fucked, but of course, since she's Delphine, it looks enchanting. She could post a picture of herself exactly like this, and people would be heart-emojiing and wanking off to it in equal numbers.

She catches my thumb in her mouth and gives it a hard suck.

"Careful," I tell her, even as my clit throbs in response. There's something about her mouth, about the way her lips are always slightly parted that gets me so hot anyway. And with those full lips wrapped around my thumb, smeared with the same lipstick that's still on my cunt—

I lean forward and give her a swat on the arse as I pull my thumb free. "Go change before you get yourself into trouble," I command, knowing full well that trouble is exactly what she wants.

And me too, if I'm honest. I would very much like for her to be in trouble.

But we have a guest—literally a Guest, looking more woeful than anyone tucking a satisfied cock away has a right to—and we also have the rest of the night. The week. The year.

Maybe longer.

She said she loves you.

Delphine gets her bag and scampers off as Auden tugs his jumper off and drops it onto the floor. He's wearing a white and gray tattersall shirt underneath, and he rolls up the sleeves to the elbow, exposing finely muscled forearms. He has the look of someone concentrating on a very small, very unimportant task so that he doesn't have to think about anything else.

And as I rearrange my knickers and romper and force myself not to watch the reflected glint of Delphine's hair as she gathers her things and disappears into the bathroom, I think I know how he feels.

She said she loves you.

And that isn't even the worst part. That isn't even the *dangerous* part.

You know what you felt when she said it.

I clear my throat, even though there's no reason to. Auden keeps fussing with his sleeves, his hair tumbling onto his forehead as he refuses to meet my gaze. But the thinness to his mouth and the shadows under his eyes are obvious no matter how much he makes his hair fall over his face.

"Guest, you look like shit," I tell him. "And you never drop by unless you're hungry or bored. And I've seen your desk—you've got too much work needing doing to be bored."

"Maybe I'm hungry then," he mumbles, still plucking at the tattersall stretched around the firm lines of his forearm.

"Auden."

He sighs, scowls down at his sleeve, and then throws his arm to the side, as if the sight of his sleeve offends him. "I may have done something wrong."

It's my experience that the less one says, the more one's interlocutor ends up sharing, so I say nothing. And sure enough, Auden gets to his feet and starts pacing, speaking in short, agitated bursts as he walks.

"I learned something. More than a month ago. About someone else. And I didn't tell him at first, because I—I—" He stabs a hand through his hair and then wheels around to face me. "Do you have any gin in here or what?"

Wordlessly, I point to a credenza that separates the living space from the home office space. Auden walks over and disappears from view, the clanking of bottles and glasses the only indicator of his continued presence. Finally, he emerges with everything he wants and he strides over to the kitchen, where he starts hunting for limes.

I fold my arms and watch him puttering around, muttering to himself and savaging innocent limes, until finally he walks back over to me, a dark look on his face and a drink in each hand.

I accept the drink, watching him over the rim of my glass as he starts pacing again.

"So the thing is," he starts, and then stops. "Well, okay. The way I see it—"

He stops again. I tip it to my lips and then wince, because it's practically all gin.

Although it is a really decent gin.

I take another sip.

Auden takes a drink too, long, gulping swallows until the entire thing is gone and he's holding an empty glass in front of my rain-streaked window. After a long moment, he says, without any warning at all, "St. Sebastian is my brother."

If I still had any gin in my mouth, I would be spraying it all over the front of my Stella McCartney romper. "*What*?"

He looks over his shoulder. "Did I finally find something that can flap the unflappable Rebecca Quartey?"

"I'm not flapping!" I protest, and then realize my free hand is doing exactly that: flapping at him. I tuck it under my thigh. "I'm just...processing. That's all. He's your *brother*?"

Auden nods, looks down at this empty glass, and then goes back to the kitchen for more gin. "Half-brother."

"I don't know if that's any better."

Auden doesn't bother with ice or tonic water this time and comes back in with a glass of room-temperature gin and a mangled lime wedge clouding up the center. "How can it not be better? We didn't grow up together, we didn't share a mother or a life or anything—"

"You're still related."

"But what does that even mean? We're not breeding stock, Bex."

"It means *something*, Auden, because if it didn't, you wouldn't be here drinking all my Bombay Sapphire and moping at the rain. What did Saint say when you told him?"

Auden frowns down at his glass. "Well, I didn't *tell* him so much as he sort of...found out. On his own."

The hand comes out from underneath my thigh to flap at him—sternly this time. "Are you telling me that *I didn't tell him at first* actually meant *I didn't tell him at all*? You knew he was your brother and you didn't think he needed to know? Auden Isaac Guest!"

Auden takes a drink, and then says, in a voice that's trying not to be defensive and failing, "I was trying to determine the best approach. I didn't want him to react...badly."

"But he still found out, and I'm supposing, based on your expression, he reacted badly anyway."

Auden's shoulders slump. "Yes."

"You shouldn't have lied to him—"

"It wasn't lying!"

"—about his own bloody DNA, no matter what it meant for the two of you. And you definitely should have told him before Beltane and all that antler nonsense."

If it's possible, his shoulders slump even more. "But then he wouldn't have been mine."

I set my glass on the table and stand up, walking over to where he stands in front of the window. The flat is all steel angles and wood planes—brick and glass everywhere else—and the space is filled with the ceaseless, echoing drum of the rain and the practically ceaseless sluice of Delphine's shower.

And still, over all that, I hear the broken sound my friend makes as he exhales.

"Have you talked to him?" I ask gently. "Since he found out?"

"Yesterday. He—he's angry."

"You can fix angry."

He takes in a long breath, staring at the rain. "Maybe. But I don't think he'll ever forgive me. And I don't think—well, it's just that he doesn't see it the way I do."

"And how do you see it?"

Auden closes his eyes. "That it doesn't matter."

I take his drink from him and have a sip out of habit, forgetting that it's all warm, limey gin. "Ugh," I say, and then I set the glass far away from him, coming back and patting him on the shoulder.

"You need to tell him you're sorry."

He sighs. "Yes."

"And you need to let him go."

"What?" Auden turns a betrayed look on me. "No! Absolutely not!"

"Auden, the two of you are related by blood. You share a father. There's no happy ending here, and honestly, maybe there never should have been one to begin with. You have too much history between the two of you, and too much pain, and now there's this on top of it all? You may not think it matters, but you certainly can't make it not matter to him. It should matter."

"But *why*?" he asks, pained. "Why? When we love each other? You didn't see him by the river this weekend, Bex, you didn't see the way he looked up at me after I caught him. Like he wanted to be in those bluebells forever. Like he wanted to stitch his soul to mine, and I can't—"

He breaks off, a ragged breath shuddering through his body, and I pat him again on the shoulder. We stand there for a moment, and I keep my eyes fixed on the rain as I feel his shoulder hitch and stutter beneath my palm, like he's swallowing down noises he can't bear to let out. I know I should hug him, but I'm not a hugger—and anyway, I sense he doesn't want it. The only embraces he wants right now are from St. Sebastian. Or Proserpina.

Speaking of... "What did Poe say? You didn't hide this from her too?"

"No. I told her. Today actually, before I left. I wanted so badly to bring her here with me to London, I need her so much, and I know she would've come if I asked, and yet—"

"You knew St. Sebastian needed her more," I finish for him.

Auden nods miserably.

He's right. And it's the same thing I would have done if I had two subs and found myself in a similar bind. "How does Poe feel about the...you know...brother thing?"

"She wasn't exactly chuffed that I hadn't told St. Sebastian about it—she excoriated me quite thoroughly, in fact. And now she has to overlook that she's in love with two of Ralph Guest's sons, when it was already hard enough being in love with only one. But the actual consanguinity doesn't seem to bother her." Auden's lips tilt up in a weak smile. "She said she thinks it's rather titillating."

"De gustibus non est disputandum," I murmur.

Auden lets out a laugh as weak as his smile as he turns to search for his glass. "Quite right."

"Auden, what do you want?" I ask as he walks over to the coffee table and retrieves his drink. "I mean, truly. What is it that you want from this?"

"Him," Auden says without hesitation, simply and firmly and also with enough despair to raise goosebumps on my arms. "I want *him*."

We stare at each other for a long moment, and it's not the boy I grew up with looking at me. It's Auden of Thornchapel, the Guest heir, the wild god.

It's a king, and I don't know how to feel about a king standing in my living room holding warm gin when kings are supposed to stay in the woods. Safely inside our little Thornchapel games.

But even kings need advisors, and so I give him my honest advice.

"Maybe you know what you want," I say. "But do you know what you're willing to lose in order to get it?"

Auden's lips part as he looks at me. And then he slowly shakes his head. "I don't—I don't think I do. Should I?"

"Yes. And be prepared to lose him anyway. *Brothers*, Auden. Brothers! *And* you lied to him about it?"

"It wasn't *lying*—oh, hello, Pickles."

Delphine has opened the door to the bathroom, letting out a cloud of steam and the animated chatter of her favorite podcast—something about romance novels and blooding?—and she emerges from the steam in a silk robe that clings to every soft curve of her. It's short enough that when she turns to close the door, I can see the delectable curves of her arse.

"Just grabbing some turmeric and beet juice before I do my oil cleanser," she says, and Auden and I both nod, as if this is a sentence that has any real meaning for us. She digs in her bag for a moment, pulls out a trendily packaged bottle of orange liquid, and then disappears back into the bathroom, like a busty phantom of self-care. But not before she loops by to drop a kiss on my cheek, which I intercept with a hand on the nape of her neck and a kiss of my own, right on her lips. Quick, hard, and ruthless, like I like. She's pink-cheeked and bashful as she walks back into the bathroom and closes the door.

After her podcast starts up again, Auden turns to me and says, "Something's changed between you two."

I finish my drink and start walking toward the kitchen. "Yes."

"Is this more than just kink?"

"More how? And don't think I don't know you're trying to change the subject."

He turns and looks at me, taking a long, insolent drink as he waits for me to answer my own question. Which I refuse to do. He may be my best friend, but Delphine is my business.

Mostly.

"You hated each other," he says after it's clear that I am not going to answer. "For years. All those awkward parties, Bex, do you remember? All those parties when you and Delphine would have to be in the same room and you'd bicker nonstop?"

"I remember it quite well, Sir Guest. As well as I remember you wrestling St. Sebastian in front of your house because you hated him so much."

His eyes darken. Another drink. "Point taken."

The look on his face is almost enough to make me feel bad for bringing up St. Sebastian again. "Look, Delphine and I don't hate each other now," I say, although even as I say it, the words feel flimsy. Disingenuous.

She said she loves you.

"You don't hate each other now," he echoes. "Is that all? Is that the only reason she's here getting kissed like *that*?"

I look at the window across from me, at the woman reflected there. Tailored clothes, lifted chin, perfect flat behind her. Everything as it should be. No chirpy blond tarts who cover sinks in lipsticks and bottles of micellar water. No shoulders hunched against unravelling feelings.

No vulnerability, no tremulous smiles, no declarations of love.

I answer how the woman in the reflection would answer. "She needs a Domme. I'd like a sub. It suits."

"Does it? You've always talked about how spoiled you've found her, and how irritating it was."

I'm irritated now, actually, although I can't exactly explain why. It makes my voice sharp when I answer, "Well, it wasn't until this year I realized I could be the one to fuck it out of her."

Auden knows me too well to let me get away with saying something like that. I watch as his reflection sets its drink down and crosses its arms. "Bex. Seriously. Is everything okay between you two?"

I love you.

Like it was nothing at all, easy as breathing.

I love you.

I make to pull my hair down out of its bun and then realize I'm doing it to fidget. And I don't fidget. "Everything's fine."

He still doesn't drop the subject. "I care about Delphine, you know," he tells me. "Very much."

"Is this the talk where you warn me, one man to another, to treat your ex-girlfriend well?"

Auden frowns. "No warnings. I don't think you need them, despite how you're acting right now."

I bristle a little at that, turning to glare at him. "And how am I acting?"

Unfortunately, Auden also knows me too well to be properly terrified of the Quartey Stare. "Like a rake," he says.

It's so far away from what I was expecting him to say that I nearly laugh. "A *rake*?"

He's giving me his crooked smile now, and dammit, he's too adorable to keep bristling at. "An inveterate rake, even. A new submissive every night before this, and now you're having one move in but it's only about the sex, no feelings. It is very rakish, you have to admit."

I part my lips to speak—and then I realize I have no idea what I want to say. I am a rake, I guess. I've certainly been acting like one with Delphine.

"I have to say this, even though I know you will anyway," Auden says, "but please take care of her. She's not as…confident…as she seems sometimes."

Of course she isn't. No human could be. No person is entirely self-assured, entirely positive, entirely poised all the time. And yet, Delphine makes everyone believe it. She makes everyone believe that she wakes up with clear skin, bouncy hair, all the answers. She makes even cynics believe that she can turn any obstacle into a caption-worthy learning moment.

She makes lovers believe she can say *I love you* and be perfectly content not hearing it said back.

She's new to all this, I remind myself. *You're the Domme. It's your job to teach her. It would have been crueler to let her believe she really loves you when you know better. When you know it was just the scene making her feel that way.*

Then why is guilt dripping like sticky tar down my throat? Making it impossible to speak?

No.

No, I don't do guilt. Guilt is an indulgence—an excuse to avoid action because it feels like some sort of penance. But it's not, it's the ignis fatuus of penance. It changes nothing and leads one nowhere.

I imagine swallowing all that guilt down, all the uncertainty—along with that breathless, brilliant, idiotic *something*—I felt when Delphine whispered those words. I push it all away until I'm myself again, and there's no guilt.

Or worse...*hope.*

"I know," I finally say. "I know."

"I wish," Auden says, and then stops, and then starts again. "I wish we were home right now. All six of us."

"Yeah," I say, suddenly feeling it too. Missing the way the rain echoes through the library, the pop of the burning logs even when it's too warm for a fire. The huffs of Sir James Frazer, and Delphine curled up in an armchair, and Becket arguing with me about something. Missing the rustling press of the trees from all sides, except to the south, where the grounds slope up past the river into louring, windy moorland.

Missing the way Delphine and I can spend hours fucking in a giant bed, half drunk and giddy with knowing there's nowhere to be in the morning, except outside on the grounds I love anyway.

She said she loves you, and for a minute, you wanted to say it back.

"Want some more gin?" Auden asks abruptly.

God. Yes, please.

"Make it a double," I say, and then decide to go help him so he doesn't forget the ice.

9

St. Sebastian

Not far from the thorn chapel and overlooking the River Thorne is a heathered ridge called Reavy Hill. There are no footpaths here, no obvious beauty spots, no standing stones or dolmens to photograph. It's a wild, gorse-ridden heap, striped with overgrown reaves on one side and rolling down to the thick woods of Thornchapel on the other. I can see the proud stone head of the house among the trees—the tower in particular looking stupidly pretty in a sea of pear-green leaves. Farther off, Thorncombe clusters around the river, a chocolate-box-worthy huddle of stone and thatch, with the medieval St. Brigid's preening in the middle of it all. It's easy to understand why the people who built the standing stones, and later the reaves and roundhouses, decided to stay in this veiled and winding vein stretching south to the sea. Even easier to understand why everyone after them stayed too. Like my mother.

Like me.

I sit perched atop a clumsy jumble of granite—which is too squat to be a landmark but still tall enough to earn you some scrapes as you climb it. Auden and I used to come here, as teenagers, flushed with stolen wine and nervous adolescent attraction.

I stare down into the trees, picking out the thorn chapel's clearing and the teasing crook of one menhir as it peeks through the branches. The rest of the clearing—the other standing stones, the crumbling chapel, the altar— is mostly hidden from view, but I still feel it there, like an extension of myself, aware, breathing, alive. Waiting for me to come back. I look up toward the house, with its glittering windows and grim crenellations.

Is it waiting for me too?

Was it always?

"Thought I might find you here," a voice says from behind me, and I turn to see a sweaty Becket climbing up onto the boulder next to me— gracefully and without a single scrape at all, despite his flimsy workout clothes, damn him.

I grunt in response and turn my eyes back on the house. It's impossible to see the front, much less which cars are in the drive, but I know Auden's already left for London. He usually leaves by late afternoon on Mondays, and anyway, the last few weeks he's been gone, it's like Thornchapel itself can sense it. The moment he leaves, you can see the trees arch and stir and shake, you can hear the breeze kick up in fretful gusts, and you can see the warblers and finches and stonechats hopping anxiously about, fussing and flapping their wings in vexation. The river throws fits: sulking and drying into trickles, then surging suddenly again, as if in a tantrum, and then finally, in defeat, abating into its usual whispers and sighs.

Auden is gone, and so even the river weeps for him.

Becket is good at long silences, and the sun has started to sink when he finally says, "Poe is looking for you, you know."

I know. My phone is in my pocket, turned off after the seventh text message she sent me. I know hiding isn't healthy, I know it's something I would have done five months ago. I know she deserves a response at the very least. And it's perverse, me hiding, because all I want to do is see her. All I want to do is crush her to my chest and fill my hands with her hair as I feel her breathe against me. In fact, I came up to Reavy Hill not to watch the sunset or the herd of wild ponies grazing and swishing their tails, but to watch the house. As if by watching the house I could somehow be closer to her, somehow soak up her comfort without having to expose anything of myself.

Because seeing her, actually seeing her—worry slithers in my belly at the mere thought. She told me via text that she knows about Auden and me, and if I look at her and I *see* her knowing…

I don't know. It just feels like something that can't be undone. The final stitch in the shroud of what Auden and I had.

"I don't have my stole, so I can't hear a confession at the moment," Becket says in a casual, *oh hey, here's a fun fact* kind of voice. "But if you wanted to talk, just as friends, I'm here."

I scrub my face with my hands, pulling down on my cheeks as if I can pull the skin away from my face. "I think I might need a confession, actually. I've sinned."

"We're all sinners," Becket says placidly. "If we didn't sin, perhaps we'd never know the gift of grace. The free and undeserved clemency of God. And maybe that would be its own kind of tragedy."

Grace.

I think of Mamá for some reason, how she would hold me and wipe my tears away when I was little, even after I scratched and kicked at her. How she'd still kiss my cheek and help me with homework and leave my clothes washed and folded in perfect squares on the bed even when I told her I hated her, I hated our life, even when I snarled and sneered at her because I was fifteen and angry and felt like I was deeply and uniquely alone. Still, she loved me.

Grace. Free and definitely undeserved.

"Shall we sin, because we are not under the law, but under grace?" I murmur. "God forbid."

"Romans," Becket says, recognizing the verse's origin immediately. "Book of the angsty."

"I'm not angsty," I say reflexively, and then Becket laughs, reaching over to pluck at my hand, where I've colored in my fingernails with a black Sharpie.

"I was bored at the library this morning," I protest, curling my fingers into my palms. I don't tell him how I wrote a capital M on each nail before scribbling over it.

"Mmhmm," Becket says, clearly still amused.

I sigh and look over at the man next to me, his classically handsome profile limned by the dipping sunlight. He's got his legs crossed like a child at school, and his eyes are dancing with more mischief than kindness.

Right now, he's not a priest. He's just a hot guy in sweaty running clothes who happens to be my friend. And five months ago, I would have dodged even the idea of having friends, because I've only ever had one friend before, and that friendship died in a Methodist graveyard after a few weeks anyway. But something has changed, I guess, because I don't run away. I don't continue on in stony silence.

I say, "I'm going to tell you something, and I need you to promise not to say a word about it. Not just to other people, but like, right now. To me. I don't think I can listen to it yet, not from someone whose job is knowing sanctity from sin."

Becket nods, his expression open but also carefully neutral. His confession face, probably.

I still feel compelled to add, "And I'm probably going to need a real confession at some point."

At that, Becket raises his eyebrows, a small smile on his lips. "Saint, I can't even get you to take the host most Sundays. I'm not fussed if you don't come to confession."

"You haven't heard what I've done yet," I mutter.

Becket touches my knee, his hand warm over my jeans. "I'll happily hear it, when you're ready," he says. "And as a priest, it's my job to tell you that confession is essential to remitting your sins and restoring the sanctifying grace inside your soul. But as your friend, I'll tell you that I don't think God always plays by his own rules. Come when you're ready, and don't let your fear be stronger than your love."

Mamá's face flashes in my mind.

"That's very wise," I say, a bit impatiently. "But the problem is my fear should be stronger."

Becket's as patient as I am impatient, and he just gives me a slow nod, like of course I know better about fear and love than a fucking priest, and I'm scrubbing my face with my hands again, like I can scrub away everything that I am. Ralph's son. Auden's brother.

A man who still wants someone he shouldn't.

"Sorry," I say. "Okay. Here it is."

I tell him. I tell him about finding the letter from Auden's lawyer, I tell him about my middle name. With my eyes fixed on the house where it rises stony and stern from the trees, I tell him about Auden finding me. About what came after.

"I safeworded," I finish. "I stopped him. But, fuck, I didn't want to. I wanted him. I wanted it, even though I knew it was wrong."

When I look over at Becket—expecting to see that neutral priest face again—his brows are drawn together and his eyes cast down, but he doesn't seem disgusted, only thoughtful. Although it's strange—when he looks up at me, I can't see *any* of what those thoughts might be, whether they're good thoughts or bad thoughts or anything. His eyes are rather like staring into the bluest part of a fire or the ocean on a calm day, and for a fierce, fleeting moment, I'm struck by how unfathomable they are. How unfathomable *he* is.

The part of me that's always hearkened to loneliness, to the wild bevels and peaks of this place, recognizes something in him, something almost the same as me but not quite.

Mamá joked once that I was like a druid, someone who absorbed lore and stories and safeguarded them for the next generation. It fit the teenage boy with stacks of fantasy novels in his room, and it fits the man who spends his days scanning RFID tags and helping pensioners with the internet.

But if I'm a druid, then Becket is something else, something baneful and holy and darkly recondite. It dances deep in his eyes, this nature, a part of Becket that's beyond manners and cheer. A part of him that was born to walk in the desert with God and God alone.

But the moment leaves me as moments do, and I'm back to being miserable about myself, and Becket keeps his word, saying nothing. There's only the breeze and the bleating sheep down by the reaves and the quiet rush of the river nearby.

"In every book I ever read," I hear myself saying, "the bastard is always angry. He hates the heir, he resents the heir, and there's no end to his despair or jealousy or bitterness—but what happens when he's also *in love* with the heir? What happens when he doesn't want what the heir *has*, but who the heir is? I always felt a certain way about this place, I always felt claimed by it, but I didn't feel at home here until *he* claimed me. Until he marked my heart and my body, and said *you're mine.* It was like everything made sense then: who I was and where I belonged and where I needed to be and everything just finally felt right for the first time since we were kids playing in the chapel. Like I'd had thorns around my heart for so long that I'd forgotten there were supposed to be roses too."

I press the heels of my hands into my eyes, replacing Thornchapel and the trees with bright, staticky sparks.

"But it was a lie," I say. "There were no roses. No flowers. Not for me."

I feel Becket's hand on my back. Not on my shoulder, but right in the middle, right in the place where you'd stroke a bird between its wings.

Without meaning to, I relax into his touch, a small shaft of warmth sinking into my chest.

"I won't say anything until you're ready to talk about it," Becket murmurs, "but I will say this: you should find Poe. She's worried about you. And nothing about your love for her has to change."

I think of Poe's fist pumping like a heart. The three of us share one love, one bleeding, prickling snarl of it, and there's no untangling it, any more than there's untangling the brambles clinging to the chapel walls in the woods below.

But he's not wrong about finding Poe. I've been a coward enough for one day, and besides, cowardice is lonely work. I miss her. She misses me. It should be that simple, and I'll make it so.

Even if it means the beginning of the end: the start of us unbrambling and rending each other ragged.

Becket stands up and stretches. Against the Dartmoor sunset, he looks like a commercial for running clothes, a magazine cover for outdoor living. There's no longer any trace of that unknowable thing lurking inside him, no trace of the Essene, the anchorite, the priest who trades in blood and flesh. He's just a boy from Virginia who grew up tall and blond and moneyed.

He holds out his hand to me and I take it, letting him help me to my feet. Our shadows are long enough that I know it will be almost full dark by the time I'm across the river.

"Are you parked close?" I ask. There's a B road only half a mile away, winding between tors, and Thorncombe is only about two miles from here. Honestly, there's hardly anything dangerous on the moors—the occasional adder and maybe some grumpy cows, depending on where you are—but the weather can turn quickly, and the darkness of night is near total, meaning it's very easy to sprain an ankle or twist a knee, and then find yourself drenched and shivering with no cell service.

"I'm on the road," he says, pointing. "And I've got my flashlight if I need it. The path is good and well-marked."

"I could always walk with you to the village and then drive you back to your car."

Becket's already leaping down off our rock, landing with the stable poise of a professional athlete. I follow, as easily as he does, if not as springily—more lynx than deer—and then he pulls me into a quick hug. Too quick for me to slouch out of it.

"It's going to be okay," he tells me. "And St. Petroc's will be unlocked. Tonight and every other night. You know you're always welcome."

I nod, my throat tight, and he bounds down the hill, bending back toward the path that snakes along the bottom of the reaves. And then I take a deep breath and walk the other way, down Reavy Hill to the River Thorne and then on to Thornchapel.

The house is quiet when I let myself inside, the quiet of a tomb or museum, with a stillness that creeps along my skin.

You're not him, I can imagine the house saying. *You're not him.*

But the creeping silence is broken when Sir James Frazer hears the south door click closed, and he comes tearing into the mudroom, back legs scrabbling on the flags as he careens around the corner, howling balefully until he sees it's just me.

Instantly, the howls change to whines as he nudges my hand and then prances near the wellies lined up against the wall. He nudges my hand again, with a meaningful sort of look, and then I ask him, "Outside?"

He answers me with another prance and a lick on my hand. I open the door again. He streaks off into the gloaming, barking at nothing and seeming like the happiest dog in the world. I prop open the door and go find Poe.

The library is barely lit when I get there—just a reading light on a table and the glow of her scanning equipment—like dusk has crept up on her without her noticing. And indeed she doesn't even seem to notice me as I slip through the doors, her head down and earbuds in her ears as she hums happily to herself. At some point she's pinned her hair up with some pens, but several strands have since fallen to hang around her face and neck, and she's kicked off her shoes, wearing a pair of fuzzy socks instead. It makes her shorter than usual, more rumpled, and more adorable for all that. For a few minutes, I just lean in the doorway and watch her work. Watch the way the shadows catch on her dark eyelashes and around her hauntingly plump mouth. Watch as she competently pages through books older than the country she was born in, as she fingers colorful lithographs, quirky typefaces, rich end papers—the minutiae book lovers live for.

I drift closer, half dreading her seeing me, half unable to resist. She's tweedy and pretty and lush, and I'm getting hard just by looking at her, but I don't know if she'll want me now, I don't know if I'm allowed to touch her, taste her, feel her—

She finally turns all the way around, reaching for a pen that's rolled to the edge of the table, and then she sees me, her eyes lighting up as she tears her earbuds free. "Saint! Thank God!" She's over to me in a few skirt-bouncing steps, flinging her arms around my waist and burying her face into my chest. "I was so worried," she mumbles into me, her fingers bunching in the thin fabric of my T-shirt. "I wanted to come find you, but Becket said that would stress you out more, so I've been trying to be understanding, but I was almost out of patience. I was considering walking down to your house and just banging on the door until you let me in."

I slide my hands around her, exhaling a long, jagged breath. Her back is warm under my hands, and her hair smells like summer—like reading a book under the shade of a big tree. Paper and wildflowers and sunshine. I fill my lungs with her, with Proserpina; I breathe her in so she'll be in my body, in my blood, bonded to my cells. I want my body to be made of her, built from her, layers and layers of Proserpina inside St. Sebastian.

I kiss her hair, and it's so silky and soft that I kiss it again. "I wasn't home," I finally say. "I had to work and then I took a walk after to clear my head."

"Saint," she whispers, finally tilting her head up to me. Even in the dim light of the library, her eyes are greener than a cat's. "Auden told me, and I— I don't even know what to say. I'm so sorry that asshole was your father, and I'm so sorry that Auden hid it from you. I'll kill him if you want, you know."

Impossibly, I feel the corner of my mouth turn up.

"Just a little murder. Not a lot." She smiles, but the smile doesn't last long. "Are you okay? Are you doing okay?"

I nod, my throat going tight again. I'm not planning on saying anything else about it at all—because I don't *want* to, I don't want to talk about it, I don't want to *feel* about it—I just want to stand here and breathe in the girl I love and never have to think about this again.

But then Poe pulls harder on my shirt, as if I'm not close enough, and I breathe in another lungful of drowsy summer flowers and somehow I *am* talking, without planning to. Somehow the words are coming out, and I can't stop them.

"I don't know if I can forgive him," I say. "I hate that he lied. I hate that it's true. I hate that I was so happy, and I hate that I feel so foolish. Like it was transparently, pathologically stupid to have believed I could have...*that*. But the thing that makes me sadder—angrier even—is knowing Ralph could have told me at any time. He could have called, written, pulled me aside that summer or any summer after, and just fucking *told* me."

St. Sebastian Perth Martinez, yes. I know who you are.

"And then Mamá—" The words have tied themselves into knots deep in my throat; I have to hide my face in Poe's hair in order to force them out. "She lied to me too, you know? And maybe that's worse? Because she lied my entire life—every single day—and then she left me, she went and died and now I can't yell at her, I can't scream at her, I can't make her fix it. I can't even ask her for the whole story, I can't even learn the entire truth. All the things you're supposed to know about where you come from and about why you're here—I don't know any of that, and I never will. It's just this *question*. This unknowable thing I'll have to live with my entire life, and on top of everything—losing Auden, reckoning with the sins I've made with him, knowing everyone has lied—it's somehow the not knowing that bothers me the most. There will always be a curtain between me and the entire truth. And every person who could possibly draw it back—Ralph, Richard, my mother—has died."

I finish with a short suck of air, having run myself clean out of breath, and then every part of me flushes hot with embarrassment. This is why I hate talking about feelings. It's like feeding stray cats—you do it once or twice, even just a few scraps of food, and then one day you have a back garden full of the little beasts licking their paws and mewling at you.

I'm about to apologize to Poe for all the emotional vomit when she looks up at me again. And there's no aversion on her face, no pity. There's a cute little line between her eyebrows as she studies my face like it's one of the library's leather tomes.

"There's got to be someone who knows," she says. "I know you said your mother didn't have very many friends in the village other than those in the Historical Society—do you think she would have confided in them? Or perhaps—you're not going to like this—but perhaps Augie knew? If he was close with your father—your real father, I mean, not your biological one—then he might know?"

"My uncle doesn't know," I say sharply. "He never would have accepted me if he hadn't thought I was Dad's—Richard's, I mean."

As soon as I say it, it feels a little unfair. Truthfully, Augie's never really set me at a distance. When I came back from Texas, he was eager to have me work for him and has been begging me to consider taking over the day to day of the company. He's always had faith in me and my work...But how much of that faith is because he thinks I'm Richard's son?

Poe rubs a hand along my back, soothing me. "And the Historical Society?"

I think of the superannuated crones and gaffers at the few society meetings Mamá managed to drag me to. "Too old to be confidantes, I think, and she wouldn't have confided family business in them anyway." And as soon as I say it, as soon as I say *family business*, I know.

"Ana María," I say with a sigh.

"Who's Ana María?"

"A cousin. My mother's cousin, actually. They were best friends growing up, studied abroad together in college. Mamá talked to her almost every day. She might know."

I'm too far past hope to think I'll find real answers, but there is relief in realizing there's something I can do, any kind of door to knock on. I let out a long breath and pull Poe in tight. "Thank you."

"You can thank me by going to the gala in a couple of weeks," she says promptly, and I stiffen in her arms, pulling away.

"No," I say.

"Please?"

"Poe."

"I know Auden's going to be there, but come for me," she says. She reaches for my hand and tugs me over to one of the long tables in the middle of the room, where she turns and hops up on the edge. She pulls me by the belt loops between her spread legs.

I nearly shudder with how good it feels to be pulled and led and made, and the brush of her thighs around my hips makes my erection hard enough to hurt. Sitting with her legs apart like this has her skirt rucked all the way up, and I can see the black cotton of her panties. Another sign Auden isn't home—otherwise she'd be bare under her skirt, available for his use any time he needed it.

"He's still going to be there too," I finally say, distractedly. Her exposed thighs are so fucking sexy, those cotton panties so tempting. Her cunt is at the perfect height; I could yank her knickers to the side, unzip my jeans, and be inside her in seconds.

With a coy little hum, she trails her own fingers up her leg, ghosting them across her pussy. "He'll be busy mingling."

"He said he wanted to show us off," I say. "He'll want you on his arm."

"He wants you on his arm too." She's teasing herself now, tracing the seam of her cunt, showing me where I could fuck.

"I'm not going, Poe," I say, my eyes on her fingers.

"Everyone's coming. Even Becket. I don't want you to be the only one not there." Her finger slides under the elastic edge of her panties and then slowly draws them back. Shadows hang like a second dress around her, but I can still see the unmistakeable glisten of her sex. I can see the small, wet place where I need so badly to be.

"I won't feel left out," I promise on a rasp, running my own hands up her thighs now. I have to touch her, I have to feel her wetness for myself. And she lets me, moving her hand so that I can push a thumb inside her.

We both inhale at the same time—her from the invasion, and me from the pure, tight feel of her. There's nothing softer than her pussy. I remember thinking that the night I lost my virginity to her, I remember thinking that if I'd known how good it felt to fuck, I never would have been able to wait so long.

"Let me," I say. Beg. "Let me inside you."

"Come to the gala."

"*Poe*," I groan.

"I'm not going back to how things were before," she says, rocking into my hand. I slide my thumb free, meaning to stop touching her altogether, but then she lets out the saddest, sexiest whimper, and I can't bear it. I push two fingers back inside, my entire body humming as she arches to me, my skin aching, my balls drawing tight.

"I'm not going back to all of us leading separate lives," Poe says. "I won't do it."

"You and Auden won't have to change anything. And if you want to— I mean, I still want to be with you."

"I know," she says. "I know you do. I want to be with you too—I love you. And I love him. But we didn't want two or three separate relationships, Saint. We wanted one."

"Yeah," I say. Bitterly. "We did."

"Auden was wrong to lie, but surely—"

I keep stroking her with firm, steady fucks of my hand, but now I meet her gaze, lifting my eyebrows. "Surely what, Poe? You can't be *okay* with—"

"I am," she interrupts. "I am okay with it. I'm pissed Auden lied to you, but you sharing a father doesn't bother me."

"Because you're not the one committing a sin."

"You don't believe in sin," she says.

And I don't answer. I no longer know if I believe in sin or not. I don't know what I believe in.

It used to be Thornchapel.

It was supposed to be Auden.

I don't know what I believe because I barely even know how I feel.

No. No, that's not true. I do know.

I feel like someone's come in with embroidery scissors and started snipping around my heart.

But the feeling eases when Poe puts her hand over my chest. I drop my head to the top of hers, and we breathe together for a moment—her palm against my bleeding heart and my fingers touching her in her sweetest place. Wordlessly, she reaches for the fly of my jeans, and I let her. I let her pop open the button on the waistband, I let her unzip me. I let her tug my pants around my hips and free my shaft.

My breath hitches as she gives me a light, barely there caress.

"Do you have a condom?" Poe whispers.

I do. I pull my fingers free and fumble in my back pocket to give it to her, and she makes a total mess of trying to open it, and I try to help, but my fingers are slick and the inside of the condom packet is slick, and we're both suddenly giggling with how stupid it is, until finally she's rolling the latex over me and I'm not giggling anymore, I'm not giggling at all. The pressure of her hands, the slippery insides of the sheath—I'm exhaling in short, rough breaths, barely able to hang on.

"Can't wait," I grunt. "Need to now."

Poe doesn't stop me; there's no talk of the gala or Auden or anything else. She slides her hands around my hips and squeezes, digging her fingers into the top of my ass, and it's just the kick of objectification and ownership I need to be truly lost. I shove inside her and groan, unable to bear how tight and warm she is, unable to bear being without it even for as long as it takes to pull out and stroke back in again.

She doesn't seem to be able to bear it either, because whenever I separate my hips from her thighs, she grips me harder, urging me closer, so the mating is close and urgent. I band an arm around her waist and fill my free hand with her curvy, plush bottom, and then I hold her tight to me as we move.

"More," she says into my ear. "Use me."

Except it's the two of us using each other, it's the both of us ordering, taking, seeking. A circle of selfishness creating a circle of submission. She commands me to fuck her dirty, she spurs me on with greedy hands and so I'm the one being used, cheapened, enjoyed solely for the thick cock to be ridden. And it's freedom. Because inside Poe's body, with her teeth on my neck and her eyes fluttering, the pain of the last two days eases somewhat.

The embroidery scissors around my heart stop snipping. There isn't the raw, angry despair coiling in my stomach. There isn't the cold, whispering voice that now I'll be alone, that I've always been alone, that I'll die alone.

There isn't the dull, bruising pulse of Auden's name in the back of my mind, thudding in time with my heart.

With her, I remember how I felt just a couple days ago, crashing through the trees and wildly in love. With her, it's always summer.

I use the hand on her backside to grind her against me in just the right way, keeping pressure on her clit, and then I lower my mouth to her ear and confess all sorts of filthy things to her. That I think of her when I fuck my toys at home, that I had to lock myself in the library bathroom and jerk off last week, just thinking about her pretty tits, about how soft they are and how tight her berry-pink nipples get. I tell her that I never want to stop fucking her, that she makes me feel so good I can't stand it, that I want to come on her backside, on her belly, on her cunt. I want to make her as dirty as she makes me, I want her to know what it's like to crave fucking like craving food or air or sleep.

With my desperate words in her ear, she comes—a fast, mean orgasm that has her clawing my back and squirming wildly in my arms. Her legs tighten around me, her cunt gives me those irresistible little flutters, sweet squeezes as if she's trying to suck my orgasm right out of my body.

I follow her immediately, sinking into that soft heat over and over and over again as I spill jagged, urgent pleasure into the latex. The orgasm is almost crushing in how good it feels; each heavy pulse sends waves of selfish bliss everywhere—tightening my thighs and tingling in my toes, racing up my spine to the nape of my neck and then buzzing down to my fingertips. Everything is dizzy, hazy, brilliant, and sweet. And for a moment, nothing hurts. For a moment, I can almost imagine a life where a day without Auden doesn't scratch scars onto the skin of my pathetic heart.

10

St. Sebastian

Once I've succumbed to the need I have for Proserpina, the rest of my self-control melts away. I let her convince me to stay the night—although I can't bear to sleep in the bed that should have been for all three of us—and so we end up sleeping in one of the guest suites instead. She's unpredictable to sleep with, sometimes afflicted with the fretful dozes of an insomniac and then other times hibernating like a little bear, but tonight she's yawning and slow-blinking before we ever get into bed. Sir James is back inside and already chuffing softly in his sleep, taking a whole corner of the bed to himself.

"Promise me you'll think about the gala," she says, crawling under the covers and snuggling right into my arms. It feels so good to hold her that I could cry. "Promise me you won't shut yourself out from everything. From the rest of us."

I have a lot of things I could say to that—defensive and bitter things, maudlin things—but instead I say the most painfully honest thing of all. "It's not about shutting myself out, Poe. It's about *him*. It's about seeing him, talking to him, brushing shoulders with him while he wears a tuxedo and smells like a forest. I can't do it. I can't see him being so...*him*, and then be okay. I just can't."

"Because you're still angry with him?" she whispers.

"Because I'm still in love with him."

"Then why separate yourself from whom you love?"

Through the window, I watch a moth-eaten cloud stretch across the sky, trying to reach the moon. It makes me feel lonely in a familiar way, in my usual way.

"Loving him is wrong," I say. "That's irreducibly true, Poe. It can't be navigated around. It's just *wrong*. But I also don't know if I can stop, and until I figure out what to do about that, I don't know how I can be near him."

"It'll break him," she murmurs on a yawn. I don't need to see her face to know her eyes are closed. "You'll break him if you stay away."

It won't be the first time.

The thought, and the sheer truth of it, makes me miserable. But what am I supposed to do? Really? Drop everything I know about right and wrong—admittedly not much—and embrace a life of iniquity with him? Eat forbidden fruit forever?

How could a love like that, unholy and unhealthy, ever survive?

Here, it could.

The thought comes unbidden, but intoxicating nonetheless. I push it away.

"Don't forget," Poe murmurs again, and then presses her closed fist to my chest, right above my heart. She falls asleep clenching her fist over and over again, the heartbeat the three of us share, and when it finally stops and she starts snoring in my arms, I gently take her hand away from my chest and try to forget the feel of it. The memory of our joined love.

But still I lie awake a long time, Thornchapel awake around me too, with owls and breezes and restless trees who miss their master.

I don't have to be at the library until after lunch, so I let myself doze later than usual, well past dawn. Poe is predictably still asleep next to me, a tangle of blankets and long, dark hair, and I spend a long time simply looking at her, savoring her closeness, her trust, the innocence of her sleeping face which never quite vanishes, even when she's awake.

But eventually I get up and treat myself to a shower and one of the new toothbrushes stocked in the bedroom's en suite, and by the time I get out, Poe is blinking against the sunlight like a sleepy kitten.

I sit down on the edge of the bed and stroke her hair away from her face. "Morning," I say.

She mumbles something mostly unintelligible, and I wish there was no real world, no other life than this, and I could just spend the day in bed with her, napping and fucking and napping some more. But she has an entire library to catalog and I have my own little kingdom of picture books and free Wi-Fi to manage, and there's something else I need to do anyway.

"I need to go," I tell her. "I just wanted to say goodbye first."

She pouts. "No. You can't leave."

"We both have to work," I say, kissing her on the nose and then nuzzling her neck. "And Sir James is ready for breakfast."

The dog in question has been trotting in and out of the room all morning, eagerly wagging his tail whenever I so much as look at the door, and it's him jumping up on the bed and snuffling wetly at Poe's face that finally has her sitting upright and opening her eyes for real.

"Hate you both," she mumbles, but then she slumps against me and lets me pet her hair for several minutes, yawning and grumbling and finally turning back into a living girl.

"Are you going now?" she asks.

"Yes." I don't mean to say more, but I'm addicted to sharing my most private thoughts now, I guess, because I add, "I'm going to look through my mom's office some more. And I'd like to call her cousin before I go to work."

She gives me a squeezing hug, but she doesn't remark on it, she doesn't exhort me to be brave or anything condescending like that. Instead, she just says, "Okay. Let me get dressed and I'll walk you out."

Like the besotted wraith I am, I drift behind her as she goes down the hall to the bedroom she shares with Auden. The same bedroom the three of us were supposed to share.

It's very hard not to imagine the version of myself who moved his threadbare T-shirts into the dressers, and left his scuffed boots next to Auden's gleaming dress shoes in the massive walk-in closet. Who already has a stack of books on the end table, who's already had to take off Auden's glasses and put them on the same end table after he fell asleep wearing them.

A whole other life, stolen away.

Except it wasn't really stolen, was it? It was never mine, it was never meant to be, it was always a lie.

I just didn't know it before.

But even with the lingering ghosts of the Life That Might Have Been, I'm still content to watch Poe move around, sleepy-eyed and sulky, fumbling for clothes and flinging socks and bras around like a teenager getting ready for school. When she goes in to use the bathroom and brush her teeth, I wander around the room, the dog at my heels.

Almost nothing has changed since the morning I found Auden's journal, save for Poe moving in her things too. She has a book on the bedside table just like I would have, and librarian habit has me picking it up and flipping through it. It's a book about ancient British religion, and after nosing through the front matter—it was published fourteen years ago through a university press—and scanning through the chapter headings, I'm about to set it back down when I see Poe's last name. Or more accurately, her mother's last name.

Introduction by Dr. Adelina Markham

Curious, I page through to the introduction, reading about Dr. Markham's background in Neolithic Mediterranean rituals and how she views the author's work on ancient British religion. One section in particular catches my eye:

The nuances of when, where, and how humans were sacrificed are vagarious and so intrinsically complex that they defy easy explication, even in a book entirely devoted to the matter. It is frustrating to the historian, of course, because we crave categorization, we crave indexing, but above all, we crave understanding. We must never forget, however, that the bones, bogs, wicker men, sacred groves, and altars all belonged to people, and people are inherently inconsistent and illogical; they are given to fear, erratic behavior, and all manner of specious thinking.

They are also hopeful, imaginative, compassionate, and profoundly selfless.

We can surmise from archaeological evidence and contemporary accounts that many victims of human sacrifice consented to their own deaths and willingly allowed themselves to be slain, often in brutal and painful ways. Why they consented is a matter for conjecture, but it seems reasonable to suppose that ritual murder was an act that straddled both violence and abnegation, and that sacrifice was an act that was seen to benefit the community and the land the community needed to survive.

Complicating our search for meaning is the gradual ebbing of the practice before the pervasion of writing into the communities that performed ritual sacrifice. In fact, one may even go so far as to say that there is a strong inverse correlation between written history and human sacrifice—that the latter declined in the face of the former, but again, why that might be is beyond what the data can tell us.

In the face of this absence, we are left with mysteries, and our only recourse is to find more mysteries to add to the record, in the hopes that somehow all these unanswered questions will elucidate themselves. And to that end, the work of Dr. Katy Davidson has been invaluable, particularly in the excavations in the Thorne Valley, where I first met Dr. Davidson as a student many years ago, and where she has conclusively proven a span of human religious activity dating back to the Neolithic. Dr. Davidson uses the Thorne Valley ritual landscape as a synecdoche for the religious life of ancient Britain as a whole, showing the transmission of ideas from the Neolithic all the way to the Roman occupation and into Saxon rule—

"I see you found my mother's introduction," Poe says from behind me. "Cheerful stuff, right?"

"It's interesting. Where did you find it?"

"I was looking for something about Estamond, actually, and I noticed this because it was so much younger than all the books around it. And then once I saw my mom's name, I obviously had to read it. But there's also a lot in there that's on brand for us." She says it in an oddly light voice, as if she's trying to make a joke, but she's too troubled to pull it off.

"I did notice your mother referenced the Thorne Valley. She was a student digging here?"

Poe lifts a shoulder. "That's what the introduction says. My father never said anything about it, but it would explain why she came here when we were children, maybe? Maybe not? But here, look at this—"

She flips to a dog-eared page toward the end of the book and points. I read:

The standing stones on the Thornchapel estate are a well-guarded secret, as is the chapel situated to the west of them. The Guest family, who have officially owned the land since the Domesday Book, but very probably for much longer, have only allowed one excavation of the site, in the late 1980s. The stones have been in place there for at least four thousand years, while the chapel is of early Norman construction. The altar inside the chapel, however, is an interesting case, as it seems to predate the standing stones, but also bears testimony to the various faiths that have been practiced there. The excavation uncovered two Neolithic jet beads, a pair of bronze divination spoons, a mix of Roman and Saxon coinage, and a small lead cruet that could have possibly been used for sacramental wine after the Guests commissioned the family chapel. This speaks to an incredible continuity of worship centered on one site, especially one so remote, and indeed, it is hard not to conjecture why that might be. Even the Romans were curious; it is said that when they first encountered the Dumnonii living in the Thorne Valley, they asked the Britons why the altar in the woods was so deeply sacred to them.

We don't know what words the Dumnonii used to explain it, but we do know how the Romans translated what they said. Convivificat.

It stirs. It resurrects.

It is perhaps no wonder the Christians felt so at home there.

I look up at Poe, and she's staring back at me with an *I know, right???* face.

"Convivificat," I say aloud, thinking of the words etched onto the altar. The lettering looked newer than Roman to me, just by the shape of the letters, but how much newer is hard to say. Long enough for the grass to grow over the altar, I suppose.

"I still don't know why she wrote it," Poe says, looking down at the book with distinct yearning. "But it's nice to know the history of it, you know?"

"And the altar."

"Isn't that part wild?" she asks. "The altar being older than everything else in that clearing?" And then she frowns to herself. "Well, other than the door, maybe."

"The door?"

She looks away from me and the book, off to the window. As if she's embarrassed. "It's going to sound very, um, bizarre, but I've seen a door. Behind the altar. Mostly in my dreams, but also glimpses of it when I'm awake, and then Auden saw it too. After Beltane."

"A door," I repeat. "Like an actual door? A door that takes up space in the real world?"

She winces. "Yeah."

I have walked every inch of that clearing in every possible weather, mood, and time of day, and I've never, *ever* seen a door behind the altar. So why does the idea of it raise goosebumps along my arms?

"Hmm." But I don't say anything else about it and neither does she.

I set down the book and we walk downstairs together, Sir James running ahead of us, and then wheeling back, and then running ahead again.

"Also I didn't mean to pressure you about the gala," Poe says as we reach the door. "If seeing Auden is too painful, then I understand. I just— surely there is some way you can stay close to each other? Even if it looks different than you thought it would?"

I kiss her.

I kiss her because I love her, and I love her hope, and I can't bear to snuff it out.

But I know the truth, and the truth is that there is no staying close to Auden Guest.

You either fall at his feet or flee into the hills. That's it.

I walk home.

The walk itself is very easy—a mile of barely used country lane, lined by ancient hedges and frowned over by enormous, creaking trees. There's some hills—but where aren't there in Dartmoor, honestly—and there's the occasional walker using the lane to jump onto the next section of public footpath, but other than that, it's an easy, lonely heaven. When I was a boy, I liked to pretend that I was on my way to the Prancing Pony; when I got older, I used to put on my headphones and listen to all sorts of sad and wistful music and imagine myself in a sad and wistful music video. Now I see it as Dr. Davidson might see it—a lane following the route of an ancient road, which follows the line of an even older path. An artery running from the valley's heart out to the village, a thread connecting the sacred to the profane.

How did Poe's mother see it, I wonder, the lane which ribboned through the trees to her eventual death? Did she know? Did she have an inkling the last time she came here? Was there a part of her that knew as she walked over the bridge and into the world of Thornchapel that she'd never see another dawn?

And my own mother? How many times must she have walked down this road—a tiny me skipping or sulking by her side—and had to pass the turn for the estate, had to listen to the whisper of the little streamlet guarding the old house from the rest of the world?

Was I conceived after a walk down this lane? Did she walk back to the village afterward feeling happy? Ashamed? Hopeful? Ralph was a monster, and my mom was perfect, and so how did they come together? How could it ever have happened?

There's some halfhearted drizzle by the time I get to the house, enough to make all the rooms gloomy and gray, and by the time I take off my jacket, kick off my boots, and hunt down an apple to eat, I feel that dull ache in my chest again. Those blunt scissors around my heart.

Snip snip snip.

I poke around my mom's office for a minute or two, not sure what I even want to find, and then I spend an embarrassing amount of time looking at the picture of Richard Davey on my mother's desk, too shy to actually pick it up. He's gingery and red-cheeked and grinning. If I concentrate very hard, I can remember clambering over him, hugging him, pulling on his beard. I can remember the sharp, painty scent of him; I can remember how he used to draw me robots and mermaids whenever I asked, which was often.

He loved me.

And I know, in an abstract sort of way, that Richard is still my father. That Ralph's DNA can mean as little as I want it to—at least when it comes to how I think of my family and who raised me.

But it still feels like something's been ripped out of my hands, something I didn't even know I was supposed to hold onto, and now I can never get it back.

Suddenly I'm backing away from the picture, I'm pressed against the wall, I'm sliding down to the floor and staring at the half-eaten apple in my hands like it holds all the answers. Like it can reassure me that I was loved and that I deserved it, and that those robots and mermaids and cuddles were given out of anything other than pity.

I wanted to do this, but later, because it's too early, it's still so early in the morning in Mexico City. But I can't stop myself from finding my phone and pulling up Ana María's number. She's a vampire, though, so maybe she hasn't even gone to bed yet. Maybe she's still awake, curled up on her couch with her latest paranormal romance and a cigarette.

I press *call* and then feel hope and dread both as I hear her pick up.

"St. Sebastian, if your mother were alive to see how you neglect your family, you know what she'd say."

"Ana María," I say in Spanish, trying to sound normal and soothing and not at all like I've been in hell the past two days. "I've been busy. I work for my uncle here—"

"I know all about you working for your uncle," she interrupts. Ana María is the kind of relative that knows everything—even when you'd rather that she not. "And I know you call your grandmother and grandfather almost every week," she goes on, "but you can't call me once in an entire year?"

I could point out that my grandparents helped raise me and also that Ana María is only a cousin—my *mom*'s cousin at that, which makes her like a second cousin. Or a cousin once removed or something. I could point out that I'm calling her *now*, so it makes very little sense to scold me about not doing the thing she wants me to do while I'm actually doing it.

But I want her help, and also I can't help but like her. She may be bossy, she may mail me selenite wands and abalone shells and smudge sticks, but she's also funny and generous and loves all the same books I do.

Also I've spent the last three months doing breathlessly filthy things out in the woods, so I'm the last person who should judge about abalone shells.

"I'm sorry, you're right, it's been too long," I apologize. "But I need your help."

"Hmph," she says, but she only manages to resist asking her next question for a few seconds. "What help?"

I take a deep breath. "I need to know about my father."

"Richard?"

"No. Not Richard."

I might be the first person in the world to successfully quiet Ana María for any length of time. And…her silence is all the confirmation I need.

"I know you know the truth," I say after a few heavy moments without either of us saying anything. "I know you know who he was."

More silence. I wonder what she's looking at right now. If she's staring at her shrine of Santa Muerte, thinking of how I'm named for her. If she's missing my mother, who was her best friend. If she's staring at the picture of Jesus on her wall—*the* picture, the only one the women in my family seem to like: a frowning, silky-bearded god with a heart of thorns.

I wonder if she's thinking of what to say to me.

There's the flick of a lighter and a long breath in. The habit she and my mother both picked up when they spent a semester studying abroad in France. When she speaks, I can practically see the smoke floating up toward the ceiling. "How did you find out?" she asks.

I can hardly say I found out after waking up sex-sore and happy in my half-brother's room, so I try to find a reasonable facsimile of the truth. "Apparently Ralph had arranged for a letter to be sent after his death. To his legitimate son." Legitimate. What a stupid word. And yet I hate all the other words even more. Acknowledged. Recognized.

Chosen.

"I just—" I don't know how to go on, because I have every question in the entire world and yet I have no questions left inside me at all. There's a hollowness where the questions should be, an empty fatalism, which just says *of course*, over and over again. Of course the one good thing I'd found, the one home, the one place for my heart—of course that would be taken away.

And of course Auden would be the one to do it.

"I don't understand," I finally manage to say. "When did they meet? How? And why would she lie about it to me? Why go through the whole charade of pretending Richard was my father if it was Ralph all along? And then the money—" I break off because suddenly the money makes sense, suddenly it all makes sense.

Of course that's why he gave her the money. *Of course.* Ralph fathered me so he paid for me. Noblesse oblige applies to bastard sons too, and as much as I imagine it hurt my mother's pride to take it, she did anyway.

Ana María takes an audible drag, holds it in for a long moment, and then sighs. "She was very young, you have to understand, just out of college, and we both—as girls, we both loved magic. Everything about it. So when she took the job working for the paper out there and one of her first assignments was profiling the festivals celebrated in Thorncombe, she was thrilled."

Another inhale, the next words coming out on the coughing exhale. "And then she met Ralph. The next thing I knew, she was seeing him every day. She was in love."

"He would have been married." I have a faint memory of Auden's parents being congratulated on their twentieth anniversary at Mass when I was sixteen. "He *was* married."

I hear Ana María take another drag, perhaps using the time to think of what to say. "Love is often wrong, St. Sebastian. It's often wrong about everything."

And what can I say to that? It's a lesson I was too stubborn to learn back when it would've done me any good.

"She knew he was married, of course, but I think she loved him too much to stop. And that was the first year he was trying to revive the old ways." Ana María pauses then. "Do I need to explain those to you?"

If I were capable of feeling anything other than empty, wasting pain, maybe I'd feel shame right now. But I'm not, so I don't. "I know them, Ana María," I tell her. "I know the old ways."

"She would hate that," my cousin says. "Your mother wanted nothing to do with them after everything happened."

"You don't sound like you hate it," I say.

She snorts. "Certainly not. I'm *proud.* But also I know you're too smart a boy to let yourself get hurt, so that's why I don't worry."

I rub idly at my chest, where those scissors keep snip-snipping my heart right out of my body.

I'm not too smart, Ana María. I let myself get hurt so badly.

She clears her throat. "That first year, the first time he tried to bring back the old ways, your mother was his May Queen. Imbolc through Samhain, every feast."

"It wasn't his wife?" I think of Auden's mother, pale and trembling whenever they visited the Abbey.

"Jennifer said Clare never loved Thornchapel, not the way Ralph did. She didn't want the rituals to happen at all, and maybe she thought if she refused to participate, then Ralph wouldn't do them at all. Which was foolish. That man did whatever he wanted."

"I saw a picture of Ralph and some other adults here at Thornchapel," I say. "It seemed—well, I think they might have been doing the same thing Ralph did with my mother, keeping the old ways and all that. Clare was there with them."

"Maybe she changed her mind? Maybe she realized that Ralph would never stop? I don't know. But I do know the year your mother was his May Queen was the year she conceived you, and after Jennifer found out she was pregnant, she stayed away from the estate and everything associated with it.

She didn't see Ralph for a very long time. Years, in fact. She refused to see him until well after Richard died."

I look up at the picture on her desk, the frame resting atop a stack of old receipts. Richard Davey, eyes crinkling and mouth wide in a happy smile, a splotch of white paint on his neck. "Do you think Ralph knew she was pregnant?"

"No," Ana María admits. "I'd almost like it better if he had so that I could hate him for that too, but he didn't know until you were twelve, and the minute he found out, he started helping. With money, I mean. He wanted to meet you, but Jennifer said he couldn't unless he was ready to claim you and actually be involved in your life. The way she saw it, you were better off thinking Richard was your father and not knowing Ralph at all if all Ralph was going to do was refuse to acknowledge you."

I'm still looking at the picture. The happy face of the man who reared me even though I wasn't biologically his. "Why did Richard do it?" I ask. "Why did he fall in love with a pregnant woman? Claim me as his own? Raise me?"

Ana María sniffs. "Women don't just cease to exist as people once we're pregnant. Your mother was beautiful and smart and bright like sunshine. She and Richard fell in love, and it was never a question to him that he would raise you."

"She was done with Ralph though, after that first year? They never...you know..."

A couple long drags on the cigarette.

Finally, "I told you earlier, St. Sebastian. Love is often wrong. And it is never, ever simple."

And with a feeling like hot needles pricking the inside of my body, I recall what my mother said to me when I left England after the attack in the graveyard.

I have to stay. I won't leave the man I love.

I thought she meant Richard Davey then. I thought she meant his grave and all the memories she'd made with Richard in the too-short years they had together. But no.

She meant Ralph.

"*How*?" I ask. "And for how long?" I search my memories, but I can't remember anything that would have ever made me think she was sneaking off to fuck Ralph Guest. She took the occasional research trip, maybe, and she left sometimes for historical society meetings, but…

I can practically hear Ana María shrug. "Jennifer hinted something awful happened to him—something he couldn't bring himself to tell her about. Something in the thorn chapel. I think it changed him. He was still a monster, but he was a broken one when he came back to your mother. And anyway, I think she couldn't help but love him still. To her, he'd always be her May King. Her lord of the manor."

I lean my head back against the bookshelves and stare up at the ceiling. I suddenly feel very foolishly and obviously like my mother, making the same mistakes, falling for the same breed of broken Guests. Except my mother's sin was loving a married man, and mine is a sin of much greater magnitude.

Jesus. No wonder she was so scared and angry when Auden and I started seeing each other. No wonder she wanted me back in Texas, far, far away from Auden's floppy hair and cool, arrogant drawl.

Too far away for him to draw on my skin or bite my lip.

Too far away for us to fall into reckless, terrible love.

Which we did anyway.

"She should have told me," I say, vehemence staining my words with anger. "She was a fucking coward."

This earns me a blistering scolding. "Do you think it was easy for her?" Ana María snaps. "Do you think it was easy raising a son on her own? Do you think she wanted to have a son with a married man who would never claim her or him? If she didn't tell you, it was because she wanted to keep you safe from all of it. She wanted to keep you away from the darkness Ralph had made."

"She was afraid of what I'd think," I say angrily. "She was afraid I'd judge her."

"Can you blame her?" Ana María demands. "Look at how you're reacting now!"

"She lied to me *my entire life!* And because of her lies, I didn't know any better, and I—"

Fell in love with Auden Guest is what I was about to say, but I manage to choke the words back before they pass my lips. Because here's something as terrible as it is true:

No one can ever, ever know.

No one can know that I fell in love with my brother, that I made vows to him beside the river. That he chased me and caught me and mounted me and that I liked it. That he, Proserpina, and I were going to live together, that he was going to be our Dominant, that we were going to be our king's priest and priestess, and we were going to be very fucking happy.

It's a crime and a sin and a stain I'll never be free of, what I've done with Auden Guest. What, even now, I ache to do with Auden Guest.

"You *what*, St. Sebastian?" Ana María asks carefully. "What happened?"

"Nothing," I mumble. "Nothing happened."

Silence hangs between us then. I stare at Richard Davey's picture, still rubbing at my chest.

My body aches the tiniest bit, and I remember what it felt like to have the wild god over me, inside me, feral and cruel and snarling with the need to fuck. My cock thickens at the memory…at the thought of it happening again.

It can never, ever happen again.

"You're too smart a boy to let yourself get hurt," my cousin tells me, repeating what she said earlier. "Tell me I'm right, St. Sebastian. Please."

"You're right," I say automatically, but I don't know if I believe it. I don't know if it's true.

Because I am very, very hurt right now, and there's a miserable, traitorous part of me that wants to go find the source of my pain and be wrecked all over again. And when I end my call with Ana María and see a text from Auden—

Come back to me.

—I very nearly cave and go find him. I want to so badly, in fact, that I leave my phone in the kitchen and go early to the library, determined to stay so busy that I'll forget all about him and how much I long to crawl back to his feet.

II

Rebecca

The day of the gala, I'm sitting in my office with a fine-point marker in my hand and my desk covered with site plans for the Severn riverfront revitalization. I'm supposed to be making revisions so my junior architect can start rendering the plan in Photoshop, but I've done nothing but stare at the slopes and bends and loops, my mind playing strange tricks on me.

Somehow the slopes have become generous curves. And the bends have become arches, sinuous and beckoning. And the loops are sliding, silky hair, catching on itself as it drapes over a pillow.

The river—flattened in the CAD drawing to a few squiggly depth indicators—becomes palpable wetness against my fingertips. It becomes the slick, gin-soaked kisses I stole from Delphine last night. The fevered moment when she took my hand and pushed a single fingertip inside of her. Not deep, not any deeper than the first knuckle, but my god, I could have been inside her past my wrist for how good it felt. Her eyes had shone up at me, brimming with so much trust I wondered if I could drown in it, and I could hear the memory of her words, a memory I kept curling my thoughts around—*I love you.*

And the inside of her, a place I had traced countless times, licked and lapped at—it was softer than I ever could have imagined, tighter too. And wetter—the kind of wet that has me wet just remembering it, squirming just from looking at a fucking CAD drawing, Jesus Christ.

I toss the marker down and stand up, pacing over to the window and scowling. The place between my legs aches now, aches enough that if I press my thighs together, pleasure sizzles up from my clit to shower sparks in my belly.

I lean my forehead against the cool glass and try not to feel miserable. I hate this, I think. I hate having the order of my thoughts rifled through, I hate the misbehavior of my body. Always, always, there had been a line drawn between work and sex. Work was the gift, and sex was the thing that kept me going when it felt like the gift would break me. Fucking was for the body and work was for the mind.

Except now my mind is invaded.

Even now I can imagine I smell her—although I know that can't be true—but still. A smell like the scent she favors—berries and violets, ripe and delicate all at once.

When I remember it, my belly hollows. I feel like my chest has been cracked open and my heart is beating out in the open air and everyone can see the ugly ordinariness of it. The thin skin of it, the greedy blue veins, the way it skips and speeds up for someone who will invariably rend it in two. Everyone will see the sloppy, idiotic organ and say *yes, she was a genius, but a fool for all that.*

I roll my forehead against the glass, imagining my chest suturing itself back together, imagining a plate of armor over it, imagining all of me encased in concrete like a radioactive tomb. Heart, thoughts, cunt—all of it suffocated with necessity and focus.

You're just worked up because you know what you're going to do this afternoon, I reassure myself. *It's just the anticipation any Domme would feel. You have your own sub now and it's normal to be excited.*

There. That's it. We're going back to the club this afternoon, and it's going to be unbearably sexy, and anyone in my place would be just as distracted. Maybe even more so. If I were Auden, I'd already have tossed off in the staff loo, so there's that at least.

Our first visit to the club went well enough, I suppose. I decided that we'd go in a voyeuristic capacity only; I wanted Delphine to acquaint herself with the space without being preoccupied with the possibility of performance. I wanted to ease her into it all, the way I hadn't eased her in our first night together in London; I wanted to keep her heart safe.

And if a consequence of that was keeping my own heart safe, could I be blamed?

At any rate, I'd forgotten that Delphine *was* a performer. That performance intoxicated her, that she found a heady meaning in it. That she craved being watched and witnessed. The entire time we'd been there, safely ensconced in a plush leather booth as we watched scene after scene on the main stage, she'd been enraptured, captivated, practically twitching to leap up onto the stage herself and fling herself at the feet of strangers as a willing victim.

It had pleased me—she would thrive there, she would love it—but there had been a small snake of jealousy moving through my guts too. Was she so willing to have another person top her? Was I just a...I don't even know, some kind of shortcut to what she needed? Was her loyalty to domination in general and not to me?

Was she with me not because I was Rebecca but because I was a mistress?

I knew I had no right to ask those questions. After all, I was the one who kept telling myself I only wanted Delphine for the submission. I was the one saying this was about kink and sex only, I was the one who told Delphine she didn't really love me. But every time she gasped as some other Dom showed off their skills, every time she leaned forward to see more of the flogging, more of the dripping wax, more of the sneers, praises, and comforts that the Doms gave their subs, the surlier I became. Eventually, I dragged Delphine home and pleasured her until she was hoarse with screaming, and even then I found myself curling around her like a dragon as she slept. Like someone would come and take her from me.

But I'm better prepared for it now. I know not to trust those jealousies—like all feelings, they're just chemicals, just oxygen and glucose flooding different parts of my brain in response to external stimuli. It's the brain of a mammal trying to avoid pain, trying to avoid the sting of rejection because social rejection meant death when we evolved. It's a system ten thousand years out of date, a system made for humans on the fringes of survival, and should obviously be ignored now.

And anyway, maybe I'm not frightened, maybe I'm merely possessive, and that's to be expected.

I have more than voyeurism planned for us today. I want to play with her before the gala, so she can have stripes underneath her gorgeous gown, so that under all her silk and chiffon will be a reddened bottom and a needy cunt, waiting for me to soothe it.

You're going to have to make her wait for it, I remind myself sternly. *You can't just give it to her the minute she bats those doe eyes at you.*

My terrible secret is that there's an urge in me, as deep as it is unfamiliar, to simply spoil her. All of the time. To pet her hair and play with her tits and kiss her pussy to my heart's content, and to withhold nothing, even the things it makes me flinch to give. My hunger for her is as bottomless as her eyes. And so I don't even know who I am anymore when I'm with her. Am I the strict Mistress, demanding perfection? The naughty Domme, spanking her for fun? An insatiable lover, keeping her up into the small hours of the night? A girlfriend, who texts her and cooks her supper and listens to her chatter about her day with photographers and business managers and fashion reps?

Something more?

Because it is something more, isn't it, when I find myself watching her face as she sleeps, when seeing certain Pantones in a prospectus makes me think of her, when certain ads on the Tube make me think of her, when working, eating, breathing—they all make me think of her.

And so it's no wonder I'm consumed today, thinking of this evening and my plans. Thinking of tonight, when she'll be trembling and slick and oh-so-sweet.

But there's one unpleasant task between me and leaving the office to go fetch her, and there's no sense in delaying it. I give up on the site plans, deciding I'll pack them up and work on them after she's asleep tonight, and I go to close my office door for a semblance of privacy. I feel foolish as I do it, but I'll feel more foolish if I don't and someone overhears us.

Not because I'm embarrassed about calling my own mother, but because I am embarrassed of myself; I'm embarrassed of how she makes me behave.

I take a deep breath and dial.

Lydia Quartey picks up the phone on the second ring, answering in English. "Becky."

She's the only one who calls me that. I take a deep breath. "Hi, Ma."

"I was hoping you'd call today," she says, and I hear paragraphs of meaning in that one sentence alone. I close my eyes a moment. I can do this.

But before I can find an easy pleasantry to lead with, Ma asks me her favorite question. "Have you been going to church?"

"I—" I hate lying, but this is a truth with a heavy cost. "As much as I'm able. I have to travel a lot over the weekends."

"The Lord says, 'Honor the Sabbath Day.' How will you honor the Lord's day if you're honoring work more? God must be first in your heart, Becky."

Tell him he can come first in my heart when his preachers stop preaching that my heart is unnatural and wrong.

I shake my head at myself. I have more control than this.

"I'll think about making more time to go. How is Ima?" I ask, knowing that turning the conversation to my grandmother will give me a few moments' respite.

My mother's words spill into a river of chatter—half English, half Ga, moving seamlessly between the two. Ima's health is just bad enough to be interesting without being dangerous, and the bad health is just prolonged enough to give my mother a flavor of martyrdom as she talks about all the help she has to give Ima now.

I'm treated to a full account of it all. Then I hear about my aunts, my cousins, my godparents, and my mother's best friend. By now I'm standing by the window again, staring down onto a lone tree growing from a bare-dirt square in the pavement below. Quartey Workshop is in a cluster of new, shiny things—glassy and open and shamelessly expensive among the still graffitied storefronts and litter-caught kerbs of the neighborhood. There's neither a park near here, nor grass. The only flowers that exist here are purchased from black buckets and wrapped in cellophane. There's only this one tree, and it looks as tired as I feel.

I miss Thornchapel like I miss Delphine. Like something vital has been pulled out of my body and blood is pooling in the cavity it left behind.

I close my eyes and think of Thornchapel while Ma talks. I think of the woods there, thick and carpeted with bluebells. I think of the river flashing bright and shallow. I think of my labyrinth, and how it will feel to walk it when it's finished.

"—and Sheila's son is in London now, you know. He's a barrister, and doing very well for himself, I hear."

She stops then, and I realize too late the trap I've wandered into.

"Oh?" I say, pitching my voice as carefully as I can.

"Well, you're not seeing anyone, and why not a dinner, just to catch up? You haven't seen each other since you were children, and now you're both in London, and I think you'd like him, Becky, he's very good-looking."

I'm not fooled by all the words she said after; that casual *you're not seeing anyone* is a hook, baited and cast into the water, and biting it is the kind of mistake I know better than to make.

Unfortunately, letting it float by without a semblance of an answer is also a mistake.

"I'll tell Sheila, of course, and make sure Daniel has your number—"

The idea of dinner with Daniel is suddenly so suffocating, so unwelcome, that I actually take a step back, as if I can put more space between myself and my mother, when she's already in Accra.

"I can't," I say. Blurt. And the silence on the other end tells me that I've bitten the hook just as she knew I would. Irritation flares, then ebbs. I wish she would just ask the questions she wants to ask. I wish she could bring herself to.

I wish I could just tell her without having to be goaded into it.

"Why can't you?" she asks, even though she's already guessed, I'm sure of it.

I shut my eyes. "I'm seeing someone."

"It must be someone special," she says slowly. "You haven't dated since you finished school."

"It is someone special," I say, and if I were less tetchy, I'd be surprised at how easily those words come out. *Someone special.* Just like that.

"*She* is someone special," I add, because if I'm going to do this, then I'm going to do this.

"Ah," my mother says faintly.

I came out as queer to her years ago, and ever since, it's been like I dug a pit between us. A shallow one, maybe, one that can be easily bridged with planks and flat stones, one that can be navigated—but it must be bridged, it must be circled. It must be talked over or around or ignored.

My mother is modern in many ways, but the rest of her family is not. Her church is not. Daniel's mother is not. Not when it comes to this.

She doesn't say anything for a long time, and I wonder if I should just end the call now. Let her stew about her foiled matchmaking, and then try again next week.

Finally, she says, "I want you to be happy. You know I do."

I do, I do know that. In fact, I know two things for certain: my mother loves me, and I love my mother. Now, if only that were enough to make it easy between us.

"I just worry," Ma says cautiously, "that you're missing a…chance."

"A chance," I say.

"You're young now, and doing well in your career, and I know it seems like you have all the time in the world to think of things other than the workshop, but time moves faster than you think. Don't you want to get married? Have children? Know that you'll have a child to take care of you when you're old?"

I shouldn't be surprised by this. Why am I surprised?

Before I can answer, Ma goes on. "There's nothing wrong with wanting…what you want," she says, and I have to close my eyes again. "But if you like boys and girls both, maybe you could…choose? To marry someone nice and have children with him? Here at home?"

Here at home.

Where openly loving another woman would be frowned upon and prayed over—at *best*. And at worst…?

I don't know my own feelings. I think I might cry, but the hot thrum in my chest is anger, not sadness. "I'm sorry. I have to go," I say. "I have to go now."

"Wait! Wait!" Her voice is desperate, and in that desperation, I hear it all. Her loneliness and her need, and also her shame. "I shouldn't have—I'm sorry. I don't want to make you upset."

I give a dry, mean laugh. "Too late."

"I just want—Becky, I want you home. I want you living here. I want to see you every day, like a mother should."

"My life is here," I state. "My work. Everything I've done for the Workshop and everything I still want to do. I can't move back home now."

"Your father could move the firm here," she says. "Both of you could come back."

Guilt gnaws at my anger. She's lonely. I know she's lonely. Her husband and only child have lived apart from her for almost two decades.

But.

"I don't think that will happen," I tell her. "London is where Daddy and I need to be."

A pause. "Does he—has he been busy this week? He hasn't called."

This is almost worse than the casual bi-erasure, the stepping into the strange whirlpool of my parents' marriage. At least I don't have to lie. "He's been commuting every day for a project in Wiltshire. He's got a lot on his plate right now."

"I see," she says. She doesn't sound like she sees at all. "And he is good? Healthy? Seeing friends?"

Another baited hook. Again, I'm grateful I don't have to lie. "He's healthy. No friends. He works and sleeps—no time for anything else."

"He should relax more," Ma murmurs, but I hear the relief in her voice, and suddenly, I'm just really fucking sad. I'm sad that my mother loves my father, and I'm sad that I'm not sure if he loves her back. I'm sad my mother is so lonely, but also that she makes being around her so difficult. I'm sad that I know for a fact that my father was unfaithful at least once, and I'm sad that I saw more raw longing in his eyes for the memory of David Markham than I've ever seen him have for his wife.

And I'm sad that while divorce is possible, it would never be easy, at least not for Ma. Her family would not make it easy on her. Hell, even my dad's family wouldn't make it easy. My father is giving Ma a gift, in a way, by staying married—economic comfort for her and her family, and freedom from scorn—and so maybe the gift outweighs the price. Who but her can say?

My watch buzzes gently against my wrist. "I have to go, Ma," I say. "I have an appointment."

"Tell your father I said hello. And to call me. And Becky?"

"Yes?"

She pauses. "I really am trying, you know. To understand."

I wish I knew the right way to respond.

I wish I could tell her that if I can't trust her with who I love, then I don't know if I can trust her at all.

But I don't want to fight. And I'm also very conscious that the reason her family and church are this way is the very place I'm standing in now. The country I'm reluctant to leave is the same country that sowed those seeds nearly two centuries ago. Colonizing, stealing, raping, converting—all of that came from *here*. From this cloudy city, from this damp island, and I don't know what it means about myself that I'm choosing it anyway. I could say, well, I was born here, raised here, schooled here—but is that really enough?

I don't know. I don't know.

I'm supposed to be the smartest person in a family of doctors, lawyers, and architects, and I still don't have the answer to this.

Anyway, I'm a coward, because I end up saying the easiest thing there is to say. "It's okay, Ma. I know you love me."

I don't know that, actually, that's the problem, but she seizes on it. "Yes, of course, Becky, of course I do. I love you more than anything, you know that. You and your father."

I should be relieved when we say goodbye, but relief is very far from me as I start packing plans into my bag. In fact, my hands are shaking as I do it, even though they weren't shaking on the call itself. Like my nervous system is finally catching up to what happened—there was no bear, no fire, no blizzard, there was only a mother, but here we are all the same, hands shaking, heart thumping, a trembling in my muscles like I've run a race.

Deep breaths, I remind myself. *It's not real.* Just an outdated brain reacting to stimuli. Just old hardware taking a long time to boot up the new software.

I brace my hands on my desk and force myself to breathe.

I'm safe. No bear. No fire. Safe.

Just my mother. Just some words.

Funny, isn't it? How words can feel like fire and teeth, and yet they're nothing at all. Nothing but vibrations hanging in the air.

After a few minutes, the trembling stops. My pulse slows, and my hands steady. My thoughts return, finally, full and functioning, ordered in the way I like. I can lift my hands off the desk and finish packing my bag. I can turn off the lights in my office and make a polite goodbye to Shahil as I leave.

It's fine. I'm fine. Everything's fine.

This is what happens.

I step into my waiting car, settling in for the drive back to my flat, trying to think of the whispering trees at Thornchapel, trying to think of Delphine's smile, her honest eyes. But my anticipation is brittle, it's flattened just like the river in my site plan, and all I can think of are my mother's words, her clinginess and her loneliness. Her own guilt and the guilt she induces in other people.

This is what happens.

This is how people can hurt someone they think they love.

12

Delphine

The club is called Justine's, and it's a meander of richly furnished rooms set into the heart of St. James—leather and wood and books, fireplaces, and small nooks for statues, and rugs so plush my feet sink into them as I stand. The light comes from the fires and sconces and the occasional chandelier; there always seem to be piano notes drifting from some distant room, punctuated with equally musical moans and cries.

Paintings hang from picture rails mounted on jewel-toned walls. Large oil works, small watercolors, portraits and landscapes and slyly erotic scenes, rendered so subtly that one hardly notices the cocks and cunts until one is staring directly at them. In the lobby, a gilt-framed painting stretches nearly from the floor to the ceiling: Cupid wrapped in silk ties and sulking while someone reaches to untie him.

Hope Comforting Love in Bondage, it's called.

When I walk into the lobby today, I'm greeted by a young man in an impeccably tailored three-piece suit, the leather waistcoat underneath his jacket the only nod to the club's true nature. He's fat, with a full face and full body, and even though I wasn't feeling self-conscious or nervous, I feel something inside my chest ease a little.

It eases even more as I see a woman my size walk through the far doorway and into a hallway. A naked man crawls behind her on hands and knees, his head down and his erect cock bobbing as he goes.

"Mistress Rebecca sends her apologies that she isn't able to meet you here herself," the concierge says. He has a puckish face, with an upturned nose and sparkling blue eyes, and a spray of freckles across his cheeks. But despite the Peter Pan look, his bearing is nothing but stillness and grace. "She asked me to show you to your room."

"Yes, of course," I say with a beam and follow him as he leads me into a hallway. He pulls back the cage on an old-fashioned lift, and then together we go up to the second floor, where I'm led to a room furnished like a study—bookshelves, a desk, a small fireplace with a statue of Pan fucking a goat on the top. The walls are painted in a dark garnet, and there's a big window teasing a view of St. James' Park—a glimpse of bright, new green in a world of gray.

But it's not a study, not truly. A study wouldn't have racks of paddles and crops set between the bookshelves, a study wouldn't have a sensible wood floor for easy cleaning. A study wouldn't have a bed set into the far corner with cuffs already dangling from the bedposts.

A study wouldn't have leather lingerie waiting for me on the primly made bed.

"She expects you to dress and wait next to the desk. Kneeling, of course. Do you need help dressing?"

I go to the bed and study the lingerie. When I was a teenager, I used to hate the sight of my clothes laid flat because they always looked so much bigger than I thought they would be. I don't feel that way nearly as often now, but there is a brief moment—an instant, nothing more—when I think: *no.*

When I think: *anything but this.*

Because this isn't truly lingerie, not really. I've modeled for plus-size lingerie brands before; I've worn my own lingerie to take cute, flirty Insta pictures in. Lace, mesh, silk, cotton so fine one can peek nipples and navels through it—all of that is workable. All of that I can do, and I have done, and I know how to angle my body and twist myself just right for the desired effects.

But the outfit Rebecca's chosen—it's nothing but straps. *Leather* straps, which means there's no give, no stretch, no forgiveness. It will press into my flesh. It will show all the places where I'm soft. There will be no twisting, no angles, no way to hide that my body is a fat body, and I don't *want* to hide that my body is a fat body, because it is and I'm proud of it, but—

But—

I don't know. I don't like how this is making me feel. This is worse than being naked somehow, this is having a lover say, *here, dress up in this slutty thing I found*, and having to show one's lover that one *can't*, that one only looks good in slutty clothes with planning and good angles and maybe a couple passes through Adobe Lightroom.

This is having to explain to a lover that one's body won't look as good as the lover imagines it will, and that feels an awful lot like saying, *my body doesn't look good at all.* I know that's not true—at least I think? I think I know that? But it feels true.

It feels brutally and humiliatingly true.

When I look up at the concierge, he says—in an offhanded sort of way, like of course it's not meant to soothe me, it's just an observation—"A mistress would be very pleased to see her pet wearing the things she chooses."

I swallow, looking back at it. It's like a snake on the bed. I'd been smiling earlier, and now I can't remember what a smile feels like on my lips. "I don't know if it will fit."

"Why don't we see?"

"I—" The idea of trying it on and then *knowing* for sure that it's as bad as I'm imagining…it's unbearable.

But before I can say no, before I can run back down the hall and take the lift to freedom, the concierge comes up to me and gently unhooks my bag from my shoulder.

"I'll assist," he says, and then he's helping me out of my jacket with quiet grace.

"I don't know…"

My bag and jacket are stowed in a discreet cupboard among the bookshelves, and then he's kneeling at my feet, unbuckling my heels with a surprising deftness. Or maybe not so surprising, given that it's a kink club. Rebecca told me last time that the employees here sometimes work as submissives or Doms, depending on the demand. Perhaps he's been trained to do this very thing. Perhaps he would do it for fun even if he wasn't paid.

My shoes deposited in the same cupboard, he then moves to help me with my clothes. "This outfit came from a very well-known atelier," he informs me, again in that casual kind of voice, "and the atelier only takes custom orders. This means your mistress ordered this specifically for you. She would have given the atelier your measurements in order to do so."

I chew on my lip as he unzips my dress. "You think so?"

The dress is tugged off, and then he steps back so I can remove my own knickers and bra. I'm not shy—photoshoots cure one of that quite quickly—but I still hesitate.

"I hate this," I say. "I hate this right now."

"My Dom sometimes makes me wear a corset," the concierge says with a rueful smile. "I hated it at first—my belly hangs below the bottom and my back spills over the top, and I just kept thinking, 'Does he want me to be thinner? Is that what this is? Or does he just want me to be embarrassed and miserable?'"

I run a fingertip along the leather. It's supple, almost like satin to the touch. "And? Did you tell him you couldn't wear it anymore?"

The concierge picks up the top part of the lingerie. "No. But I asked him what he wanted with me in a corset, and do you know what he said?"

I shake my head.

"He said he wanted to fuck me in it," the concierge says with a laugh. "It was hot to him. *I* was hot to him. That simple."

That simple.

I close my eyes. I should be over this. Why am I not over this?

"Let's just try it on," he says calmly. "If it doesn't fit, then we will explain everything to your mistress."

"What if it fits, but I still don't like it?" I whisper.

He gives me a sympathetic look. "If you were going to push yourself to become braver—if you were going to perform exposure therapy on yourself so that you could wear whatever the hell you wanted—why wouldn't you do it with someone who'll reward you with orgasms?"

"I do like orgasms."

"Of course you do," he says. "Now lift your arms. There you go. Oh, your hair too, I don't want it to get caught."

Together he and I get the top on. The straps crisscross up to my tits, making leather cups that can be unlaced down the middle to expose my nipples, and the straps stretch up from those cups to create a halter, which effectively collars my neck.

The concierge cinches me up from the back, and then we turn to look at the mirror. I catch my breath.

Shockingly…it fits. And it fits well. I don't know when Rebecca managed to find my measurements, or how, but somehow all the straps and laces work together to cup my tits enticingly, and with plenty of support.

"Now the bottoms," the concierge says, and these I need less help with, but he still laces up one side while I lace up the other. When the concierge buckles them to the top, I can feel where they crisscross my bottom and bite into my flesh. Not much—it's too well fitted for that—but some, because it's inevitable. "Look," he says, turning me to the mirror. "Look at yourself."

I look again, and blush. The bottoms are made to expose my sex, and so framed by all the precisely cut leather is a delta of gold curls, silky and trimmed enough to show the pink seam where I split open. My hair is an equally golden waterfall of sleek waves, sliding against itself as I move this way and that.

"You look like a Disney princess who was cursed into slutitude," the concierge says fondly. "Your mistress will be very pleased."

Will she? I turned in the mirror some more, wondering. There's no hiding the convexities of me like this—but there's also no hiding that I've listened to her, that I've done as she asks. Her will binds my body along with the leather; in fact, the leather is her will, the leather is Rebecca's command, her hunger, her possession of me.

How can I hate it then?

I still feel uncertain as the concierge tidies up the bed and then leaves. I kneel by the desk, ducking my head so that I'm surrounded by a curtain of blond hair.

I stare down at my thighs, which are pale and dimpled and flecked with a handful of stray freckles, and I wait.

I don't have to wait long.

After only a few minutes on the floor, the door opens and I hear Rebecca enter. Even if I wasn't expecting her, I'd still know those footsteps. Deliberate, precise, and yet fluid for all that. Almost dancer-like, although Rebecca would never do anything so frivolous as dance. The only time I'd seen her do it was in the thorn chapel, her feet bare and her eyes sparkling with firelight and champagne.

Rebecca strides toward me, and I try to imagine what will happen next. She'll say she's pleased maybe, and I'll get to feel that sweet warmth in my chest at making her happy. Or maybe she won't say anything at all, but have me present my body for inspection, and I'll know I've pleased her by the curl of her mouth or by the satisfied flick of her eyes.

I'm not ready for what actually happens.

Rebecca makes a punched, gasping noise like she's about to fall from some great height, a noise that's as needy as it is stunned, and I'm surprised into looking up at her.

We meet eyes across the room, and for a moment, we're both still, her lips parted and her eyes glittering, and before I even know what's happening, before I can prepare to be bossed around, made to crawl, paddled on the backside, whatever, she's on me. She's in front of me and she's yanking me up by the leather straps of my bodice and then she's devouring my mouth like a woman starved. She's molding her lips to mine as her hands find my hair, my waist, my arse, and she's seizing me to her like she'll rip this city apart if she can't use me right now. Like she'll set the world on fire if I'm not hers.

The kiss is like no other kiss we've shared. There's a feral life to it, a desolation, and when I open my lips to say something—I don't even know what—she steals inside my mouth with her tongue, and all my words leave me anyway. She's too hot, too soft and slick, and each stroke of her tongue against mine sends thrills chasing through me, skating down my spine to the soles of my feet and skipping to the tips of my fingers. Breathing is an impossible thing, it's all stolen wet gasps and shuddering exhales, and I'm dizzy, I'm so dizzy with it, but in the best possible way, like being on a sailboat that's turning too fast, like dancing at a club so hard I can't breathe, like watching thorns bite into my hand as they make me bleed.

Rebecca makes another one of those punched gasps, like the very existence of me is enough to bruise her, and then we're moving, she's pushing me as she kisses me, and I'm shoved against a bookshelf hard enough to make a book rock off the edge of the shelf and fall to the floor. We both ignore it, too lost in each other, too desperate for more. No single kiss is enough—so much so that the moment a kiss starts, we're already chasing the next one, and the next, already grabbing, already seeking, tilting, taking.

I'm not supposed to grab. I'm not supposed to take. It's not why I've been trussed up in leather and made to kneel. But every time I use my teeth, every time I squeeze a slender hip, cup a firm breast, I'm rewarded with growls and scratching embraces and eager presses of her pelvis against me, and so how can I stop? How can I stop when she's like this—wild and insensate with wanting me?

"You," she breathes, tearing away from my mouth and ripping at my bodice with shaking fingers. She can't even wait to get a cup all the way unlaced before she shoves her hand inside to feel me, and then she can't even wait to properly feel me before she's replacing her fingers with her mouth, seeking out my soft flesh amid the leather and then making a satisfied noise when she finds it. Growling with pleasure when she draws my nipple into her mouth and it's already tight and hard for her.

"You," she says again, a groan, a plea, her normally deft fingers frantic and desperate as they unlace my other cup, and then once both my tits are exposed, she can't seem to pick where she wants to be. Sucking on my breasts or my neck, biting my jaw, licking into my mouth. Her hands everywhere, restless and greedy, squeezing at my hips and bottom and thighs and stomach and all the places I've let shame live for years and years, and I almost want to laugh, because so many tears and therapy sessions and Xanax pills and an entire influencer career has gone into my feelings about those parts of me, and still it's never, ever occurred to me that those parts of me could make me *happy*. That they could make a lover happy. That someone could be so fucking wound up and horny over me that they go mad and slam me against a bookshelf so they can maul me properly.

"Mistress. Rebecca…" They're not even words, they're breaths instead. She's replaced my oxygen with the sounds of her name.

And then her hands find my mound—they find where the leather opens to frame my cunt—and she shudders so hard that all the breath seems to leave her in one shredded exhale. Her fingers play over the unyielding leather, over my curls, tracing the slutty outlines of it. She finds where my clit has swollen past my lips, a pouty little bud, and she plays with it a moment. It's a toy meant for her, not for me, and knowing that has me whimpering, mindless, begging for more with pawing hands and arching hips.

"So wet," she murmurs. "So wet for me."

Her hand comes up and she takes in a short, quivering breath as she presses her fingers to my lips. I lick them, tasting myself, at the same time she starts licking too. Our lips and tongues meet between her fingers, a tangle of slippery kisses that taste of me. And her. Of sex and faintly of mint.

I squirm as we kiss through her fingers, heat pooling so low and fiery in my belly that I can't believe I haven't gone up in flames. My cunt aches without her touch; I know it will ache more *with* her touch but that doesn't stop me from chasing it, from rubbing against her, from making small keening noises in the back of my throat.

There's this beautiful suffering right behind my clitoris, right in the heart of me, a twinging and yearning inside my body. It's agony, but it's the kind of agony that's the opposite of hurt. It's the kind of agony that makes me feel more alive than I've ever been, and it's because of her. It's because she's raw and ravenous, powerful and demanding. Sovereign.

And it's as I catch a glimpse of her eyes—dark and avid and exposed—it's as I hear her breath hitching with my name—*Delph, pet, pet, oh Delph*—that I realize the Rebecca we always see, the Rebecca we take for granted as being calm and untouchable always, she's not the real Rebecca, not really. The real Rebecca has messy joys and hungers, the real Rebecca is more like Thornchapel than the orderly corporate gardens she designs.

She is fierce and alive and unconfined, and I want her always like this, always this ruthless and ferocious with me.

I drink her in as she steals kisses, as she returns to suck viciously at my breasts while she palms my sex. I drink her in, and I pray that this is real, that this hungry woman won't slip away from me and retreat back into her shell. Into the place where I cannot reach her, I cannot know her. Into the place where I can't even tell her I love her without her dismissing me.

The next idea comes to me so clearly and urgently that I have no choice but to listen. My body will allow nothing less, and I think I've been wanting this for a long time but haven't known how to ask for it.

I spread my legs more and reach for her hand, and I press her fingers all the way past my folds and into my opening. We freeze there a minute, both of us rocked by the feeling of her fingers only a knuckle deep.

More, my greedy sex demands. *More and more and more.*

Rebecca meets my eyes. The afternoon sunlight slants in gray and cloudy, and it adds a silvery shine to her high cheekbones, her small, queenly nose. I can see the pulse banging at the side of her throat, and I can see as she swallows once, as if for control.

"You're sure, pet?" she says hoarsely.

"Yes—" That's all the negotiation we have. I haven't even finished saying the word, and she's over my mouth again with a searing kiss. As I open my lips to let her tongue slip inside, she slides her fingers deeper. Another inch, slippery but still hard-won.

I can't concentrate on kissing now. Pleasure roils from my center, pleasure mixed with a trace of pain.

I worried—I still worry. What if the pain makes me feel like I did in Audra Bishop's garden? What if my body doesn't know the difference between what happened to me then and what's happening now? My therapist warned me, my support group warned me, and now all these warnings froth up like soap bubbles in my mind—

Only to pop one by one as Rebecca fucks me with filthy, expert intensity. The trace of pain only grows as she finally fits her fingers in to the bottom knuckles, stretching me in places I've ignored for years, and stokes the slow, unbearable ache in my core. But the pain feels good too—it's wanted, it feels just as wonderful as being spanked or flogged or bound. It weights down the pleasure so it's not so oppressively delicious.

Like salt on caramel, like chili powder or cinnamon in hot chocolate.

And I should have known. I should have trusted.

Nothing from Rebecca could ever feel bad.

Rebecca buries her head in my neck and feasts on my jaw, my throat, the skin between my neck and my shoulder, fucking me between the legs all the while, her clever fingers changing to slow, grinding strokes with twisting and a pressure against my front wall that has my eyelids fluttering. The heel of her palm grazes and grinds against my bundle of nerves as she goes, and she only stops kissing me in order to look down every few moments. Her expression is one of base, biological greed as she watches her hand moving in and out of me, as she plays with her submissive's cunt like I know she's been wanting to for weeks.

The orgasm, when it comes, kicks me in the chest and buckles my knees. The pleasure twists and twines around her fingers until it's no longer pleasure at all, but something even better. Something necessary and perfect and human and also divine—something I feel in my soul as much as I feel in my sex—something that cuts through me like floss, cuts me right in two.

Hard, hot contractions grab at my womb; curling waves of sweet sensation spiral out from my clit and cover me everywhere, everywhere, everywhere. I feel this climax in my thighs and belly and chest, I feel it in my tingling lips and in my seizing lungs and near-sightless eyes. I'm overpowered by it, consumed, and I don't even realize I've crumpled to the floor until I hear the thud of Rebecca's shoes being toed off, until I hear the impatient zipper of her cigarette pants, and she's crawling over me, straddling me and finding my hand so she can use it how she wants. She's so wet, so fucking wet—wet enough that I think she must have been thinking of this all day, for hours and hours. And it's so unlike her to be like she is right now—no formality, no plan, no toys or ties. No, it's only us, struggling for kisses as she rides my fingers, struggling for that indefinable *more*—more friction, more teeth, more taste, more of each other. Nothing is enough, not a kiss, not a buck of her hips, not a rub of my thumb over her clit, none of it is enough until we've tasted each other's hearts.

That's what's different today, I think dizzily.

Rebecca's heart is here. It's beating outside her chest.

It's seeking mine.

She comes like a woman being unwound from the outside in, she comes like someone on a clattering, rocketing roller coaster—laughing, gasping, terrified but alive. She comes like it's the only thing she's ever wanted in this life, and she milks each and every jolt, riding my hand until it cramps a little, until her body is finished and until her slick channel is completely and utterly still.

Until my hand is soaked and she can finally take a long, deep, very relaxed breath.

She slides off of me and tumbles to my side, looking more mussed and well-fucked than I've ever seen her. Her eyes slide closed and her long lashes rest on her cheeks like a doll's. A smile plays at her mouth.

"I had such plans," she murmurs, eyes still closed.

I arrange myself next to her, so our sides touch. The floor is hard and cool and we're sticky and smell like sex, but I don't care. My heart is flailing against my ribs. My stomach is floating somewhere in my chest.

She doesn't love you, I remind myself.

But oh—oh how it feels like she might right now.

It feels so much like she might.

Rebecca's eyes open and she gives me a fond, lazy grin—the kind of grin I've never seen her wear before. It opens her face completely, showing off that delicate jaw and those inky eyes, revealing a hidden dimple tucked into her cheek and displaying the mathematically perfect curve of her lower lip, the two subtle arches of her cupid's bow. She has a mouth that would make a makeup artist weep with joy; she's got the kind of bone structure that women chase for years with scalpels and contour kits.

And yet she's never looked more beautiful to me than she does right now. Loose and smiling at the world like she's about to roll it like a marble between her palms.

"I walked in and saw you in that outfit, and my cerebral cortex forgot how to cortex."

"You like it?" I ask shyly. I don't know why I need to hear it, why I crave anything more than seeing her turn into a greedy fiend for me, but I do.

Rebecca turns and props herself up on her elbow. She runs a hand over my half-exposed breasts, over the places where the straps meet over my belly, over my naked cunt. Even lying down on my back, the leather makes a topography of me. Rivers of leather, hills of silky, bisque body. Swells and valleys, all softness. A map of Delphine.

"You look like dessert," she says.

"Yeah?"

"Like I want to eat you alive." She ducks her head to nuzzle at my breast. I feel her mouth pull on my nipple, hot and wet, and my clit jumps in response. "God, I want to fuck you again in this. Like right away."

A warmth nestles in my chest at her words; it surrounds my thudding, hopeful heart. Maybe the concierge was right: it's that simple.

Although maybe that's not right either. It's not simple at all…but it's worth it anyway.

And what more can I ask for than that?

Soothed and stirred by Rebecca's touch, by her mouthing over my breast and toying with my cunt, I say, "I worship you even more like this."

Rebecca lifts her head. The window is behind her, and her eyes are unreadable. Shadowed. "Like what?" she asks.

There's a wary note in her words. It wasn't there before.

I ignore it. Why would she be wary? We just had the best sex ever, and we're in a happy, clumsy tangle on the floor—wariness has no place here.

"Like, I don't know, looser and everything. Rougher. It was like you were worked up about something and then took it out on me. Like you were letting me help you. I loved it."

For a single moment—for one mercilessly short moment—I see something wistful flit through her eyes, like she's looking at something she's wanted her entire life and it would cost her everything to reach out and take it.

I love you. I almost say it, unwelcome though it might be, because *not* saying it feels wrong. It feels like an impiety. It feels like not smiling when the sun is on my face or not drinking when a champagne flute is tipped to my lips.

I love you.

But the words die on my tongue, because Rebecca's face shutters and her gaze cools. When she speaks, her voice is distant. Not upset or brittle, just...distant. Like she's locked that wild, hungry queen somewhere deep inside of herself, and I'm outside at the gates, not allowed in.

"We should get ready for the gala," she says, rolling up with the ease of a dancer and getting to her feet. The hand she offers me feels impersonal. Perfunctory. Even though it's the same hand that was just inside me. The first hand ever to be inside me.

I think I'm going to cry.

"Rebecca," I say, and I hate that my voice isn't like hers, that it's not steady and aloof, that it shakes a little.

She doesn't look at me as she pulls on her knickers and her pants. "We don't want to be late. I'll take you back to the flat now."

I think I should say something here, I should do something. If someone asked me on a live video for advice, I would tell that person to speak their truth. Set boundaries. All that good stuff my therapist talks about.

But it turns out those nice-sounding self-care maxims don't apply here. Because what good will crying do? Accusing? Clinging?

No, I have known Rebecca nearly all my life, and I know the worst thing I can do is pull at her hem and beg for attention—or guilt her into more affection. At best, I'd get pity. At worst—well, I don't even want to think about the worst. I don't think I'd survive it.

So I nod at my mistress, swallow down my misery, and start to get dressed.

I3

Delphine

Harcourt + Trask's annual gala is in the courtyard of Somerset House, a Neoclassical venue and arts center on the Strand—and also a place I know Auden personally likes very much. He used to drag me here in the winter, when the courtyard is turned into an ice skating rink, and we'd skate until our cheeks hurt from laughing and our ears hurt with the cold.

Theoretically the gala is for charity, but in the years since I've been going, it's mainly a chance for the beau monde to show off new frocks and lovers, and I'm no exception. I've spent all spring figuring out which dress I want to wear—not to mention the last month or so picking out a dress for Rebecca, since she was planning on wearing something she already had, and that was simply not going to work for me.

And so here we are a few hours later, crammed into a car while Rebecca scowls at her phone and I perch on the edge of my seat so as not to wrinkle my gown (a sculpted off-the-shoulder dress in a vibrant red, which hugs every curve and then pleats artfully at my feet).

My lips are painted in the always-dashing Ruby Woo, and my hair is pulled back at one side with a long, diamond-studded clip I borrowed from my mother. It hangs down in sleek waves, and I've caught Rebecca's eyes lingering on it more than once, like she's imagining what it would look like wrapped around her fist.

God, I wish she'd do it. Pull my hair. Dirty my dress. Smear my lipstick.

Anything other than the cold reserve that's settled over her since our time at the club.

Idiot that I am, I keep trying to make small talk. "My parents will be there, you know."

"Mm," she says, not lifting her eyes from her phone.

"And it's the first event we're doing…together. It might get noticed."

I'm lying. It *will* get noticed. Enough so that my manager emailed over a publicity kit to Rebecca in anticipation of tonight—specific sound bites she was to give if the press called the next day, the emails and phone numbers of people she was to refer media inquiries to.

We have a solid social media strategy in place: a scheduled post tomorrow morning with a picture of us snuggled together on a library sofa at Thornchapel. Then a gradual integration of her into my stories, and then my manager will start lining up interviews, depending on the interest and available outlets. Because so many fat-friendly brands are also queer friendly, my team feels like my relationship with Rebecca won't impact my existing business relationships, so most of our plan has focused on wider public perception, safety, and preparation for bullying, trolling, and worse.

"Rebecca? Are you sure you're still okay with it?"

"With what?" she asks distractedly.

"We're going to this event together. It might work its way into the press. It will definitely be on social media."

Rebecca doesn't lift her eyes from her phone. Given how fast her thumbs are moving, I presume she's typing an email. "I don't care about social media."

I've never understood this attitude. At all. "It will care about you," I tell her. "And the press is ceaselessly invasive when it wants to be."

"I'll be fine," Rebecca says. "I saw the publicity kit." She looks up, and her expression softens a little. "I'm proud to be with you, pet. It's my honor."

"I know," I say. "I just feel rather beastly about it. If I had a different job, we could be a normal enough couple."

That might be a lie too. My fame came at first because I'm a Dansey, because my family is the kind of wealthy that people love to gossip about, and because all Danseys live to be rich and pretty and admired. A daughter of society showing up on the arm of a world-famous architect—who is a woman—would have always sparked interest. But add in my actual platform, the modeling work, the podcast I'm launching, and it's beyond inevitable. Our relationship—whatever it actually is—will be public domain and there's very little I can do about that.

"And your father will be okay with it? They'll know you work for him, and so his name will come up too."

"He'll be okay with it," she says. And then rubs at her forehead, looking suddenly very tired. "I don't know about my mother though."

"Does she not know about me?"

"She does." And that's all the answer Rebecca seems willing to give, because she says nothing more until we arrive at Somerset House.

There's a red carpet going into the event, which is mostly an opportunity for the guests to bask in their single claim to public attention—money—and is also an excellent opportunity for Rebecca and me to debut as a couple. She's dressed in a white dress, precisely tailored and cupping her small, high breasts perfectly, and also setting off the lean lines of her stomach and hips.

She is patient through all the pictures, even though I can tell she's uncomfortable being so visible and being expected to perform. I squeeze her hand to let her know I'm here, and she squeezes back. And when she gives me an impromptu kiss at the end of the red carpet, much to the ecstatic scuffle and flash of the photographers, it's real and warm and earnest. There's something like apology in her eyes.

"Let's get some bubbles," she says and pulls me into the gala itself.

There's to be dinner later in the clusters of clear tents spread across the courtyard, and of course there will be dancing in the largest tent. They've left the ground fountain turned on and people are milling around the water's edge, shaking hands and waving over servers for more drinks and generally just being rich knobheads. It doesn't bother me—it's the devil I know, after all—but Rebecca seems like she wishes she could vanish into the ground and reappear back at her office, where she could at least be getting some work done.

I find her a drink as quickly as possible, guiding her to the side of the fountain where we can watch it splash without being interrupted. As I thought, the sound of water seems to relax her, the fluid geometry of the jets all arrayed in soldierly rows, spurting up in endless, translucent columns. She studies it a moment, and I know her mind is diagnosing the mechanics of it, the logistics, examining how she could do it better, cleaner, more integrated with the landscape and the river only a stone's throw away.

"Oh, there's Poe and Auden!" I say excitedly, trying to wave them over and failing. There're too many people and too much noise for them to hear me.

"Thank God," mutters Rebecca. "You and Auden aren't allowed to escape and have pedantic conversations in the corner, understood? This is his firm's gala and he needs to mingle, and *you* need to mingle on behalf of your firm too."

There's an amused tilt to her lips now, like she's watching a baby kitten attack her booted foot and she's decided to indulge it because it's so adorable with its tiny claws and teeth. "Oh, is that so?" she says.

"Yes—oh, there's Becket too. It's too bad Saint isn't coming."

"He's currently furious with Auden."

I look over at Rebecca, but she doesn't elaborate, and anyway, I'm tugging her toward our friends, ready to say hello and also to make sure Poe is dressed exactly the way I styled her.

Proserpina like a curvy doll—with long, dark doll curls and porcelain doll skin and big doll eyes, and honestly, I wish she'd let me dress her more often. She's in a real rut with all those Modcloth dresses and cardigans, and it's a shame, because she's got such a *body* and such Victorian fairy-tale features, I could have so much fun with her.

She's in the strapless champagne-colored dress I picked out, her bright green eyes glowing, her hair pulled into a lush updo that shows off the arch of her throat and her square shoulders. And Auden is perfect next to her, as he always is—his tuxedo almost painstakingly fitted to his hale proportions, his hair swept back off his forehead in a way that would make any other man look vain, but on Auden it only looks right. As if the world should see the high, noble lines of his face, the marble-statue features of him.

But even though they look like a picture together, it's not their clothes or their hair that I notice as we get closer. It's how Auden leans in to whisper in Poe's ear, how he holds a small remote in his hand, how she blushes and trembles and holds onto him for balance.

"He's got a remote vibrator inside of her," Rebecca says approvingly. "I'd like to do that with you someday."

I flush with sudden heat. The performer in me likes that idea a lot—being in public, pleasure buzzing through me as I'm helpless to do anything but endure it as silently as I can.

Rebecca traces a line up my neck. "Soon, pet," she promises, and I can almost imagine that her distance this afternoon was a dream, that it never happened. Maybe she's not my raw queen again, but I'll take this—the friendly Domme, the considerate girlfriend. I can live with that.

Auden—in front of everyone, not seeming to care how it might look—wraps his hand around Poe's throat and then—tenderly, sweetly—bites her cheek. "Go on now," I hear him say, and I realize he's sending her off to Becket. With a vibrator in her pussy and a bite mark across her cheek.

Looking dazed, she goes, and he smiles after her. The smile of the Thorn King.

And I think I'm jealous of Poe Markham. Not because she gets to be bitten and bidden by Auden, but because he looks at her with unguarded love and appetite. Because she knows he loves her more than anything.

"Sir Guest," Rebecca greets him, and he moves his forest eyes over to us.

"Quartey. Delly." He kisses Rebecca's cheek and then kisses mine. His lips on my cheek are firm and warm, and when he pulls back, his eyes are fond and sad all at once.

I think of the way he bit Poe's cheek. I think of how he watched her as she walked away. And I think of how it felt to watch Rebecca slip away from me this afternoon. How it felt to welcome her inside my body, to have the most urgent and unfiltered sex we've ever had, and then to look over and see a stranger in her place.

What if I'd stayed with him?

It's a stray thought, one that can be batted away like a moth, one that can be wiped away with a thumb like bleeding lipstick. I'm not in love with him, because I'm in love with someone else.

I just wish I'd known how much it hurt to love someone for real. I wish I'd known how much it hurts to be the one waiting.

I should have been kinder to him. But I look over at him now, talking seriously with Rebecca, his eyes flicking over to Poe in a way that betrays where his real attention lies, and I think maybe I was kind after all. I know

Auden would've never cheated, never strayed, but if we'd stayed engaged, maybe he would've burned, like St. Paul talks about in the Bible.

Auden would've married the wrong person, and oh, how he would have burned for it.

And me? Without Rebecca, I never would have caught on fire at all.

"Why is the priest here?" Rebecca is asking Auden. "Doesn't he have a flock to tend to?"

Auden takes Rebecca's glass and helps himself to a drink. She flicks him on the cheek for it, and he just laughs before he answers her. "He's on the board of the DevonSafe foundation, which helps shelter domestic violence victims. Harcourt + Trask is currently designing three secure shelters for the foundation, as a pro bono contribution, and they're the beneficiary of this year's gala, so naturally we invited the board to come."

We turn and watch as Becket sees Poe and takes her hand to kiss it. The gesture is gallant—more Virginia money than Virgin Mary—looking all the stranger because he's wearing his priest's clothes. They're flawless and crisp and a black so Cimmerian that I know he'll look stunning in every picture taken tonight—but they're a priest's clothes, nonetheless. His collar flashes snow-white at his throat, and when his black jacket parts, I can see the corner of a small Bible poking from his pocket.

Becket offers his arm, and there's a lost kind of smile on his mouth when Poe accepts his offer and tucks her hand into his elbow. Together they start walking toward us, Becket's head bent solicitously over Poe's so he can listen to whatever she's saying.

"Guest," Rebecca says. "I think your priest is in love with your submissive."

I look over at Auden, not sure what I expect to see. One of his crooked smiles maybe, his first line of defense when it comes to showing his real emotions, or perhaps a dismissive laugh, or maybe one of his smirks, as crooked as a smile but curling with bitterness at the edges.

But he only looks thoughtful, and maybe a little sad. "I know," he says. "I know."

Becket stands out among the crowd—a pillar of blue-eyed flame clad in coal—and I can see how much attention he's drawing as he walks toward us. I can see the swiveling heads, the darting eyes, the ensuing whispers. *Did you see that? Did you see him?*

The perils of being a handsome priest, I suppose, but I'm more concerned about the way he's looking at Poe while everyone else is looking at him.

"He needs to be careful," I say. "A fit priest is bound to make waves. But a fit priest looking swoony over a woman like Poe is going to make trouble for him."

Auden nods, and for the first time tonight, he looks concerned. Because there is no mistaking the look on Becket's face as he strolls next to Poe, and if we can see it, other people can too.

I scan the side of the courtyard we're standing in, making sure I don't see any cell phones out and taking pictures, making sure I don't see any of the worst gossips circulating through the tuxedoed horde, and that's when I see him from across the fountain, looking lost and angry—and rather romantic standing alone like that, with his hands in his tuxedo pockets and with the jets of the fountain walling him off from the rest of us, like he's been imprisoned behind towers of warped glass.

His hair falls dramatically into his face, and his lip piercing glints in the fading twilight of the city. *Sigh.* I wish he'd let me style him too.

"I thought Saint wasn't supposed to come tonight," I say.

I4

St. Sebastian

*T*his is a mistake.

This is a mistake and I knew it was mistake and I did it anyway.

I meant what I told Poe. I had no plans to come to this gala. I had no plans to see Auden at all, maybe ever again, because it just *hurts*. Too fucking much. I can barely even think of him, I can barely stand living in Thorncombe and watching the trees stir while he's gone. Watching them preen and flutter happily when he's back home again.

For the last two weeks, I'd avoided Thornchapel when he was there, I'd dodged his texts and his calls. When he didn't show up at the library or at one of Augie's worksites, I was foolish enough to feel some kind of relief. Not because I didn't ache for him, but because I ached for him too much. Too much to pretend I was okay in front of other people.

But he didn't come, and I thought—well, I thought maybe he was finally giving me what I asked for. Maybe he was giving me space. Maybe he'd decided I was right, maybe he'd finally concluded that we could never be together, and he was already moving on with Poe.

I tried not to hate that possibility too much, I really did.

The evenings were longer, stretching toward summer, and so many nights I found myself up on Reavy Hill again, staring down into the forest and tracing the outlines of Thornchapel with my eyes. I roamed through the woods and spent hours in the chapel, plucking wildflowers out by their stems and tracing thorns with the pad of my thumb.

I stared at the altar, at the perpetually damp stone, set among bluebells and soft shoots of new grass. It had been a grave after all; the new grass was a testament to what had been discovered and dug up, and anyway, there was just something about it. Something that wasn't quite alive, but wasn't quite *un*alive either.

Convivificat.

I would stare at the altar and try not to think of Auden. I would think of Poe's door, of her mother's foreword about human sacrifice. I would think about Lammas, I would think about Samhain coming after it. I would think about the summer solstice and whether I should go with Poe to her mother's funeral, even though money was tight and Auden would be there. I would think about Ralph and my mother, and wonder what they did in these woods.

I would wonder if the trees would reach for me when I left too.

So the days passed, lonely and ephemeral save for the time I spent with Poe, and I almost believed it was over. Auden had stopped texting and calling, and he hadn't come after me, and this was the end. This was actually the end of us, and it turns out that it was no one's fault but a dead man's.

I tried not to feel disappointed. I tried not to imagine Auden striding after me in the thorn chapel and pushing me into the spring grass as he crawled over me. I tried not to imagine him pinning me to a wall with a forearm on my neck as he unfastened his pants and stepped between my legs.

I tried not to imagine his hand over my mouth so that I couldn't say the words that would make him go.

This was sickness and I was sick with it. I wanted him to burn our boundaries to ashes and rule over me anyway. I wanted him to take me and make me. I wanted Beltane, I wanted sides heaving and skin slick as I ran from the god in the forest, I wanted the same thing Auden told me he wanted the day after—forever.

I wanted *him*.

But then I'd think of my mother or Ana María or our friends. I'd think of the inside of St. Petroc's Church—hushed and holy—and I'd think about what I believed. What I had to believe. Being sick doesn't excuse shit.

And then the tuxedo came.

It came like a dress in some kind of romcom, zipped into a garment bag and hung in my bedroom, a box of gleaming dress shoes underneath it. For a moment after I walked in, damp and smelling of flowers from the chapel, I couldn't actually discern what it was. I'd never worn anything that needed a garment bag, I'd never even worn clothes that needed dry cleaning. But when I pulled the zipper down to expose a Hugo Boss tuxedo, with a gala invitation pinned neatly to its collar, I felt a corrupt thrill run through me.

This was from Auden.

I couldn't help it, I tried the tuxedo on. And the shoes. The fit was faultless—the hem of the pants shivering on the laces of my shoe, the shoulders perfectly trim, the sleeves tailored right to the bones of my wrists.

I normally hated anything more formal than a T-shirt and jeans, I really did. But this…

I felt like Cinderella. Like bi-boy Cinderella, and what if I went to the ball? Just to *see* him, nothing more? What could it hurt?

If I was Cinderella, then Becket was my fairy godmother. After he dropped Sir James off at Abby's house, he helped me arrange last minute transportation, since there wasn't a snowflake's chance in hell that I was driving in London, and he offered his hotel room for the night —both to get ready in and to crash in after the gala. He helped me dress, he fastened my cufflinks for me, he loaned me a pair of dress socks when he saw the holey boot socks I'd brought to wear with the dress shoes.

And now here I am. Regretting everything.

Becket's gone ahead to find our friends, but I've hung back, feeling useless and stupid among all these elegant people. Men saunter by, clearly at ease in their ten-thousand-pound suits, and women mince next to them in spindly heels, moving with the practiced concentration of ballet dancers. Words of money drift through the air like cigar smoke. Horse breeding, vacations in the Seychelles, real-estate investment in Croatia. Did we see what the Japanese stock market did this morning? Have we seen the latest symphony performance—Bartók again, how quotidian? Have we heard what happened to the Foxhill-Spencer's au pair—scandalous really, but what else does one expect from an au pair?

I hate it, and I hate this courtyard, which is a coffin of stone, with the stony twilight sky as its lid, and I hate this city, and I hate these people.

I hate myself most of all for coming.

I turn, thinking I'll leave, I'll stop playing Cinderella and I'll go back to Becket's hotel, but then that's when I see him through the watery bars of the fountain. I see him and then I falter.

He looks like a prince.

I'm used to him looking like the lord of the manor. I'm even familiar with him as my wild god—a being of hungry eyes and even hungrier appetites—running down prey through the trees to slake his needs.

But this—this right here is almost too much. Him in the immaculate tuxedo, him tall and lean and narrow-hipped, him with a watch glinting on his wrist and a glass of clear liquor in his hand. Everything about him so clearly and painfully belongs—everything about him is so clearly and painfully *Guest*.

He was born to inherit this world, he doesn't need our forest games and our lanterns in the night. Thornchapel is his and this world of money and boredom is also his, and everything that he could ever want is already his, will be his the moment he bothers to reach for it.

He's a prince and I'm a pauper. Rich boy, poor boy. And though we issued from the same bitter loins, though we are joined by our very essence, it is him who has the world at his fingertips and it is me who has a designated hook in the staff room of the local library.

I'm not jealous, but I hate it. I hate that at every turn, fate seems to be saying *he is not for you*. I hate that my only inheritance has been sacrifice. I didn't gain a house or the land I love. I didn't gain money or a new name.

I simply lost *him*.

I still mean to leave, and I'm trying to tear my eyes away when he sees me. I know Becket didn't tell him I was coming, so I expect his surprise. I expect the part of his lips and the blink of his eyes. But what I don't expect— what I have no defense ready for—is his pleasure. The parted lips slowly easing into a satisfied smile, and the lifting of a single brow. He puts a hand in his pocket as he lifts his glass to me and then puts it to his lips and takes a drink. Like fucking Gatsby.

The sight of Auden pleased, the sight of him in victory, it's too much, it's scotch straight from the bottle, it's holding a sparkler and letting the sparks shower bright and fizzling against your hand. The very reality of him chokes me, burns me, all of it in the worst way, because it's the way that makes me beg for *more, God please, more*.

I spin away, not sure if I'm going to leave, not sure if I can stay, strung as always between the ache of being near Auden and the ache of being far away, and it's as I'm spinning that I run right into Poe.

"Hi," she says, smiling up at me. She takes me by the lapels and gives me a soft kiss.

She smells like the flowers in the thorn chapel right now, and this *dress*—this fucking dress. Her breasts are bound high and tight by the strapless bodice, pushing them up and making delicious swells and curves that I want to trace with my tongue. Her nipped-in waist and healthy hips are hugged by the silk too, presenting all the places she's the most grabbable, the places where someone could seize her and haul her off to a corner to be enjoyed.

"You look incredible," I breathe. *Like a princess,* I almost say, but then I don't, because it's too close to Auden being a prince, too close to the ways they fit together so easily and he and I never will.

She makes a purring noise, sliding her hands down my tuxedo-clad torso. "You're not looking so bad yourself," she says, and I know it's no accident that her fingertips graze my semi as she drops them from my stomach.

"Poe," I groan quietly.

"We could find a nice, dark coat room," she whispers. "Just for a few minutes."

My cock kicks in my pants at the thought. I pull my lip piercing into my mouth. "Yeah?" I ask.

"Yeah," she says, eyes sparkling. She takes my hand, presumably to lead me off somewhere and have her way with me, but Delphine is approaching us with two older people trailing behind, a genuine smile on her face and her mouth already open to call out to us.

Next to me, Poe heaves an unhappy sigh. I try to subtly adjust my jacket to keep my cock hidden. But we both stay put and wait for Delphine to reach us.

"Just who I was looking for!" she exclaims. "Proserpina Markham, St. Sebastian Martinez, this is my mother and father. Freddie and Daisy Dansey."

The two adults next to her have already stepped forward, both of them tall and flaxen-haired, both of them very attractive. They have red-hued cheeks and lines around their eyes, like they spend their days drinking and laughing in the sun. They *look* wealthy, they look like the kind of wealth that predates William Pitt the Elder, but I immediately like them anyway. When

Freddie shakes my hand, he does it warmly, and when Daisy presses her fingers in mine, it's impossible not to return her welcoming grin.

I've often found Delphine's boozy chirpiness rather endearing, if alien to me, but it's even more endearing now, seeing that she's come by it honestly. And when Freddie gives her a quick, affectionate kiss on the temple, I see that she's always known love, always always, and it reminds me that I have too. I may never know how to feel about Ralph Guest, but I will always have known the fierce, protective love of Jennifer Martinez.

"It's a pleasure to meet you both," Daisy says. "We just love meeting Delphine's friends, and now our Pickles is dating Samson Quartey's daughter! Just think, you two have grown up together and now you're in love..."

Delphine clears her throat a little and takes a drink. "In love is a bit premature, Mummy, honestly. We only just started dating."

"Nonsense, I saw how you were looking at her. Wedding bells any day, I say."

"*Mummy*," Delphine groans. "I just ended an engagement. I can hardly jump into another one right now. What would Nanna think?"

While they spar, Freddie smiles at me, tilting his body in that unmistakable way that says *I'm about to initiate small talk.*

I brace.

"I knew your mother," he says so only I can hear. "She was a truly wonderful person. I was—well, I was very sad to hear of her passing."

"Oh," I say, feeling like he's just given me a kindness and a laceration at the same time. "Um, thank you. And yes, it was hard. It's still hard."

He studies me a moment. "Delphine still spends a lot of time at Thornchapel. All of you do."

"I mean, I live there—well, not *there* there, but in Thorncombe. It's where my mother lived too."

Freddie nods, slowly. He has a face so symmetrical and pleasing that it's hard to imagine anything bad ever happening to him. And yet there's a haunted look in his eyes when he says, "Daisy and I know Thornchapel well. We spent a summer there once, when Delphine was young."

I know. I remember you there.

But I don't speak, because I don't know if he knows that I remember. I don't know if he remembers that I was there at all. But I do say, "How did you know my mother? If you don't mind me asking?"

Freddie looks down at his drink. And then he looks up at me. He seems to be searching my face for something, some answer to a question I can't even begin to guess at. "I grew up with Ralph and Ingram Hess, you see. School chums and all that. When he decided—I don't know how much you know about what Ralph wanted to do at Thornchapel—but when he decided to start, I was there. Ingram Hess too. And your mother."

Poe is next to me, Delphine and Daisy are next to her, they are teasing and laughing and they might as well be a million miles away. "Mr. Dansey…"

His voice is pained. "Freddie. Please. Please don't—" He stops, like he's not sure what he wants to say next. "I—I knew your mother well, St. Sebastian. I don't want there to be distance between us."

I can guess what he means when he says he knew my mother well, and now I wish I had my own drink, Jesus Christ.

"The festivals," I say, some morbid part of me needing to know. "You celebrated the feasts in the woods."

He nods slowly. "Yes."

"With my mother."

I wonder what he is thinking of now. Of the past? And if so, which one? The one with my mother? Or the more recent past, with Poe's parents? Is he thinking of the present? Of his own daughter in the thorn chapel, chasing after the same things that made their generation so broken, so sour, so dead?

"You understand then," he says, his words slower than his nod. "You understand what the feasts were."

"Yes."

At that, his eyes do flick over to Delphine, and I see him wrestle with something. Protectiveness, probably, because I see the concern in his forehead and around his mouth as he looks back at me. "I'm not sure how much is my place to say, St. Sebastian. I'm not sure how much your mother told you."

"Nothing," I say, surprised at how tired I sound. "She told me nothing. But I learned—later—she was the May Queen that year. The year she became pregnant with me."

Again, Freddie is searching my eyes, my face, hunting for something. How much I actually know.

"And I know Ralph is my real father," I say, giving him the answer he's looking for. I'm not sure why I tell him this—we've only just met and it's one of the worst things that's ever happened to me, which is honestly a pretty high bar, and it's also intensely private. Private enough that speaking it out loud gives me a near-illicit thrill, like I've just touched a painting in a museum. Like I've just lit up a joint. I say it again, almost buzzed off the sheer impropriety of it. "I'm Ralph Guest's son."

Freddie chews on his lip, and this time his eyes go to his wife, who is still chatting animatedly with Poe. "I know Ralph wouldn't have wanted—"

But whatever he's about to say, whether comforting or damning, I don't know, because we're joined then by Becket, Rebecca, and Auden.

Auden shakes Freddie's hand and kisses Daisy's cheek—clearly the broken engagement hadn't fractured the warm sentiment between Auden and his ex-fiancée's parents. Becket does the same, reminding me that Freddie had grown up with his father, and then Rebecca is clucked over by Daisy as if Daisy already considers her a daughter-in-law. Rebecca tolerates it well, although I catch her exchanging more than one wry glance with Auden, as if Auden had already warned her what it was like to be a new member of the Dansey family.

But it is Auden my eyes go to, and it's Auden I hear, Auden who is at the center of everything just by existing. He laughs and takes sips of gin, and he's all easy charm like he doesn't need to bruise and scratch when he's behind closed doors, like he doesn't hold my throat in his grip, even when he's miles and miles away.

He meets my stare, his teeth digging into his lower lip, and I know what he's thinking, I know he's remembering biting *my* lower lip, I know he's thinking of my piercing and what it means, what it's meant from the beginning. I know that he wants to bite me right now, and I can't tell him I don't want it. I can't even tell him I didn't come here exactly for that purpose, because I don't know *why* I came at all.

And it's so hard to remember all my good intentions, my lectures to myself about my mother, about sin, when I'm looking at his cruel, beautiful mouth.

"Excuse me," I say abruptly to everyone. "I need to—" The words and their accompanying gesture is pointless because I'm already walking away, I'm already striding with long, hurried strides to the other side of the fountain, to the escape promised by an open doorway on the far end of the courtyard. Some kind of art exhibition, I think. I'll go in there and catch my breath and figure out how to leave, because there's no way I can stay. There's no fucking way. Not when just looking at Auden's mouth makes me want to weep.

And it might have worked, this impromptu escape of mine, it might have worked with any other man besides Auden Guest. Because he may well be a prince of galas and understatedly expensive wristwatches, but the hunt is still in his blood.

I've only made it nine or ten steps before I become aware of his following me, of his footsteps arrogant and predatory behind mine.

I speed up, walking faster, my hands in my pockets as I duck through patricians and politicians, darting through clumps and clouds of people as quickly as I can without being rude. I think of Beltane, of the woods, of running through the woods of Thornchapel as Auden chased me and the sunlight shafted golden and hazy through the trees. We're walking instead of running, maybe, and the forest is a forest of people and not whispering trees, but there's no mistaking that it's the same thing. I'm being stalked through this party just like he stalked me then. And if he catches me...

I don't know what I want to happen when I finally mount the shallow steps and enter the building. I know what I *should* want, I know what my mother would hope that I wanted. I know what is right and moral to want.

But if I want that—if I want what's right and what's moral—then why am I still here? Why am I playing the part of prey, why am I thinking of antlers and bluebells when I'm wearing a tuxedo and wending my way through installations of wheat and barley woven into the shapes of houses, people, animals?

The exhibit is deserted, emptied of everyone except the grain people frozen in their poses—watering gardens, walking next to cattle, bundling sheaves of wheat. The gala goers must all be outside, enjoying the mild evening and free booze, and I presume the exhibit is closed to the public during the event. My footsteps echo through the big, wood-floored rooms.

I hear the echo of another's footsteps behind me. Far enough away that I have time.

Close enough that my cock is hard.

Finally, I stop. I stop in a room that is nearly all installation—a mounded structure made of woven grain with a narrow passage for an entrance. I doubt I'm allowed to, but I move into the passage, having to turn sideways to fit, and push myself into the center of the structure, emerging with a few bits of straw clinging to my tuxedo and dusting the tops of my shoes. A bright light shines into the passage I just came in from, and above me, the ceiling is arched and ribbed like the vaults of a cathedral—except the vaults are made of willow rods and grain instead of stone. The ceiling is dropping wheat heads and barley spikes onto the floor.

It smells of summer inside.

The structure is only half a structure; the gallery wall bisects the chamber halfway in. The wall is painted a plain white and still marked with the hanging screws of whatever exhibit was here last.

I press myself against it and try to decide how to feel when Auden can't find me.

Except, of course, he does find me.

I wasn't fast enough, or he could hear me shuffling through the passage, or it's where he would have hidden if he were the type of man to hide. It doesn't matter, because the minute I hear his footsteps coming closer, everything about my body comes alive. My organ is so swollen now that it presses against my zipper. I know if I pulled it out, it would be wet at the tip.

He steps out of the passage without a single fleck of straw or grain on him, his expression carnivorous. "St. Sebastian," he says.

15

St. Sebastian

"I didn't come here for you," I say.

It's a lie, we both know that, but I have to say it anyway. "I didn't come here for this."

"I think you did," Auden says softly. "I think you came here for exactly this."

He steps closer. The grain chamber muffles the noise some, which makes the room feel even smaller. A cloister of barley. A cell of wheat.

He steps closer again, close enough to reach out and run a long finger up my lapel, which he does now. "Do you like your tuxedo?"

"I'm going to have to clean the barley off it before I return it."

Auden's forehead wrinkles. "Return it?"

"To wherever you rented it from?"

Auden looks appalled. "I didn't *rent* you a tuxedo, St. Sebastian. Give me some credit." His mouth pulls into a moue of offended pride.

Rich boy.

I look down to where his hand still caresses my lapel. It's hypnotic to watch his fingertips ghosting over the fabric, lingering over the neatly tailored peaks, dancing over the single button that keeps the jacket closed.

"Grosgrain," he says after a minute, his eyes on the lapel now too. "Instead of satin. I thought it suited you better."

"I don't know what grosgrain is," I tell him. His fingers are plucking at my jacket button, each little tug and pull of the fabric like a whispering kiss along my middle. If he popped the button open, there'd be nothing between his hands and my stomach but my dress shirt.

"It's silk," he says, "but it's been pulled and twisted into something rough and strong. Unlike other fabrics, grosgrain shows its bones." And then my jacket button releases and his hands are inside, sliding up my stomach to my chest. When his palms drag over my nipples, obviously bunched into tiny points even with the shirt between us, he lets out a long-suffering sigh. As if I should be ashamed I've been denying him the pleasure of this.

"This shirt is Egyptian cotton," he tells me. "It has the longest fibers of any of the cotton breeds. It makes the fabric stronger, but softer too. Almost silky. Do you feel it? The silkiness?"

His hands are everywhere under my jacket now, rubbing along my spine and shaping the blades of my shoulders, tracing the waistband of my trousers, pushing gently against my navel. I can't bear to look at his haughty, handsome face, and so I have to close my eyes.

"Yes," I whisper. "I feel it."

"The tuxedo itself is made of wool," he says, his hands moving down to my hips, and then around to my ass. He doesn't linger there, and neither does he pause over the obvious ridge of my erection, but my body hums as if he's already inside of me, as if he's already wrapped a strong hand around my staff and started squeezing. "Sturdy but so finely carded that you could almost believe it a cousin to silk. Listen to my tuxedo against yours—it's barely a whisper, isn't it? It's like a breeze in the evening or the wash of the river when the water is low. Barely any noise at all."

He's stepped into me in order to prove his point—his thighs moving against mine, his closed jacket brushing against my open one—and my eyes are still closed and I'm shuddering, shuddering, shuddering.

"And our shoes," he murmurs, his voice so close that I know his mouth is hovering near my jaw, "are calf leather. Made in Italy. Supple—" One of his shoes nudges against mine, forcing me to step out to the side. "—but robust." His other shoe pushes against my foot and then my legs are spread wide enough that he can fit both of his between mine. I'm unsteady like this, off balance with my back against the wall and my feet planted wide, and so I have no choice but to press against Auden's touch. His hands sliding under my jacket to grip my shoulders and triceps, his hips pinned firmly to mine. I can feel his cock, hard and stretching to his hip.

"Rich boy," I say.

"Maybe," he says back, and then his lips are on my neck. Right above my collar, hot and hard, a kiss immediately turning into a vicious, toe-curling suck.

"We can't," I say, finally opening my eyes. His face is buried in my neck, and so I can see the back curve of his head—caramel hair, thick and gleaming—framed by the barley ceiling. "We can't, Auden."

"Then why did you come?" he says into my neck, biting me hard enough that I feel it in my marrow. My cock jolts in neglected agony, as if it's trying to get closer to Auden, as if it's seeking its owner. "Why did you come here at all if you don't want this?"

Why doesn't he understand? *Wanting* is exactly the problem when it comes to him. Wanting is why I can't trust myself around him, it's why I'm here shivering against a wall while he brands me with his mouth instead of safely at home where I can't be tempted.

Auden seems to realize this the moment he asks the question anyway. I feel his lips curl against my neck. "You do want it, though, don't you?" He pulls away enough that his fingers can find the buttons of my shirt. They slide between the buttons, teasing little touches against the flat skin near my navel. And then he deftly unbuttons the three above my waistband. "Look at how you tremble when I touch you, stubborn boy. Look at how you flutter those long, gorgeous eyelashes and nibble on that lip piercing. I think you more than want this, I think you need it. I think you need it from me."

I can't stifle the noise I make when he unfastens my trouser button or when he unzips me. My cock pushes against the sudden freedom, seeking the cool air, seeking the wicked heat of Auden's hand.

"I don't want to want it," I mumble, my head dropping onto his shoulder as he finally takes me in his hand. "I shouldn't. We're—we're not right for wanting each other."

Auden strokes my throbbing cock like it's his favorite pet. "It doesn't have to be a transgression," he soothes me. "Who has to know we're brothers? *Half*-brothers? We didn't grow up together. We didn't know until just weeks ago. We can forget. I know we can forget it if we try hard enough."

When I look down, I can see it all. His hand with its large, elegant wristwatch slowly jacking me off, the crisp lines of his tuxedo as he shuttles his grip up and down my aching sex. His fingers curled around the grosgrain lapel, turning my tux into an expensive, tailored prison.

"We didn't know," he repeats, his touch patient but wicked. "We didn't grow up together."

But the thing that terrifies me?

I think I would have loved him anyway.

Even if we had known for years. Even if we had learned the truth when we were sixteen.

There's no dose of Auden that inoculates you to him, there's no amount of him that breeds familiarity. I could have seen his face every day and I still would have worshipped the graceful arrogance of his features; I could have spent every waking moment with him and I still would've been hungry for any spare word thrown my way.

And there's nothing I wouldn't have done for him when we were sixteen, there was nothing too shameless for me, nothing too obscene, and I just can't imagine that sixteen-year-old Saint would have felt any differently if he'd known Auden was his brother. But that doesn't make it right, it doesn't make it any less twisted to do now.

Maybe it's *more* twisted knowing that. Maybe it's worse.

Oh God, it's definitely worse.

"Auden, we can't."

He doesn't loosen his grip. He doesn't stop stroking. My cock is so hard now that I can feel my heartbeat in it.

"*Auden.*"

"You know how to stop me."

I do. I do know how. But once again, I can't make the words come out.

Auden knows it too. He seals his smiling mouth over mine, taking his kiss like a king takes tribute. "You look so fucking pretty like this," he murmurs into my mouth. "All undone for me, all tormented. Your cock out and hard for my hand while you keep telling me we can't."

Said cock surges in his hold, and I can feel his pride surge right back in response. "Turn around, stubborn boy."

I should say no.

No—not *no.* Auden would let me bleat all the *nos* and *we can'ts* I wanted, he'd allow these little reflexes of conscience, because that's what they'd be: reflexes. If I said *no* to him, I'd have to do it in the language we agreed to speak together. With the words agreed on precisely because they were not reflexes, because they had to be thought about and searched for and chosen.

I should say *may I*, and end this. I should because I want to, because I know it's the right thing to do, because if I don't, I'll regret it the rest of my days.

He's turning me now, releasing his grip on my cock so that he can take hold of my hips and spin me toward the wall, and my entire body is humming, singing, alive. Goosebumps erupt every place he touches, he's sowing responsiveness like a farmer sows seeds, and the noise he makes when he presses his entire body against mine could feed me for years. His lips find my neck above my collar, and he fists my dick again, his own erection grinding openly against me.

"Nothing underneath your trousers, I notice," he says. His free hand is under my jacket, under my shirt, he's gone from squeezing my hip to searching out the muscled swell of my thigh, the firm curve of my bottom. I have to close my eyes against the pleasure. "Is that on purpose? Did you do it to tease me? Did you do it because you hoped you'd end up here, your zipper open and me about to open mine?"

I could stop this. I should stop this. I'm going to stop this.

In fact, Auden even dares me to stop him. Once with his words—*say it, my sweet, suffering martyr, and I'll stop*—and over and over again with his body. A pause before the expensive wool is pulled down over my hips. A moment of stillness before a warm fingertip presses against the place I open. A lull in the kisses along my neck as he reaches for something in the inner pocket of his jacket.

I know what he's doing. I know exactly what he's doing. And still I don't speak.

Auden—the same man who packed reusable water bottles for our sylvan antler-fuck—is no less prepared now. I hear a packet crinkling, the rustle of deliberate movement, and then something else that has me rolling my forehead against the wall in agony: the slick slide of him preparing his shaft for me.

"You had lube in your pocket," I say. I want it to be an accusation, but I only sound dreamy and besotted, even to my own ears.

Auden's voice sounds amused when he speaks. "You can't blame a boy for hoping."

Slippery fingers find the most private place in my body and enter, sending me up to my toes. The head of my now-neglected erection is leaving smears of clear seed on the exhibit wall, and when Auden slides his fingers free and pulls my hips back to present my entrance to him, I could cry with relief.

I missed this. I missed this, I missed this, I missed this.

There's the wet, gliding kiss of his crown over my rim, then the moment the kiss becomes a snug pressure, and then the moment the pressure becomes an invasion. My fingers scratch and flex against the wall as he pierces me, and I can't breathe, I can't move. My lips are parted in a kind of noiseless grunt, an apnea of lust and pain.

But he is not noiseless, no, not my arrogant gala princeling. "So sweet," he drawls, sliding out enough so he can thrust all the way in. "Sweet, suffering boy. Sweet, stubborn boy."

He makes a grunt of his own when he finally fills me to the hilt.

I know what he must see when he looks down because I feel it, I feel the snugness of where he's fit himself inside me, I feel the lean muscles of his abs and hips when he presses in. I feel the pricey rumple of our tuxedo jackets and dress shirts and the indecent open air against my backside and thighs.

He's fucking me against a wall inside an art installation while gala guests tipple and chatter nearby. He's fucking me in a tux, with our girlfriend outside, with *all* our friends outside, and he's fucking me with an angry, plundering rhythm that lets me know he has no plans for this to be quick. No plans for this to be easy.

By the time he lets me come, I'll be exactly the way he likes me. Broken open with his name on my lips.

"Now then," he says, still drawling, still cool. "This isn't so bad, is it? No lightning strikes, St. Sebastian. No bolt from heaven, no hail of fire, no plagues. We are so civilized, are we not?" He asks that right as he gives me a hard thrust, which makes my dress shoes slide on the polished gallery floor.

"You know what we are, and civilized isn't it," I say, my voice hitching with each and every stroke. "This is not what civilized men do." Maybe there have been men like us at the edges of the world, on frontiers, and in the wild, lonely places. Maybe we're not the first brothers to do this—but that doesn't make it civilized. Far from it.

This is a need that shies away from the light of day. This is a hunger that has to be secret.

"Then we'll make our own civilization," Auden says arrogantly. "One where you're mine."

"We can't," I mumble. My head hangs down, my hair drifting in my face. My hands are braced against the wall and I want so much to drop one down and start stroking myself, but it feels important to resist the urge to do it. Like if I don't participate in making myself come, then I'm not really at fault, I can't be blamed.

"You keep saying that," he says, his hand sliding up my chest to wrap around my throat. He tugs me back, makes me straighten up enough for him to nip at my earlobe. He can't really piston into me at this angle, but he can still rut, he can still grind. I'm still speared so thoroughly that I swear he's all the way into my belly.

I'm still so hard and my balls are still so tight that I know I'm going to go off soon, and he'll have won. He'll have proven to us both that our unholy lusts can't be denied or curbed.

Only, what? Two weeks without each other? And now he's fallen on me like a wolf and I've welcomed him with open arms. Shown him my throat, my belly, all my vulnerable places. My stupid, degenerate heart, ready for eating.

"I keep saying it because it's true." I close my eyes as his teeth catch on the lobe of my ear, on the skin right below it.

He nuzzles my neck. My jaw.

His cock is the most beautiful thing I've ever felt.

"Show me," he whispers. "Show me the sin in this."

I can't. And not because it's not there, but because the sin isn't scrawled on our faces or trumpeted in our words. It's written in our blood and scratched onto our bones.

"I love you," he tells me, and I don't know if I can survive it, this feeling like I'm being scythed down just like the barley and the wheat around us. I don't know if I can survive him.

"Say it back to me," he begs. His voice has lost some of that coolness now, some of its indolence. He sounds a little breathless, a little rough. "Tell me what I want to hear."

Still spoiled though. Rich boy.

"You already know what you want to hear," I say, eyes still closed. "You already know how I feel."

His hand finds my cock and he gives it quick, vicious strokes, pulling me up to my toes every time he squeezes his fist to the tip, and following my hips with his own every time I rise up so there's no escaping his fuck.

"You're not playing fair," I complain between grunts. My lower belly is poured full of heat and my erection is so swollen that I feel like I might split apart. Every single muscle is wire-tight and thrumming. "You're resorting to tricks."

"I never promised fair. I never promised that I wouldn't use tricks."

"You said there would be rules."

"For you and my little bride," he murmurs wickedly. His hand is too much. His thick cock wedged against my prostate is too much. "Not for me. I am the king and you are mine to keep and to fuck. I make the rules. And the rule right now is you have to tell me you love me."

I should have known. I should have known he wouldn't leave here without taking everything. I should have known he wouldn't let me hide from this.

"Fine, I love you. Are you happy?"

He reaches for something else in his pocket, and once he has it, he kisses my neck again. "I'll be happy when you're in my house. In my bed. In my arms. I'll be happy when I can fuck you whenever I need. I'll be happy when I can feel that piercing against my cock whenever I want. I'll be happy when you, Poe, and I are truly, actually together, the way we all know we're supposed to be."

"We're not supposed to be anything, we're—"

"I know what we are," he interrupts. "It doesn't change that you're mine. It doesn't change that you want to be mine."

"And you?"

"Well, I'm yours, of course," he says simply. "Yours to eat and ruin too."

It's too much. The hand, the fuck, his words. His thorny, cannibal heart.

I grunt as the pleasure finally takes me, as it snaps through me hard and cutting and keen, and as the first pulse surges up, Auden's hand is replaced with a handkerchief. He catches my climax with the soft, expensive-feeling cotton, standing patiently as I spurt out every last drop.

The orgasm goes on a shamefully long time, pulse after pulse, so thick and forceful that he can see how much I loved this, how much my depraved body hungered to be used in just this way and only by him. It would knock my feet out from underneath me, it would bend me double, it would have me boneless and staggering to the floor, but he holds me up as he finishes tenderly milking my orgasm, he keeps me upright not only so I can empty into his handkerchief, but so he can stay inside me as I do. So he can feel every seize and shiver and clench of my groin as I release.

"Good boy," he whispers, giving me an approving nip on the neck as I slowly stutter to a finish. "I didn't want you to dirty your tux with what you let me do to you."

The handkerchief disappears, and then his bare hand returns to pet me. Fondly. Appreciatively. "Now hold still, I need to come."

His cock is wedged tightly inside of me, he's jammed in so thick and so deep, and every rock of his hips has him shivering, murmuring to himself, squeezing my hips and cock and biceps at turns, as if to reassure himself that I'm really here, he's really fucking me, he's really using his stubborn boy the way he needs. And here I am doing the same thing—trying to memorize the feel of his lips on my neck, the fit of his erection inside me, the low rumble of his pleasure-words under his breath as he eases his needs with my body. I want to stuff myself so full of him that even when we're apart, I can feel his hands and hear his voice. His possession most of all—that is what I must never forget. I must never forget how it feels to be whole.

He comes with a ragged sigh, one hand on my throat and the other wrapped tight around my waist. I feel him inside me, I feel each and every throb, and without a condom, I can feel the slick heat of his release too. His orgasm feels as good as mine, which sounds like it shouldn't be true, and yet it is, it is. Feeling his satisfaction, his jerking, pulsing animal pleasure—it eases something inside *me*. It scratches some itch I can't describe—service, submission, love, *something*—and it makes me feel like I've just swallowed the sun.

Plus it makes me hard all over again.

"One more," he says gently. "I can't send you out there like this." I feel him reach for something else in his pocket, and after the tearing of a wrapper, I look down to see him rolling a condom on over my renewed erection. He's like Mary Poppins with that inner tuxedo pocket.

"I'm afraid you've already defiled my handkerchief," he explains as he rolls the latex all the way to my base. "And walking around with cum on your tux is rather infra dig."

I think I laugh a little, a soft puff of air that has my body clenching around his erection, which hasn't softened one bit since he came.

He takes in a sharp breath at the abrupt squeeze of my channel around him, and then he's moving fast, hard, rough, his earlier release easing his way and making his fuck slick and wet. And he matches his own pleasure with mine; he fists my latex-covered cock and jerks me like I jerk myself at home. Brutally. Impatiently. With a ruthless pace and a cruel grip.

I don't stand a chance.

The merciless ride against my prostate, the elegant, watch-wearing fist I'm fucking, the vulgar selfishness of the man behind me using me like this— there's no way I ever stood a chance. My second orgasm rips through my guts and tears through my groin, and I fill the condom with long, heavy jolts; I empty all of myself into that primal, aching moment, my heart pushing up to the vaulted ceiling of barley and wheat and floating there as Auden finishes inside me. He chases every drop, every swell and pulse, he denies himself nothing.

He would deny me nothing too, I think. If I let him have me.

I can't let him have me.

My heart tumbles to my feet, flopping and shivering wetly around the spiky awns and kernels and stalks already drifting dry and dead on the floor. My eyelids are burning even as he carefully slides the condom off and puts it somewhere, even as he extricates himself and uses something—his handkerchief again?—to catch any spend as he pulls free.

It wasn't as if I'd forgotten all my protests, all my reasons and fears, when I let Auden fuck me. It was only that I wanted Auden more than I wanted to be good. And now that we're no longer joined, now that we'll have to step back and fix our clothes and leave this chambered tomb of barley, the horror of what I've done—knowingly this time, knowing who he is to me—crowds up into my throat and chokes me.

Is it always going to be like this? Me pushing him away, hiding, denying, until our control snaps and we fall on each other like hungry animals? Is it entirely hopeless? Should I stop resisting? I can't live without his love, and yet succumbing to it will always be wrong, our family and friends would think it wrong, *everyone* would think it wrong.

Our desires are so forbidden, they shouldn't even be shaped in words. In thoughts. They shouldn't even be acknowledged, except to a priest under the cover of confession.

Auden has tidied up behind me, and I know I should pull my tux together too. I just can't, I can't move from right here with my forehead and hands braced against the wall. If I move, if I turn and I see him, I will start to cry. And I may not have much to my name, but I'd still like to have some dignity. Some pride.

But again, I underestimate Auden's attunement to me, his acute perception. His hands on my body as he puts my tuxedo to rights are solicitous and calming, like he's coaxing a skittish horse into staying still for him. When he's done dressing me, he gently turns me around.

"Oh, St. Sebastian," he says, because I'm already crying, dammit, the shame and the misery of it all is too much. I think I could cry for the rest of my life and still have sorrow yet to spill.

"Come here," he whispers, and I come, stepping into his arms and clutching his jacket like a child. The minute his arms slide around me—strong and certain and a little bit acquisitive—I cry even harder, as if his comfort doesn't shore up my walls but rather weakens them, and within seconds, I can barely breathe, I can barely think, all I can do is hold on to him as I cry and cry and cry, as I grieve every single second of a life which seems determined to rip the people I love away from me.

We end up on the ground, I don't know how. I only know that one moment we're standing, and then the next I'm in his arms on the floor, sitting between his sturdy thighs and nestled into his chest. He holds me tight, he drops kiss after kiss onto my hair, he croons things so low that I can't hear them, I can only feel them as they rumble through his chest and throat.

I can't remember someone ever holding me like this, ever, not even my mother or Richard Davey, even though they must have when I was little. But having Auden hold me and the weight of my unhappiness so easily, like I and it weigh nothing, having him cradling me and tending me like there's nothing in the world he'd rather do—it's a gift I cling to greedily. This one thing can be mine right now, this one solace.

I'm not sure how long I cry. Long enough that the breast of his tuxedo jacket is wet and one of my feet has gone numb from having my legs draped over his thigh. Long enough that I feel disoriented when I stop, dizzy from all those juddering, seizing inhales and wild, uncontrolled exhales. But it hasn't been long enough that Auden's arms have grown tired. I'm still held as tightly to his chest as ever.

Silence creeps back into our little tomb of grain, filling up the space where my sobs had been. There is only our breathing and Auden's heart beating steadily against my ear and my occasional sniffles. I feel very small like this, even though I'm not small, even though my legs are as long and muscular as his, even though I fill his arms.

I feel a strange, sad peace. A numb kind of safety.

I wish we never had to leave this room.

I reach up and stroke the line of Auden's lapel. "Did you get me a tuxedo just so you could fuck me in it at a swanky party?"

"Well, obviously," he says wryly. Tenderly.

I look up at him. And then I notice his bowtie is gone. "What happened here?" I ask, lifting my hand to stroke the exposed hollow of his throat.

"As I've mentioned, you've already made use of my handkerchief, and I didn't want to send you back into the fray still dripping with me." The corner of his mouth tugs up. "Or rather, I *wanted* to, but I wasn't going to."

"So you used your bowtie?" I ask incredulously. "What happened to not being infrared or whatever?"

"Infra *dig*," he corrects, "and in my case, everyone will assume my sartorial transgressions are for the sake of being roguishly fashionable."

He's probably not wrong. With his collar open and his throat naked, he's still the cool, arrogant prince from earlier. Just more rakish now, a little more dangerous. A little more like the wild god he is inside.

"Are you saying I don't look roguishly fashionable when I transgress?" I ask.

Auden gives a soft laugh and tugs on my lip piercing. "You always look perfect to me, and that's what matters. Anyway, I think we can both agree there's a material difference between losing a bowtie and having semen spattered on your trousers."

We fall quiet again, Auden still using his thumb to toy with my labret. "Tell me why you were crying," he says.

My voice is tired. Hoarse from the tears.

"You already know why."

There's an abrupt stillness to him now. "Do I?"

"Auden."

He presses his face into my hair. Not to comfort me, but for himself now, as if he can't bear this. "Will you hate me for loving you?" he asks brokenly.

"I don't know."

He pauses. "Will you hate yourself?"

That. That I do have the answer to.

"Yes."

A long moment. A moment that stretches through us and through the years and years we've been tied together and into a past that neither of us were there to see or change. A moment filled with shadows and silhouettes— our father, my mother, our little bride. Our friends. A proud house in the wind-scoured moors, and a ruined chapel in the woods.

"Then no more," Auden says, and his words are guarded and carefully pronounced. But when I push out of his arms to sit up and look him in the face, his eyes are filled with a raw agony that flays me alive.

"Auden," I say again, not sure what I'm going to say next, but knowing I have to stop him from looking like that or we're both going to die. "We—"

He shakes his head, reaches out to touch my mouth again. The place where he first marked me, a prince and pauper wrestling in a cloud of lavender and baby's breath. "It's enough now. I love you and Proserpina with a hunger like I could eat the world and not be full. But I love you too much to push you. I love you too much to let you hate yourself."

I don't have an answer to that. I don't have anything that would make him feel better.

Because he *would* push me and I *would* hate myself.

He gives me a sad smile, like he knows all this without me having to speak it aloud. "I told Rebecca about our father, and you know what she told me? She told me that I needed to know what I wanted and what I was willing to lose in order to get it."

"And?" I ask, my voice still hoarse. "What do you want?"

"You, St. Sebastian. I want *you*. And I don't mean for sex, even though that's part of it, I mean that I want your face and your voice and the way you smile when you think no one is looking. I want to talk to you and see you, I want to come home and know you'll be there. I want to go on walks with you and argue about books with you, and just—do *everything* with you. Live with you and grow old with you and die with you. That's what I want. That's what I will die without and what I refuse to give up now."

That agony is still in his eyes, sparkling green and brown in our art exhibit sanctuary, but the agony no longer cuts me down. It lures me in, beckoning me to a place of pain we share together.

"Be my brother, St. Sebastian," he says. "No kissing. No kink. No fucking. But come to the house and live with me. Share my inheritance. Share our bride. Surely that's—it's not unheard of, is it? It's not a sin? Two brothers living together? Loving the same woman?"

My breath is caught in my throat. A knot of hope and pain. "We could be together then."

"Yes," Auden says, with what would be eagerness if there wasn't still so much longing written across those elegant features.

"We could have each other." I'm almost stunned at the simplicity of it, the near inevitability of it. "It would be the way it was always meant to be between us."

Auden's mouth twists a little. "I wouldn't go that far."

"We could love each other," I say, ignoring him, something deep green and glossy unfurling inside me. Something born of winter finally seeing the light. "We could have the rest of our lives together."

"All the parts of love, save for one."

"And we'd still be a three."

Auden nods, a tired, kingly finality. "We'd still be a three."

I feel stupid that I haven't thought of this before, that I haven't begged for it or spoken it into being or even imagined that it could be a solution. It's the answer to everything, it's balm from Gilead at last. We'll have each other. We'll have Poe.

What else could possibly matter?

How hard could it possibly be to resist the carnal blossoms of our desires when the roots are fed elsewhere? With his attention, with his time— I surely won't need his cruelty then, nor his crude lusts. I won't crave them when so much else is being given to me.

"Yes," I say. "Yes. I'll move in. I'll be at Thornchapel. I'll be your...your brother. For real now."

The smile he gives me then. Like the chapel itself—haunting, beautiful, broken and whole all at once. His smile is the center of the world. "Good."

He gets to his feet and helps me up, and together we dust off all the bits of harvest detritus from our tuxedos. He keeps his touch impersonal, and quick, but I'm so, so aware of him as he brushes off the back of my trousers, the sides of my thighs. Not an hour ago, he would have used this as an excuse to maul me. To get me hard. Now it is nothing more than what one friend would do for another. Platonic solicitude.

It feels strange. Nearly as wrong as anything else, but maybe I'll get used to it.

We slide out of the small barley tomb and emerge into a gallery that's still as vacant and empty as ever.

"I suppose we should get back," I say, turning to find Auden staring at my mouth like he wants to eat it.

"One last kiss," he says, lifting his eyes to mine. There's no power in them now, no arrogance. Only pure, young longing. "Please, St. Sebastian. I want...I want to kiss you one last time."

He's not even finished before I'm in his arms, slotting my lips against his, opening for him as I always do. His tongue is hot, silky, and he strokes my tongue expertly with it, exploring every corner of a mouth that no longer belongs to him. He drinks his fill of me, one hand in my hair and the other at the small of my back, and for a single perfect instant, everything is how it is supposed to be. *We're* how we're supposed to be.

He gives my tongue a lingering caress with his, and then he nips at my bottom lip, sucking it and the piercing into his mouth. When he pulls away, he takes my heart with him.

He looks at me with swollen lips and glittering eyes. Without his bowtie, I can see his pulse thrumming like mad in his throat. "Shall we?" he asks, gesturing toward the door.

And, convincing myself that this is the right thing, that this is the only thing to be done, the only way we can have most of everything and only a little nothing, I swallow and nod.

"Ready when you are."

Part Two

Midsummer

16

Midsummer
St. Sebastian

He doesn't remember precisely how he came to be in a car with Auden and Poe driving down I-70, but he would never dream of complaining about it. The windows are down, the radio is blaring something loud and fun, and Poe's hair is everywhere—a storm of hair, dark and silky—as she drives and sings and eventually goads Auden into singing too.

His voice is terrible, hers too, and St. Sebastian leans his head against the backseat window and smiles as he listens to them. Outside, stretches of Kansas flash by—green fields, greener pastures, broken by lines of stunted, prairie-hardy trees and shallow creeks with cows crowding the edges. This isn't home—this isn't sunlight glinting off glass and waving off asphalt, this isn't a sidewalk ready to scald bare feet, paletas dripping onto your hands if you don't eat them fast enough, the splash of a pool, the smell of chlorine, the hot sand of Burger's Lake—all of that is Texas's and Texas's alone.

But it reminds him of home. The heat, the sun, the tar-ribboned interstate. The cows in their fields too, standing up to their bellies in muddy ponds or crowding under the shade of the one tree big enough to cast a shadow.

Prairie. It's the prairie in summer, and even though St. Sebastian doesn't think of the prairie as his home, even though his version of the prairie is made of mega highways and air conditioners humming like giant metal bees, he still feels himself breathe easier here.

It's the vitamin D, Poe will tell him later, once they've finished their drive from the airport and settled into her father's living room with cold beers and panting dogs sprawled between them. *No way are we getting enough at Thornchapel.*

Maybe it is. Maybe he's been craving the sun and the heat, the slow-rolling summer that bakes and bakes and bakes, doing its little chemistries inside his cells and making him stronger. Or maybe it's the open sky, so far away and such a sweet blue that it's impossible to believe in clouds and storms and wind, even when Poe points out trees snapped like sticks from a tornado last year. Or maybe it's the open road, straight and wide and mostly empty, a runway to a horizon so distant that it feels like a movie set, a backdrop, a painting propped against the real horizon somewhere closer by.

Whatever it is, he's still smiling as they roll into Lawrence—another car with Delphine, Rebecca, and Becket behind them—driving through a cozy downtown of brick storefronts and winding to the foot of a big hill.

Above them, there's the University of Kansas, perched on the hilltop, glimpses of bright limestone and red roofs. Here at the base of the hill are narrow streets of old Italianate houses, fussy Victorian Baroques, low-slung Craftsmans, all jostling among mature oaks and maples and sweet gums, with dogwoods and crabapple trees squatting between. When they park and start spilling out of their cars, stretching and scratching themselves, Delphine twirls a slow circle in the middle of the shady street.

"I thought there'd be cowboys here," she says.

"Just drunk college kids and hippies, mostly," Poe says, popping open the trunk of the car. "Well, and the professors aren't drunk or hippies. Usually. Daddy!" This last she directs to a tall, thin man who's just emerged from the two-story house in front of them. She skips right into his arms and they hug for a long moment.

Saint looks over to see Auden staring at the fatherly embrace, an almost-puzzled knit to his brow, and he thinks that for all of Auden's gifts—the money and the house and the education fit for a prince—Auden's never felt the affectionate embrace of a father happy to see his son.

Even Saint had that, for a little while at least.

David Markham finally releases Poe, although he keeps her close as he greets the rest of them, his eyes lingering on each and every one of their faces—especially Rebecca's. Rebecca notices and clears her throat.

"Ah, yes," David says, blushing a little above his beard. He has light, brownish hair and blueish eyes behind trendy glasses, and there's so little of him in Poe—except for those easily pinked cheeks and the button of his nose. And then in the way he talks, which is precise and somehow also tangential and meandering at the same time, as if his mind has so many rooms crammed full of so many thoughts that he has mentally sprint between them all in order to communicate. "Welcome to the house, come on in—let me show you where you're staying, there's plenty of room and I'm a deep sleeper as Poe can tell you, so no need to keep quiet when you're coming in or out. I'm teaching a summer course, so I'll be gone most of today and tomorrow, but the day of the funeral of course, I'll be home, and the day after—it's Intro to Religious Studies, I could teach it in my sleep, normally they give it to a lecturer, but I wanted to stay busy this summer, there's never enough work it seems, with the house so quiet, although I could get another dog, I suppose. Are you thirsty?"

They all look at each other, then back to David.

"Very," Auden says politely, and they go inside.

Rebecca and Delphine took a guest room, as did Becket. Saint opted for a couch in the attic, and Auden dropped his and Poe's bags in Poe's girlhood room. David frowned at that, but said nothing. Perhaps he felt comforted by the presence of only one twin-sized bed in the room, thinking someone would sleep in a sleeping bag or end up on a couch downstairs, which was rather foolish in Saint's opinion. Auden Guest would sleep wherever he wanted to sleep, even if that meant using Proserpina as a warm, curvy blanket.

After dinner, they ended up at a bar a few blocks away, which is where they sat now. The three Brits perched on their stools, looking inordinately out of place in their pleats and presses and Italian leather belts, while Saint and Poe fought over the beer menu and Becket checked his phone.

"Trouble at the parish?" Saint asked.

Becket shook his head. "Everything's fine. But I've never taken a vacation before and it's unnerving not to be there. A deacon is leading the Chaplet and Rosary recitations, and they're sending in a priest from Bristol to do the Mass I'm missing, but what if he can't find something in the sacristy? Or someone forgets to lock up and teenagers get in—" He breaks off, blowing out a breath. He's wearing a chambray button-up, white pants, and deck shoes. He looks like he left a yacht behind, not a tiny forest church.

"I need a drink," he mutters, and then edges off his stool to walk up to the bar.

Meanwhile, Delphine is trying and failing to find a good selfie angle. The neon beer signs and giant televisions airing baseball games are fucking with her light.

"What would you like?" Rebecca asks.

"Bubbles," Delphine says, still tilting her head this way and that as she holds out her phone in front of her. "And a cocktail too, the cutest one they have. Not to drink—just for me to take a picture of. Okay, well, maybe to drink too."

Rebecca sighs, but she goes without protest. After a minute, Delphine hops off her stool too to go search for a better selfie spot in the room.

Auden is squinting at a sign behind the bar, and he finally pulls out his clear-framed glasses so he can read it. "Rock Chalk Jay...hawk?" he pronounces carefully. Then he looks at Poe, his face as expectant as a Latin pupil's after a recitation.

Poe's laughing and is presumably about to explain what a jayhawk is when a woman approaches the table. She's olive-skinned and dark-haired, with kohl-rimmed eyes and a septum piercing. She's dressed in black boots, a black miniskirt, with a red shirt that says *Fire Walk with Me*.

"Little doll," the woman says warmly.

"Mistress Emily," Poe says, and she ducks her head in a way that makes Saint think of kneeling.

"You didn't say you were coming back," Emily chastises, and Saint notices a faint note of disapproval in her tone. He remembers that this is the ex-girlfriend, the ex-Mistress. The one who gave Proserpina stripes on her ass to wear across the ocean. He looks at her more closely, suddenly aware of his own boots, the glinting metal in his own face. Poe seems to have a type.

"It's for my mother's funeral," Poe says. "We found her remains in England this spring, and now she'll be laid to rest here." She sounds matter-of-fact as she explains it. A librarian of her own tragedy. Far away from the sobbing girl he held in his arms the morning they found her mother.

Saint thinks about how people can be like this—impersonal and efficient, even when they are also capable of screaming into the fog. Even when they have to be beaten and fucked in order to use their heart properly again.

How can you ever know a person when they are always changing, stronger on some days, softer on others? She is like the ritual landscape described in

Dr. Davidson's book, Saint thinks. Secrets upon secrets upon secrets, buried under flowers and thorns.

Emily's demeanor changes at Poe's explanation, softening a little. "Oh, sweet doll. I'm so sorry."

Auden's hand covers Poe's on the table, offering comfort and staking claim all at once.

Emily doesn't fail to notice this, and a small, tight smile pulls at her mouth. "I don't think we've met before," she says, extending a hand to Auden. "I'm Emily Genovese."

"Auden Guest," he says, returning her handshake. His expression is polite, his mouth shaped into amiability, but something burns in the air around him. "And this is St. Sebastian Martinez."

Saint offers his hand too, and Emily nods. "It's nice to meet you both. Are you…friends of Poe's?"

Auden's face doesn't change, but there's no hesitation when he answers. "She's mine."

Emily has the look of someone whose suspicions are being confirmed. "Ah," she responds.

"And she's dating St. Sebastian too," Auden adds, always careful to include Saint.

They're both careful, these days. The last five weeks have been nothing but care. Tiptoeing around the past. Dancing around the future.

"*Ah*," Emily says. "I see."

"It's good to see you," Poe says, clearly trying to break the tension. "Are you still going to Orthia's these days? That's our old kink club," she says to Saint and Auden by way of explanation.

Emily nods, her eyes scanning over where Auden's hand is still curled possessively over Poe's. She seems to come to a decision. "I was actually going to go tonight," she says. "Do you want to come? I could get your group in for free."

The air around Auden burns brighter, hotter, and both Poe and Saint feel it. Poe turns and smiles at her king, who can't hide his interest. Saint wishes he'd already ordered a drink so he could down it now.

"If all of us can go," Poe says, "then we'd love to."

Orthia's is neither glamorous nor grimy. It's in a converted warehouse next to the Kansas River, underlit, under-furnished, but meticulously clean. It's laid out with all the composition and Feng shui of an exterior door expo—curtained stalls that can be either private or public run through the warehouse in two long corridors; there're plastic totes crammed with assorted items stuffed into corners and behind tables; and someone sits in a folding chair at the front door and officially makes them members of what, for legal reasons, is considered a social club. In the remaining space, there is a makeshift bar, a low stage surrounded by leather benches and chairs, and then plenty of equipment scattered about, for people to play with in full view.

It's where they're at now, Poe and Delphine stripped to their underthings and cuffed side by side to St. Andrew's crosses, while Rebecca and Auden peruse the impact play implements like children inside a toy store. Becket claimed jet lag and didn't come, and Saint hovers at the edges of the scene, restless and annoyed with himself. He knew there'd be no place for him here, he knew that he wouldn't be the one cuffed to a cross and made to endure Auden's cruelty, and yet still he came. Why? Is he so masochistic that he'll use anything to hurt himself, even watching Poe get something he'll never, ever get again?

Apparently, yes.

Which would surprise nobody, he supposes.

The warehouse is dim, pounding with music that can only be described as music for people who wish they were vampires, and so Saint doesn't bother to hide his expression as Auden finally selects a flogger and then steps up to Poe to whisper in her ear. He doesn't bother to muffle the groan he makes when Auden bites Poe's shoulder and then has to visibly adjust himself. He doesn't conceal a single thing as Auden starts flogging the woman they both love—lightly at first, and then harder, and then faster, until Poe is shivering. Until Poe's body has started twisting with delicious confusion, until she both shies away and chases the sensation, unsure of what she needs.

Auden's sure though. He changes floggers, something heavier now with sharp, angled tips. It's not the kind of flogger that will make you bleed, but it's not too far away from that kind of flogger either. The first hit has Poe's knees buckling, and her moan carries over all the heavy bass and snarling female vocals, hitting Saint right in the stomach.

She'd moaned like that this morning, but so softly it was barely audible, after Saint slipped into the airplane bathroom behind her and fingered her so slowly that by the time she orgasmed, a flight attendant had come by and straightened their seats. Later tonight, he'll come too. Even if it means fucking her on the twin bed while Auden watches.

No, he reminds himself. *Brothers.*

But it's so hard, because he has no practice being a brother, and neither does Auden, and anyway, what happens when two brothers are in love with the same woman? Surely there's *some* leeway then?

Watching, maybe? Helping? Maybe even being inside her together?

Which makes it sound like Poe is a toy to be shared, and that's not it at all (except when that's the game she's playing with Auden). But she is the single unbrotherly ribbon tying them together, and so sometimes Saint finds himself trying to reach Auden's body through hers. Searching out every small cruelty Auden's marked her with and then kissing it, worshiping it, murmuring litanies of prayer into her skin.

These past five weeks living with Poe and Auden, he has been deliriously happy...and also tattooed with so much yearning on the inside of his skin that he wonders how no one else sees it.

Well, Poe had seen it. At least once.

That day had been a hot one, and they'd spent the morning in the laziest possible way, splashing in the indoor pool. He'd been watching the way the water slid and sluiced over the lean corrugations of Auden's chest and stomach, he'd been marking the dark hair trailing from Auden's navel down into the waistband of his trunks.

He was miserable. And then a laughing Auden had pounced on Poe and playfully guided her hand into his swimming shorts. There'd only been a glimpse, a flash really, of a hard cock, straight and proud and jutting up with male arrogance, but then Poe wrapped her hand around it.

Auden's gaze had met Saint's, his eyes loud with all the things they'd agreed not to say.

It should be you here too, those eyes said. *It should be you both.*

Saint abruptly couldn't exist in that pool a single moment longer. He muttered an excuse and then fled up into the hills. He sat staring down into the trees wearing nothing but damp trunks and unlaced boots until Poe found him and sat down next to him. Her hair was still wet and her cheeks were flushed, and Saint had wondered if Auden had fucked her before he let her leave.

But she said nothing about Auden when she spoke. Instead, she asked, "Am I enough?"

Saint had looked at her then, feeling horror and guilt and panic, and she'd held up a hand. "I'm not trying to coax compliments out of you, or plea for proofs of love. I don't want to be that girl, okay? I just need to know the truth. Because right now I have half of two men, and if it wasn't hard enough watching you both suffer, it's compounded by the fact that I can't heal it for either of you. I'll never be him, Saint. And I'll never begrudge you loving him or missing that part of your love, but I also have to be enough on my own. I won't settle for anything less."

"Poe—"

"And before you ask, I've just had this same talk with Auden," she said. "I don't mind being in between, St. Sebastian. But I can't be instead of."

Her eyes had been a blazing green then, like an alchemist's fire, and he'd pulled her into his lap, he'd kissed her, he'd told her the truth—that she was enough, that she was everything, she was an infinity of love and his infinity was sewn to hers. But that it was the same with Auden too, and even in this new life of brotherhood—sharing days, dinners, drinks by the fire, seeing each other in the hallway, reading in the garden with a bottle of wine passed between them—he still missed that last piece of their love. The piece they agreed to bury together.

Except it wouldn't stay dead, and Saint didn't know how to fix that. Maybe he never would.

Poe had nodded then, understanding. She, too, had a heart made for two people. Only her love was permitted, while theirs was a sin of blood.

He'd reached under her dress and found her naked underneath it. He'd freed his shaft and had her ride his lap under the golden May sun until they'd both felt like themselves again.

And so the three of them had managed to cope, managed to share a house and a life for the last month. Managed to share all the parts of love, save for one.

In five weeks, he's learned this: with Poe he is complete, and without Auden he is not. He doesn't know how both things can be true at once, but they are.

In the here and now, Auden gives Poe a break. He goes up to the cross to kiss her cheek, her sweat-misted forehead, he gives her a drink of water and murmurs things in her ear until she nods, her eyelids fluttering. And then he leaves her for a moment, coming up to St. Sebastian with the kind of direct steps that says Auden knew where he was all along.

"Emily says we can fuck here," Auden says. He's a little breathless from the flogging himself, his color high and his eyes sparkling.

"And so you're going to fuck her."

Hunger is all over him. "Yes."

"You don't need anyone's permission but hers," Saint says. He says it as placidly as he can, even though he's not feeling placid about it at all.

"I'm not here to ask permission," Auden clarifies, in the sort of amused tone that says *permission, how adorable of you.* "I'm here to ask if you want to join me."

Saint flicks his eyes over to his former lover, his former king. "Auden."

"It's inevitable, St. Sebastian, and you know that as well as I do."

"I don't know that," Saint says. "I don't know that at all."

"It's not us together, stubborn boy. It's us with *her.* Surely that's allowed."

If it was truly allowed, then why hadn't they done it yet? Saint wants to ask. Because they've jumped right into everything else that's allowed—living together and eating together and arguing about books together. But this is toeing the line, and Auden knows it. Saint can tell by that autocratic bearing, that lifted chin. The insolence stamped all over his features, a testament to ancestors who took every green field and fluffy flock they wanted to take and damn the consequences.

"Can you truly tell me if brothers don't do this?" Auden asks.

It's a game they've been playing, one they've played since the day after the gala when Saint moved into the house—not into Auden's bedroom as had once been the plan, but into the bedroom next door.

Auden had walked in and looked at the haphazard heaps of clothes and things that Saint had brought from the semi, and said, in a voice so quiet and raw that Saint had nearly died, "I want to hold you right now."

Saint had croaked back, "Then hold me. Brothers hug, you know."

A week later, they'd been watching Poe and Becket stroll around the walled garden while Sir James Frazer tried to eat butterflies. "Do brothers hold hands sometimes?" Auden asked.

"Brothers hold hands," Saint decided, and they'd laced their fingers together in the sun and watched the flowers and the dog and the smitten priest and they'd said nothing, but Saint had felt the imprint of Auden's fingers and the heat of his palm for hours and hours afterward.

So many other things to learn. Did brothers share whisky glasses? Slices of cake? Did brothers sit next to each other on the couch? Hip to hip? Head on the other's shoulder? What if they'd had something to drink by that point? What if the world was floating and sweetly spinning and there was also a hand on an ankle, a knee, a thigh? Was that allowed? Did brothers do that?

And when the woman they loved came to bed already well-pleasured by the other, did brothers savor the slickness inside her, did they hunt for bites and chafes left by the other, did they imagine another set of hands, another set of firm thighs and powerful arms to surround her with? Did they sometimes whisper things into their woman's ear to pass on to the other— *make sure to bite him back, swallow him deep, show him your throat. Make him come so hard I hear it.*

Did brothers do that?

And now Auden is pushing them even further.

Saint looks at the woman shivering on the cross, her back red and angry, her panties unable to contain the full, ripe curve of her bottom. He knows if he cupped the heat between those cheeks, he'd find her wet and open. He would nudge in and she'd be tight enough to curl his toes.

"I know you want to," Auden whispers. "You could go first. I wouldn't touch."

"You'd watch though," Saint says. It's the line they haven't really stepped across yet. There's been kissing Poe in front of each other, some playful petting maybe, but actually seeing each other mate…

"Yes," Auden answers. "I'd watch."

They look at each other. They both want it. Saint knows Auden is hard—was hard from the moment he started fingering the falls of the flogger—and Saint is too hard to deny himself anything.

"Maybe brothers watch," Saint says. Hoarsely.

"And take turns."

"And take turns," Saint echoes.

"And they help."

Saint can already see it—Auden's hands playing over Poe's tits, rubbing Poe's clit, maybe even seizing Saint by the hips and helping him find just the right angle to make Poe scream.

"You don't play fair," Saint says, but he steps forward anyway, letting Auden lead him over to the cross.

Auden's voice is amused again.

"Why would I play fair?"

17

Midsummer

Becket

enturies ago, when Masses could be bought and sold for any old cause and chantries could be founded by any nobleman with a heavy purse and a healthy fear of hell, priests were often required to say Mass at least once a day, sometimes even two or three times a day. In fact, many medieval churches were built with multiple altars simply to manage the surfeit of Masses needing said.

Becket would have made a very good medieval priest.

He wouldn't mind saying Mass every day, or more, and even more so, he wouldn't mind working in a chantry, speaking prayers for the dead behind a screen of lacy, ornate stone. Perhaps he should have been a monk, so he could order his days around prayers and rites, so he could spend all of his time with God and God alone, but no, he's no monk. The sacraments mean too much to him; he is a priest through and through.

Anyway, he has his breviary, he has his daily offices, there is enough prayer to anchor him. Because while the zeal has eased, it hasn't left him and perhaps it never will, and so it's through prayer that he finds himself centered and calmed. It's through the motions, the tasks, the unyielding liturgies, that he feels his hungers and fears ease. Without these little pearls of divinity strung through his day, he'd be lost. His heart was made to live inside God's, hour by hour by hour, and if he had to leave...

No. He won't have to leave.

He doesn't try to reconcile what he's done with the exhaustive, molecular laws of the church. He knows when he confesses—which he will—that his confessor will think him in a state of grave sin. He knows that his confessor will remind him that a priest is not allowed to perform sacramental rites while his soul is apart from God. He knows the ways any other priest will see what's happened in the thorn chapel, he knows the words they'll use—sin and separation, blasphemy and lust. False gods, sacrilege, heresy. Fornication. The sin of Sodom.

Sins that cry to Heaven for vengeance.

These are all grave sins according to canon law, and yet he does not feel a gravity, he does not feel a danger. It's helped him love God more, not less, and it has made him happier and healthier and more whole.

How can that be grave? Mortal?

But still, he must confess, right? He loves this vocation, he loves this church, he even loves its fussy little rules, its centuries upon centuries of thought about what it means to lead a holy life. He may not agree with all of those thoughts, he may not agree with even half, but he does agree that these things must be thought about.

And who will change this place if not him and people like him?

The problem with confession is that he must be repented of his acts, he must plan on doing them no more, and is he truly ready for that?

Ready to say goodbye to the thorn chapel?

The others have slept late, were still stretched over guest beds and sofas when he woke to the pink glimmer of dawn outside his window. Instead of waking them, he decided to go for a run, and after that, he went to the Catholic Church only a few blocks away to pray his daily office in the sanctuary there. When he started, it was fully morning and a cluster of old ladies were praying the rosary in the front two pews.

Now he is alone, save for a lone man kneeling with his head ducked in the back.

Even though Becket is finished with his prayers, he finds he's not ready to leave. The church is a cheerful place of Romanesque arches and fake barrel vaults, recently refurbished and chilly with air conditioning. It couldn't be further away from St. Petroc's damp stone and leaded glass, and it's easier to think here. Easier to sift through what must be done.

He has to honor his ardor for God, but how? How can he give up stained glass for the broken walls of the chapel? Why should he have to make that choice?

He doesn't.

He won't.

"Excuse me," a voice says, and Becket realizes he's been so deep in his own thoughts that he didn't notice the praying man from earlier approaching him.

"Hello," Becket says.

Sunlight glows through a window, turning the man's blond hair into a jeweled halo. His features are sculpted with a stern beauty usually reserved for statues of demigods.

"I think I've been waiting for you," the man says, and then he sits down with a muscular grace. He's wearing a priest's collared shirt and black slacks, but he's also got on a dark pink cardigan, paired with a decent amount of stubble, and he looks like he's just wandered out of a locally owned coffee shop where he was reading a Russian novel or something equally sapient and pretentious.

"Waiting for me?" Becket asks, but as soon as he asks, he feels it—the brush of the man's soul against his own.

It's another soul of zeal, another heart of fire.

Becket meets the man's dark eyes and decides to ask a different question. "Why have you been waiting for me?"

"I'm here to hear your confession."

They are not in a reconciliation room or a confessional. Becket didn't come here for this, and in fact, he was thinking he wouldn't do this until later. Much later.

And he has questions—so many questions—but he is used to questions at least, he has heard the other-drums in the forest and watched his friend transform into the Thorn King. If this man says he has been waiting for Becket's confession, how can Becket say he's wrong?

Becket thinks for a moment. "I'm not sure how repentant I am," he says.

The man pulls a stole out of his cardigan pocket. It's reversible—one side white, one side purple—and it's the purple side he arranges facing up after he kisses it and puts it over his shoulders. "We do a disservice to penance by conceiving of it as a static state. I've learned from a good friend that sometimes it's a journey. Sometimes it leads to unexpected places."

"And my journey is to begin now?"

The man inclines his head but doesn't speak.

Becket looks over at him. "I don't want to make a mockery of this sacrament by pretending shame or transformation. I don't intend to change what I'm doing."

"And yet you are torn. You have two hearts where there should only be one."

Becket's lips part with surprise. "Yes."

"What sins there are, there is new life also. But one does not feed the other."

Becket moves his eyes away, to the small niche set into the wall next to him. It's filled with a carving from the Stations of the Cross: Veronica Wiping the Face of Jesus. "Then what does feed new life?" he asks.

"Choice."

Choice.

Beyond this niche, there is another Station, and then another. Jesus falling, falling again, Jesus stripped, nailed, killed. But it wasn't a journey of passivity.

It was a journey of choice.

The man's hand rests on top of Becket's. Warm, big. Again Becket feels the man's soul, clean like snow and hot like flames. "I used to feel the same as you—that there could be no confession without purity of purpose. But now I believe sometimes the feet must move for the heart to follow. And I also believe we won't make a mockery of this," the man says. "Together, we will make it holy."

It is impossible not to believe this man. It's impossible to resist his goodness, his faith. His fervent clarity. "What is your name?" Becket asks. He needs to know, he needs to have something to cling to before he wades into the thorn-edged whirlpools of his deeds.

"Jordan Brady," the priest says.

Becket smiles at him. "I'm glad you were here today, Father Brady."

Jordan nods. His hand is still on Becket's, and the weight of it is reassuring, comforting. Like being shepherded.

Becket lets himself melt into the feeling and takes a deep breath.

"Bless me, Father, for I have sinned," he says, and then he begins to speak.

18

Midsummer

Delphine

Delphine feels like she's lived entire lives in this room.

She's shackled to a leather-upholstered thing which is mostly bed, but partly bench, and studded all over with convenient bolts and eyes and hooks for binding down submissives. There're no walls as such, just the facsimile of walls made with cheap black curtains, and the ceiling is the warehouse's ceiling—so high above her that she can barely make out the metal girders holding it up.

She can't remember any noise that's not the cool snap of Rebecca's voice or the harsh buzz of the vibrator. She can't remember any smell other than the bouquet of sex and Rebecca's own scent—mossy, botanical, green.

She can't remember any other feeling than this: acute, miserable pleasure.

"Once more," Rebecca says, and Delphine strains against her bonds.

"I can't," she pants. She's already come three times, and the orgasms from that vibrator are *mean*. Mean, mean, mean. Sharp and greedy and bright.

"Oh, I think you can," Rebecca says calmly. Her braids are pulled up in a high pony, and they swish over her shoulder as she leans down to tap Delphine's open mouth. "What did you say this lipstick was called again?"

"Violet Fury," Delphine manages. "It's Fenty."

"It's slutty. I like it."

Rebecca had let Delphine pack for her, and so tonight her Mistress is dressed in an outfit much sexier than what she normally wears. Tight jeans, shiny black heels, a cropped leather jacket. When Rebecca leans over to wedge the vibrating wand against Delphine's pussy again, the sides of the jacket part and move open, revealing nothing but a lacy red bralette underneath.

Despite her calm voice and amused expression, Rebecca's body is less coy—her stomach caves and swells with quick, urgent breaths. Her dark nipples are hard and jutting against all that red lace. And in her jeans is the final thing Delphine had packed for her. Rebecca had been shocked, since Delphine has shied away from anything but Rebecca's fingers since the night of the gala, but her mistress was too tantalized by the possibility of getting to use it that she didn't question why.

Which was good, because Delphine didn't know if she could actually explain why she wanted to pack it, or why suddenly the idea of Rebecca wearing it now made her wet and squirmy instead of cold and apprehensive. It came on like spring, the easing of her anxiety; one day there was mud, cold and bare, and the next day there were daffodil shoots, tender and clean. Like the last three years of talk therapy and group sessions and the occasional anti-anxiety med had been all for tilling and planting and weeding, and now finally there was a bloom, a harvest on the horizon.

Anyway, she packed it and Rebecca pretended that she wasn't turned on by her sub asking for such a thing, and now Rebecca is wearing it tonight:

a slim pink cock tucked up against her fly. Delphine fondled it so much on the way here that the moment they parked the car, Rebecca bent Delphine over the bonnet and spanked her bottom for bad manners.

Delphine could have cried with happiness.

"I'm glad we came back tonight," Delphine says. Auden, Saint, and Poe are back at Poe's father's house, having the awkwardest "meet our girlfriend's dad" dinner of all time, and Becket went to Clinton Lake for a walk in the moonlight, leaving Delphine and Rebecca alone to their devices. It took them less than a minute to decide they wanted to go back to Orthia's, and off they'd scampered, giggling the whole drive there like teenagers sneaking off to snog.

"Me too," Rebecca says, her eyes raking over Delphine's naked frame. "Me too."

"Can I come in?" someone asks.

Rebecca eyes blaze over Delphine's body once more and then she straightens up and sighs. "Yes," she answers, and Emily Genovese saunters in, all boots and eyeliner and attitude.

"I just wanted to play the part of hostess and make sure you had everything you needed," Emily says. "And also to tell you Poe invited me to the funeral, so I'll see you tomorrow too. Fuck, your submissive is pretty."

"I know," Rebecca replies, pride and wariness in her voice.

"May I?" Emily asks, gesturing at Delphine, and it's Rebecca's turn to be the hostess. She nods once, eyes narrowed, and steps back, allowing Emily to run an appreciative hand over Delphine's tits and stomach. "Pussy too?" she inquires, asking both of them now.

Delphine surprises herself by answering, "Yes." She can feel Rebecca's surprise too. Even though she's had Rebecca's fingers inside her multiple times, it's not something she's ever expressed an interest in sharing. But something about tonight, about Emily's no-nonsense attraction to her—it just feels right.

And then when Emily slides experienced fingers into her, it feels so good that Delphine thinks she might be able to come again, even without the wand.

Emily's voice is raw with lust as she works her fingers in and out of Delphine and leans down to lick a hot stripe up the curves of Delphine's stomach. "You are very lucky," she says to Rebecca.

"I know," Rebecca answers, promptly enough, but her voice sounds strange to Delphine's ears. As if she's struggling to be polite.

Emily gives Delphine's cunt a final stroke and then a farewell sort of pat. "This is the kind of submissive I dream of having," she says. There's no mistaking the desire stamped all over her face as she looks down at Delphine on the bed. "I could play with you for years and still want more, sweetheart. You're the kind of doll a girl decides to marry."

She bends down and gives Delphine a deep, searching kiss. Delphine finds herself chasing it as Emily pulls away, that last word like a hook in her chest.

Marry.

Of course she doesn't want to marry Emily—she hardly knows her—but to have someone look at her naked body and not only want to fuck her, but marry her, keep her, love her, and display that love to the world...

She's never felt this before, this shimmering blade of possibility. These reachable, beckoning futures where she's desired and claimed.

Auden loved the girl he grew up with. Rebecca enjoys having her around for sex and companionship. But someone looking at the woman she is now and saying *mine forever*—it would be incredible. Heady. If it were even an ounce of what she's feeling now in the wake of Emily's words, it would be worth dying for.

"Pet," Rebecca says after Emily's gone. "Do you want to keep going?"

"Yes," Delphine answers.

There's a ferocious glimmer in Rebecca's eyes. Maybe she didn't like that Emily took such liberties with her? Maybe she was jealous of the kiss? But

Delphine can't really regret either thing when Rebecca bends down and gives one of Delphine's nipples a hard suck.

And when she looks up at Delphine, Delphine sees in her face the same desperation she saw all those weeks ago before the gala. A look like she's about to fly apart atom by trembling atom if she doesn't devour Delphine right now.

"Anything you want," she whispers. "Anything. You can do it to me."

Rebecca needs no further invitation, she's already mounting the bed and crawling over Delphine. Long fingers find her hair, Rebecca's jacket moves over her tits and stomach in a whisper of leather and zipper teeth, and then Rebecca settles her pelvis against Delphine's. The long ridge of her cock lines up with Delphine's sex, and she gives a soft, ragged groan.

"Pretty pet," Rebecca murmurs, kissing Delphine with quick, fierce kisses. "Spoiled kitten."

"Fuck me," Delphine blurts, and then bites her lip. It's not her place to demand things, not when they're in a scene, but it feels so good to have Rebecca there, it feels better than good. For a moment, she feels like a teenager, horny and innocent, just chasing what feels delicious.

And Rebecca's cock nudging at her pussy feels better than delicious. It feels like she's being kissed on every nerve ending. It feels like she's being turned inside out.

Rebecca meets her gaze, and Delphine sees she's too aroused to argue. "Say your safeword if it gets to be too much," she says, and then her hand drops down to her fly. One-handed, she frees the pink length and adjusts the harness so the shaft can jut out at the angle she wants.

The sight of the cock pushing through Rebecca's jeans has Delphine's toes curling. And when Rebecca fists it to drag it through Delphine's slick furrow, Delphine thinks she might die. She never thought—she didn't know—how can something that gets her so worked up have been a secret to herself? How did she not know how badly she would want this? How hard she would pant for it?

"Ready," Rebecca murmurs, and Delphine can't tell if it's a question or just Rebecca talking to herself like she does sometimes when she's really worked up, and then she starts to push in.

The pressure of it bows Delphine's back, pressing her stomach and tits to the leather-clad woman above her. Rebecca dips her head to kiss Delphine on the lips, on the soft skin between her breasts, on the pebbled flesh of her areolae, back and forth between them until Delphine is wordless, mindless, trying to spread her legs even farther apart, and failing because her ankles are still cuffed to the bed.

"That's it," Rebecca says with a smoldering look. She gives Delphine's nipple a wet, sloppy kiss, her hips starting to churn faster and faster between Delphine's thighs. "That's it, sweet kitten. Do it for me. Feel it for me."

The pressure—it's so much more than usual, so much deeper—but it's not pain, not quite. Delphine's not sure how it feels, except that every second when she thinks *ouch* is matched by a following second when she thinks *ooh*.

Rebecca reaches down to press a firm thumb against Delphine's clit. "How is it?" she whispers, smiling again as she watches Delphine's head thrash slowly from side to side. "Good?"

"Yes but—I think, oh God, I think I might need to wee—"

"You won't," Rebecca soothes. Her dick doesn't stop, her thumb doesn't stop. Everything below Delphine's navel feels strung so tight that she's almost scared she'll snap in half. "I promise."

"But—"

"Look down, pet. Look at what I'm doing to you."

She looks down. Over the swell of her stomach she can see the dick moving in and out, shining and slick. She can see how depraved this looks, her spread naked and wanton for a Mistress's taking, and she can see how much Rebecca likes it. She can see the breathless part of Rebecca's mouth, the quivering clench of the lean muscles in her belly as she thrusts. And Rebecca is fucking her so hard that one high heel falls away from her foot and clatters to the ground, and she keeps going, keeps fucking with that relentless, insatiable cock.

And her eyes…Delphine doesn't think she's ever seen eyes like this. Dark as onyx in the low club light, molten as they pore over her. Those eyes are promising so much right now, and Delphine lets herself imagine those promises are real as the pressure between her legs resolves into a rolling, thundering tide and sweeps her out to sea.

"Sweet kitten," Rebecca says hoarsely, watching Delphine whimper and arch against the advancing pleasure. "Just let it happen. Let it, let it—"

The pleasure breaks, and Delphine's scream reverberates up to the girders. It takes hold of her—cunt, thighs, belly—pulling everything into its toothy, delirious grip and shaking her in it, like a cat with a toy. She feels at its mercy, she has no choice but to succumb to the sharpness of it and the strength of it, and she thinks she could laugh with joy even as she's still screaming like she's being mauled alive.

Rebecca doesn't let up, she ruts into Delphine until Delphine sinks back into the bed, limp and dizzy, her temples wet with tears she didn't even realize she'd cried.

"There, there, darling pet," Rebecca's murmuring to her, kissing the tears away. There's some hurried wriggling—Rebecca's pulling her jeans down past her backside, down to her knees, and Delphine thinks of horny teenagers again, so desperate to fuck they do it in the backseats of cars, in night-shadowed parks, and behind school buildings. And indeed, Rebecca is desperate now—she unfastens the harness until it's slipped down to her knees and then fumbles with the dildo until it's free of its moorings. Still wet with Delphine, the dildo slides into Rebecca easily and she holds it in place with her left hand as her right finds her clit and strokes.

It takes less than a minute. A laughing shiver moves through her, and she rides the toy as eagerly as she rode Delphine just a second ago, the leather of her jacket creaking and her thighs tensing and her breath coming in short, happy pants.

Seeing Rebecca come is better than anything. Better than Prosecco, better than a new tube of lipstick still perfectly curved and pointed, better than a good bra, a swimsuit that fits, waking up with good light and clear skin. It's better even than coming herself.

Spent and breathless, Rebecca falls to her side next to Delphine and slowly pulls the toy free.

Delphine can't help but enjoy the moment. Rebecca so rarely cuddles, and even when it does happen, it's usually when she thinks Delphine is asleep.

"That was proper good," Rebecca says, kissing Delphine's shoulder. Her hand rests on Delphine's belly and it's still wet from her climax.

"Brilliant," Delphine agrees. Rebecca kisses her shoulder again, and then nuzzles her neck, and Delphine thinks she couldn't be happier, that life couldn't be better.

"You could do this more, you know," Delphine says without thinking.

"Fuck you with my dick? Yes, please."

"No," Delphine laughs. "The snuggling. The nuzzling. I like being nuzzled."

Rebecca sits up with a sigh, bending over her lap to work the toy cock out of its harness. "I'm not that person, Delph. You know that."

Auden was.

Emily might be.

The disloyal thoughts rip through her so fast she can't stop them. She blinks up at the ceiling. "Do you think—could you be that person?"

Rebecca's silence stretches into eternity, and then she asks, carefully, "Do you want me to be?"

Delphine doesn't know. She wants her to be Rebecca, no one else. She also doesn't know how much longer she can love someone who doesn't love her back.

Toy cock freed, Rebecca stands up and zips up her jeans. She sticks the toy in her back pocket while she sets to work freeing Delphine's wrists and ankles from the cuffs. She looks like a rebel from the 1950s—jeans, leather jacket, moody scowl—but instead of a comb in her back pocket, she has a dildo. A random, demented part of Delphine's brain thinks it would make a hilarious Instagram story.

"I'm not asking you to love me," Delphine finally says, after she's completely freed. Rebecca hands her a glass bottle of water and then retreats to the corner, where she sits on a spanking bench and puts the fallen shoe back on her foot. At the word *love*, she lifts her head, like a deer scenting a wolf.

"Delph…"

"I just—I don't want to be the fat girl you boff and then nothing else. Sometimes I'm scared that I'm like a novelty for you, just another kind of girl on the checklist, and that you're already sick of me, and I know even just saying this out loud is going to upset you, but I can't help it. I have to know—could you ever love me?"

Rebecca's eyes are no longer hot. They are cold. So very cold.

"This is the scene talking," she says, standing up. "Hormones. You'll feel better in an hour or so."

"Don't patronize me."

"Delph, *enough.*"

Delphine stands up too and ducks quickly for her clothes before Rebecca can see her face. She doesn't want Rebecca to see her cry. Not *these* kinds of tears at least, the unsexy kind.

Rebecca seems to realize that her tone was too sharp and walks over to her submissive. "Pet, look—"

"It's fine," Delphine says. Her hair is a curtain around her face as she scoops her things off the floor. She reminds herself that she chose this with her eyes wide open. She chose the woman who used to have a new submissive every night.

She wanted to be easy, right? Why can't she just be easy?

Be easy.

"It's fine," Delphine says again, keeping her voice lifted and as cheery as she can. She straightens up and tries for a smile. "We should probably get back to the house though. The funeral is so early in the morning."

Rebecca takes a step toward her. Stops. "Do you—do you want help getting dressed?"

"Actually," Delphine says, her throat already clenching shut and her eyes burning. *Be easy, be easy.* "Maybe you could ask Emily what we need to do to clean up? Just to hasten our exit?"

Rebecca is a good Domme, and so Delphine can tell she's reluctant to leave. But she's too polite—and maybe too relieved—to fight Delphine on this. With a nod, she pulls the curtain aside and steps outside their stall. And the minute she leaves, Delphine sinks down to the floor and cries, alone and as silently as she possibly can.

19

Midsummer

Rebecca

She's not really paying attention to the funeral until her dad walks in.

Until that moment, it's a standard Catholic service as far as she can make out. Lots of white people standing in silence, sitting in silence, kneeling in silence, lots of droning hymns and restrained chants. But the priest keeps it moving at a steady clip—enough so that Rebecca imagines they'll be done in under an hour—and there is no collection plate passed around, so the situation is mostly bearable. The worst part is how much she wants to touch Delphine, how much she needs to, and can't. She doesn't care one jot about offending the priest; she spent enough weeks in Accra being dragged to church and listening to preachers rail against homosexuality before going home to their extramarital mistresses that she's lost all fucks to give when it comes to protecting the sensibilities of holy men.

But she doesn't know this place, and if she doesn't know it, she can't be sure Delphine will be safe. And that, more than her own safety, keeps her hands cautiously wrapped around the hymnal, even as they itch to find Delphine and pull her close.

It's after Proserpina gets to the lectern and begins reading, that Rebecca hears the door to the sanctuary open, in the quiet way of someone trying to sneak in unnoticed. And they would have gone unnoticed too, but Proserpina pauses in her reading of Psalm 121—

I lift my eyes to the hills…

From where will my help come?—

And then looks over at Rebecca, eyes wide. Rebecca turns and looks over her shoulder herself, and her hands go loose around the hymnal.

Samson Quartey is here. In Kansas.

And she knows, beyond a shadow of a doubt, that it has nothing to do with her.

The potluck after the service is subdued and soulless. There's not much Rebecca misses about Ghanaian church, but she finds she misses the funerals. The wailers, the extravagant coffins, the drinking—there's something visceral about it, like it turns grief into something that can be seen and heard and tasted. But there's no taste to this, no sound.

The grief here is wet cement. It sits heavy in the room, it pulls at everyone's shoes, and they all do their best to walk around it, to pretend it's not there. No one says Adelina's name. No one is raising toasts to her, crying for her. In fact, Poe and her father are doing their very best *not* to cry, their very best to keep a polite, unemotional facade.

Unemotional! At a *funeral.*

Rebecca is the least emotional person in the world, and even she knows a funeral is a time for feelings.

"Why are you making a face?" Saint asks, tipping a bottle of beer to his lips. He's the only one drinking except for Poe, who mutely accepted a glass of whisky Auden had sourced from somewhere, and Delphine, who is chatting with Becket and Emily Genovese near the door. The way Emily keeps looking at Delphine—like Delphine is her future ex-wife—is also making Rebecca feel very sour.

Rebecca immediately stops making the face. "I'm not making a face."

"You were," Saint says. "But it was a subtle one. I think only your friends would be able to tell, and maybe your dad."

Her dad. Here.

Jesus *Lord*, as her mother would say.

"I didn't know he was going to come."

"He and David Markham seem friendly."

She looks over at her supposed friend. "I'm only just starting to like you. Tread lightly."

His eyes smile at that, even if his mouth doesn't quite. He's wearing a slightly nicer pair of jeans and a black button-up shirt undoubtedly borrowed from Auden. Same boots as usual. "I think it's nice."

Rebecca looks across the room, to where her father and David stand talking in low voices to one another. They haven't done anything remotely inappropriate in the context of the funeral—no embrace, no hands touching, nothing except for long looks and exclusive conversation—but it's written all over them. It was written on David's face when the funeral ended and he finally turned to see Samson there. Twelve years of longing. A love that didn't die, even when the people around it did.

Is that nice?

She doesn't actually know the answer. Because seeing her dad's eyes bright and animated for David Markham…seeing the way his body is angled toward him, the way he keeps shoving his hand in his suit pocket, as if he has to keep himself from reaching for his former lover…

It should be nice, it should be sweet.

Instead, Rebecca is remembering every hard thing there is to remember about her parents' marriage, about her father, about her mother, about being a bisexual teenager locked in a flat with an unfeeling parent who never made her feel good enough.

Instead, she feels bitter.

Why does he get to be in love? After all these years of treating love like an invasive species. A tulip tree with branches covered in beautiful lies?

Her phone buzzes in the pocket of her black jumpsuit, and she pulls it out and sighs at the screen.

"Your mother again?" Saint asks. Her mother has been calling since last night.

Rebecca lets it go to voicemail, as she has for the last twelve hours, and nods. Then grabs Saint's beer from him and takes a drink. "They're still married, you know," Rebecca says and passes the beer back. "They've lived apart since I was eight, and yet…I don't know."

Saint isn't like Poe—he doesn't push for answers, not really. He just dips his chin in acknowledgement. And for some reason, it makes Rebecca open up more.

"It's not common back home. Divorce. It *can* happen, it can be done, and if Daddy ever hit Ma, Ma's family would be the first to help her pack up her things—but divorce for the reason of not loving each other anymore? For not being compatible? Even for infidelity on the husband's part? It's rare. There'd be fallout. She'd have to deal with the whispers, and the faces—"

"The faces?" Saint asks.

"The *faces*," Rebecca emphasizes. "The faces they'll make when she goes to visit his family, and she *will* have to keep visiting his family. The faces her own family might make—the aunties especially, they will have all the faces whenever she walks into a room. And it will be like that for years."

"Why doesn't she just move, then? Move away? To London, to be near you?" Saint asks.

"She could," Rebecca says. Rebecca actually would, in her mother's shoes, because nothing is worth sacrificing emotional independence for, not even family. "But she'd be leaving behind her entire family. All her friends.

Her church. Everything that gives her meaning, except for me, is in Accra. And my father doesn't just take care of her—he takes care of her mother and her mother's sisters and one of my aunties—they all depend on him, and always will. If they got a divorce, life would look a lot harder for more people than just her."

Saint nods again.

"So they're still married. And I thought—well, my dad has never made a fool of her, you see, even when it would have been easy to, with him in London and her at home. So I thought that was the status quo. I thought the Quartey family would always look the way it did when I was growing up, with the three of us politely pretending everything was okay."

"And now your father isn't pretending anymore," Saint says.

Her throat goes tight—a sudden, abrupt cinch that feels dangerously like she might start crying if she says something. And so she doesn't say anything.

"Come on," Saint says, standing up and offering his hand. "Let's beat the rush and go back to the Markhams' house now. They've got better booze there, at least."

She looks up and sees Emily Genovese toying with one of Delphine's big, blond curls. Delphine is letting her. And then her phone rings again.

She silences it with an irate squeeze. She takes Saint's hand. "Let's go."

If Rebecca sat down and imagined a professor's house, it would look like David Markham's. The rooms are lined with built-in shelves, so overcrowded with books that they sag, and—with no regard for safety—even the old, green-tiled fireplace is surrounded by books. Stacks on the mantel, stacks around the hearth.

The dusty remnants of Adelina's life as an archaeologist are scattered at intervals throughout—pottery sherds, arrowheads, coins—the kind of stuff one can keep because it's too unremarkable for proper study. And on the coffee table and kitchen counter and kitchen table—stacks of papers to grade, like David had taken a clump of papers to work through and then abandoned them halfway through the project.

The windows are edged with geometric stained glass, there's a set of wide, creaky stairs, and antique light fixtures that predate the world wars. And of course, there are the dogs. Three big ones haunting the kitchen like fuzzy, overheated ghosts, sleeping on their sides and panting on the kitchen tile, even with the air conditioner roaring full blast. They follow one breathlessly for caresses and pats, they insist on sharing the sofas with humans, they shed everywhere. An automatic vacuum occasionally ventures out to suck up the fur, but there's too much and the floors are too crowded with stacks of books and reams of photocopies for anything to be cleaned with any degree of efficiency.

Almost nothing about the place appeals to Rebecca, except the back garden—*yard,* as Saint corrects her, stretching out the *ARRRR* like a pirate —which is filled with soft summer grass and two big oaks, old and shady and perfect for climbing. It's the kind of outdoor space she's seen in movies or on telly, perfect for an all-American barbecue, ready and waiting for the quintessential all-American family. It was the kind of back garden she used to dream of as a girl. Like if only they had a place like *that,* they would be the perfect family there. They would smile at each other and grill burgers and sleep in the same house after they ate.

She would have traded their expensive city lofts in the U.K. and Ghana both for those two trees and that hail-battered barbecue grill.

Since Saint and Rebecca arrived at the house, more people have followed, and now she's sitting alone on the back deck, watching the warm wind blow through the leaves while guests talk and eat around her. The mood has eased a bit since the church—there's more talking and drinking now, at least—but Rebecca's mood hasn't eased in the least. She's very aware of her father sitting next to David, their heads bent together.

Rebecca is also very aware of Emily Genovese flirting with Rebecca's own submissive in front of her own eyes, fetching her drinks and hovering near her elbow while they talk to Poe and Auden and Saint. She's not sure what to do about this, because her impulse is to haul Delphine off and do something depraved, but she feels vaguely certain it's not good funeral etiquette to do such a thing.

"Rebecca," her father says. He's come up to her without her noticing. Rebecca has a thousand things she'd like to say to him. She's aware that nine hundred and ninety-nine of them are unfair, and so she takes a drink instead of speaking at all.

He sighs, sitting on the patio chair next to her, and says in Ga, "You are angry with me."

"I'm not. You have every right to come to your friend's funeral."

"That's right, I do," he says, a touch coolly. "But we both know that's not what you're angry about."

She's not going to do this. She's not going to do this.

"Rebecca," Daddy says, and this time, the coolness is real. This is his *you're disappointing me* voice. This is his *these marks are not good enough, you're not putting in the hours* voice. And something inside of her breaks— maybe it had started breaking last night with Delphine, maybe it started when she talked on the phone with her mother. Maybe it had started two decades ago, as Tea Set Barbie worshipped Red Dress Barbie to the soundtrack of her parents yelling at each other.

Rebecca turns to him and she doesn't care that her eyes are wet and her voice is strange. "You're here for him."

Her father doesn't answer, which of course, is its own answer.

She swallows the rest of her drink and stands up. If she doesn't, she'll scream at him. She'll say *where was this queer father when his queer daughter was alone and afraid?* She'll say *how come you can be brave for yourself now, but not for me then?*

"Ma's been calling," is what she does say. "You should call her back. She misses you." She starts to step away.

"I offered your mother a divorce," her father says.

She stops walking. "What?"

When he speaks now, his words are a mix of English and Ga, moving back and forth between both. "Yesterday, after I decided to be here for David. I called and told her I was going to see him again, and I offered her a divorce."

A divorce. All those missed calls on the phone—Rebecca knows why they're there now. She thinks through what else he said. "Wait—see him *again*? She already knew about you two?"

Her father nods, that frown still on his mouth. He's still handsome with it, he's the kind of handsome that looks better stern or sad. There'd never been a shortage of men or women in London pining for him—even clients at the Workshop, even employees—but he's never indulged even one. Rebecca thought it was for her own sake, or her mother's, but now she wonders if it was for the memory of David Markham alone.

"That summer at Thornchapel—I took one look at him and I knew. I called your mother and told her everything, and I also offered her a divorce, just as I have now. She said no then."

"And now?"

Her father sighs. "She's thinking about it. I would give her a very healthy alimony. She could support Ima and the aunties still. She would stay comfortable."

Rebecca doesn't respond.

"It's past time. You know it. I know it. She knows it too, even if she's worried about other things."

"You've always been unhappy together," Rebecca says finally. "I know that."

"I was her last choice. Did I ever tell you that?"

Rebecca pauses. Shakes her head.

There's a relaxing to his mouth now, as if he's thinking of the past with some hard-earned fondness, nostalgia for the silly simplicities of youth. "She had so many beaux. She was the name on everyone's lips, the girl every mother was trying to matchmake her son to. I was just an apprentice architect, fresh out of school and from a family that wasn't quite good enough."

Rebecca has never heard this. In fact, she realizes, she knows nothing of her parents' marriage at all, save for the misery and the strain. "So how did you end up married?"

Her father sighs. "The boy she really loved married her best friend instead, around the same time I found a job in London. I think it was London more than me she wanted then—the escape from all the gossip and prying eyes—but I didn't care. I'd take her any way I could get her. I did love her then, you understand, even though she never loved me."

"She loves you," Rebecca murmurs. "She wouldn't act the way she does if she didn't. She asks after you all the time. She misses you."

Samson Quartey shakes his head. "She thinks she needs me. That's different than love."

Rebecca's eyes slide to Delphine, who is a living ray of sunshine on the deck, currently telling everyone a hilarious story about Auden falling in the River Cam at a party.

Is that what's happening with Delphine? Is Delphine her own Tea Set Barbie? She needs the feeling of worshipfulness and awe that a good Mistress can provide?

Rebecca's father keeps talking, drawing her attention back to him. "I know I was not the best father when you came out to me. I didn't have...You have to understand, when I was your age, it was not possible for me to do what you did. I didn't come out to my parents when I realized I liked men too; I hid it from them, and even from myself, for many years. I had no idea how to act when you told me, how to talk to you about it, because so few in my generation do. But I want you to know—if I've never told you, which I realize I haven't—I'm proud of you. So, so proud."

Rebecca stares down at him, her blood feeling hot and cold all at once. "What?"

He meets her gaze. Steadily. Lovingly. "I'm proud of you. You are not only brilliant, but you are brave. You chose a person to love, and you're telling the world about her. It's what I should have done long ago, and now instead, I've wasted years I didn't have."

"You're proud of me?" she whispers.

He stands up. And for the first time in years, he folds her into his arms and holds her to his chest. Braids cover her face, her cup is crushed into his ribs, but she stays there, bewildered and tense, like a captured bird.

"I am proud," he tells her. "And sorry. More sorry than you'll ever know. But I am learning from you. It's because of you and Freddie and Daisy's daughter that I decided to come here. That I decided to do the right thing by your mother and myself. Life's too short not to love who we love." He pulls away and touches her cheek, the way he used to do when she was little and he'd make her find the horizon. "You taught me that, you know. You gave that to me."

And with a kiss on her forehead, he leaves to go find David Markham, leaves her alone there with an empty cup and an aching chest.

You chose a person to love.

He's wrong about that part. Delphine doesn't love her, she loves the kink, and Rebecca is wise enough not to conflate the two.

And anyway, Rebecca would know if *she* loved *Delphine*, right? She would feel it, it would be apparent to her. She sees how Becket looks at Poe—like Poe is running around with half his internal organs and only just now told him—and she knows she doesn't look at Delphine like that. She knows that even though she wants to drag Delphine away from Emily Genovese and make love to her in a dark corner until she's limp and purring—she knows that even though she can barely breathe when Delphine isn't near her—she knows that even though Delphine makes her frantic, feral, vulnerable, unspooled—that's not love. It's nothing like love.

It can't be love, because she doesn't do that.

It's lust, is all. Possession. Good kink.

But, Rebecca thinks, straightening her shoulders and heading for the other side of the deck, Delphine belongs to *her*. And she's not a novelty, she's not something that Rebecca will ever, *ever* get sick of, and the sooner she understands that, the better off that pretty, easily welted bottom will be.

"Excuse me," Rebecca cuts in smoothly to the group, smiling at Emily Genovese as she puts a hand on the back of her submissive's neck. And without another word, she guides Delphine away from the post-funeral chatter and to the upstairs guest room, where she fucks Delphine in her cute plum funeral dress until Delphine's cries are hoarse and Rebecca feels in control again.

She collapses onto the bed next to Delphine and gathers her happy, loose-limbed slut close, petting her and kissing her.

She'll have to go back down soon. She'll have to face her father and David Markham again, and she'll have to call her mother back, finally. But she has her Delphine, and her father said he was proud of her, and for the first time in a very long time, her mouth stays curved in a smile after the sex is over.

And she can honestly tell Ma she went to church today.

In the words of her mother, *praise the Lord.*

20

Midsummer

Auden

"Is it strange that we're both sitting here with you, when it was our father who very probably killed your mother?" Auden's voice breaks into the hot summer air, joining the lapping of the lake and the unending whirr of the cicadas.

In front of them, Becket and Rebecca are arguing about the best way to start a fire with the limited resources they have. Delphine is standing over them, interjecting with things she's finding on Google with her phone. On the lake, the sinking sun has painted a path of orangey-pink arrowing east to the hills.

He turns to look at Poe, who's staring at him with some surprise. Her mouth is parted, showing off the tempting crease in her full lower lip, and without thinking, Auden reaches up to press against it with his thumb. His crease. His lip. His Poe.

"I'm sorry if that's a cruel thing to ask," he says. "But I can't stop thinking about it. If our father had never met your mother, you wouldn't have gone to her funeral today. And now here you are with not just one but two of his sons. In your place, I don't think I could endure it. I don't think I could forgive me or St. Sebastian for bearing the blood of Ralph Guest."

Poe looks down, long lashes sweeping over her heat-flushed cheeks. "I've been thinking about it too."

St. Sebastian shifts on the other side of her. They're all sitting on a blanket spread over the ground, coolbox packed full of drinks and food nearby, their shoes kicked off and their naked feet in the grass. They're here because, as the evening wore on and the Markhams' funeral guests trickled away, it became increasingly apparent that Samson and David needed to talk privately. Proserpina suggested they go to a spot she knew on the nearby lake and watch the midsummer sun set, and Rebecca quickly seconded with palpable relief.

"For what it's worth—" Auden starts, but Proserpina holds up her hand.

"Don't say you're sorry."

"But I am, Proserpina. So fucking sorry."

A breeze kicks up and sends the hair not tucked into the knot at her neck flying around her face.

"Me too," St. Sebastian adds softly, and she sighs.

"It's not your fault. And no—stop. I'm not just saying that. It's actually not your fault. Any more than it was Becket's for having been there for part of it. I don't blame any of you."

She looks out over the lake. Nearby, Becket finally gets the fire going, and Delphine whoops.

"If my mother and your father hadn't met, then *we* wouldn't have met. And I keep thinking—how could her tragedy have been my happiness? Her end, my beginning?"

No one has a response to that, save for the cicadas, who seem to have a response to everything.

"It's a question for Becket," Auden says.

"Or it's a question without an answer," she says.

"Or that."

Becket calls out that he's going to follow the overgrown trail to see where it will lead, and Delphine and Rebecca spread out their blanket on the other side of the fire. Trees, thrumming with the cicadas' chirr, surround them on all sides except for the east, where the lake ruffles under the last of the sun.

They're in a spot Poe says almost no one uses, and they're utterly alone—no people, or cars, or boats anywhere. It's almost like Thornchapel in a way, and Auden finds himself grateful for tonight. Just to be alone with his friends. With his little bride and his St. Sebastian.

Proserpina takes in a deep breath, and Auden can almost imagine the trees and lake breathing with her, inhaling and expanding and reaching, and then she lets the breath go, and the world sighs with her.

Auden knows that breath, because he's breathed it himself both at Thornchapel and in the graveyard of St. Brigid's.

It's a breath of resignation. It's a breath for all the breaths her mother can no longer take. It's a breath at the beginning of a new life she'll have to start again and again, each time she remembers, each time she forgets. She's been practicing it for twelve years, and that's why Auden trusts the look in her eyes when she puts her hand over his and tilts her head at Saint.

"Are you sure?" he murmurs. They talked about what they would do tonight—they talked about it before they left England, actually—but Auden knows how depleting a funeral can be, and anyway, the plan had been to be in her room, with walls and a door. Not in the warm open air.

But he can also read the restlessness building in her, he can see her need for something distracting and Saturnalian and vital. She's itching for something he can give, and he was born to give her everything.

"I'm sure," she says firmly, and that's that.

"St. Sebastian, we have something for you," Auden says, leaning forward to look at his half-brother.

St. Sebastian looks confused. "Something for me?"

"It's your birthday today," Poe reminds him softly. "We didn't forget, you know."

St. Sebastian looks like he's not sure what to say or do—which is fine, because Auden is sure enough for all of them. Auden gets up from where he's seated and takes the few steps over to St. Sebastian, so that he's standing right behind where he sits. On the other side of the fire, Delphine and Rebecca are already amorously occupied, and so Auden feels no compunctions about what comes next.

"Lie down," Auden tells him. "On your back."

St. Sebastian pulls his lip piercing into his mouth, looking uncertain. "Auden...I—"

"Lie. *Down.*" Auden uses the voice he's so careful not to use with Saint anymore. The voice that he used on Beltane. The voice he used that summer.

When he uses it, he expects to be obeyed—but if he's not, he'll happily fight St. Sebastian into submission. He'll happily wrestle him down to the blanket and pin him there. *Happily.*

But St. Sebastian obeys. A flush dusts his cheekbones as he releases his piercing from his teeth and slowly lays himself back so that he's completely supine. When he's done, his T-shirt has pulled up from the belted waistband of his jeans just enough to reveal a sliver of stomach. Light bronze and firm, with a narrow trail of hair leading down from his navel.

Auden's mouth actually waters at the sight of it. *Waters.* Like he's seeing a meal he's been kept away from for months and months and years. He would pay all the money he has, sell off every asset he owns, just to bite that stomach right now.

No. Think of the gallery. The gallery with its fake Maeshowe tomb made of grain. The gallery where he held a sobbing St. Sebastian in his arms—

where Auden made St. Sebastian sob because he had been selfish and needy. Because he had been a bad Dom and a bad lover. A bad brother.

Never again, Auden had vowed as he held St. Sebastian's shuddering frame. *Never again*. He would die first. Die before he made Saint cry like that again.

St. Sebastian had been martyr enough for a thousand lifetimes, and now it was Auden's turn.

However, that didn't mean Auden's hunger had abated. No, no, not at all. Not the hunger, nor the possessiveness, nor the love. All of it seemed to grow and grow, fed by its own starvation, until Auden's blood felt like it was made from molten metal and his bones from sharpened swords. Walking hurt, working hurt, *existing* hurt when St. Sebastian wasn't completely his.

So he's been cheating. A little.

It was Poe's idea at first. After he confessed all this to her, kneeling at her feet as he sometimes did, and letting her be the priestess to his king, she reminded him that she and Emily had been kinky and in love for eighteen months without having sex.

There are ways you can still care for him, she said. *Little ways he can still be yours.*

So Auden had St. Sebastian's car serviced, and the render on the front of his mother's house repaired. He refilled St. Sebastian's drinks when they sat in the library, he told Saint to go to bed when it was time, he drove him to the library when he was at Thornchapel and picked him up when his shift ended. He bought Saint's plane ticket to America and then savored his sullen protests for no other reason than it gave him an excuse to use *that* voice and then see St. Sebastian's flushed response to it.

And sometimes, when he was very, very bad—when he felt like his bones would cut right through his flesh with wanting this man so much—he would do worse. He would make St. Sebastian get drinks for *him*, he would stretch out his legs on the sofa so that Saint would have no choice but to sit on the floor beneath him. He would make Saint wait for him when they needed to go someplace—five minutes, ten minutes, once even a full half an hour—and then he would finally show up, insouciant and drawling, cock throbbing at St. Sebastian's flashing eyes and angry pout. Because of course St. Sebastian waited for him anyway.

Of course he sat on the floor and fetched Auden his drinks.

Of course he had to pretend it didn't make him hard too.

It's a dangerous game to play, Auden knows that. He wants this to be forever—he needs this to be forever—and so he has to keep St. Sebastian safe from the worst of his needs. From the worst of *both* their needs. But surely these little nibbles and licks of dominance are okay? Surely what he's about to do next won't hurt anyone? Surely it will be a little relief valve for both of them, a way to blunt the teeth of their cravings for a little while?

It's just an innocent little birthday gift, that's all. Nothing like what they did in the gallery.

Auden deliberately, unhurriedly, steps to St. Sebastian's side. And he just as deliberately, just as unhurriedly, lifts his bare foot and then rests it on St. Sebastian's chest.

St. Sebastian goes totally still. Auden can't even feel him breathe under his foot.

"I thought," Auden says, "Proserpina might want a little help giving you your birthday present."

This isn't actually Poe's present to Saint—that is back at her father's house, a signed first edition of a fantasy novel he loves—nor is it actually his, but that's apart from the point. The point is how St. Sebastian's ribs judder and shake as he finally manages to drag in a breath. The point is the swelling ridge behind St. Sebastian's zipper.

Poe herself crawls between Saint's legs and perches there on her knees, a small smile on her lips. "I did want some help," she says. "I thought I could make you come harder if Auden held you down while I sucked you."

The noise St. Sebastian makes then—like death would be easier to endure. Now Auden is smiling too.

He presses the ball of his foot even harder against Saint's chest. Not hard enough to bruise or even really to hurt, but hard enough that he can feel the firm resistance of his pectoral muscle. The bones underneath.

"We did agree," Auden says, looking down at the boy trapped beneath his foot, "that you should get to pick where you come, because it is your birthday and all. You can of course make use of Poe's mouth, but you could also make use of her cunt, isn't that right, little bride? Why don't you show him his options?"

Poe shows him. She spreads her knees apart and lifts the hem of her dress—a different dress than she wore to the service today. It's a white sundress with little daisies printed on it that falls past her knees when she's standing, the picture of summer sweetness, which makes it all the sluttier when she pulls the skirt up to her hips to reveal the naked pussy underneath. She's groomed herself completely bare, and so there's no hiding her soft lips, her clit, where she splits open to show a beckoning shadow, dark pink and dewy.

She also opens her mouth—wet tongue, plush lips, all of it waiting to be used—and Auden has a dizzy moment when he can't believe this is real. That she is his, and his in the way he felt ashamed of needing for so long.

St. Sebastian lifts his head to stare at her, his chest seizing fast and urgent under Auden's foot. "Fuck," he groans, head falling back. "Both. Both *please.*"

Poe gives Auden a look, which Auden returns as smugly as possible. They'd taken bets earlier on what Saint would choose and Poe thought he'd only want a blowjob. Auden knew better. Poe's body inspires desperation, it calls to gluttony; a person looks at her and needs to do everything, taste everything, feel everything. Of course, St. Sebastian would pick both.

"Start with your mouth," Auden tells her. "Go slow."

St. Sebastian's eyes are dark mirrors reflecting back the sunset as Poe unbuckles him, unzips him, and finally exposes his erection. He rolls under

Auden's foot, hissing a little as Poe gives him a long, hot stripe with her tongue.

His eyes search Auden's face, and he doesn't have to ask the question out loud for Auden to know what it is.

Do brothers do this?

Auden nods at him.

Saint's eyes flutter closed as Proserpina takes him into her mouth. The foot on his chest keeps him from arching, but his hands reach down for her, and Auden can't have that. He kneels down, easy and fast, and pins St. Sebastian's wandering hands up by his head.

He also rests a knee on Saint's chest while he's down there—not strictly necessary to keep him pinned at this point, but still fun.

Saint blinks up at him—trapped, flushed, beautiful. "You're holding me down," he says, a little dazedly.

"Does it feel good?" Auden asks.

"What do you think?" Saint mutters, but there's no venom to it. His eyes drop to the front of Auden's shorts. "Does it feel good for you?"

Auden raises an eyebrow. His own erection could probably be seen across the lake at this point. "What do you think?"

Saint rolls his eyes but nearly smiles.

Auden shifts a little so he can watch Poe between his half-brother's legs. Her dress is pooled around her in a way that seems fresh and prim and a little princess-y, but there's nothing prim about her mouth right now. No, that mouth is all wickedness, licking up and down St. Sebastian's stiffened cock, sucking it into her mouth, trailing soft kisses around the base and the curves of his testicles.

Auden's own cock aches and aches and aches. Already he can feel arousal beading at the tip, begging to be licked off too. And it's not only at the sight—which is beyond erotic—but the knowledge that it's happening at *his* command. That pink tongue, the naked pussy underneath the innocent dress. The body currently roiling in agonized pleasure underneath him.

"Your cunt now," says Auden. "Make it fast."

Poe scrambles to obey, getting to her knees and then straddling Saint's hips. Her daisy-patterned skirt is everywhere, blowing in the breeze against Auden's knee and waving around her thighs, and she has to use one hand to hold the excess fabric against her hip as her other hand takes St. Sebastian and guides him to her opening.

Wet. She's so wet that they can hear it the moment Saint's tip glides against her. And when she positions him just right, angles him just so, they hear it as Saint enters her.

Saint strains underneath Auden, and Poe moans, slumping forward and bracing her hands on Saint's stomach.

Auden growls. He needs to fuck, the need for it is clawing inside him, but no—no, he needs this more. The beautiful boy writhing and panting under his knee. The beautiful girl arching and shivering next to him.

He moves his hands, one to St. Sebastian's throat and the other to the knot at the nape of Poe's neck, so he has both of them, he's gripping both of them, he's guiding and restraining and *making* both of them. And he feels when they both reach their peak, when they both go trembling, reaching, shivering, tumbling over together under his touch.

He could come like this. Just like this. Just with his knee on Saint's chest and his hand full of Poe's hair.

He doesn't though. As much as he wants to, he wants this more. He wants this moment more. Their bliss he savors as if it were his. He drinks in Poe's soft cries and Saint's tortured gasps, their joyous torment under the midsummer sky. He feels it thrumming along his skin like it's his own pleasure, his own release, even as his dick impatiently reminds him that it isn't.

Auden makes sure they're both finished before he carefully eases off St. Sebastian and lets go of them both. They are limp and sweat-misted; he is tense and tight and he can feel his pulse in his cock, it's that swollen and ready, but his chest is loose and light and happy. He can feel the happiness around his eyes and mouth.

"You're still hard," St. Sebastian says, rolling onto his side to prop up on an elbow.

"This was a birthday present for you," Auden says, "not me."

St. Sebastian seems to think about this for a moment. "What if, for my birthday, I want to see you come?"

"On my tits?" Poe adds eagerly, climbing between them and laying on her back. Before Auden can even truly digest what's happening, she's untied the halter of her dress and tugged the bodice down, exposing her breasts, which are pale and soft and generous, tipped with tight, rosy nipples, and dotted with fading bite marks.

His bite marks.

Fuck.

This wasn't the plan, this was never the plan, but Auden suddenly can't bring himself to care about the plan, not when Poe's pressing her tits together like that, not when Saint is dipping his head to kiss the crescent-shaped imprints of Auden's teeth all along the undersides.

He's more aroused than even he knew, because his hands are shaking too much to open the button of his shorts, and he keeps fumbling with it and fumbling, fumbling, until Saint reaches up and opens it for him, his warm fingers brushing along the skin of Auden's stomach as he does. Auden can't breathe as Saint pulls down his zipper too, working his shorts open until there's nothing between Auden's cock and the open air save for his boxer briefs.

"You have to do it," Saint whispers. "I can't—I shouldn't—"

Because brothers don't. Brothers don't do what Auden wants St. Sebastian to do right now, and that's reach past the elastic waistband and draw out his cock for him.

Damn their father to hell for his lies.

Auden tugs the waistband of his boxer briefs down himself and fists his shaft, looking down at Poe. Her fuckable mouth, her sexy tits. All of her so brilliant and beautiful and more precious to him than his own life, and he loves her so much, he loves Saint so much, he wishes they knew, he wishes he could properly explain it to them. He wishes they could understand that when he bites, when he bruises, when he is cruel, it's only because he's given them his own heart for biting and bruising, it's only because his life is completely theirs already, to stomp on and macerate. It's a kind of homeostasis, a kind of loop—they own him, so he gets to own them in return. They hold his spirit, and so he can hold their bodies.

His wild and thorny heart beats for them and them alone.

"You both are my life," he tells them, because there should be no secrets tonight. "My entire life."

It takes nothing—two strokes, maybe less—and the orgasm roars through him, barreling up his length and erupting past his fist to spatter Poe in white ropes of seed. It feels yanked from the very soles of his feet, from the deepest pits of him, every drop of his essence offered up as proof of his need for them, unending, unbearable, unbelievably good and agonizing all at once. It goes on, pulse after pulse, until Poe's breasts are liberally striped with his cum, like he's double-marked the territory he's already marked with bites, and then some, because there's semen on her upper belly and along her cheek and mouth as well.

"Fuck," he whispers, as his organ gives a final throb and gives up one last pearl of fluid. "*Fuck.*"

He drops to the blanket on the other side of Proserpina and pulls her into his chest, not caring about the cum, not caring about anything but holding her. On the other side of her, St. Sebastian watches him with glittering eyes. Behind him is the fire, and behind that are Delphine and Rebecca, still consumed with each other.

St. Sebastian wraps an arm around Poe's waist, his fingers pressing into Auden's bare stomach. It's the closest to happy Auden's been since Beltane.

"Happy birthday, St. Sebastian," Poe finally says. And they lay there for a long time, not moving or bothering to clean up until the sun has finally sunk behind the hills and the stars have come out to light the sky.

Later that night, when all the sex is done and the coolbox is empty of drinks, Auden sees St. Sebastian drift away from the group—currently telling each other ghost stories—and he gets up to follow.

The mostly full moon hangs high above the lake, and the cicadas have quieted some, and so as Auden follows Saint down to the beach, the loudest sound is the lake itself, chopping and sighing in the breeze, which is cooler now than it was. Cool enough that Auden has goosebumps, although as always, Saint seems unaffected.

"I lied earlier," Auden says as he approaches Saint at the edge of the water.

Saint looks unsurprised both that Auden followed him and that Auden lied. "What about this time?"

That stings a little, but Auden deserves it.

"Your birthday present," he answers. "It wasn't just what we did earlier. I have another gift for you." And he reaches into his pocket and pulls out a small bundle of silk cinched tight with a ribbon.

He hands it to him, letting his fingertips linger over Saint's palm as he puts the bundle there.

"You didn't have to get me anything. Even the scene—you didn't have to do any of that."

"I wanted to," Auden says simply. "Now open it."

Saint carefully unties the bow of the ribbon and unwinds it from the bundle. The silk falls open to reveal a ring, which gleams like a circle of moonlight in his palm. He picks it up between his thumb and forefinger and studies it, pulling out his phone and turning on its flashlight to see it properly.

Auden knows what he'll see engraved into the silver. The ornate capital G with a thorn-studded vine coiled around its outer curve.

G for *Guest.*

Thorns for Thornchapel.

St. Sebastian's face doesn't change, but Auden feels suddenly nervous, suddenly exposed. He's never had to share the burden of being a Guest before, and he knows he's fucking it up, he knows he's going about it all wrong. St. Sebastian already has a family. A good one—two good ones, if he counts the Daveys. Saint doesn't need the tainted silver of a poisoned line.

"It was our grandfather's," Auden says quickly, feeling like any moment Saint will hand it back to him or throw it in the water or drop it in the dirt. "I barely knew him—he died when I was very young—but he was a good man. He wasn't like our father. He loved his wife, he gave to charity, he was a man of true faith. When he died, my grandmother gave me his ring, and told me she knew I'd be worthy of it, and Thornchapel, so long as I had even a tithe of his spirit. I used to cling to that idea, you know? That there was more in my blood than only my father—that there was my grandfather, who was good, and my grandmother, and all kinds of ancestors I didn't know, but who might have been good also. And if they were there in my blood, maybe I could be good too. Maybe I would be better than my father."

St. Sebastian turns off the flashlight, but he doesn't drop the ring in the dirt. He doesn't hand it back.

"I know this whole thing is shit. You being my brother, being Ralph's son, having to confront all the baggage the Guest family comes with. But I wanted you to have a small thing that proves there is some good at Thornchapel…I wanted you to know that a Guest could be a good person."

St. Sebastian looks up at Auden then, and his eyes are like the lake at night, dark and restless and deep. "I already know a Guest can be a good person, Auden," he says softly. "Because you are good."

And he slides the ring onto his thumb.

He pulls Auden into a hug. A tight embrace, with no room between them, and of all the depraved things Auden wishes to do with this man, the fucking, the crawling, the crying—the one thing he yearns to do the most is not depraved at all.

He wants to kiss him. Slow and sweet, under the moon, next to the lake. He wants to taste his lips and feel his breath and hold his beautiful martyr close.

St. Sebastian breaks the hug before Auden can do it, toying with the ring on his thumb. "Thank you," he says, and then he climbs back up toward the fire, somehow quieter in boots than Auden could ever be even barefoot, and this time, Auden doesn't follow.

He sits on a log and stares at the water for a long time, thinking of the kiss he didn't take, and thinking of the years that lay ahead, and the price this love will extract from him before all is said and done. And when he does finally stand up and rejoin the group, it's with a troubled mind.

For the first time in six weeks, he has the very real fear that he won't be able to do this. That his control and his desire not to hurt Saint won't be enough, and all of them will suffer for it.

I won't let it happen, he thinks as he helps them clean up by the fire. *I won't.*

But what if he does?

What then?

21

Midsummer

Proserpina

In the dream, she sits on a blanket in front of the Equinox stones.

In front of her is Thornchapel, looking like a postcard, as immoveable and natural to its landscape as the rocky tors on the horizon. And behind her is Dartmoor in summer: blooming moors rucked up around granite crags; deep, wooded seams tracing rivers and streams; flower-speckled meadows and contented sheep, all divided by walls made of hedge or stone.

"Proceed with your question," a woman says next to her, and Proserpina realizes she was in the middle of a conversation with her.

"I'm not sure what I was going to say," Poe murmurs.

The woman reaches out and covers Poe's hand with hers. "Yes, you are," the woman says. She has bright green eyes and dark, dark hair. She's wearing a buttercup-yellow dress that spills around her tucked legs, and a small bracelet of wildflowers.

Estamond.

"You were going to ask me a question, remember?" Estamond prompts. "About John Barleycorn?"

Right, yes. As soon as Estamond says the name aloud, Poe knows she's right. She'd heard the name in the village earlier, and... "Who's John Barleycorn?" she asks.

Estamond's hand around hers tightens, and her voice goes low and serious. "John Barleycorn is a memory," she says, looking right into Poe's eyes.

This isn't like the time she said it to Randolph Guest, Poe somehow knows. This isn't a dismissal. It's a warning.

"Remember," Estamond says urgently. "Remember this. You must, because it will happen again."

"I'll remember," Poe promises.

Estamond's hand goes slack on hers, the sky goes dark. Suddenly, she's standing in front of the altar in the thorn chapel, and Estamond's lying on top of it, the torc around her neck and a small knife in the grass.

The altar is how it was before Poe's mother was found—covered in a gentle swell of earth and grass—and the door, the door is behind it—it's open—

Poe opens her mouth to scream, and Estamond says, in a voice as dead as old bones, "It will happen again."

Poe screams. And screams and screams.

John Barleycorn is a memory.

"Poe," a voice says. Male, American, young. "Poe, wake up. It's just a dream."

John Barleycorn is a memory.

Who is John Barleycorn?

Poe bolts upright in her bed, nearly smacking Becket in the face with her forehead as she does.

"Goodness," Becket says mildly, and then pulls her close to his chest when he sees her shaken expression. "Hey, you're okay. *Shh.* I'm here."

Poe presses her face into Becket's shoulder, the dream still too real to shake off. She can still feel Estamond's dead hand in hers, limp and cool, and she can still see the door—open and waiting. Covered in roses blacker than midnight.

"Your father sent me up," Becket says, stroking her hair. "He wanted you to know that the guests will be here soon."

Poe nods against his shoulder. Her mother's funeral the day before hadn't been large by any means—Adelina had been gone for twelve years after all—but a few friends who had been close had flown in, along with some family, including Poe's favorite aunt Sarah—a businesswoman from New York. They're coming to the house for lunch today before they leave town again, and it's her job to play hostess. Which she doesn't mind at all, but it does mean getting up and putting on real clothes.

With a long sigh, she straightens away from Becket and swings her feet to the floor. "Okay," she says, shaking off the dream and the memory of the altar and Estamond. "I'm up."

It's another sunny day, hot and relentless, and most of the guests choose to stay in the air conditioning, balancing plates on their laps and setting cups on the floor at their feet as they talk in low murmurs in the living room and sitting room.

Poe mingles as best she can, trying to make sure everyone is comfortable and fed and that her friends aren't bored. Which they aren't. Early on, Rebecca found her burning a batch of cupcakes in the kitchen and ordered her out, taking over the job and conscripting St. Sebastian into helping after he unwisely slouched into the kitchen to hide. Becket, Auden, and Delphine, on the other hand, are completely at ease and charming everyone they talk with, keeping the conversations light and flowing.

After an hour or so of circulating, Poe finally sits down and has something to eat. She's shoveling potato salad into her mouth when an older black woman sits down next to her, a beer bottle in one hand.

"Hello, Proserpina," she says. "I wanted to make sure I had a chance to introduce myself before this was all over. Your mother was one of my favorite students a long time ago, and I was lucky enough to later count her among my colleagues." She extends a hand. "Katy Davidson."

Poe hurriedly swallows and sets down her food. "Dr. Davidson! Yes!"

Dr. Davidson smiles at her. "I take it you heard about me from your mother? If so, I promise I wasn't as bad as she probably made me sound. Every student thinks their first excavation director is a dragon until they go on to supervise a site themselves."

"No, no, nothing like that," Poe assures her. "But I read your book last month, the one about ancient British religion?"

Dr. Davidson gives her a kind look. "I hate to ask this, but which one? I have a few."

"*The Hunt and the Hearth: Perspectives on Ritual Practice in the British Isles from the Neolithic to the Saxon Age,*" Poe recites promptly. And then seeing Dr. Davidson's expression, she adds, "I'm a librarian. Sorry."

"Don't apologize. And yes, of course it would be that one you read. Adelina wrote the foreword."

"She did." Poe pauses, not sure exactly how to phrase her next question, not sure if it's even appropriate. "In the foreword, she mentioned that her first dig was with you, in the Thorne Valley. When she was there—I know it was a long time ago—but do you remember if she seemed…overly interested in the valley? Preoccupied with it, maybe?"

Dr. Davidson raises an eyebrow. "You mean, did she seem like she'd want to come back there on her own, years later?"

Poe should feel a little self-conscious for how quickly Dr. Davidson reads into her question, but she doesn't. "Yes."

"We were excavating kistvaens up by Kernstow Farm," Dr. Davidson says. "Naturally she was interested in the house and the area around it, knowing her family came from there. I would have found it strange if she wasn't."

"And Thornchapel?" Poe presses. "Did she seem interested in Thornchapel then?"

Dr. Davidson pauses to think. "She did seem interested. Which I understand must seem ominous now, in light of where she died, but at the time, it was very unremarkable. I'm the only archaeologist who's ever had permission to dig there, you know, just the once in the late eighties. The dig was years over by then, but I got permission from Ralph Guest to give the students a tour there one day, just so I could show them the standing stones. Adelina hardly stood out to me for wanting to know more about it. It didn't hurt that Ralph Guest was also very handsome." She tips the neck of her bottle toward the doorway to the sitting room, where Auden is leaning casually against a bookcase and charming the hell out of some old professor. "Just like his son. I think the students fell in love with Ralph as much as the chapel. He was married, of course, and couldn't have been more scrupulous about it, so I don't mean to imply any encouragement on his part. But still, he made an impression."

She doesn't know, Proserpina thinks. *She doesn't know that Ralph wasn't scrupulous at all.*

Her dad has been deliberately vague about Adelina's death—telling family and friends only that she was murdered and the case is technically unsolved. It's cleaner that way, given that the police weren't able to officially name Ralph as the murderer due to lack of evidence, and given that it would only drag Auden's name through the mud by association. And it also means that all of the amorous connections between Ralph and her mother could be buried along with her, protecting them from pointless whispers and lurid gossip.

Which means Poe keeps her voice as light and innocent as possible when she asks her next question. "And my mother? She seemed in love with him too?"

"Well, yes," the archeologist replies. "But again, so did everyone else."

"I see." And Poe really does see. If she'd been her mother, young and excited and abroad, and she'd come to Thornchapel and met a man who looked like Auden...

Yes, she would have fallen in love with him too.

"Thornchapel has that effect on people," Poe adds. "It makes everything seem like—like a secret. One that's waiting just for you."

"A secret," Dr. Davidson says, nodding and then taking a drink. "Yes."

"I only knew my mom as a child, but I do remember that about her. She loved secrets. She always said that's why she chose her field—she could have her pick of secrets to find."

Dr. Davidson looks at her thoughtfully. "You know, when Adelina came to my dig that year, she was in the same place a lot of students are toward the end of their undergrad. She wasn't sure where she wanted to concentrate her studies, and she wasn't even sure if she wanted to stay in academia afterward, or maybe move to commercial archeology and earn actual money. But I think she found something in the Thorne Valley that led her to the ancient Mediterranean. Can you guess what it was?"

Poe remembers her mother's foreword. "Human sacrifice." She makes a face, which the professor laughs at.

"You know what's interesting, though," Dr. Davidson says, nodding at the bookshelves across the room. "I see a Bible there. I see Homer, I see Livy. Abraham and Isaac, Iphigenia and the vestal virgins. In a time when almost all history was oral, when almost nothing was recorded, these stories persisted and survived. They reverberated through the memories of generations. And of course—" Dr. Davidson nods at the crucifix hanging on the wall "—I can think of one human sacrifice that created an entirely new religion."

"Well, but that's not—it's not the same," Poe says. Even though the more she thinks about it, the less she's sure.

"Maybe not," Dr. Davidson agrees with a shrug. "In the purest sense of history, Jesus would have been an executed criminal. But you have to agree that the theology of the crucifixion is a sacrificial theology. One where Jesus consented for his blood to be shed for humanity's absolution, where his life was a price paid for the lives of others. That is human sacrifice—human self-sacrifice—and that brings me to the point I'm trying to make, which is that there is something more to ritual murder than horror. Can you guess what it is?"

Poe shakes her head. It's hard to think of anything other than horror when it comes to killing another person.

"*Power*," Dr. Davidson says. "The horror the ancients felt—that *we* feel—that is a kind of power. The inspiration millions have taken from the oblation on the cross—that is a kind of power. Fear, legacy, exhortation, security, absolution—power, power, power. That power is what drew your mother to study it. That power is why the memory of ritualized murder stays with us, even though the practice itself is long over."

But is it over? Poe wants to ask. Estamond killed herself in the thorn chapel. Ralph Guest killed her mother. According to her father and even Reverend Dartham, people have been going to the thorn chapel far more recently than the Bronze Age. And not just *people*, but her own family. And Auden's.

Remember, Estamond had said. *It will happen again.*

Poe picks up her drink and considers. She's not afraid of asking questions, especially of teachers, but "questions inspired by dreams" is new territory for her.

Oh, what the hell. "Do you know anything about someone named John Barleycorn?" she asks.

The archeologist studies her for a moment. "Superficially, a folk character," she says. "Burns has a poem about him, based on even older poems and songs. A man named John Barleycorn is cut, crushed, burned, and then his blood is drunk by his killers, and it gives them courage and heart."

Poe sees immediately. "So he's not really a person at all. He's the plant! Scythed and ground into grain."

"And brewed into delicious beer," Dr. Davidson says, lifting her own bottle of John Barleycorn's blood. "It makes for a good drinking song. But in the drinking songs, some might see the imprint of a deeper meaning. An older meaning."

"John Barleycorn is a memory," Poe murmurs.

Dr. Davidson looks surprised. "Exactly so. He represents the harvest—the cycle of sowing, growing, and reaping. He represents the spirit of the grain, which to the pre-Christian Europeans, was a real entity who needed a place to house himself when the grain was cut down. The practice of corn dollies—or leaving a hollow sheaf in the fields, depending on your geography—comes from this idea. The dolly or the sheaf would house the spirit of the grain through the winter, and then during sowing season, it would be plowed under the first furrow of spring, thus returning the god into the ground to grow again. The last grain to be harvested is the first to be sown, harvest into planting into harvest again. Death feeding life, and so on. I assume the human sacrifice subtext is plenty apparent here?"

Poe nods.

"The idea of the Year King is an enduring one, even if it's lacking in actual evidence," Dr. Davidson continues. "That a king is tied to the land in such a visceral way that his death is necessary to feed it. He must not grow old, he must not grow weak—he must be cut down when he is healthy and strong and vital—and then be fed back to the land that fed him. As the poem goes, John Barleycorn must die."

John Barleycorn is a memory. She understands why Dream-Estamond meant it as a warning now. Because Poe knows about Year Kings...about Thorn Kings. Which means the memory of John Barleycorn is the memory of *them*, and she thinks again of Estamond bending the torc around her neck, walking to the thorn chapel alone in the dark.

"Dr. Davidson," Poe asks, and then stops. And then starts again. "Do you have any theories as to why people would do this? Like, if they lived...recently. Not in ancient times."

The older woman takes a drink, already shaking her head. "They *don't* do this if they lived recently," she says. "This isn't a modern practice, Proserpina. It's not even a pre-modern one. The idea of human ritual murder was already abhorred by the time of Christ, that's how old it is. And at any rate, I only deal in what I can touch and what I can see. I can give you facts. If you want religion, you'll have to go to your father."

"You promised."

The lunch is over and all the guests—excluding Samson Quartey—are gone. The house has been tidied up, the dogs are napping, and Poe's just cornered her father and Samson talking on the deck.

"You promised," Poe reminds her father when he turns to face her. "You said if I came home, you'd tell me why you and Mom went to Thornchapel. You said you'd tell me what you were doing that summer."

She expects him to defer, to deflect. She expects him to hedge away from answering like he has so many times before. But he doesn't do any of that. Instead, he looks over to Rebecca's father, who nods at him, and it's the kind of nod that makes Poe think they've already discussed this.

"You're right," David Markham says. "But I think all of you deserve to hear it, all together."

It takes close to thirty minutes, but eventually everyone is gathered in the living room, sitting on overstuffed sofas and chairs—except for Auden, who sits on the floor so that everyone else can have a seat. His lap and legs are immediately covered with dogs looking for ear scratches, which he furnishes with a small smile and several low croons.

David insists that everyone has a drink, and while he's pouring whisky and gin for his guests, Poe hears Delphine say to Rebecca, "Did you hear Emily Genovese say yesterday she's coming to London next month? For a film festival?"

Rebecca's voice is tense when she answers. "I didn't."

"Maybe we should take her out to dinner," Delphine muses. "Or see if she'd like to come to Justine's! That would be a nice way to welcome to her to London, since she let us play at Orthia's."

"Sounds brilliant," Rebecca mutters.

Poe only has a second to wonder why Rebecca doesn't seem to like Emily before Poe's father is seated on a sofa next to Samson. They look cute together, in a mismatched kind of way—Samson in carefully pressed pants and a sport coat, and Poe's dad in jeans and a fraying University of Kansas T-shirt.

David takes a drink and says to Samson, "I wish the others were here."

"You mean our parents," Becket says from his chair, nodding down to Delphine. Neither the Hesses nor the Danseys were able to come to Kansas for the funeral.

"They should be the ones to tell you," Poe's father says uncomfortably.

"They've had their chance," Samson disagrees. "Just like we did, David. Our kids are adults now, and they're *there*. They should know."

Poe's father sighs. "Yes."

"Dad," Poe says, "just tell us. We already—" She stops at Rebecca's expression of panic. Right. Their dads don't need to know everything. Definitely not the naked parts. "We've already guessed a lot of it. We know that you were all, um, polyamorous."

"Really?" Delphine asks, sitting up straighter. "I didn't know that!"

Rebecca, meanwhile, looks like she wishes her chair would eat her alive. Poe can commiserate.

"But we don't have to talk about that part," Poe says quickly. "I just want to know the rest of what happened and why you were there."

Her father takes a drink, definitely for courage, and then after a moment, he starts.

"It began innocently, believe it or not," he says. "That year—the year we all stayed there—Adelina and I were in the country for a conference in Bristol. Poe, you were staying with my parents, and we decided to take a few days before the event and explore a little, see some of the places your mother had been as a student. We went to Kernstow Farm, and we hiked around the tors, and then we went to Thorncombe. They were celebrating May Day."

"Beltane," Delphine says.

David nods, and if he's surprised his daughter's friend knows about Beltane, he doesn't show it. "Ralph was there too, presiding over the celebrations. Your mother—she was never shy—when she recognized him, she went up and re-introduced herself. After she mentioned her family came from the valley originally, that she was a Kernstow, he was so friendly. So charming. He invited us to come to Thornchapel, where he'd be hosting a small May Day celebration of his own."

"So you just went with a stranger to a strange house in order to go to a mysterious celebration?" Poe asks. It sounds like something *she* would do, not her fussy, bookish dad.

"Your mother had been there before," David points out. "And I am a professor of religious studies. It seemed like a privilege to be invited, and anyway, your mother and I always tried to say yes to new experiences. Just a few years before, some Polish friends of ours invited us to their village's Dozynki festival, and your mother helped make the wreath—"

Samson puts his hand on David's knee with the affection of someone familiar with his tangents. David clears his throat. "Ah, sorry. Story for another time."

"So you went to Thornchapel on Beltane," Poe says. "And were you there, Mr. Quartey?"

Samson shakes his head. "Not yet."

"Ingram and Helena were though," David says, looking at Becket.

"And my parents?" Delphine asks.

David nods.

Poe doesn't want to know. Except she kind of does.

Except she definitely doesn't.

Except—

Delphine puts everyone out of their misery. "Did you all have sex that night?" she asks, tilting her head.

Poe's father blushes a little above his stubble. He pushes his glasses up his nose. "Well…"

"Dad! You'd only just met them that day! What the hell?"

"Poe, don't slut-shame your father," chides Delphine.

"I'm *not* slut-shaming—"

"You are a little," Becket says.

"I think," Samson cuts in calmly, "your father was explaining how Ralph came to invite your parents to stay for the summer."

"Right," David says, shooting Samson a grateful look. "So your mother and I had a lovely time that night—"

"Ew," Poe says.

"—but we did have to leave the next day for our conference. When we got home afterward, Ralph called, and invited us to stay the summer. He was already hosting the Danseys and the Hesses, and we'd be welcome to bring you since all the kids would be there. We'd get to stay in a beautiful house, free of charge, give Poe a summer abroad, and have complete access to the Thornchapel library—which obviously was a dream come true. There're books there that you can't find anywhere else—local religion for me, local history for your mother—and we'd be able to use the grounds too. There was the maze, the garden, the thorn chapel…"

"And all the sex you wanted to have," Delphine pipes up. "Don't forget that."

Poe makes a face.

"Well, uh, yes," says David. "That was part of it."

"Wait, Daddy, how did we end up staying there?" Rebecca interrupts to ask Samson. "If you weren't there on Beltane?"

"He'd commissioned me to draft up a proposal for the grounds, to see what it would look like if they were properly opened up to visitors. During that first visit, I met David, and…" Samson falters a little, meeting David's gaze and then looking away. "I think Ralph knew. He was perceptive like that, very gifted at reading people's thoughts. He invited us to stay the summer as well—I could work in peace, with a break from all the noise and hustle of London—and Rebecca, you could be with your peers, with children it would have been good for you to associate with. How could I say no?"

"But really you wanted to stay to see Poe's father," Rebecca says. The words are blunt, but her tone is not.

The look Samson gives her is honest. Vulnerable. He laces his fingers through David's, and David squeezes them tight. "Yes," Samson says.

Rebecca glances away, but she doesn't seem unhappy, only pensive.

"I have a question," Auden says politely from the floor. "If that's all right."

"Of course," says Poe's dad.

"I know that both of you were there for largely emotional reasons, and that a fair amount of your time was spent recreationally," Auden says.

"That's tactfully put," mutters Poe.

"But I know that you were also working on something together," Auden goes on. "In the library. Almost all summer long, all of you were locked in there, and we weren't allowed in. And I spent enough time trying to eavesdrop at the keyhole to know that you were actually talking and reading in there, not just…"

"Recreating?" offers Delphine.

"Right."

David goes to take a drink and realizes his glass is empty.

"I'll get it," Samson says, reaching for the drinks globe next to the sofa. He pulls the whisky bottle free and makes to tip to David's glass, but David snatches the bottle by the neck and drinks from it instead.

"Your dad is kind of a wreck," Saint says into Poe's ear. "Papers everywhere, drinking from the bottle. In love with your friend's dad."

"He's a widowed professor with tenure," Poe whispers back. "What do you expect?"

Fortified by the liquor, David hands the bottle back to a vaguely alarmed Samson. "Okay. Okay. Do you want to tell them, Sam?"

"Sam," Rebecca repeats under her breath. "*Sam.*"

Samson touches his knee. "You start. I'll help."

David covers the hand on his knee and then takes a deep breath. "Okay. So. When we were finally settled there, it was early July. I learned that Ralph—along with the Danseys and the Hesses—had been trying to revive some of the older practices of Thornchapel, like we did on Beltane, but all year round. Your mother and I became fascinated by this, we became just as obsessed as Ralph, just as eager as he was to learn every secret the thorn chapel had. When he said—when he asked us to help him try something—it was impossible to say no."

"You have to understand what Ralph was like," Samson says. "What it was like to be there with him, at Thornchapel. It was like being in a dream."

"Like fairyland," David says. "And Ralph was the fairy king. Offering you everything you ever wanted. Sex and magic and mysteries."

"What was it that he wanted you to try?" Becket asks.

"He'd heard a story," Samson says. "An old one, from someone in the village, that there was a door to—well, it sounds ridiculous to say it now—but that there was a door to Faerie somewhere on the Thornchapel grounds. Anyone else would have dismissed it as nonsensical folklore, but not Ralph. He felt powerfully that the story was rooted in some truth."

"There was a song the people in Thorncombe sometimes sang," Poe's father says. "*Here and there/king and door. Cup and spear/corn and war.* Ralph felt like there had to be a connection."

Poe is staring down at her hand—the same hand that held Estamond's in her dream. She knows that song. She knows that song because Estamond knew it. Because the Kernstows knew it. And lived by it.

"And then he found the journals by Reverend Dartham."

At Dartham's name, all their heads snap up.

"Dartham? Really?" Becket asks, leaning forward.

"Yes, really." Poe's dad studies them for a moment. "How do you know about him?"

"I've cataloged his book in the library at Thornchapel," Poe says smoothly, before anyone else can elaborate more. "And I showed everyone after I was done. It was very interesting."

"I'm sure it was," David says, eyes narrowed.

"Ralph stumbled upon Dartham's journals at a historical society when he was searching for local fairy tales," Samson says, picking up the thread of the story. "He thought he could use the fairy tales to triangulate the precise nature of the door. Instead he found something better—Dartham's interviews with the people living in the valley."

"When the door appeared, according to those interviews," David says, "the Guests were supposed to go to the altar in the woods. Ralph felt certain that meant the door was near the altar itself. You've been to the thorn chapel by now, I'm sure, and I'm sure you've noticed the problem: there is no door there."

Auden meets Poe's eyes from across the room. She shakes her head very slightly.

"Ralph wasn't deterred. He thought he could manifest the door," Samson says. "That it would appear if he engaged with the thorn chapel in the right way. He thought if he could find an earlier version of the rituals, if he could discover how it was done centuries ago…"

"And he had your mother," David adds. His voice goes a little heavier then. A little angrier. "He believed a Kernstow was necessary, that it needed to be a Guest and Kernstow in the chapel together in order to make whatever ritual he found work fully."

"We spent weeks combing that library, looking for a way to make the door appear," Samson says. He looks down at his hands and shakes his head. "It sounds like madness now. Foolishness. Doors that don't exist, spending every night...together. But at the time—" He falls silent, as if he can't quite find the words to explain it.

"At the time," David says after a minute, "it felt like the only thing that was real. As if only Thornchapel was real life, and everything else was a dream. Your mother—she felt that way most of all."

Poe meets his eyes and then she has to look away. It was easy to dismiss her father's fears for her when she'd heard them over the phone, but being right here, face to face, listening to him talk about her mother—she understands now. She understands why he's scared.

Because he knows she is just as in love with Thornchapel as her mother was.

"And so what happened?" Saint asks. He's leaning back against the couch, his booted feet planted firmly on the floor and an arm around Poe. "Did you find anything in the library?"

"We did," David answers. "*The Record of Thornechapel Customs.* We decided we'd follow its instructions for Lammas as closely as we could."

None of the six look at each other when David mentions the *Record*, which Poe is grateful for.

"And did it work?" Saint presses. "Did you see the door?"

Neither Samson nor David answers for a moment. And then David wordlessly reaches for the bottle, which Samson hands him.

"If everything until that point had been a dream," Samson says quietly, "then that was when we woke up."

Silence—except for the sound of snoring dogs—fills the room.

"The door was and is the single most terrifying thing I've ever seen," David says after a while. "It wasn't there when we began, and then it just— *was*. Right there in the half-crumbled stone wall. Surrounded by roses so dark they looked black."

Poe thinks of her dream. She knows exactly what those roses look like.

"But the most frightening thing about the door wasn't only that it was there," Samson says. "But that it was open."

"Open," Becket says. His voice is strange.

"Open," David confirms. "Dangerous."

"It was wrong," Samson says softly. "Whatever that door is, it's not meant to be open. Perhaps it's not meant to *be* at all."

"What happened next?" Delphine asks, rapt. "Did you try to close it?"

"Your father tried, Delphine," David replies. "He reached an arm through the doorway to pull it closed, but—"

"He collapsed," Samson finishes for David. "Unconscious, and he was asleep for nearly a full day after."

"We fought after he tried," Poe's father recalls, his voice going even heavier still. "We all fought. Bitterly."

"We couldn't agree on what to do."

"To brick it up."

"To try to find an expert—"

"—a scientist—"

"—the government—"

"—anyone who knew more—"

"I wanted to leave it the way it was," Samson says. "I wanted to walk away. If God has put that door there, then it is not for men to meddle with."

"And I wanted it studied by people with plastic suits and ticking meters and lanyards with government IDs on them."

"And Mom?" Poe asks. "What did Mom want?"

David sighs. "She wanted what Ralph wanted. To try to close the door on Samhain."

A palpable chill settles over the room. They're all very, very aware of when Adelina died.

Auden, of all people, is the one to ask. "And how did my father think he could close the door?"

Poe remembers her dream weeks ago, her dream of Estamond going to the altar on her own.

If you don't do it at Lammastide, then it will be done at Samhain.

"Sacrifice," Poe says. "The door is shut with a sacrifice."

One of them—Becket maybe—lets out an unhappy exhale.

Auden sets his jaw and looks down at the dog whose head he's stroking. Agitation and shame are sketched all over his face, in the tense lines of his shoulders and arms.

"Ralph didn't tell us that at the time," David says after a long minute. "And honestly, I don't think it had even occurred to him by then. To really do it, I mean."

"He only said that he thought doing the Samhain ceremony as described in the *Record* would close it, and your mother agreed with him, Proserpina," Samson says. "And the Hesses. Freddie wanted nothing more to do with it, however, after what happened to him, and Daisy agreed."

"By that point, things had already started to go wrong between us anyway," Poe's father says. "There were too many of us, maybe, or not enough. Some of us—like Samson and Clare—had no experience with polyamory, and maybe the rest of us had had too much."

"It was Ralph, mostly," Samson says, rubbing a soothing hand on David's back. "He wanted Adelina. It was all that mattered to him. He was willing to do anything, hurt anybody, so long as he could possess her."

Across the room, Auden meets Poe's eyes again. There's a haunted look to them that Poe doesn't like.

Samson continues, addressing them all now, "Because of Ralph, we were ready to fall apart at the slightest push—which the door gave us."

"We couldn't agree, we couldn't stop fighting. Your mother didn't want to leave, but I convinced her we had to. Look at what happened to Freddie! What if you kids found your way out to the door and were hurt by it? What if Ralph never saw reason? What was the point in staying when it was so dangerous for all of us? We left two days after Lammas."

"As did I," Samson says. "The Hesses and Danseys weren't far behind." David looks out the window to the front yard. There are cars parked outside, joggers on the road, moms with strollers on the sidewalk.

"The farther away we were from Thornchapel, the sillier it all started to seem," he says slowly. "Who cared about a door in the woods? Why did it matter? Let it stay open. It wasn't hurting anything. I should have known then."

He looks over to Poe, his blue eyes full of pain. "I should have known she would go back—" He breaks off. Samson slides an arm around his shoulders and pulls him close.

"You couldn't have stopped her, David," Samson murmurs. "She was determined."

"I still wonder…did she know?" David asks. He's asking everyone and no one—his daughter and the son of his wife's killer. "Did she know what he was going to do? Did he tell her? Or did he simply beg her to come back to help him close it?"

Auden clears his throat. "I don't—I don't know if the police mentioned to you. But when they were searching through my father's things, they looked through his phone records. They found a call from a phone number here in Kansas, registered to the University. It was her old faculty number, not her current one, and it wasn't her cell phone, which is why you wouldn't have found it when you were investigating her phone records the year she disappeared."

Poe's father looks down at the scotch. "Yes."

"The records show the call was short," Auden says quietly. "Less than ten minutes. If it's any comfort at all, and I understand that it may not be, I think she couldn't have known what my father intended. I think she called to check on him, and he begged her to come back, and she did—because she was a good person, and because she loved Thornchapel, and because she wanted to help."

David nods, blinking fast, and Poe's eyes are burning too. She suddenly misses her mother so much that she can't breathe, that she can't speak, that her throat and her chest are knotted tight.

"Thank you for sharing all this with us," Auden goes on. "I know—I know it's not worth much. But I am truly sorry for what my father did to your family. I would give anything to undo it."

"I don't hold you accountable for Ralph's sins," David says heavily. "I hold Ralph accountable. And that cursed place. If only we'd refused to celebrate Lammas there…the door wouldn't have opened. No one would have needed to die."

He gives a tearful, unhappy look to Poe. "And your mother might still be alive."

Part Three

22

Proserpina

We can't go out there again," Auden says as he paces in front of the fireplace, one hand stabbed into his hair and the other balled at his side.

Rain lashes against the tall library windows, as if the very sky is mirroring Auden's mood, and even though it's almost July, the space is filled with a dim, stormy gloom. Every so often, thunder cracks and rolls over the moors and down to the house, rattling the panes in the windows and sending Sir James Frazer to his feet to bark indignantly at the air.

"I'm not going to argue with you," Rebecca says. She's sitting on a sofa with Delphine's head in her lap, and she strokes her submissive's hair while she talks. "But I do think we need to qualify what we mean when we say *go.*"

Murmurs of agreement come from around the room. From everyone except me.

"Do we mean only for Lammas?" Rebecca continues. "Do we mean no rituals at all? Do we mean we shouldn't go out there at any time, for any reason?"

Auden drops his hand from his hair. "I don't know," he says. "Definitely not for Lammas. As for the rest…"

He looks over to me, and I look down at my hands, which are currently fussing with the hem of my dress. I know he's trying to protect me, and I'm grateful.

I also have no idea what to do.

It's been three days since we returned home from Kansas. Three days since my father and Samson told us their story, and three days since we learned what they did in the thorn chapel that summer. I also told the group everything Dr. Davidson told me, and confessed my dreams of Estamond and her death.

We agreed to talk about it once we met back here at Thornchapel, but now that we're here, I feel more confused than ever.

It should be a simple solution. Easy math. Avoid the thorn chapel, and nothing bad will happen to us like it did to my mother and Estamond. The end.

But then why do I feel so uneasy?

"Do we actually believe in this, though?" Saint asks after a moment. He's standing behind the sofa, as still as Auden is in motion. "It's not that I think your dads were lying," he says to me and Rebecca, "but it's hard for me to imagine the door is a real thing. And even harder for me to imagine that—if it *is* real—that it could possibly matter to us. The only reason it mattered for your mother, Poe, was because of Auden's father, and we're not murdering psychopaths like him. No offense, Auden."

"None taken," says Auden mildly. "Although I feel compelled to remind you that he's your father too."

"I'd be sad not to have Lammas in the thorn chapel," Delphine says from Rebecca's lap. "It's not like we're going to go starkers and decide to kill each other. It's just a door. So what if it shows up? We'll just pretend it's not there."

"I don't think we'll have to pretend very hard, Delphine," Saint says.

"Because you don't think it's real," Becket clarifies.

"Because even if it is real—which is a very big if—there's no guarantee it will manifest again. And even if it does, it doesn't have to be terrible. We get to assign the meanings we want to it and all that. Isn't that right, Father Hess?"

"Some meanings are inherent to themselves, Mr. Martinez," replies Becket.

"You mean the meanings of *magic, invisible doors*?"

"Well, if you're going to be reductive about it, then—"

"Look, my father wouldn't have told us about this if it weren't true," interrupts Rebecca. "He doesn't deal in fantasy or delusion. I had to ask him to stop reading the *Harry Potter* books aloud to me when I was a girl because he kept pausing to explain that the magic at Hogwarts was logically impossible and also that Dumbledore was criminally negligent in the care of children. The man does not exaggerate and he doesn't credit anything he hasn't personally seen or experienced. If he says there is a door, then there is. And if he says it's dangerous, then it is."

"You don't want to go out there either?" asks Delphine, tilting her head to look at her Mistress.

Rebecca sighs. "Delph—"

"Sometimes things are dangerous," Becket says. "But that doesn't mean they're bad. Arguably the best things in life are dangerous, because they have the power to be."

"Or—lone voice of dissent here—they're not dangerous at all," Saint says, "and we're letting old ghost stories scare us away from something we enjoy doing."

"Since when are you pro-chapel?" Auden asks. "You've always been reluctant to go out there before."

"Probably since you fucked him there, Auden," Rebecca says dryly.

Saint glowers at her from behind the sofa.

"Maybe it doesn't matter," I say. The others turn to look at me; outside, the rain surges against the window, turning the library into a colossal drum made of stone and books and glass.

"What do you mean?" Rebecca asks.

I glance over at Auden. Of all of us, he's the only one who's truly seen the door in waking life, and he's the only one who might understand. "I think the door might appear whether we go there on Lammas or not. I don't think it's beholden to us or our actions."

"That's excellent news, then," Saint says. "If it doesn't give a shit about what we do, then no one has to be human-sacrificed to it anyway."

Auden glares at him, his eyes dipping meaningfully to me. "Let's not make light of this. People have died."

"But I still don't understand what harm a manky old door is," Delphine protests. She's held out her arm for Rebecca to caress now, and Rebecca obliges—a wry, amused smile at her lips as she does, like she's too charmed to stop herself from doing it. "Can't we just ignore the door, like Saint said?"

Auden's hazel eyes meet mine in the storm-infused murk, and I know what he's thinking. It's all well and good to feel like the door doesn't matter when you're here, but when you're *there*—when it's in front of you...

"We can ignore it because we're not going out there," Auden finally says. "Not for Lammas. Not for any other ritual. As far as I'm concerned, we're done with all of it."

Delphine sits up and glares at him. "You don't get to decide that for us!"

"Someone has to," says Auden, his mouth set like a king's.

"And that someone should be you?" Delphine pushes, her tone outraged.

"Yes, for fuck's sake, *yes!*" Auden yells as lightning splits the sky outside. For a moment, the world is bright and sharp, and then it's plunged back into gloom as the answering thunder roars overhead. "Don't you see?" he asks.

"It was my father who killed Poe's mother, it is my family that owns this land and has been doing horrible things with it for centuries. This is my responsibility, and I refuse—I mean, absolutely *refuse*, Delly—to let one other person get hurt. I'm not doing it. And if that makes me draconian, if that makes me unreasonable and a ruiner of fun, then so fucking be it. I'd rather have you all miserable and safe than hedonistic and dead. Am I very understood?"

For a few seconds, the only sound in the room is that of the rain against the glass and the low roll of thunder over the hills outside.

I think of our parents—all arguing viciously about what to do—and I wonder if we're about to erupt in the same kind of a sour tumult. If the next person to speak is going to tell Auden to fuck off, that he's not the boss of us, that he has no right to choose for us, and then we'll be fighting for real.

I wonder if this is the end for our strange little group, our small, kinky kingdom out here in the moors, and dread curdles in my stomach.

But the moment passes.

Becket concedes first. "If you think it's for the best, then of course we agree with you."

"And we can be hedonistic here at the house," Rebecca reminds us all as the rain against the window abates a little. "Without the chapel."

Delphine issues a huffy, "*Fine.*"

Saint nods, but he doesn't speak.

Auden puts a shaking hand to the mantel and leans his forehead against it. He looks like he wants to close his eyes and sleep for a hundred years. "Thank you."

"It's your birthday," I remember aloud, looking up at him. "Lammas. I'd forgotten."

He rolls his head a little on his hand so he can give me a self-deprecating smile. "I promise I can survive not having an outdoor orgy for my birthday."

"But we could still do something special. Maybe it would feel less like we were missing out on something if we did."

"Yes!" Delphine exclaims, grumpiness instantly gone. "I shall appoint myself the official Auden Guest birthday coordinator then, if there are no objections? No? That's what I thought."

"No objections," Rebecca says. "You always make everything so easy."

Delphine blinks once and then shoves to her feet, like she can't bear to be sitting still for a minute more. "Where do we think Abby is with supper?" she asks brightly. "I should go check."

Rebecca watches her leave, her expression fading into something tight and closed off. Sir James lifts his head to watch her go, but then looks up at Auden and, reassured his master isn't leaving, stays where he is.

Becket stands up. "Anyone want a drink?"

"Me," Saint says, following Becket over to the antique sideboard that serves as the library's drinks bar. "Poe, you want anything?"

"In a minute," I say. Auden is leaving the room—quietly, like he does when he doesn't want anyone to notice—and Sir James is now up and at his heels.

"I'll take one," Rebecca says, getting to her feet. "Something stiff. Do *not* make a joke about that, St. Sebastian."

"Wouldn't dream of it," says Saint.

"Uh-huh."

Becket turns on some sad-boy indie music just as Delphine returns to tell us Abby will be bringing supper into the library within the hour. She doesn't go immediately to Rebecca's side, but instead wanders over to the window. Something that Rebecca observes over the rim of her glass, her face unreadable.

When Saint and Becket start arguing about the music and when Rebecca answers a call on her phone, I get to my feet and leave. It's not a choice really, more like a compulsion, an instinct that won't be denied.

I go after Auden.

The storm precludes some of the usual hiding places around the estate, but I think he would have gone to the tower anyway. He seems to seek it out when he's upset, this place where he used to hide from his father, and this isn't the first time I've come up here to find him standing at the window, looking out over the grounds. The only difference is today those grounds are veiled in rain—even the steep rise up to the moors is utterly shrouded from view—and he's not standing at all, he's sitting on the floor and staring at his hands.

The dim light coming through the windows casts stained glass roses on the floor and across the long sprawl of Auden's legs. The thorns are the color of pine needles in winter, the petals the color of old blood. The air itself is tarnished silver, nearly bronze.

Sir James is curled on one side of his master, his head resting on his paws.

I make to sit on the other side of Auden, just to be near him, but the moment I get close, he grabs me and hauls me into his lap. I'm crushed to his chest, and he buries his face in my hair.

"Little bride."

"You left," I say, trying to nuzzle him back.

"I was upset," he says, his voice muffled by my hair.

"About the door?"

He pulls away and shakes his head.

"No. Or rather, not only about the door." He finds my wrists with his hands, circling them and pulling them between us.

His eyes are on where his thumbs and middle fingers meet over my pulse points. He says, in a voice barely audible over the rain, "I've been thinking since we left your father's house. About everything. About what happened to your mother. What happened to Jennifer Martinez and everyone else who got close to him. And what if I'm like that too? What if I'm like him?"

There's no question whom he means. "You're not," I tell him. "I promise, you're not."

"But look at what I do to you," he whispers. He tightens his grip on my wrists until the pain flickers up my arms.

"You know I like it," I say.

"I don't mean the kink, Proserpina."

Suddenly I'm on my back with him over me, my wrists pinned to the floor on either side of my head. My skirt has fallen up to expose my sex, and it gives a wet kick at our position. At having my Sir over me and restraining me, at having his tormented eyes on mine and his jaw tight with something we only barely have the words for.

"I mean *this*," he says. "I mean that when I look at you, the first word I think is not your name, it's 'mine.' When I say 'I love you,' I mean 'you're mine.' When I hold you down, when I tie you up, when I fuck you, that is what my body is telling yours: mine, mine, mine."

I'm arching underneath him—not in distress, but in need. "I am yours," I whisper back.

"What if you shouldn't be?"

"Don't be ridiculous, Auden. When I see you, I need you, when I'm with you, I kneel. When you're touching me, I'm whole, and I don't care how fucked up it is, I don't care if it's wrong, if it's twisted, if we're all kinds of broken, this is what I want. *You* are what I want."

Auden's eyes move over my squirming form, leaving heat in their wake. He stares at my pussy for a minute. "Open your legs," he says.

I obey immediately, because they belong to him, just as my cunt does, just as my entire body does.

He lets go of a wrist and uses one hand to open his pants. But he doesn't go inside me, no matter how much I writhe and beg for him to. Instead, he rubs his crown against me, up and down my wet seam, denying us.

"This is what you want?" he asks.

"Yes, Sir."

He ducks his head to bite the exposed upper curve of my breast, hard enough to make me cry out. "And this?"

"Yes."

He moves up, releases my wrist. I'm flipped to my stomach, and before I can even catch my breath, he's on top of me again, this time pushing inside with a hard thrust that drives the breath right out of my body.

"And this?" he asks, shoving all the way in. The fit is so tight like this, snug and a little bit painful and a whole lot wonderful. I press my face into the floor and breathe as pleasure and pain sparkle up from my cunt to light my blood on fire.

"This too? You truly want to be loved like this?"

"You know I do," I whisper into the floor. "Please…"

"Please what?" he asks. He pushes my legs together to make it tighter for him, planting his knees on the outside of my own. "You want to come?"

"Yes, Sir," I gasp. Each thrust feels like it's going into my belly, into my chest. I could come just like this, even without direct pressure on my clit, if only he'd keep going—

He stops.

"Auden, no," I beg as he slides out. "Please, don't—"

"But you wanted it, hmm?" He leans down to bite the back of my neck, and I shudder underneath him. "You wanted me?"

"*Please…*"

I feel his hand on his erection, shuttling slowly up and down his length. He's fucking his hand instead of me.

"Auden!"

He slaps my bottom so fast and so hard that I squeak in surprise. "No. I say when you come. I say when this perfect little body feels release. Because you are mine, and that's what you wanted, right?"

"I know what you're doing," I say, turning my face to speak. "It won't work."

"And what am I doing, little bride? Enlighten me."

"You know you can't scare me with pain because I get off on it, and so you think you can scare me with selfishness. But it won't work, Auden. Your selfishness gets me off too. *You* get me off—your will, your desires—they are mine now, as well as yours. And I know the secret anyway, which is that you're not selfish. Not really."

"Oh, is that so?" His hand is still working his organ, his knuckles grazing the curve of my bottom as he jacks himself off. "I'm not selfish?"

"Not like how you're worried—*oh*—"

He slides back in, one hand sliding under my stomach to lift my hips slightly off the ground. I realize what he's doing—he's making sure there's no stimulation against my clit so I can't come. Mean. He's so *mean*.

"How can you be so wet and agreeable when you know what I'm going to deny you?"

"I don't know," I whimper, trying to arch against him, trying to rock into his hand, trying to chase down any friction I can get.

"How can you still love me when I mistreat you so?"

"Because it's fucking hot, Auden, please—"

"No," he says. Smugly. Breathlessly. Then he comes with a sharp breath and low moan, his shaft throbbing inside of me as it releases.

It was the act of telling me *no*, of denying me, that brought on his orgasm, as much as it was my body, and it's so hot. It's so damn hot.

"Fuck, you feel good," he murmurs, his cock jerking a final time. "You always feel so good."

"Sir—"

He pulls out, leaving me empty and aching, wet from his release. "You can come when I say so. *How* I say so. And not a moment sooner."

"So not right now?"

Another slap on the backside, hard enough that I know I'll be sporting a bright red handprint for the next hour. "Just for that, it won't be tonight. Or tomorrow."

I roll over to look at him as he sets his clothing to rights, keeping my sex shamelessly exposed—hoping he'll change his mind, but knowing he won't.

No, he's too mean for that, and also too good a Dominant.

His eyes do drop down between my legs however, as if he's drinking in the sight, and after he's finished zipping himself up, he says, "Stay just like that. I like looking at you."

So I stay on the floor with my legs spread and my skirt up, his orgasm slowly leaking back out. He sits on a trunk directly in front of me to enjoy the view, periodically reaching down to run an admiring finger through the mess he made. My clit is so swollen, I can feel every stir and puff of air against it, and I can't help but rock against his hand whenever he deigns to touch me—something he takes advantage of, toying with my needy berry until my pleasure starts to build, and then backing off and watching with satisfaction as I wiggle and whine.

"You know you're not selfish," I say after a long few minutes of this. I say it even though every nerve ending south of my belly button currently disagrees, and even though the fresh erection visible in the leg of his trousers proves he's enjoying my agony like only a mildly sadistic person can.

But it's true. He's not selfish.

"How can you possibly say that? You're spread out on the floor with my semen dripping out of you, displayed for my liking."

"You know what I mean."

He sighs, looking down as his hair tumbles in front of his forehead. "There's no material difference between my father's selfishness and mine, Poe. I want you as thoroughly and as horribly as he wanted your mother, and God knows I still want St. Sebastian, even though I'll burn in hell for it. How is that not the worst kind of selfishness? Doing everything in my power to possess the daughter of the woman my father killed? Barely able to keep myself from hauling my own brother off to bed?"

"But you do keep yourself from doing it," I say, pushing up to my elbows so I can better see his face. "Even though I know you don't personally believe you'll go to hell for it. You do it for him, because it's what he needs, and that's not selfishness, Auden. That's love. And as for me, we already know I want to be possessed by you. Your father didn't want love *or* possession; he wanted to fill an emptiness inside himself, and that's not what you're doing or who you are."

Auden doesn't look reassured. "But what if it is me? How can I tell the difference?"

The world outside has darkened even more, and the roses falling over his messy hair and elegant hands are more black than red. Just like the roses around the door in the chapel.

I think of Estamond—a woman who had a child with her own brother, a woman who never refused sex or pleasure or fun, but who also paid the highest price so no one else around her would have to.

"The difference is in what you do," I answer. "Not how you feel."

"In my choices then." A small, sad smile pulls at his mouth. He reaches for me. "Come here, wise girl."

I come, settling onto his lap and practically purring at the contact.

"I trust you," I tell him, tilting my head up to kiss his throat. "I trust you even if you don't trust yourself."

His arms tighten around me. "I don't deserve that."

"You do."

"Promise—Proserpina, you have to promise me something." His voice is that of a man harrowed. A man sacked like an ancient city. "If I ever go too far, if I ever really hurt someone the way he hurt people—you have to promise me you'll leave. I mean it."

I stiffen and try to sit up, but he won't let me, he keeps me against his chest. "You know you won't," I say. "I know you won't."

"You have to promise," he begs. He sounds pillaged and ravaged and more than a burning city now, he's a world on fire. He presses his face into my hair. "Please, little bride. Please don't let me hurt you. Please don't let me hurt St. Sebastian. If I turn into my father, you have to go away from me."

"We have safewords for that," I say. "Neither Saint nor I would ever let you get that far. We wouldn't even let you start."

"Promise," he insists. "Promise to leave. I have to—I have to know you'll keep yourself safe, that you won't make excuses for me, that you won't linger just to be hurt again. Please, Proserpina."

I know the man whose arms are around me, and I know his heart. I know he would never hurt someone the way his father did.

"Of course, Auden," I murmur. He finally lets me turn, and I brush my lips over his firm, sculpted mouth, sighing as he opens to me. "I promise."

23

Proserpina

"If Auden doesn't let you come soon, *I'm* going to be the one to die," Saint says. He keeps his voice low because he's about to leave for work, and the renovation crew is periodically coming through where we're standing with their mysterious reels and unlabeled buckets. "How much longer is this going to last?"

"I don't know," I say, too miserable to even whine about it properly. Auden's denied me climaxes before, but never this long—a week since that rainy evening in the tower—a week of fucking, spanking, all kinds of kinky sex, all kinds of fun orgasms for *him* and none for me. I'm not even allowed to come with St. Sebastian, which Saint is not happy about. And not a little jealous of.

He misses being Auden's. He even misses the misery.

Saint opens one of the front doors, letting in a world of green and gold. Thornchapel in summer. Birds sing in the trees, and there're so many bees buzzing around the roses on the front of the house that the air itself thrums with them.

"It's too bad we're not doing anything for Lammas," Saint says, stepping out. I follow him as he walks toward the lane leading to the village. "You could use it more than ever."

"Are you still upset we're not doing a rite in the chapel?"

One shoulder comes up, drops back down. "Why shouldn't I be?"

I look over at him as we walk. The trees are so thick and leafy that only ripples and dapples of sunlight make it down to us. They glint off Saint's lip piercing and off the dark, dark brown of his eyes. "You don't believe in anything," I point out. "Not God, not church, not magic, and not...whatever we do in the thorn chapel."

He stops.

"Why do I have to believe in something to want to do it?" he asks me. We're standing on the narrow bridge over a small rill, and he keeps his eyes on the water as he speaks. "Isn't wanting to do it enough of a reason on its own?"

"Sure. But it's not a very strong reason."

His phone goes off: an alarm letting him know his shift is in twenty minutes. St. Sebastian is many things, but he is never late for work. He silences it without pulling it out of his pocket.

"How about this," he says, lifting his eyes to mine. "If I believe in anything, it's this place. It's the thorn chapel. And it's you."

I can hear what he doesn't say. It's in the way he reaches up, as if unconsciously, to touch his lip.

And it's him.

He believes in Auden too.

"It's the closest thing to faith I know, what I feel for this place and the people here. That's why I don't want to give it up."

And how can I argue with that? I let out a breath. "That's fair."

"It's fair for you not to want to do it too," he says softly. "Given what happened."

And I definitely can't argue with that either.

He leans in and kisses me, his piercing cool against my lips, his breath warm. His tongue perfect. He kisses me until we're shuddering against each other and his phone alarms at him again.

"I have to go to work," he whispers against my mouth. "But tonight…"

"Tonight," I promise, as he pulls reluctantly away. "You'll have me for as long as you want me."

"I better." He gives me a final, smoldering look, and then I'm left alone on the bridge, with nothing but my own work and a week of pent-up climaxes to keep me company.

"You have to let me have an orgasm. You *have* to."

"You know," says Auden over the phone, "I've never thought of it that way before. What a compelling argument you present, Proserpina."

I lean against the outside of the car I borrowed from Auden, and then jump away. The metal is hot under the July sun.

"I'm dying," I whine to him, turning to face the Kernstow farmhouse. "It's been a week."

"It's been eight days and four hours and approximately twenty minutes since you came last," corrects Auden.

Huh. So it has.

"You have a good memory."

"Only for the most crucial things." Auden's voice is amused. "Is that wind I hear? Are you outside?"

"Saint won't be home until nearly ten, and I was finished with my work for the day. I thought I'd come up to the farm for a while." I've been coming here sometimes, just to walk along the ridge or sit on the old stone fence and watch the sheep. The wildflowers and blooming heather have done nothing to make it less lonely—if anything, the vibrant life around the crumbling farmhouse only highlights how desolate it is—but it reminds me of my mother all the same.

She was here once. She walked here and dug near here. She was happy and curious and alive near here.

"Be careful, Proserpina," Auden says. I hear whirring on his end—whirring from the large format printer at his office—and I know he's still at work. "I wish you weren't alone."

"I'll be careful if you promise to go home on time tonight. Oh, and if you let me come."

"So many demands," he says tranquilly.

"Auden, *please*," I say, walking up to the abandoned farmhouse, wildflowers bobbing tall and sweet around me as I walk, tickling my calves. "I'm dying. Saint is dying. You won't be home for another two days, and I've been very good, Sir, please."

I hear a door close where he's at, as if he's shut himself into an office so he can't be heard. "You do beg so prettily," he says. "But no."

I don't bother to stifle my groan.

"What a brat you are," he says, sounding delighted. "I can't wait to get back to Thornchapel. How many paddles do you think that groan was worth? How many minutes of being flogged?"

I hesitate. "…which flogger?"

"Buffalo hide," he says, already sounding like he's relishing it. "Or the rubber one."

Fuck. "I don't like the rubber one."

"I'll be sure to use it then."

Well, I walked right into that. I decide to switch tactics. "You could come home early," I say. "I'd let you tie me up and flog me with the rubber flogger until I'm begging to come."

I can hear the crooked smile in Auden's voice when he answers. "An alluring proposition with two logical weaknesses. Firstly, you're mine to tie up and torture any time I like, whether or not you *let* me. Secondly, you're already begging me to come. I hardly need to go to any effort for that particular pleasure, do I now?"

"You're so *mean*."

"You told me you liked that."

This entire conversation has me as worked up as I was fooling around with Saint this morning, and Auden isn't even *here*. It's just his voice, sultry and arrogant, coming all the way from London.

"Here's what I'm going to do, darling brat. I'm going to give you a choice. You can come tonight—and tonight only—but each orgasm will have a price, determined by me and unknown to you until I make you pay it. But if you choose not to come, you'll be rewarded—again, a thing of my choosing and unknown to you. Does that seem fair?"

I think about this.

"No."

His laughter is abrupt and boyish and perfect, and I just miss him so fucking much, my chest hurts with it. "Are you sure you can't come home anyway?" I say.

He must hear the loneliness in my voice. "I would if I could," he says, his laughter changing into pure longing. "You know, it's not too late for you to come out here…"

"I know." Every time Auden leaves for London, he asks me to come with him. To stay in his townhouse and eat at fancy restaurants and have lots of kinky sex. And every time he asks, I say no.

Because my work is at Thornchapel. Because Saint is at Thornchapel.

I'd feel wrong the entire time I was without both.

That doesn't make it easier to be apart from Auden, though.

"Soon," he assures me. "I'll come home in two days, and leave all kinds of marks on that lovely body of yours."

"And in the meantime, it's up to me whether or not I want to risk whatever diabolical punishments you're dreaming up?"

"Only if you'd like to come," he says evilly.

Only Auden could make a liberty feel like a restraint, like a persecution.

"Are you going to have fun thinking about me deliberating over this?" I ask.

"Proserpina, we both know you're going to deliberate for about three seconds before you find St. Sebastian and make him fuck you. You like orgasms *and* punishment too much. No, I'm going to be having fun anticipating exactly what I'm going to do to you, and how much you're going to hate it and love it all at the same time."

I'm breathless by now. "Or I could do it right here," I whisper. "Right now. On the phone with you. I'm in a dress and I could just stick my fingers in my panties and come for you."

His pause lets me know he likes that idea a lot. But he's stronger than I am. "If you do it, I won't be complicit," he says, "no matter how tempting the reality of listening to you get yourself off would be. I want you to choose naughtiness all on your own."

"All the better to punish me for?"

"Clever girl."

I sigh. "Fine."

"Fine what?"

"Fine, *Sir.*"

I can hear his satisfaction all the way from London. "That's more like it. Text me when you're safely home again."

I agree that I will, and we hang up. For a moment, I stand in front of the farmhouse, feeling so in love I can't stand it. Getting to start the day with Saint, some delicious torment from Auden...

I feel like Dartmoor itself right now. Sweeping and open, in heady bloom.

In the full fulgor of happy summer.

I'm smiling to myself when I duck through the doorway and nearly trip over a priest sitting on the floor.

"Jesus!" I mutter, catching myself before I actually tumble over onto the dirt-covered flags. "Becket, what the hell?"

Becket doesn't answer me.

After so many times coming here alone, of being here with no one else, seeing another person inside the broken farmhouse is unsettling. Not because it belongs to me as a Kernstow descendant, necessarily, but because it's the kind of place that doesn't belong to anybody at all. Like the moors themselves, or like the empty tombs up on the ridge.

The early evening sun is still bright and hot and eager, sending thick shafts of golden light into the mossy ground floor of the farmhouse. Becket sits just out of reach of the sunshine, his legs crossed and his hands in his lap. In front of him is the old hearth of the house, carved with the antlered god.

His eyes stay on the etching even after I nearly fall on top of him, even after I say his name.

"Becket?" I kneel next to him. "Is everything okay?"

He still doesn't answer. His eyes are so blue they barely look real. Like fires from another world.

I look at the god chiseled into the hearth, wondering if I'm missing something, if it's changed somehow since the last time I've been here, but it hasn't changed. It's still the horned god, still carved in simple, abstract lines, his stick-figure legs crossed as Becket's are and antlers twining out from the vaguely humanoid shape of his head. Swirling spirals rest on each outstretched hand, mirror images of each other—one spiraling clockwise and the other counterclockwise. The outer curves of the spirals disappear into the god's arms, connecting them to him in the most elemental way.

One spiral represents life. The other represents death.

"Becket," I say, turning back to him. His face doesn't change, his eyes don't leave the carving. The pulse at the base of his neck beats fast and hard, though, and I can see the heaving of his chest and the sweat misting along his hairline. He's in an athletic T-shirt and shorts, his running shoes on, and he must have run here from the rectory—over five miles away.

Worry fills me. I touch his knee. "Becket? Hey. Becket, it's me."

His lips part, but his eyes don't slide away from the god. Those eyes are so blue, so very blue, and goosebumps erupt all over my arms and legs.

I put a hand to his shoulder, whispering his name, then I move it to his heart. He doesn't react, doesn't seem to see me, and so I lean in and put my lips to his.

Our mouths brush together, parted and breathy, and for a moment, I think it hasn't worked, that I haven't broken him free of whatever trance he's in...but then I feel his firm lips move the slightest bit under mine. His tongue flicks cautiously against the crease in my lower lip.

I seize the movement, kissing him back hard enough that he groans and slides his fingers through my hair. He takes command of the kiss in that expert way of his, and the kiss goes from hesitant to seductive in mere instants.

I melt into him, an eternal whore for confidence and control. It's not quite Auden's mastery, or even Saint's burning desperation, but it's still wonderful, it still lights me up. I straddle his lap and rock my hips against him—all of the need stoked by my phone call with Auden surging to the surface—and Becket answers me, his hands finding my tits, my throat, my backside.

"Proserpina," he murmurs, pulling back to blink at me. His eyes are a normal blue now—a human blue—and they're focused and clear. They see me. "Why are you here?"

"Why are *you* here?" I counter as I reach up to stroke his hair. It's normally styled in a well-behaved coiffe, but his run and the summer heat has turned it into an untidy mass of gold. It's just long enough that I can rub it between my fingertips. "And what were you doing? You seemed...distant."

"I must have gotten lost in prayer," he says. A rueful smile pulls at the corner of his mouth. "Hazard of the job. Like getting lost in a book for you, I'm sure."

I smile back at him, but uneasiness twines through my thoughts. I don't think I've ever—even in my most absorbed moments—been so lost that I didn't notice someone tripping over me and calling my name. So lost that my eyes became bright and strange.

"Let's go outside," I suggest, getting to my feet and helping him up. He unfolds into six feet of trim, handsome priest, and he smiles down at me once he's standing.

"I missed you," he says, cradling my hand in both of his.

"It's only been a few days," I respond, trying to tease and also walking at the same time, so that we move away from the hearth and into the sun.

I glance back at the carving of the god and fight off the urge to shiver. The urge to physically shake off the memory of Becket's stilled body and near-violet eyes.

"Yes, but that was at church, and so I couldn't do this." He pulls me close and kisses me again, and I let him, each skilled stroke of his tongue reminding me of the charming, thoughtful friend I know and love. *It's just Becket*, the kisses reassure me. *The same Becket as always.*

After a few minutes, he breaks away and takes my hand again, and we walk past the house and up to the ridge above it. There's a public footpath snaking along the crest of the moors, and just beyond the path, a cluster of kistvaens: boxes of stone sunk into the earth, long empty of whatever and whomever they once held. They are the same kistvaens my mother studied as a student. Perhaps the same kistvaens that the ancestors to the Kernstows buried their dead in.

We stop in the middle of the trail, near an exposed shelf of stone, and Becket turns to look down at the farmhouse. It looks like a painting you'd hang in your bathroom right now, a watercolor of a place perfect in its own dereliction, but I suddenly don't want to see it anymore, I don't want to think about it.

The look on Becket's face as he stared at the hearth…

"It's strange, though," Becket murmurs as he looks at the farm. "I barely remember coming here. I know I must have run or walked, but I don't recall doing either…I don't remember getting dressed or locking up the church. I was home, and then I was here, with you."

That *is* strange, but I can't say that to him. I should say something reassuring instead. "I don't remember getting dressed most mornings either," I offer up. "Habit and all that."

"Mm," he says, not sounding comforted or convinced.

"Becket," I say. "Look at me."

Unlike in the farmhouse, he does look at me, and he does it as soon as I ask him to.

"I'm here," I tell him, because it's the only thing I can give him, maybe the only thing any of us can truly offer to someone else. "I'm here with you. Maybe you don't remember before, but you remember right now with me, right?"

He takes a deep breath. "Of course."

I pull him over to the stone shelf and make him sit down. I sit next to him and wrap an arm around his back. I want to ask him so many questions, like if he's lost time here at the farmhouse before, and what he was thinking when he stared at the hearth, and if all of this started when we started going to the chapel in the woods. But I manage to keep quiet, even though it nearly kills me.

"Poe," he says after a minute. "You said a while back that if I ever needed to show you—"

I'm kissing him before he can finish, climbing back into his lap. It feels so much better in the sunshine, away from the cheerless murk of the farmhouse, and his response feels better too—gratified surprise followed by a heavy shudder that moves through his entire body.

The same Becket as always.

"You can always show me," I whisper, nipping at his lip. "Any time."

His hands—the same hands that page through holy books and hold chalices aloft—find my ass, and pull me so my sex is settled firmly against his. There's nothing but my panties and his thin athletic clothes between us, so every hard, eager inch of him is discernible. Instinctively I rock and rock and rock against him, chasing the friction, savoring everything about him— his hardness, his heat, his sculpted mouth made for prayers and pleasure.

"I feel so clear with you," he says, kissing my jaw. "Like everything is real."

"Real? *Oh*—" One of his hands has slid between us and moved under my skirt, stroking my pussy over the cotton of my panties. Thoughts shiver right out of my mind like water on a hot pan, and I can't hold on to a single one while he's touching me like this. It's been so long since I've been touched properly—instead of teased to heighten my agony like Auden's been doing— and my body is so primed, so ready for it, that I think I might be able to come just like this. Come just from the soft sanding of his fingers over my panties.

"Should I be asking Auden's permission?" Becket asks, biting the lobe of my ear.

"He said I could come today," I manage. He also said I'd be punished for it, but that's almost as much an enticement as the climax itself, if I'm honest.

A gust of wind buffets around us, warm and ruffling my skirt up around us, and I remember where we're at. Remember that the stone digging into my bare knees is not a Thornchapel stone and that the sun around us is not Thornchapel's sun. We're not tucked away into our little world of make-believe and sex, where we can do whatever we want and the consequences never come.

"Becket, we shouldn't—not here—"

"There's no one," he whispers, kissing my neck. "We'll be fast."

I look around us, my pulse thudding against his tongue as he flicks it over my throat. He's right—there's no one to be seen. Just the perennial sheep and a herd of ponies in the distance. We can't even be seen from the road leading to the farmhouse from here.

But.

"It's summer in Dartmoor," I protest weakly, my voice breaking as Becket's fingers find their way past my panties. I'm so wet that my skin is slippery to the touch, and it takes no effort for him to slide a finger inside of me. "S-someone is bound to be w-walking along—oh God—Becket—"

His thumb is on my clit now, and it'll take nothing to send me over the brink, nothing at all. I'm almost there already, the muscles between my legs clenching tight, my thighs trembling around his hips.

"We'll be fast," he promises again.

And then he pulls back to meet my eyes. His are a turbulent blue, as if he's fighting off whatever he was feeling in front of the hearth, and I can feel the fight all over his body, in his thighs and chest and arms and even in the hand between my legs. Like he's consumed with something and can only just keep himself from being burned alive by it.

"Please, Poe," he whispers. "Please."

I press a hand to the side of his face. "Will it help…whatever this is?"

He closes his eyes. "Yes."

"Will you tell me what it is?"

His voice is honest when he answers. "I don't know."

He opens his eyes again, and I can't bear to see them like this, near-violet and hazy with a torment I don't understand. "Okay," I whisper. "Okay."

Relief shivers through him, clearing his eyes, parting his lips. "Thank you," he breathes.

I rise up on my knees, still arching into his touch as he continues to finger me while I find the waistband of his shorts and the tight boxer briefs he wears underneath them. Within seconds, his cock is exposed—straight and thick, roped with two twisting veins and surrounded by trim golden hair. I look around us one last time—see no one and nothing but heather and rocks and sheep—press my soft place against Becket and push down.

He holds my panties to the side as I screw myself slowly onto him, his other hand wrapped around his root to assist me, and soon he's all the way inside. This position has him so deep, it sends delicious pressure everywhere, and I have to squirm and squirm to endure it.

"So good," he murmurs, staring up at me. His eyes are open like an early morning sky now. "You feel so good."

"Becket, I need—" He's only just got inside me and I'm so close, but I need more, I need dirtier. *Hurtier.* Even being outside—even riding a priest with my bare knees on the ground and the wind whipping around us—isn't quite enough.

I have an idea. I find his hand and I wrap it around my throat. "Hold me tight," I tell him. "Keep me how you want me."

Becket's hand isn't as tight as Auden's would be, but it still works, it still makes me feel like I'm being forced. Like I'm being made. My body reacts instantly, flooding me with even more heat and urgency, everything between my legs going so tight I can barely breathe.

"God," Becket says, his pupils dilating as he watches me shiver in response. It doesn't sound like a curse when he says it, it sounds like a prayer, like worship, and I love it, I love him and his heart that beats for ecstasy and ecstasy alone.

Becket keeps his hand on my throat, his thumb pressed gently to my windpipe as I begin moving in earnest, circling and grinding, chasing the sweet sparkle of my clit against the base of his cock. The wind flutters through his hair and his dark blond eyelashes, pulls his shirt tight against the firm curves of his muscles. He's at odds with the landscape around us, with the world of rough moors and wild empty meadows. His jaw is too perfectly chiseled, his cheekbones and nose too refined. His hand around my throat is a hand for smoothing robes and pouring wine, for red-inked pages and prayer beads cool to the touch.

He is too cultivated, too civilized. Except then I think of his eyes glowing in the farmhouse, and a voice inside me whispers, *not so civilized after all.*

The uneasiness that comes with the thought should invade my arousal, it should cool me down. More evidence that I was born pervy though: because in this moment, the fear doesn't invade me at all, it *pervades* me, it twists through me and fills me up, it turns everything dangerous and uncertain. And danger and uncertainty get me off like nothing else.

For a moment, I'm poised at the edge, my movements growing jerky and urgent, and then as I stare into his eyes—which even now move from blue to a deep, unearthly indigo—I come with a low and broken whimper. Eight days of denial, eight days of longing, all of it cresting and roaring through me like a merciless wave, yanking me out to sea.

My body surges and tightens around Becket's erection, and I writhe through the contractions, squirm and pant and moan, not caring what I sound like or how loud I am, not even noticing—there is nothing but the wind and the jolting, agonized pleasure below my navel. Nothing but sex and the rock digging into my bare knees. Nothing but the hand around my throat and the memory of Auden's voice and Becket's otherworldly eyes.

"Yes," he breathes. "Yes. That's it. Keep going. Keep going."

The climax rolls on and then I feel Becket's muscles quivering against me, I see his eyes flutter closed. "Fuck," he mumbles. "Oh fuck. I—"

He doesn't have to tell me he's coming, because his cock announces that for him. Swelling and jerking heavily inside me, filling me with his seed. The long throbs are mirrored in the grip on my throat—tightening, loosening, tightening again—his eyes opening so he can watch my face as he pumps me full. It's erotic as hell, and I think I could come again, I think I could find another peak, if only he keeps holding my throat, if only I keep moving—

A dog runs behind me, barking happily, and Becket freezes. Voices come from just on the other side of the ridge, which means they won't be able to see us yet, but in just a few seconds…

Ever the gentleman, Becket helps me to my feet before he tucks his still-twitching erection away, and I mumble a hurried *thanks* as I smooth my skirt down.

But I look up, and with a sinking sensation in my stomach, I realize it's too late.

The hikers, a man and a woman, have crested the hill just in time to see me crawl off Becket's lap, just in time to see him adjust his shorts. There can be no mistaking that we were fooling around—at *best*. And it wouldn't be difficult to guess what we were doing at worst.

"Uh, hello," I say weakly, giving a limp wave. My panties are still pulled to the side, and there's no way to adjust them—or worry about my flushed cheeks or disheveled hair. Warm seed threatens to run out of me and I clench my thighs together to keep it from running down my legs.

Becket stands up, and turns, and even in profile, I can see the shock that ripples through him and pales his skin. It's the same shock that ripples through the couple as they recognize him.

"Father Hess?" the woman asks tentatively, looking back and forth between us. And shit—now I recognize her too. She's in the choir at St. Petroc's. Her husband helps tend the cemetery there.

They go to Becket's church.

And they saw us having sex.

Fuck.

"Georgie," Becket says, his voice warm, but also laced with uncertainty. "How are you?"

"Fine," she asks, still looking over to me. I'm sure she recognizes me from Mass. From the front pew, where I sit holding hands with Auden.

God, what she must think of me.

I've so rarely felt shame that isn't the fun kind that I almost don't recognize it at first. I don't recognize the feeling like my stomach has sunk between my feet and like my cheeks have caught fire and like I want to cry.

It's only as I press my thighs together even harder—the insides of them growing slick—that it hits home.

I'm ashamed.

Ashamed and guilty—because judging by the look on Georgie's face, she knows exactly what we were doing, and the unhappy shock in her eyes tells me she's not going to forget about it any time soon.

And maybe she shouldn't—maybe no one should forget a misbehaving priest. Maybe no one should forgive one.

God. Why didn't I stop us? Why didn't I fight harder to move somewhere else? To go somewhere private? We're so used to being the gods of our own little world that we've forgotten the real one, and now we'll have to pay for our hubris. We'll have to reap what we've sown, except it will be Becket doing the reaping, it will be Becket paying the price for both our sins.

I blink back hot, guilty tears as Georgie says, "As you can see, we were just out for a stroll. It was good seeing you." She and her husband start walking again, their dog running back up the path to meet them, tail wagging. They don't look back at us.

As farewells go, it's rather brusque, but I'm relieved nonetheless. I don't think I can stand here another minute with Becket's seed running down my thighs and my skin burning like it's already been dipped in brimstone.

Becket finally turns to me, exhaling heavily. His eyes downcast.

"Becket," I say softly, and then stop. I don't know what I can say to make this better. We fucked up.

And the cost—the cost could be something it would kill him to pay.

"Do you mind driving me to the rectory?" he asks, not meeting my gaze. "I don't feel like running back just now."

"Of course. Do you—would you rather come to Thornchapel instead?"

He shakes his head. "I think I need to spend some time alone right now."

"Okay," I say. I want to hug him, hold his hand, do *something*, but what can I do? Haven't I already fucked things up enough by touching him in the first place?

We start walking down the farm's side of the ridge, through the wildflowers and down the lane to where the car is parked.

"Will it be okay?" I ask. "Do you think it will be okay?"

Becket takes a long time to answer.

The silence between us is filled with bleating sheep and trilling birds and a playful, tossing wind, and it's so hard to believe that anything could be bad now, not with the world sounding like this.

"I don't know if things will be okay," Becket says finally, his voice hollow.

"But I also don't know if they should be."

24

St. Sebastian

At first, it was like gin, the feeling of loving him after knowing the truth.

It was just another burn, another kind of heat to add to the glow of the library fire and the warmth of Poe's kisses.

Dizzying, maybe. Forbidden, definitely.

But translucent. You could hold it up to the light and say, *see? I've only had this much sin tonight.*

Or perhaps it was like scotch. Drinking it would cost me more than I could afford, but then what else would burn as good going down?

I tried not to care that we couldn't seem to resist these little sips of each other. I tried to write it off the same way I wrote off an extra drink or two at the end of the night. Who did it hurt if sometimes he made me sit on the floor by his feet or if sometimes he held my hand while we walked down to the river? What did it really matter if we trembled when we hugged each other good night, if sometimes he let his lips ghost over the shell of my ear as we did?

It didn't matter, of course it didn't. And it hurt nothing and no one for him to treat us both to those small acts of dominance, for me to pine after him the same way I've done for years.

Except I was wrong, it did hurt someone.

It hurt *us*.

After we come back from Kansas, something changes. Something I can't define. Perhaps it was the time we shared Poe at Emily's club, or maybe it was hearing the full story of what Ralph had done in the thorn chapel. Or maybe it was the ring, a confirmation and a kindness and a taunt, all in one. Or maybe it has nothing to do with any of those things—maybe it's simply spring passing into real summer, when everything goes hot and lush anyway.

Whatever it is, it's no longer a sweet, sipping burn. It no longer pours itself into the cracks and empty spaces left behind by everything else, it's no longer light and mutable and easily contained.

It thickens. It pervades. Instead of a burn, it's a crush, and instead of a sin, it becomes the fabric of my days.

What do I breathe? Wanting him.

What do I drink? What do I eat? Wanting him, wanting him.

Every element is him now, every act is suffused with the memory of his touch and his voice, and it's as if the pain feeds itself, as if it feeds me, because it only grows stronger, and me along with it. Poets write about growing weak with heartbreak, about wasting away, but I solidify, I grow in the face of my own starvation. Summer means long hours for Augie, it means my hands grow rougher and my body grows bigger. And every fiber of muscle, every lock of hair, is grown with the sear of wanting a man I can never have.

Thornchapel knows it too.

Storms threaten but never break. The air grows so sultry and oppressive that even our shady stone manor is nearly unbearable inside. I take to swimming in the river whenever I can because the indoor pool is too cloying. Poe starts wearing bikini tops and skirts while she works—tops that are so easy to untie and peel away from her skin...

The trees are full now, the hills are green. The gorse flowers golden and the heather purple, and the ponies and the sheep and the cattle are high up on the slopes, grazing the upper pastures and occasionally congregating on roads already clogged with summer tourists.

July is in its full promise, plump and ripe and ready. Everything has glutted itself so thoroughly on sun and water that there is nothing left to do but doze, hot and sated and a tiny bit miserable.

Our moods worsen. Auden stalks through the house like a wolf, scowling at everything that isn't Proserpina or scotch. The heat makes Poe sleepier and that makes her crankier, and to make up for it, she works in the library every minute she's awake.

And I feel like I am sixteen again, like there is a fist in my heart and no amount of working, wandering, or jerking off will make it go away. I work from dawn till dusk between the library and Augie, I bury myself in Proserpina every chance I get, any free moment is out ranging the woods and swimming in the river, and still.

Still.

Proserpina was right earlier this year. Whatever the three of us share can't be segmented or portioned out, there is no cutting or slicing sections of it away. It is a cage of brambles around all of us, inside all of us—the thorns have grown straight through our flesh and bitten into our hearts and there is no chance at extrication now.

All the parts of love save for one?

Did we really believe that could work? As if I could excise one share of my love from the other? As if I could chip away at one facet and expect the rest of the gem to remain intact?

No.

It was a lie, and no one wanted it to be truer than me. But we are miserable inside of it, hungry and rough, biting at each other with words and dark glances, prowling after each other, stalking the other's steps only to snap and snarl when we finally catch our quarry.

Nothing helps. Nothing will ever help the torment of needing my father's son like this.

And still the storms will not break.

25

Delphine

Just make it inside.

> *All you have to do is make it inside.*

My hands shake as I unlock the lower door to Rebecca's flat. They shake so much that I drop the keys on the pavement at first; they shake so much that I struggle to fit them into the lock and turn it. And then when I'm inside, I find I can barely see the trendy, industrial stairs in front of me. I find I can barely walk.

Just make it upstairs. Just make it to the shower.

When I manage to trip my way up to the flat and see I'm alone, relief quivers through me so violently that I have to stop walking. I have to drop to my knees, my bag sliding off my elbow and spilling tubes of lipstick and a bottle of half-drunk kombucha onto the reclaimed wood planks of Rebecca's floor.

Breathe.

Breathe.

The floor helps. The floor is where I feel loved and held—where I kneel for the woman I love—and even knowing she doesn't love me, even knowing she can't ever, ever see me like this, I still feel better down here. Not good, sure, and definitely not okay.

But better.

Breathe. Make it to the shower.

I can crawl now, I can make myself move. Slowly I make it to the bathroom, every limb trembling, my stomach and chest juddering with long, ugly noises that aren't quite sobs and aren't quite moans either, but some hellish keen in between. Thank God I'm alone, thank God, thank God.

I never want Rebecca to see me like this.

When I get to the bathroom, I force myself to stand. My feet hurt from the heels I wore this morning for the photoshoot, and my skin burns and prickles so much that I think parts of me are bleeding.

But that's not why I'm crying. That's not why I had to crawl across the floor.

I shove off the romper I wore to the photoshoot and kick off my sandals. I glance up in the mirror and see myself naked—my skin covered in angry red marks from the clips and tape and pins—and see my hair and makeup still as pristine and perfect as they were an hour ago at the studio. My lips still painted in a bright, vital red.

Lady Danger.

Usually one of my favorites, but today, it looks too much like Cherry Tree, which means I flinch at my own reflection.

I grab a clean flannel and rub at my mouth, desperate to scrape it off, to *feel* it scraped off, and then I swipe a bottle of micellar water off the vanity and step into the large shower, turning it as hot as I can stand and sinking to the floor as the water sluices down, flattening my hair and streaming over my back and shoulders. And all the while I wipe roughly at my face, using the micellar water to clean everything off, every last stitch of makeup. Like if

I can clean my skin, then I can clean my insides too. Clean my shaking, ugly guts.

It was supposed to be a photoshoot like any other photoshoot. In fact, it *was* a photoshoot like any other photoshoot. A brand I'd modeled for before, with a photographer I liked. When I woke up this morning—early, earlier even than Rebecca for once—I'd felt nothing but excitement. Modeling is *hard*, it's often painful, it's often awkward, and even with a fat-positive company and photographer, it's hours and hours of reckoning with one's body in clothes that don't always fit and under bright lights that hide nothing. It's hard not to hear every shitty comment that someone's posted on my Instagram aloud in my head. It's hard not to hear my *own* shitty thoughts aloud in my head.

And yet, for all that's hard and miserable about modeling, I love it. The beeps of the camera, the clicks of the shutter, the sharp, chemical scent of hairspray. The thrill that never goes away from being dolled up, being petted and praised, being posed and directed and made to suffer in tiny ways.

Which, now that I think about it, was probably a sign I would end up being a kinky girl.

And anyway, there's also the satisfaction of getting to model clothes made for bodies like mine. Every time I do it, I'm taking part in something new and huge and exciting—I'm changing the world. Maybe I'm not shepherding souls like Becket or building things like Auden. Maybe I'm not a genius like Rebecca or clever like Poe, but I am doing *something*. Something that would have meant the world to a baby teenager Delphine, still trying to shop at all the same stores her friends did, still trying to pretend she didn't spend hours picking her clothes because nothing she owned ever, ever, ever made her feel pretty.

So today should have been wonderful. Even better because tomorrow night was a big exhibition at Justine's, and so after all that hard but good work, my Mistress would reward me with a hard but good scene in front of the entire club.

But today wasn't wonderful. And it was because of the cherries.

I should have told my manager about them, I know I should have. I should have told my assistant or my publicist. I definitely should have told my therapist. I should have told so many people, but I didn't, because when it's not bothering me, when I haven't thought about cherries for hours and hours and even days, it seems like such an insignificant problem. Something I can ignore when it pops up.

Something that *of course* I can just deal with, because it's trivial and fucking ridiculous.

But then when it is bothering me, I can't ignore it, it's not trivial at all, all I want to do is hide, hide, hide from the world and myself and my own mind. All I am is ashamed and crazy, and my therapist hates the word *crazy*—

But when I'm like this, when the cherries are in my mind and my thoughts are going cherry tree cherry tree cherry tree and I can feel wet grass against my shoulder blades and see the cloud-covered moon behind heavy, monstrous shadows—

When I can feel a tongue shoved wet and squirming into my mouth—when I can see a face in the moonlight as it lifts its head, its mouth smeared with Cherry Tree—its lips stained with the same color I'd so happily and carefully applied just two hours earlier—my lipstick, on *him*—cherry tree cherry tree cherry tree—

I *feel* crazy. I *feel* crazed. Frantic, unconsolable, unreasonable.

Driven mad by something that's entirely in my mind.

How can I tell people? How can I tell them and have it make sense? I can't, because it doesn't make sense. It makes no sense that I can easily muster the actual words *rape* and *assault*, that I can talk about what happened, that I can describe it and sound normal and well-adjusted and calm. And yet the mere memory of the lipstick I was wearing that night plunges me into panic.

The mere *memory* of it.

It sends me straight back there, back to that garden, and then breathing is impossible and my skin burns and my heart pounds and I can't feel my fingers, my lips, my anything other than the roiling, metallic tightness in my chest. Nothing is real except the desperate, desperate feeling that I'm about to die.

I'm ashamed of it. And that's why I haven't been able to tell anyone, not even a therapist or a lover or a friend. Not even Auden, not even Rebecca, not even my mother.

Not even when I feel like I'm full of cherries on the inside, a pretty doll stuffed full of shiny fruit. Like when I open my mouth to speak, cherries will fall out instead of words.

Like even my tears will be red and sweet.

I should have said no when I saw the cherry-patterned swimsuit. I should have faked a diva fit, faked sick, faked *something*. I should have pulled my manager aside and made her deal with it.

So many things I should have done and didn't. I didn't want to be dramatic. I didn't want to let anybody down. I didn't want to *bother* anyone.

And so, while my mind screamed itself hoarse, while my shoulder blades tickled with the memory of wet grass and my heart tried to slam its way out of my chest, I let the stylist help me into the swimsuit. I let them touch up my lipstick—a red which all of a sudden seemed perilously close to Cherry Tree—I let them fluff my hair. I held my shoulders back, I popped my bottom out, I tilted my pelvis back so my thighs wouldn't press together as much. I kept my angles dynamic, my mouth warm, my eyes intimate.

I gave them everything they wanted, even though I could feel each and every cherry on that swimsuit sinking through the fabric and branding itself into my flesh. Onto my tits and my arse, onto my hips and my cunt. Acid-etched cherries all over my skin.

But I smiled and posed and tossed my hair anyway, even as my skin was scored with cherry upon cherry, because that's what they wanted, because I didn't want to let anyone down.

Because I wanted to be easy.

Just like I wanted to be easy for Rebecca, and look what a mess that's become.

But is that such a crime? I wonder, staring down at the lipstick-smeared flannel in my hands. Is it so bad to want to be easy for someone one loves? To want to spare them the worst of one's demons? To absolve them of trying to fix the unfixable and trying to share the unsharable?

It can't be. I refuse to believe it is.

I did the right thing today, and I powered through. I only hope—well, I don't remember the rest of the shoot really—so I just hope I didn't seem off. I hope no one could see how the stupid cherries from a stupid bikini scorched themselves onto my skin.

"Delph?" I hear a voice call over the noise of the shower. "Pet?"

Rebecca.

Oh bleeding hell.

I scramble to my feet just in time for her to walk into the bathroom, looking polished and ravishing in a tailored black jumpsuit. She stops at the entrance to the shower—a large, subway-tiled walk-in with benches and multiple showerheads—and tilts her head at me. "Delph?" she asks, sounding concerned.

"Bex!" I chirp as brightly as I can, forcing a smile. "You should be at work!"

"I have the afternoon off for my hair appointment," she says slowly as she searches my face. I know she's missing nothing—not the puffy eyes, nor the abraded and swollen lips. "I thought I'd come home and see you before I went. Are you all right?"

"Oh yes," I say, still forcing the brightness out. Sunny, happy, *easy easy.* "It was capital."

She frowns down at the flannel in my hands. "You always say not to remove makeup that way."

"Photoshoot makeup," I say, coaxing a laugh up. "There's something the stylist used that was making me swell up and itch, so I needed to scrub it off."

"Ah," Rebecca says, immediately sympathetic. "That's terrible—I hope your manager gave them a talking to."

"Oh yes, you know Kendra. She tore them a new arsehole."

Rebecca nods, seeming satisfied, and it's funny, isn't it, how easy it is to lie after enough practice. How easily people will believe one, especially if one lies with a smile on one's face.

"I should probably get going," Rebecca says, but she doesn't move. Her eyes are on my body instead—where the water trickles over my shoulders and down my breasts to drip off my nipples. Her fingers curl in on themselves, like she's trying very hard not to reach for me, and I see the quick dart of her tongue as she licks at her upper lip.

Warmth—so unlike the churning, cherry-shaped heat I've been feeling all day—floods me. I feel hot and alive in a good way, in the best way, and suddenly I want Rebecca more than I want anything. I want her to curl her fingers into *me*, I want her to lick *me*.

I sink to my knees again, and this time it's not because I can't walk. This time it's my choice.

When I kneel to the woman I love, I exist again. I get to have feelings that aren't cherries, I get to have choices that aren't escape or survive.

"Don't flirt," Rebecca chides me. But her pupils have dilated into liquid pools of hunger, and she takes a step closer.

"It wouldn't take long," I whisper, peering up at her from under my wet eyelashes.

She laughs, and a dimple I almost never see flashes in her cheek. "Since when has not long with you ever been enough for me?"

I smile up at her, sliding my knees apart so that she can see between my legs.

Her eyes drop to my pussy and her smile fades into a hungry expression. "I thought I told you not to flirt."

"Can you blame me?"

"I have an appointment."

I spread my knees even more. "I could help you relax before you go."

She comes closer. She's wearing cobalt Blahnik flats I bought for her last month after I'd finally had enough of looking at the horrible wool things she normally wore. I picked them because they have a raised vamp that exposes the top of her feet, the delicate cambers of her tarsals and metatarsals, and even now I want to lean down and press my lips there. Show her my devotion.

But then she lifts her foot to step forward and panic flares through me. "Stop! You can't get those wet!"

Rebecca laughs again, a low, throaty *ha*. But she does stop, just out of range of the spattering water. "Have I finally found something stronger than your lust?"

"They're Blahniks and they're *suede*."

"And you're adorable and you're *ridiculous*." She leans forward enough to tug on a wet lock of my hair. "I really do need to go."

The idea of her leaving, of not having her hands, her kisses, her pain— it sears me with abrupt fear. "Tonight then? We could play tonight?"

Her mouth twists in regret. "I'm going to be home too late to play, I think."

I sulk. "You're going to make me wait until tomorrow."

"Delph," sighs Rebecca, "I'll probably have to work late tomorrow to make up for lost time. I'm missing this afternoon and evening as it is—"

Alarm blares through me. "Tomorrow night is the exhibition at Justine's. You promised we could go."

"Oh," she says. "Right." But she doesn't look enthusiastic.

"Bex," I say, trying to sound cool. Trying to be easy. "I've been looking forward to this for weeks."

And I have been. I've been so excited to scene publicly at our club, where everyone can see us. All the submissives Rebecca has taken home, all the Dominants she's friends with—she'd claim me in front of all of them. Everyone would know I was hers and I wouldn't have to wonder anymore if she was...hiding me...somehow. Keeping me as a convenient fuck.

If Rebecca flaunts me in front of everyone, then I'll know I'm not just a novelty, not just the fat girl on her boffing bucket list. I'll know she's proud to have me as her own.

"I know," Rebecca says. "But there will be more nights like it soon, I'm sure."

I can see it now—I can see how she'll dodge the next night, and the next, and the next after it, until we never do it at all. Until she's hidden me forever, because I'm embarrassing and ugly and afraid of cherries—

Stop.

Stop it.

I'm feeling hurt right now, that's all—and sometimes when I'm hurting, it's like I want to injure myself *more*, like I want to rip my own existence up and grind the pieces of it into the ground, because it's easier to press on my own bruises and peel off my own skin than it is to turn my wounds into words.

But I try now. It's what my therapist would say to do. It's what Rebecca herself would say to do.

"I really want to go," I say, feeling stupid and awkward and needy. "It's important to me."

Rebecca stares down at me, her dark eyes studying my face. She so rarely misses anything, but I hope she does now, because I don't want her to see what a beastly, clingy mess I am inside. I hope all she sees is a pretty submissive eager to have lots of kinky fun.

And maybe she does, because her face softens. "Of course, pet. I do need to work later than usual, but I can meet you there to save time, yeah?"

My shoulders drop in relief. "Yeah."

"Come here," she says.

I move toward her on my knees, and in a graceful move, she bends to take my hand and pull me to my feet.

"Bex, no, you're going to get wet—"

I'm in her arms anyway, and she's nipping at my jaw, which from her is a caress of purest affection. She keeps me pressed against her, soaking through her jumpsuit, as she says, "If it's important to you, it's important to me. I'll do my best to make it."

I drop my head onto her shoulder, wishing I were stronger and better. Wishing I didn't need her approval and her public validation so much. "Okay."

She starts to pull away but then goes rigid. "What," she asks, in a tight and furious tone, "is this?"

Confused, I straighten up to see her glaring at me, and before I can ask what she means, she turns me around so I'm facing the back of the shower.

A finger traces a line of inflamed skin and I wince a little. "They have to use gaffer tape sometimes instead of a bra depending on what I'm wearing," I explain. "It irritates my skin a little."

"And this?" Her finger stops at a spot above my hip, tapping a cluster of aching pinpricks.

"They had to pin a dress to make it fit." I flush a little, remembering it. The dress had been a flouncy retro number with a crinoline under the skirt, and it had taken me actually yelping aloud for the stylist to realize she wasn't stabbing the pins into a thick hunk of dress and crinoline, but into my flesh.

"And this here? It looks like someone clamped your back."

"A dress clip."

"And your feet?"

I look down, to where bruises have started to come up around my toes and where raw red skin has started to bleed on the backs of my heels.

"The heels weren't my size."

They were too small, so they'd slathered Vaseline on my feet and shoved them on, pair after pair.

Rebecca turns me around. Her hands are kind, but there's nothing gentle in her face when I see it. "I can't believe Kendra would let this happen to you," she says with fury in her voice. "I can't believe any of them would just let this *happen*."

"It's normal," I try to reassure her. "It's so normal. And I don't mind the pain, I never have."

"Maybe not," she says with a scowl. "But that doesn't make this okay, even for a masochist."

I lap up her concern, her protectiveness, even as defensiveness hums through me. "It's part of the job. If I don't put up with it, then there're a hundred other girls who will, just waiting to take my place."

"But none of those other girls are mine. You are."

I practically melt at hearing her say I'm hers. "I know."

"Do you know?" she asks, one brow raising into a perfectly curved arch. "Because if you do, then you should also know that I'm the only one who gets to put marks on your body. I'm the only one who gets to hurt you, is that clear?"

I'm still melting. I'm still defensive. I'm a mess, all clamoring, querulous contradictions. "You know I love being yours, Bex. Mistress." I add the last part after I see the dangerous glint in her eyes. "But I also love my job. I can't jeopardize it by being fussy or difficult."

"There has to be a way that you can still do shoots and not look like you've been in a bad dungeon after," she says. "You are *mine alone* to hurt. Mine to pleasure, and mine to keep safe. No one touches you unless I allow it."

I open my mouth to argue some more—the sentiment itself is very sexy, but my job doesn't work like that, it just doesn't—when she presses her lips to mine in farewell.

"I have to go, pet. Be good."

"Tomorrow night?" I plead into her kiss. "Please?"

"Tomorrow night," she promises. "I know you want it. And I think—" she slides a hand between my legs, her fingers grazing against my clit and making me shiver "—you need it too."

I do, I do. I do need it, I need all of it, I think—to come, yes, but also to have that shivery kind of hurt which turns all other hurts into soft, manageable things. Just like kneeling, the hurt gives me back my choices and my strength. It reminds me that someone sees me and cares about me enough to help me digest my pain.

I nod, closing my eyes to savor her touch. "Tomorrow night." I'm already clinging to the idea of it like I clung to the idea of getting in the shower earlier.

A small squeeze on my most intimate skin, and then my mistress is gone, leaving me alone with a wet flannel and a still running shower.

And the knowledge that more than twenty-four hours separate me from shuddering, blissful relief.

26

Delphine

After my shower, I want to drink a bottle of champagne and sleep for sixteen hours, but I can't. I have a podcast interview later this afternoon, and a conference call with a publicist from a charity I rep, and then I have my biweekly phone call with Mummy and Daddy. They're on some pseudo-business, pseudo-holiday trip to Cyprus, and are already sunburnt and blotto by the time I ring. But they're still as sweet as ever, and when I change into pajamas and curl up in Rebecca's big bed alone, I find myself truly and achingly homesick.

Not for home necessarily, but for Mummy and Daddy and Gimlet and Rumswizzle, our springer spaniels. For laying on the sofa with my head in my mother's lap, for listening to Daddy read something aloud to us while Gimlet snores next to him.

I hug a pillow and fall asleep before Rebecca gets home.

When I wake up the next morning, she's already woken up, dressed, and gone.

My head hurts from too much sleep, but I burrow back under the blankets anyway. I feel empty and gummy inside, like mascara left uncapped on a sink. Like a jam jar with only a thin layer left at the bottom.

Just make it until tonight.

I close my eyes and imagine, in great detail, being tied up, cropped, paddled, flogged, anything, anything with my Mistress. I imagine what it will feel like on the stage with her, all eyes on us, knowing once and for all that even if she doesn't love me, at least she's not ashamed of me. I imagine how good it will feel to turn all this chaotic emptiness into something explicit and distinct—turn something intangible into welted stripes no wider than my thumb, into pink handprints, into rope marks, into ruined knickers. Something I can point to and say, *see this? I chose this. I felt this. And someone I love helped me feel it.*

I stay in bed long into the afternoon, wrapped in fantasies of tonight.

Emily Genovese: I see you.

I look up from my phone to see Emily striding across the lobby of Justine's, and I greet her with my customary kiss to the cheek, which seems to take her by surprise. But she's smiling when I pull back.

"Thank you for inviting me tonight," she says. "This is much better than dinner alone at my airport hotel."

"It's my turn to be hospitable," I say, struggling to sound cheerful. "How was your film festival?"

"Equal parts dull and brilliant." Emily searches my face, her smile fading. "Is everything okay? You seem upset."

It's rude, it's shockingly rude. And yet something in me blooms under the scrutiny of her stare and the directness of her question. "The last two days have been…disagreeable," I admit.

She tilts her head to study me even more, and I flush. Not entirely with displeasure.

"Where is your Mistress?" she asks finally. "Or do you often come here without her?"

"Oh, never," I say quickly, not wanting her to get the wrong impression. "We always come together, and she's coming tonight too. She had to stay at work late, so I'm just waiting for her to arrive so we can go in together."

"Ah, of course," Emily says. Her voice is smooth and easy, a Hollywood voice, and it's hard not to watch her mouth as she speaks. She's painted her lips in a deep matte black, and it highlights how soft and full they are. How flawless her skin is.

She's dressed for the occasion too, wearing her usual black boots and fishnets, but with a red vinyl miniskirt and matching halter top. It hides nothing of the convexities and soft places of her body; there're swells of skin between her skirt and her top and where the top cuts into her back and near her armpits—and yet she's not shy or self-conscious in the least. She knows she's totally lush, she knows everyone around her thinks so, and she receives it as her due.

"I'll wait with you," Emily continues. "No sense in walking away from the prettiest girl in the club."

I shouldn't flush again at that. She's being flirty and I have a Mistress slash girlfriend slash…something.

But I do. I do flush. It's strange to feel, because my face is still tight and swollen from so much crying yesterday, and I spent today feeling numb and odd and like maybe I wasn't even real. But Emily is the first person since yesterday to make me feel human and not all empty and gummy. And if not full again, like I *could* be full again. Someday.

"Will you and your Mistress take part in the exhibition tonight?" Emily asks.

It's small talk, I know it is, and Emily has no way of knowing that her casual question has an anything but casual answer. I try to respond in a steady voice, a voice of someone who didn't spend the day listening to her eyelashes scrape across a pillow. "Yes, I am very much hoping so. But we haven't—we haven't scened publicly here before."

Emily's dark eyes dip over my flouncy white skirt and sheer white top, which reveals the black lacy bra underneath. "A shame," she murmurs. "The people here have been missing something truly special."

If only Rebecca felt the same way, a disloyal voice whispers, but I quash it as fast as I can. "We simply haven't had the time," I explain. It sounds weak, even to my own ears, and Emily's eyebrow rises the smallest bit.

"But you've had time to scene privately?" she asks. Then she holds up a hand. "I'm being nosy, I'm sorry. Not everyone likes to play in public."

But I think I do, I want to say.

I think I'd like it more than anything.

"At any rate, you look like it would do you some good," she says bluntly, and again, I should bristle at that, but I don't, because she's right.

"It would do me some good," I reply. "It would be marvelous."

The lobby is starting to empty of people now—most of the guests are heading toward the theater below—and I glance at my phone again. It's almost time for the exhibition to begin and Rebecca isn't here. Nor has she answered my phone calls or texts.

I'm starting to feel strange again, and I know, I just *know*, that if I could kneel in front of Rebecca, I'd feel better. If she were here, if she could bite my jaw or swat my bottom or tug my hair—if I could see her glimmering eyes and barely there smile—I'd feel okay again, capable, clear.

But she's not here. And as Emily and I stand in the now-deserted lobby and the minutes pass, I realize that for the first time since I've known her—the first time in at least twelve years—the ever-punctual Rebecca Quartey is going to be late.

Applause and music drift up the stairs from the theater, and I glance at my phone again.

"Maybe there's traffic?" Emily suggests kindly.

"Probably the traffic," I agree. Rebecca would never be late unless something was totally out of her control. "She'll be here any minute."

"Of course she will," Emily says. "But there's no sense in you being late to something you want to attend. Why don't you text her that she can meet you inside? I'm sure she'll understand."

"I don't know," I say, wavering. "She really will be here any minute…"

"You've been looking forward to this?" Emily asks.

"Very much." *Very much* doesn't even begin to cover it.

Emily nods. Her black hair is hanging over her shoulders in full, shiny waves, and when she nods, it slides over itself like a fairy-tale princess's. "Then she wouldn't want you to miss any of it on her account."

I could easily see Rebecca walking in, already tutting when she sees me standing here like a twit. She'd tell me I should have gone in without her, and she'd be right, because it is rather silly to miss something I want to do merely because she was late.

"You're right," I declare, and Emily's black lips curve up in a smile.

"I'm always right," she says.

I lead her to the desk in the lobby—which looks like the front desk at a smart hotel—and arrange for her guest membership. While she gets that sorted, I text Rebecca.

Going in since it's started, but I'll make sure to take a seat by the door so you can find me! xx

There's no response. I chew on my lip a moment, and then remember my lipstick and stop. I have the sudden worry that she's not okay, that she's been hurt or fallen ill, that she's been in an accident…

I'm worried, Bex. Let me know if you're okay. xx

The text comes half a second later.

I'm fine.

My heart flips over as I read it. And then immediately sinks back down to my feet. I decide to try calling one last time—and then I'm sent to voicemail after only a ring.

I look down at the phone like there's been some sort of misunderstanding, but no. That's Rebecca's voicemail message I'm hearing, and after only four seconds on the line. Which means she sent me there. Which means she's not injured, which means she's not away from her phone.

She just doesn't want to talk to me.

I…have no idea what to make of this.

A sad, lonely kind of panic starts buzzing around the edges of my mind.

"Which way?" Emily asks. I look up to see her finished and standing next to me, the thin white wristband on her wrist indicating her guest status at the club. She'll be able to play publicly and in the private rooms, but only with members of the club.

I force myself to lower the phone. To smile as brightly as I can.

"This way."

The theater underneath Justine's is all prewar glamor and Jazz Age luxury. Circular booths upholstered in buttery leather surround red-clothed tables, which are lit by small fringed lamps. Globed pendant lights hang from the ceiling, burning a faint gold, and the whole room is adorned in a custom silk wallpaper depicting various sex acts from mythology and history: Catherine the Great having her feet tickled; Enki ejaculating the Tigris and Euphrates rivers; Edward VII fornicating by aid of his special sex chair; Pasiphaë and the bull.

At the front of the room is a low stage framed by velvet curtains in a deep-hued garnet, and the usual kinky furniture staples are front and center—racks of toys, padded benches, crosses. A slender woman with light brown skin and straight black hair purrs the night's agenda into a microphone as Emily and I slide into the last unoccupied booth toward the back.

I check my phone again. Nothing more from Rebecca.

The panic at the edges of my mind buzzes louder now.

The exhibition works on a volunteer basis, our host is explaining, and anybody can come up and display whatever they like—a particularly tidy little sub, a talent for Florentine flogging, even the more outre kinks like autofellatio or fire play—all that's needed is clear, sober consent from the participants and an adherence to the club's rules, which ban scat, watersports, some types of breath play, and most types of blood play. She cedes the stage to polite applause.

A server wearing nothing but a cock ring brings us shallow coupes of fizzing champagne while the first volunteers mount the stage—an older woman and a young man with a leather collar around his neck. She cuffs the man to the spanking bench and starts perusing the selection of paddles hanging from one of the racks.

Emily clinks her coupe glass lightly against mine. "Here's to a night of fun," she whispers, her dark-lipped smile evil and beautiful in the dark. I try to smile back, but my eyes slide to the empty doorway instead, as if I expect Rebecca to be standing there, tall and stern and perfect.

She's not.

The sub gets paddled, his cock reddened and ready between his legs as his Domme beats him, and then she uncuffs him and allows him to ejaculate onto her boots. The equipment—and the Domme's boots—are cleaned and the next volunteers come up.

And the next.

More coupe glasses of champagne are handed out. A woman fucks her sub with a strap-on and I squirm in my seat. We're given finger foods and hors d'oeuvres.

And still no Rebecca.

I check my phone I don't know how many times. I send text after text—trying to be easy and calm and not clingy—but I don't feel easy *or* calm right now. I feel like I want to cry. I feel like I want to crawl under the table and hide.

Rebecca is never late. Rebecca never sends me straight to voicemail.

I'm fine, she said. Nothing else. No excuses, no apologies, nothing at all.

Am I being stood up? Was I right all this time that she didn't want to scene publicly with me because she was embarrassed? Does she want to hide me from her friends? I can live without her loving me—I think—but I don't know if I can live with being an embarrassment.

But maybe I'm wrong? She did allow me to put the two of us on Instagram; we've been photographed together countless times at events and out in the city—it would be difficult to get more public than we've been in the last month. But then why would it be hard for her to show me off here? Is it because she couldn't care less about tabloids and social media, but she does care about her peers here at the club?

"Delphine," Emily says softly. She carefully pries the champagne coupe from my fingers; my hand has been shaking so badly that I've been sloshing the drink over the sides. She uses a napkin to wipe at my hand and wrist, and it's so soothing to be taken care of like this, it's so comforting. My breathing evens out the tiniest bit.

"Are you okay?" she asks. "We don't need to stay if you aren't."

"I'm okay," I lie, because I'm not okay, but I also want to stay. I want to see the people here, and I want them to see me. I want to belong to this stylish club of stylish deviants, and I don't want to wait anymore.

"Let's go up there," Emily says suddenly. "You and me."

I let out a short, inelegant huff of a laugh. "What?"

"You wanted this," Emily says, leaning forward. "You deserve to have this, and you *can* have it, even if your mistress isn't here. I'll go up there with you."

"But—"

"Doesn't Rebecca share you anyway? Sometimes?"

I take a sip of champagne, unable to phrase an answer. Because—yes—there's Thornchapel, where all of us have kissed and petted and fucked to some extent. And also because—no. Rebecca doesn't share me here in London. And she hasn't even shared me at Thornchapel since I officially became hers.

"You should be shown off. Anyone would be proud to show you off, including me," Emily continues in a quiet voice. "I know she would feel the same."

"I don't know about that," I mutter, taking another sip. If she were proud, she'd be here right now. Or at the very least she wouldn't have given me the brush-off.

"What's your favorite punishment?" Emily asks.

"Spanking. But I don't—"

"Ah, spanking. A simple girl, I like it. Let's go up there and get you spanked."

"I can't," I say with finality. Even as I think *why can't I?*

I've been with other people at Thornchapel, and Emily is Poe's ex and friend, which surely makes her an honorary part of our circle? And it's not as if Emily and I are going to kiss or have sex. It would be a little platonic spanking between friends.

I'm fine, Rebecca said.

Well, I'm not. I'm not fine. My panic is turning into shame, which is turning into anger. Why shouldn't I get to have this? Just because Rebecca can't be bothered? How is that fair?

"Only spanking?" I ask, looking at Emily.

Her eyes glitter with victory in the dim light. "Only spanking."

I'm the only one who gets to hurt you, is that clear?

The memory of Rebecca's voice filters through my thoughts, but I push it away. This isn't what she meant, I justify to myself. She meant about my work—she was talking about taking care of myself at work. Not a harmless light spanking.

"Let's do it," I say and then finish off my champagne.

Emily only smiles.

The scene on stage finishes after only a few more moments, and then the emcee for the night asks for any other volunteers while the stage is cleaned behind her. Emily stands, and so do I, and heads swivel as we walk down through the booths and tables to the shallow steps at the side of the stage.

Up here, under the bright lights, in front of all these eager, lust-filled eyes, a giddy kind of joy suffuses me. It's humming, it's electric; I feel every cell in my body spark up and hum with energy. And when Emily confidently issues orders and I obey, I spark even more. I ignite like a Catherine wheel, all color and glitter and heat.

I love this. I love being right *here.*

It should be Rebecca here with me.

The thought barely has time to register, because I'm already bent over the spanking bench—a pleasantly comfortable model with a padded riser for my knees and a second padded surface at waist level for me to bend over and lie on. Once I'm arranged, I rest my head on my folded arms and turn so I can see the crowd. So I can see them seeing me.

Emily flips up my short skirt with flourish, and I don't even need to see the audience—I can *feel* their reaction. Their murmurs, their shiftings in their seats. They like seeing my bottom exposed like this. They like seeing *me* exposed like this, patiently and sweetly humiliated.

There is a stillness that comes, then, after I kneel and after I'm presented to them.

It's like the stillness before a rifle shot, with fog in the air and damp Scottish heather scratching at my boots. It's like the pause before the first swipe of lipstick over my mouth.

It's the first barely-there hiss of water against a boat's hull, just as it starts to move.

The quiver that shivers through me settles low in my belly and takes root between my legs. It's trepidation and delight and reckless anticipation.

The first strike is so sudden, so swift, that I don't even have time to react before the second one hits in the exact same spot. I let out a surprised *oh,* and the crowd stirs again, watching and watching with eager eyes.

Emily moves to the other cheek, and then back again, alternating sides but stuttering her rhythm so I can't guess where and when she'll hit next. There's no regularity, no certainty, no mental comfort. My comfort will come from her, and only when she allows it.

And she can read me with eerie precision: when I flinch, she waits, when I cry out, she strikes again, faster and harder. Heat stings across my skin and settles beneath the surface. I feel parts of my body that I hardly think about otherwise—the blood flushing up in the shape of her hands, the muscles quivering underneath. The hollow architecture of my skeleton jouncing with each strike. The parts of my body that move when she hits me, and the parts that don't. My breasts flattened underneath me, my heart beating like a drum behind them, my lungs dilating inside my ribs, my teeth clicking together on the particularly nasty spanks.

The crowd is beyond warmed up now, they're hot, they're hot and restless with me. They breathe when I breathe, they gasp when I gasp. When I open my eyes and peer past the lights into the first few rows, I see people openly petting and sucking each other while they watch me.

I am their living pornography—their object of lust and their shameful catharsis all at once.

I love it so much that I don't know if I'll ever be able to unfold myself and walk off this stage. Maybe I can stay here, maybe I can live in this moment forever—

Emily finishes with a flurry so fast and vicious that I begin to cry. Big tears, lots of them, spilling effortlessly down my face, and it feels so good, not only for the release from the pain, but for the release from the empty, numb anguish of earlier today. Of yesterday.

It's a release that's almost like orgasm, but even more intimate for how vulnerable it is, how witnessed it is.

How savored it is.

I cry and the people watching moan—in envy or in appetite or both— and we're bound together by it. By the witnessing and the savoring.

I'm smiling into my arms as I cry.

Emily smooths her hand over my bottom. It wasn't a bad spanking—certainly not the kind that calls for cold packs or arnica—but after anything like this, I need to be petted and soothed. I need to be called a good girl. I need to be loved on.

And she does, she does all the things I need. She rubs my sore skin as she leans down to murmur tender appreciations, she carefully rearranges my skirt to restore my modesty, she helps me back to my feet. She doesn't fondle me, she doesn't palm anywhere she shouldn't.

She doesn't do anything wrong.

And yet the minute I straighten up and blink out into the audience, *everything* feels wrong.

Guilt comes crashing down onto me; it breaks over my head and shakes me down to my marrow, leaving the rubble of the last ten minutes in a heap around my feet.

Shame comes next, then more loneliness than ever.

And I know exactly why. It's because the moment I shifted position and stood, the moment my thighs pressed together, I could feel how wet I'd become. I could feel how my nipples pushed and pebbled against the lace of my bra and snagged against my sheer blouse.

I told myself before we came up here that it was supposed to be a friendly spanking, that there was nothing sexual or improper about it…and now here I am with a ready body and a racing heart standing next to someone who's not Rebecca.

The wrongness of it sends me abruptly off the stage, down the steps, and hurrying through the tables to find a way out of here—a way to anywhere, I don't even care. A hallway, the lobby, the street. I can't be in here a single second longer, and I only just barely force myself to move calmly, to keep my face serene, before I find the exit at the back of the theatre and take the stairs up to the main floor. I know I left Emily on the stage, I know that might have looked strange, but I'm past caring, I'm past everything—

"Delphine, wait."

Emily's voice echoes across the marble-floored lobby. I force myself to stop. I force myself to turn.

When she sees my face, her lips part. "Are you okay?"

"No, I'm—I'm not quite okay."

She searches my face. "I didn't push you too hard? Take it too far?"

No.

No, Emily's only sin was helping me commit my own.

I shake my head. "You didn't take it too far. You didn't…take liberties."

"Then why—"

"I liked it too much," I cut in. It's impolite, I was raised never to be impolite—or at least to use impoliteness with a certain kind of sophistication if the weapon was called for—but I can't help the way the truth spills out of me. "I love her, Emily. I didn't think—I shouldn't have liked it like that."

Emily's face softens. Even with the septum piercing and the black lipstick, she looks kind. Gentle. "It's a physiological response, Delphine," she says. "One you've been training yourself to have for a long time. It doesn't make you culpable of anything."

I'm already shaking my head. "I got up there with you. I knelt for you. I'm culpable."

Emily takes a step forward. "Don't flagellate yourself over this," she chastens. "That's our job. Anyway, Rebecca will understand completely when you explain it to her. Unless…"

She's so close now that I can count her eyelashes, that I can pick out the golden striations in her brown eyes.

"Unless what?" I whisper.

"Unless you want to do something you can't explain." And then she leans forward and kisses me.

The kiss is warm and assertive. In that way, it's like kissing Rebecca.

But in every other way, it's not.

Rebecca tastes like mint, and Emily tastes like coffee. Rebecca peppers her kisses with nips and bites, and Emily prefers to stroke inside my mouth with her tongue. Rebecca loves to grab and seize at me—my wrists, my hips, my hair—and Emily only runs her hands up my arms, as if she's mapping me for future exploration.

I receive the kiss passively at first, utterly floored by it, but by the time my mind has caught up, my body is already racing ahead, responding to her lips and tongue with matching flickers and strokes, ready to deepen the kiss, ready to press against her.

It's a nice kiss from a fit woman. But it's not the woman I want kisses from, it's not her, it's not Rebecca. With a gasp, I tear away from Emily and stagger back, my fingers coming up to my lips.

"I'm sorry," I say. "I love her and I—I can't do that."

Emily reaches for me, she opens her mouth—now smeared with my own lipstick, pink over black—but I don't wait to hear what she has to say. I can't. I wheel around and go outside, where the evening light still hangs in a rosy shroud over the city and where I find one of the club's footman outside.

"Hello, yes, so sorry to bother you. But could you get my things for me from inside? And help me call my car? I need to leave, and I can't go back inside."

27

Rebecca

Everything changed three years ago.

Everything and nothing at all.

When I heard the key turn in the lock that night, I was sitting in my flat with a glass of wine and another two hours of work to do before I could call it a day. Then, as it is now, only one other person had a key, so I didn't bother getting up. It would be Auden, probably hungry or bored or wanting to gossip, too sober to entertain himself or too drunk to eat a kebab alone. I was used to his unannounced visits.

Which meant I was unprepared for whom I saw coming up the stairs. For the flaxen hair, and the doll face, and the curves right out of some Teutonic milkmaid fantasy.

Delphine Dansey.

Dislike surged instantly: she was everything that made me impatient. She was every vapid, moneyed, horse-owning girl that had nettled me at school. Every effete client too ridiculous and entitled to listen to the reality of soil composition and hill slopes and which climate conditions could support imported tropical plants.

Delphine was emblematic of the whole lot to me. Vain, superficial, callous, and callow. That she was beautiful only made it worse; that she was cheerful only made it worse than that. Everyone believed her to be some kind of perfect English rose, and only I knew the truth: she was a brat.

Luckily for Delphine, and even luckier for me, my thoughts move quickly. And so from the first glimpse of her golden hair to the sight of her face, I remembered she was Auden's good friend, and I remembered what had happened to her last spring. I remembered the trial.

I got to my feet, but I didn't say anything.

Auden was behind her, one hand on the small of her back, the other holding his phone as they mounted the stairs. When he looked up from his phone and saw me, his entire body seemed to quake with relief.

"Rebecca," he said. The flat was all open spaces and hard surfaces, so I could hear him easily, even though he spoke in the quiet, forced tones of someone trying very, very hard to keep it together.

Concern flooded through me. My friend could be many things—bitter, restless, melancholic—but he never, *ever* looked like he was about to break. Even at his worst moments, the times when I knew his father had hit him, when his mother had caused a drunken scene, when he had worn himself down to the bone to prove himself at school or his new firm—even then, he moved through life with a sepia-toned elegance and genteel control.

More than once it had occurred to me that he might enjoy my same deviant tastes, because that control, that restraint—it wasn't all inherited Guest decorum and educated finish, oh no. It was innate to him, inborn. Authority, hubris, insolence. Streaks of cruelty. As deep in him as his vision, his discipline, his loyalty. As deep as his fiercely moral view of the world and everyone in it.

"Do you need to sit…" The invitation died on my lips. It was meant for Auden, but once I saw Delphine's face, I knew that she wasn't okay either, I knew that she needed to sit more.

Her luxurious gold waves hung limply around her face, lank with lack of washing and flat with sleeping. Her face was stripped bare of makeup—which wasn't concerning by itself—but her eyes had deep smudges underneath and her lips were frightfully chapped and split. She was wearing wrinkled rich-girl pajamas—silk and lapelled, with buttons marching up between braless breasts—and a pair of expensive trainers without socks.

I slid my eyes over to Auden's, and what I saw there was desperation.

"I didn't have—" His hand left Delphine's back to stab anxiously through his hair, which settled back over his forehead the minute his fingers left it. "I'm so sorry, Quartey. I didn't have anywhere else to go."

Delphine didn't seem to react to this, not much anyway. She heaved a little sigh and then drifted farther into the room, standing there like the world's most pathetic mannequin.

"Guest," I said. "Get yourself a drink."

"I can't," he murmured, looking down at the phone.

"Did you drive?"

"Yes."

"Are you leaving again?" I looked over to Delphine, who still stood in the middle of the room. It bothered me to see her motionless. To see her dull. Always she was laughing and chattering and beaming, always always, and I'd thought I hated it, but—

This was worse. Much worse.

"Delphine," I said, my voice coming out sharper than I'd planned. "Sit down."

I hadn't meant it to come out like a command, but perhaps I was more upset than I realized. I took in a breath to apologize—to soften the order and make it more of a suggestion—but she surprised me and Auden both when she dutifully walked over to one of the sofas and sat. She stared straight ahead, eyes focused on nothing, her lush mouth in a dead, expressionless shape.

If someone had asked me what I would have felt to see Delphine Dansey like this—grimy and grotty and blank—I would've said that I would feel pity, and maybe disdain. Maybe a distant sort of compassion, in the global Buddhist sense of the word.

But that's not what I felt looking at her.

I felt fear.

Fear so powerful it climbed up my throat. Fear like I hadn't felt since the first night Daddy and I stayed in London without Ma, in a brand-new flat without furniture or food or plants or both my parents.

"Stay there," I told her—pointlessly, because she obviously wasn't moving under her own willpower. Then I walked to the kitchen and gestured for Auden to follow me.

"What's happening?" I asked him once we got there. "The trial's over, isn't it? Shouldn't she be relieved? Happy?"

Auden rubbed his face with a hand. His other hand hadn't stopped clutching his phone since the moment he came up the stairs.

"She's not doing well," said Auden quietly. "I've been staying with her when I can—it's technically against the rules—but everyone at the Grange has been letting it slide, considering the circumstances. She's been seeing a therapist here in London once a week, she's been able to make most of her classes. And at the trial—she rallied, didn't she? She was so focused. So sharp. Which is why when Mum took ill, I thought I could come down—" He broke off, guilt twisting at his mouth.

I touched his shoulder. "Your mother isn't well?"

"Pneumonia," Auden said without emotion. "Aspirated her own sick after drinking too much. She was managing, but things have gotten worse. They're moving her to critical care."

"Auden."

"It doesn't look...The doctors have suggested I stay near her, you see." His voice almost broke then, but he managed to keep it steady. "Just in case."

"Auden."

He ignored me. I wasn't rebuffed by it; I would have done the same had someone tried to comfort me while I was explaining something so painful.

"So I decided I should run up to Cambridge to get a few things, since I'd be staying in London longer than I'd planned," he continued. "I'd only been gone four days, and I'd talked with Delly on the phone twice a day during that time. I thought...You have to understand, she sounded like herself." He looked at me pleadingly. "I thought she was doing okay without me, I swear I did."

I looked past him to the beautiful girl staring out my window like she'd never seen a window before. "And then you got to Cambridge and found her like this," I surmised.

"It was always the plan to check on her, but I thought—I really thought she was coping on her own."

"Where are her parents?" I asked, suddenly feeling protective of her. "Why haven't they been checking in with their daughter?"

"They went to the Maldives after the trial. Freddie had some meeting there. They tried to make Delphine come too, but she didn't want to miss school. They've been calling her every day too, but—"

"She's fooled them as well."

"Yes, I think so. Because if they knew she was like this, they'd be home as fast as they could get here. My guess is that she didn't want to disrupt her father's work. She doesn't want to be a bother."

I studied the girl across the room. Even in her depression, she looked like money, like a future bride for an earl or a businessman with a private jet. And yet, we had this in common.

I understood utterly what it was to tiptoe around a father's work, to want to be easy for one's parents.

"I didn't know what to do, Rebecca—I don't think she's eaten, I couldn't get her to eat. So I did the only thing I could think of and called her therapist here."

"And?"

"We just met. She was—well, *evaluated* is the word they used. I had to lie and pretend to be her boyfriend."

I switched my gaze back to him, dropping my hand from his shoulder. "Is that a lie?"

He nodded, then scrunched his nose. "I don't want it to be, but it's more important that I be here when she needs me, however she needs me. The rest should wait."

I privately agreed. "And what did the therapist say? After the evaluation?"

Auden looked like he was reciting from a carefully recorded memory. "She's not ideating self-harm. She's not catatonic. She concedes a need to care for herself and has agreed to try. But her affect is flat, and clearly she's struggling to care for herself, so she's close to needing inpatient treatment."

I was more relieved than I could say that Delphine wasn't thinking about hurting herself. But worry still gnawed me. "Jesus. What happens now?"

"She has to see Dr. Joy every day, at least for the next week, until she can determine Delphine's getting better on an outpatient basis. She has an appointment with her psychiatrist tomorrow morning to discuss calibrating her medicine. And she—"

Even in the city gloaming, his hazel eyes were bright and vivid as he gazed pleadingly at me. "She can't be alone, Rebecca."

The dilemma assembled itself immediately. "And you need to be with your mother."

"I've called Freddie and Daisy. They're trying to get a flight back as soon as possible, but it's the rainy season, and all the flights for the next few days have been cancelled, and so..."

I let out a long breath. I'd excelled at maths always. My father liked to say that I could multiply before I could read, that I knew the counting words in three languages before I was two years old. It was probably a father's boasting, but still, I'd always solved any mathematical problem set before me. And this problem only had one solution.

"Go be with your mother," I told him. "I'll work from home and stay with her until her parents can get back."

He slumped, but the relief in his face was short-lived.

Of course it was. His mother was dying.

"Go," I repeated. "I've got this."

"I have some of her things," he said, swallowing and nodding. "A holdall in my car. I didn't know what she would like, but you know, some knickers and clothes and things. Her phone and phone charger."

"Drop it in the hall, and then go to your mum. When you have a free minute, text me the appointment times and I'll make sure she's there."

Auden came close, pulled me abruptly into an embrace so tight I could hardly breathe. I sensed it was more for him than for me. "Thank you," he whispered. "I know she's not your favorite person."

I hugged him back. "You know me better than anyone, Auden Guest. Do you truly think I'd let her or you suffer when I could help?"

He pulled back to look at my face. "No," he said after a minute. "No, I know you wouldn't. But this is also a heavy thing to lay at your feet, and I want you to know I'm grateful."

"You're family, Auden. This is what families do." Families take in the people who need help, they take in siblings and niblings and cousins and the cousins of cousins. They care for their old, their sick, the ones who need a favor and the ones who've used up all their favors already.

I considered Auden my family, and that meant my help, my home, and my time were his to ask for.

I gave him a final squeeze and then I made a shooing motion that was so much Ma's it actually alarmed me for a moment. One person to take care of, and suddenly I was my mother, ready to flutter around and mutter half-prayers, half-grumbles to myself.

"Go get the bag," I told him. "Then go to the hospital. I'll take care of everything else."

It started with a glass of water.

The thing was, I was no more qualified to watch over another human being than I was to perform brain surgery or fly a helicopter. My only experience caring for other people was within the paradigm of kink, where the rules were clear and the limits even clearer.

Kink and Delphine had one thing in common though: the consequences for fucking up were dire.

I did not want to fuck up. Not only because I was Rebecca Quartey and I didn't do fuckups, and not only because it was important for me to help Auden—but because the thought of Delphine not getting better, the thought of her slowly leaking away through invisible punctures I couldn't patch, twisted my belly and flooded my mouth with metallic-tasting panic. She had to get better. She had to have the sun in her face once again. I'd make sure of it.

Pretend she's a sub in your care, Rebecca. Where would you start?

I examined her, automatically running through the metrics I use during and after a scene. Hydration, blood sugar, temperature, comfort, mood.

The truth was, I'd never had a sub who seemed to be failing every single metric, and anxiety nibbled at my thoughts. What if I couldn't help her? What if I failed?

I took a deep breath and then another one after that. *Start at the beginning, Miss Genius. What metric needs addressed first?*

Her lips were chapped.

Okay.

Chapped lips were a problem I could solve.

I filled a glass of cool water, found some no-nonsense lip balm, and then walked over to the sofa.

It took her some time to look up at me, and when she did, what I saw in her eyes stole my breath away.

Or rather, it was what I didn't see that scared me, because her eyes were empty.

Normally a light, halcyon honey-gold, they were the color of dust today. The color of cracked and lifeless earth.

I'd meant to be gentle, to coax her. Maybe I'd thought I'd reason with her, to use the looming reality of inpatient treatment to stir her into agency again.

But the panic took me so hard in that moment that I defaulted to instinct. I defaulted to the only way I knew to care for someone else.

"Drink this," I ordered brusquely, extending the glass. "Take breaks, but finish it all."

For a moment, my words seemed to hang in the air, and I wished I could yank them back into myself. What in God's name was wrong with me, talking like this? Giving explicit instructions like she was my submissive for the night?

I was about to qualify it, about to add more words to try to make it less a command and more an invitation, when she took the glass and tipped it obediently to her lips.

And when she did—a flash in her eyes.

Not quite gold again, not quite honey. But something like it.

I thought about this as she finished the glass as I'd instructed her to—with breaks, but in one sitting.

Was it so aberrant to think of her as a sub? It was no replacement for professional care, of course not, but she would be getting that anyway, so was it so strange to think that maybe here with me, I could give her aftercare or something like it?

This wasn't maths. It was science.

So I decided to test my hypothesis.

"When you're finished," I said, when she had only a little water left in the glass, "you will take a shower. You will wash your hair and you will brush your teeth, and then apply this lip balm after. I'll set aside clothes for you on my bed. Is this acceptable?"

I watched her face as she nodded and took the offered lip balm in her hand. There was something moving in her eyes again.

"Delphine, while you're here, I need you to answer me aloud so I know you're comfortable doing what I've asked. When I ask you a question, you can answer with 'yes, Rebecca' or 'no, Rebecca.' You can even ask me questions yourself or disagree—but it must be out loud. Are you okay with this?"

"Yes, Rebecca," murmured Delphine.

She finished her water and I held my hand out for the glass, which she handed to me.

"The shower is that way. There is spare shampoo and conditioner for guests in the vanity." I hoped it wasn't obvious that my guests were all of the fucking variety, but I supposed she'd deduce that soon enough from the individually wrapped toothbrushes and the half-empty condom box.

"Yes, Rebecca," said Delphine obediently, and she went to the bathroom as I'd asked. I watched her walk, thinking for a moment.

"May I check on you? While you're showering?"

She stopped and looked back at me. There was no affront in her eyes, no bristling or defensiveness. I wouldn't have been offended if she said no. It would be an invasion of privacy, a witness to nakedness. A tacit admission that I didn't trust her for too long by herself.

But something like relief seemed to pull at her mouth, and there was almost a smile on her lips when she ducked her eyes to the floor and said, "Yes, Rebecca."

Auden had not done a bad job packing for her. He had taken comfortable clothes, plenty of knickers and comfy socks, plenty of bras, and even her makeup bag and hairbrush. For a man whose life was crumbling, he had maintained an admirable attention to detail. I set out things for her on my bed, and popped my head through the door once, just to make sure she was getting on okay. Then I came back out and waited for her to finish her shower. And waited.

And waited.

It was my first introduction to the Delphine Shower, which is long enough to empty rivers and drain lakes. If I'd known then how much she liked to play in the shower—how delighted she gets when I push her against the tile and seal my mouth over hers—then it would have been much, much harder to wait.

As it was, I was mostly thinking about the water bill and whether or not I'd left her enough towels.

I eventually gave up waiting and went back to my wine and work, finishing up the most urgent of it, and sending out emails to let the office know I'd be working from home for the next few days, due to a personal emergency. My father replied instantly to the one I sent him; I didn't realize I was clenching my jaw as I read it until I held the wineglass to my lips and had to drink.

As a Quartey, you are part of this company's essential operations, he had written back. *You are not permitted personal emergencies.*

The rest of his email was just as brusque, a few more lines indicating that he expected me to produce as much work from home as I would at the office, and that being the daughter of the company's founder did not mean I was exempt from following company policy regarding leave.

Nothing I did was ever good enough, was it? I could festoon my walls with diplomas, my shelves with professional awards, I could bring in contracts that would make every other London firm salivate, and it still wasn't enough. It wasn't enough that I worked constantly, tirelessly, that the only thing I had outside the Workshop was the occasional stolen night of kinky sex—

"Rebecca?" Delphine called from the doorway to the bathroom. "I'm coming out now."

She was wearing nothing but a towel, her skin flushed and pink, and her hair was in wet waves around her shoulders, clinging to her skin. The towel was short and her hips spread the bottom of it open the tiniest bit. When she walked to the bed, I could see the tempting curves of her backside.

Tempting? Delphine Dansey?

What was wrong with me?

I shook it off, closing my laptop and determined to finish out this day as efficiently as humanly possible. After Delphine emerged from the bathroom a second time—dressed in her fresh clothes—I asked her how she felt.

"The same," she said after a minute. "I feel the same."

"Are you hungry?"

"No."

"When's the last time you've eaten?"

"I don't remember."

It was important for me to know how long she'd been without food, but I decided not to push. "Could you eat now?"

That earned me a shrug, which earned her me crossing my arms. "Out loud please."

Her eyes lifted to mine, dark in the nighttime glow of the loft. "I could, Rebecca."

That settled it. I asked her then if there was anything she felt like eating and anything she couldn't eat—no and no, were the answers—and so I got her another glass of water and thought for a moment.

My experience feeding subs stopped at giving them bananas or chocolate to help with blood sugar drops after a scene. Maybe the occasional "help yourself to whatever's in the fridge" if they spent the night and I needed to leave for work before they were dressed and ready to go. But that she needed to eat was apparent to me.

Fuck it.

I'd feed her what Ma would feed me—what she made whenever I was sick or stressed or sad. I picked up my phone and called my favorite Ghanaian restaurant.

"Black Stars," the voice answered promptly.

"Auntie, it's Rebecca," I said, walking into the kitchen. "Can I get light soup and fufu delivered, please?"

"It's late," Auntie Yaa says, even though I know they'll be open for hours yet to serve the hungry clubgoers after they're done drinking and dancing. "You should be eating dinner earlier than now. Is your father working you too hard again?"

I smiled tiredly into the phone. "When isn't he?"

"And is this just for you, Rebecca?" Her voice was businesslike, but not businesslike enough that I knew my answer wouldn't be logged away as potential gossip.

"No, Auntie, it's for two."

She made a low *mmmm* noise. "Who is he? Does he have a good job? What is his family like?"

He. I sometimes forgot how they always assumed *he.*

"It's just a friend, Auntie."

"You young people. Always the same. 'Just a friend.' 'Just hooking up.' 'Just hanging out.' You need to *marry.* Settle down. Make little babies for Auntie Yaa to feed fufu to." I could hear her moving around on her end, I could hear the ring of the till, the congenial shout of voices in the kitchen. The music of Black Stars.

"I'll send Kofi with the fufu," she said. "Have fun with your *friend.*"

A lifetime of aunties had taught me when it was wisest to be a submissive. When arguing will only earn you more pain—even if that pain was just the hassle of being scolded on the phone. "Thank you, Auntie. I will."

We hung up then. She had my card on file along with my address, and I knew the food would either be here in twenty minutes or it would be here in an hour and twenty minutes, and so there was no sense in asking when to expect it.

I set my phone down and walked over to where Delphine stood near the window. For the first time since I'd met her, she didn't seem to need to fill the silence, and for the first time since I met her, I wished she would.

But after a long time, I looked over to see that she had drifted closer to me. Her eyes were still down on the street, which on a weekday was mostly empty, and she was still silent. But she was close enough now that I could touch her if I wanted. Close enough that I could see the goosebumps on her arms. I had the strangest urge to run my fingertips over them. To smooth my palm over her skin and warm her up again.

And then the doorbell rang.

Kofi.

I went down and got the food, thanked him, and then brought the soup up to the kitchen to serve it. Delphine moved of her own volition for the first time that night, coming over to the kitchen island, her cute nose twitching as she took in the peppery aroma of the soup.

"What's this?" she asked, peering down at the bowl I put in front of her.

"Fufu with light soup." I got her a fresh glass of water. She would need it. "It's comfort food. Here, watch." I showed her how to pinch off pieces of the soft, doughy fufu and use it to soak up the soup, which was made with tomatoes, onions, eggplant, chicken, garlic, ginger, spices, and—

"Oh g-golly—" Delphine coughed, sputtering.

—and shito peppers. Probably a couple Scotch Bonnets too, if I knew Auntie. I pushed the water glass closer to Delphine, and she took it gratefully, looking up at me over the rim with the look of a puppy who'd just been kicked.

"It's quite spicy," I conceded. "But you'll feel better soon. You'll see."

Delphine set the glass down and looked at her bowl with trepidation. "Are you sure?"

"It's comfort food. Whenever I was sick, my mother made this for me, and I always felt better after eating it. Probably because whenever you eat fufu, the next thing you want to do is take a long nap, and who doesn't feel better after a long nap?"

Delphine's mouth twitched. Almost a smile. "Fair dues."

"Go on," I urged her. "Have some more."

"And no—no spoon?"

I gave her a look. A look I gave both subs and interns at the office when they deserved it. "Fufu is the spoon. Come on, Delph."

The nickname slid between my lips before I could stop it, and it seemed to take us both by surprise. Nicknames were for friends, and we weren't that, we would never be friends. Yes, I was helping her, yes, I was feeding her my favorite food, yes, she was seeing parts of my life that only romantic conquests and Auden Guest saw. But that didn't mean I *liked* her. That didn't mean she was *Delph* to me.

I hid my discomfort by bending back over the bowl and eating again.

After a moment, she did too, her cheeks turning pink and her pert little nose slowly turning a bright red. She was in a tank top and pajama bottoms, and the tank top was low enough to expose the top part of her chest, which was also a little flushed with the spice. But she ate it all—enough to make even Ma happy—and I was a little discomfited by how happy I felt about it myself. A satisfaction had swelled in my chest at seeing her eat, at seeing her color return. The same satisfaction I felt during a good scene, during good sex. A primal, carnal pleasure.

This is dangerous, Rebecca, a voice warned me. I ignored it.

I was hardly in any danger of becoming besotted with Delphine Dansey.

"You'll wash your hands and brush your teeth again," I told her. "And then it's time for bed. Our fufu nap."

"Yes, Rebecca." She did as I asked, and I cleaned up after us, went and brushed my own teeth. I put my hair up in my bonnet and changed into pajamas in the bathroom. I went to my bed to grab a pillow and then started off toward the living area.

"Where are you going?" Delphine asked.

I turned and looked back at her. She was standing next to the bed, seeming very lost and very sweet. I had the sudden, powerful urge to take her into my arms, and I had to force myself to stay where I was.

"I thought I'd sleep on the sofa while you were here," I explained. "So you didn't have to share the bed."

"I don't want to sleep alone," she said sadly.

It was the first thing she'd told me she wanted since she came here.

My body was a riot of confusion—part of me rebelled at the idea of sharing my bed with her, and the other part of me kindled to life, thinking of plush curves and warm secrets.

But it would be better to say no, right? More proper?

More thoughtful and host-like?

But it turned out that it wasn't up to me, not really. One look at her face, with those mournful eyes and that delicate pout, and I was already heading back to bed. "I just want you to know that I talk in my sleep," I warned her. "And sometimes I steal blankets. And I don't snuggle."

Delphine was already tucking herself into bed, bothered not at all by my prickly qualifications. "Yes, Rebecca," she said.

And when I woke up the next morning, I found her snuggled against me, her hair on my pillow and her arm and leg curled over me, as if I were a long teddy bear given to her to cuddle.

I waited for the irritation to come. The discomfort.

It never did.

Instead, I laid there for a very long time, listening to her breathe.

And so it went.

I asked direct questions, I gave direct orders. Shower, eat, drink, sleep. Just as I would a sub stuck in permanent subspace.

I made sure she wasn't cold; I let her cuddle me when she wanted, which was an increasing amount. When I worked during the day, she would find her way to the floor by my chair, resting her shoulder against my knee while she read books on her phone. When I stood at the windows, she'd come next to me and take my hand. When we slept, we slept close and intertwined, and when we ate, we ate together.

I took her to her daily appointments, I checked in with Auden and her parents, I kept up with work. Slowly, she stirred to life again, talking more, smiling more, *doing* more, and by the time the rains lifted enough that the Danseys could fly home to her daughter, she was almost herself again. Enough herself that her therapist graduated her to every three days instead of every day.

On the day the Danseys came to pick her up from my flat, I helped her pack her holdall and fed her one last meal—homemade jollof rice, leftovers from last night. I found my hands shaking as I cleared away our final meal together. My stomach was lined with lead.

It had only been a week. And yet in that week, I'd grown so used to her that the idea of parting felt like a bisection, a severing of something vital.

She would have people who loved her once she was gone, I knew that. She would have professionals helping her find her strength. But whose feet would she sit by during the day? And who would she snuggle innocently into at night? Who would take care of all the parts of her—not just the daughter, not just the client—but the woman who liked to read at a friend's feet and nap in the sun?

I told myself that was why I was upset that she was leaving, that it was impersonal worry and nothing more. It had nothing to do with *me*, nothing to do with missing her, not at all.

And yet when I walked her to the door and prepared to open it for her parents and said, "Come back if you need to," I meant it almost as a plea. Almost like a prayer.

And when she said, "Yes, Rebecca, I will," I had the strangest thought.

It was that she did too.

28

Rebecca

The headache is a living thing, and its intention is to kill me.

It was there when I fell asleep after getting my hair done, and there when I woke up this morning before Delphine. It followed me to work, it kneaded at my scalp as I drank coffee and answered the first round of emails. And somewhere between the first meeting of the day and the second, it grew a soul and teeth. It grew fingers and fingertips. It grew trailing, squeezing tentacles, and it squeezed my temples, my eyes, the cavities of my upper sinuses.

My scalp stings like it's being turned inside out. My stomach swirls uneasily, not sure what to make of the pain.

I remind myself that it's only the occipital and trigeminal nerves registering compression. It's biology, it's mechanics. Nerves and nerve endings passing news of the pain like children in a whispering game.

Pressure, electricity, chemicals. Pain doesn't exist, only the perception of it does.

Which is to say, ironically enough, the headache is all in my head.

"Rebecca, are you listening?" my father asks. It's only the two of us in here reviewing the Severn riverfront budget, but of course he would demand my full and utter attention.

I look up from the file I have open in front of me, trying to force myself to focus again. "My apologies. I have a headache."

I wait for his inevitable frown, for the quiet, firm reminder that work doesn't wait for headaches. I'm ready for it, for the cool disapproval that always accompanies anything that might be a hindrance to focus and productivity.

So when he covers my hand with his own and meets my eyes, I'm staggered. Even more so when he asks, in a genuinely concerned tone, "Are you feeling well? Do you need to take the rest of the day off?"

The rest of the day *off*? Who is this man and where is the real Samson Quartey?

"What? Daddy, no. It's just my hair. It always hurts for a couple days after I have it done."

A line appears between his brows. "It does?"

I let out a puff of air that's half amused disbelief and half genuine irritation. "*Yes*, Daddy. Every time."

"Oh," he says, looking puzzled. "I see."

I look down at the fatherly hand folded over my own, not sure what to do. For years he's resisted any show of paternal affection in the office, and now he's touching my hand like he wants me to feel comforted, and I don't know what to make of it.

I thought this was what I wanted—I could have sworn it was—just one single unconditionally given crumb of love. But now that I have it, I don't know what to do with it, I don't know how to feel. I should feel happy? Or grateful?

Relieved?

But all I feel is my headache.

I pull my hand back. "I'll be fine," I say. "Let's keep going."

The rest of the day is no better.

Our site in Wiltshire has started to flood. A German company won a project we were bidding for on the Isle of Wight. The team working on the final parts of the Thornchapel maze removal are encountering more rock under the soil than we planned for and they need me to sign off on bigger equipment.

And I'm worried about Delphine. Something was wrong yesterday, in the shower, something was *off*, but I didn't have time to delve, and anyway, it seemed rude to pry if she didn't want to tell me. But then why didn't she want to tell me? And is it even fair to expect her to open up when I don't do the same with her? When I haven't told her about my parents' potential divorce, about how hard it is to be my mother's daughter, how lonely I feel even when I'm in a room full of people?

When I tell her she's wrong when she says she loves me?

God. Of course she doesn't feel comfortable telling me what's upsetting her. Not when I've treated any talk of emotion from her as complete anathema.

Tonight, I decide, pressing my fingertips to my eyes. I really want to massage my temples, but it would only make the headache worse. *I'll fix it tonight.*

She wants to go to the club for the exhibition. We'll play there, and when we get home, I'll insist she opens up to me and tells me what was bothering her yesterday. I'll fix it, like I have to fix everything.

I try to ignore the lacy tendril of bitterness that accompanies that last thought. I'm not bitter. It's fine. It's fine.

It's all fine.

So if it's fine, then will you do the same? Will you open up to her? About your parents? About how hard you work and how it never seems to be enough for anyone? About how you wish that people would be there for you for a change?

I scowl across my desk, as if the thought has crawled out of my head and taken shape in front of me.

What craven thinking, what cowardice. Wanting to dump my pointless and clichéd fusses on the lap of someone I care about when I can carry them just as easily by myself. As if the small, stupid dissatisfactions of my life aren't weaknesses enough on their own. As if I must compound the sins by making them Delphine's problem too.

No. No, I refuse to do that. I may not go to church anymore, but I know what's moral and what's right, and burdening other people isn't it.

"Rebecca," Shahil says, sticking his head through the door. "There's someone from a rural green energy company on the phone, and they're saying they'd previously secured permission to run lines through the lacrosse field at the Wiltshire school. Should I put them through?"

I stare at him a minute, my headache fusing with the potential crisis at hand. "And they only just now bothered to remember this? And the council couldn't have told us this last year?"

Shahil is very skilled at the rueful assistant shrug—the *I'm on your side, those fucking twats* shrug. "Would you like me to close the door?"

"I'd like you," I say, my scalp screaming and my eyes pricking with the tears I always get with a bad headache, "to drive to Wiltshire and politely murder everyone who had a hand in these planning permissions."

"Certainly," Shahil says cheerfully. "I can't drive though. Shall I walk instead?"

"Yes. A pilgrimage, like in Chaucer. Find a saucy widow to walk with you."

He grins. "I do like experienced women. Shall I put them through now?"

"*Ugh*. Fine."

"And would you like me to bring you ibuprofen for your headache?"

I glare at him. "No."

"You'd feel better…"

"My stomach lining in ten years wouldn't." Taking a pain reliever feels like a concession, a dangerous one. A surrender to weakness, and I already have enough weakness slithering inside me.

I refuse to admit entrance to any more.

"Put the arseholes through," I say, bracing my elbows on my desk and pushing my fingertips against my forehead.

The call eats into my afternoon, necessitating a new conference call with the council, someone from the boarding school, and for some unknown reason, a concerned citizen who wants to lodge a complaint about the proposed walking path that will loop behind her garden. By the time I've finished, the afternoon has edged into evening, Shahil has gone home along with the rest of the office, and my head hurts worse than ever.

I hang up the phone and realize my eyes are leaking with the hot but effortless tears that come from physical pain. I could kiss away a sub's tears forever, but I hate crying myself, it feels like an indulgence, a waste of energy when I could be carrying on with whatever needs done. But my head hurts *so badly* and I'm fuming about this Wiltshire problem and I'm still confused by my father and the person he's becoming and how it *isn't fair* that he gets to change after he's already made me who I am—

My phone rings, and I'm about to ignore it. I can't right now. I'm crying and my head hurts and I can't.

Except that I see it's my mother calling, and the only thing heavier than my headache is guilt.

Sticky, unfiltered daughter guilt.

I have to answer.

It's a video call, so I hurriedly wipe at my face so she can't see I was crying. I don't have the energy to fend off her questions right now. I don't think I can pretend to be okay.

But it turns out I needn't have bothered, because when I answer, the first thing I see is my mother crying herself.

"Oh Ma," I say.

"Becky," she says through her tears. "I told your father I would agree to his divorce."

His divorce. This does not bode well.

"And what will I say to everyone?" she cries. "How will I tell them?"

It feels like all the hair is being ripped out of my scalp all at once, and it takes everything I have not to snap at her that she's worried about the wrong things, that if she's more worried about perception than reality, she should've been divorced years ago. But I don't say that, I don't know how, and my mother keeps going before I can speak anyway.

She's angry, she's fearful, she's guilty. She should have come up to London; she should have put her foot down and insisted Daddy and I move back home. What will happen to her now—but also I shouldn't worry about her, she'll be fine—but also why am I not more worried about her? Why do I always take his side? But also I should make sure to comfort him now that he'll be divorced, I should make sure he's well fed and that he's going to church, because who else will? Not some professor across the ocean, that's for sure.

At some point, the headache gets too much and I tell Ma I'm still listening but need to rest my head on my desk for a moment. And so we stay like that for I don't know how long—me with my head on my arms, sorely wishing I'd taken Shahil up on his offer of ibuprofen, tears leaking onto a stack of international lacrosse field comps I'd had an intern collate for me—and my mother cataloging how lonely she'll be, how widespread and pernicious the gossip will be, what Ima will say.

"Ima didn't want me to marry him at all, you know," Ma says as I lift my head just in time to see a text from Delphine pop on the screen.

I'm worried, Bex. Let me know if you're okay. xx

I look out the window to where the world has gone the gold-orange of mid-evening. I've been at the office for nearly twelve hours at this point.

I tap out a quick: **I'm fine,** as Ma asks, "Becky, are you listening? I don't want to bother you if you're busy."

Anger and guilt combine to make a noxious slurry in my blood.

Anger because I know *I don't want to bother you* is Mother-Speak for *I know everything else in your life is more important to you than me, and you'll never appreciate me as much as I deserve.*

And the guilt because it still works. It still fucking works.

"No, Ma, I'm listening, it's just a notification—"

A double screen appears on my phone. One is my mother—tearful, watchful—and the other is a laughing girl holding a lit sparkler, dark green Thornchapel trees all around her. She had me take the picture for her Instagram, and I remember being irritated at the time because it interrupted the email I was composing on the terrace while she and Poe played with the sparklers. But now whenever I see it, my heart stutters.

It's beautiful and happy and summery and bright and a little bit sexy and a little bit silly and it's *her.* It's just her. Pretty and playful and sweet.

And she's calling me. Right now.

"Maybe I should move up to London," Ma says, heaving a dramatic breath. "Maybe it's time. I'll be alone, of course, unless I move in with my daughter."

Static crackles in my mind as I imagine trying to live with my mother in a loft that has no walls.

I swipe away Delphine's call only a second after it pops up, giving Ma my full attention. "You can't live with me," I say seriously. It's the first direct and honest thing I've said to her all night. "I don't have *rooms,* Ma. It's all open. And my girlfriend is living with me."

Ma sniffs. "It's not as if you're married—she can move back into her own place—unless—" Her eyes widen with meaning, and I sigh.

"We're not getting married. But I don't want her to move out. Especially not when I think you don't really want to move in."

"You don't know what I want," she says tightly.

"Maybe." My headache has finally squeezed off the air supply to my self-restraint; it's dead. RIP restraint. "But I don't think you know what you want either."

"*Becky.*"

"You haven't known what you've wanted for such a long time that your first reaction to getting divorced is wondering how other people will feel about it."

My mother purses her lips. "I don't like being spoken to in this way."

"And I don't like being between you and Daddy! I don't like feeling like I'm your only friend, when we both know that's not true! I don't like having to talk around whom I date to make you more comfortable!" I'm caustic, spiky. I'm a human mace swung by a knight. "You're unhappy, and I think you hate knowing that other people are happy without you."

"That's not fair!" Ma says, crying harder. "And this is no way to speak to your mother! Your father has poisoned you against me, he took you away and now he's made you hate me—"

"I don't hate you," I interrupt. My eyes are hot and wet with fresh tears of my own. "That's your problem—you think all your unhappiness is because you aren't loved well enough by everyone else. But it's no one else's job to make you happy, Ma, and it never has been. I'm sorry that you and Daddy couldn't make it work. I'm sorry that we couldn't stay in the same city and have the things we all needed. But we can't keep using the past as an excuse for misery in the present."

Ma doesn't respond for a long time. She's staring past her screen, and she's still crying, but it's softer now, only the tears and not the sobs.

I close my eyes. Shame has followed my outburst, but there's relief too. I've wanted to say these things for so long, and now they're said. Now they're out there.

"Are you miserable, Rebecca?" my mother whispers. It's my full name that has me opening my eyes. She says it like a mother should say it—like she grew me from scratch, like she labored over every bone and organ and liter of blood that went into making me.

It's surprising how quickly the answer comes. With the headache and my terrible day and my pervading loneliness and having to fix everything and this phone call, and yet—

"I don't…I don't think I am, actually. I think I'm happy. Or something very like it."

"Why?"

She asks it like she really wants to know. Like she's hoping I have an answer for this, some small candle she can borrow to light her way.

I think of Delphine that evening with the sparkler, laughing with her bare feet in the soft grass. I think of her in my bed, sleepy and pliant as I curl possessively around her. I think of her kneeling in front of me, her honey eyes clear and trusting.

I think of her. Just her.

Delphine Dansey, sunshine girl and socialite.

My former enemy, my brat. My kitten.

"Because of her," I say, and it comes out so easily that the words that follow next feel inevitable. "I love her."

I love her.

All this time I thought she was Tea Set Barbie, staring worshipfully up at me, the Red Dress Barbie. But no, I had it all wrong, it was always the other way around.

It was me worshiping her, it was me enamored with her utter sweetness and symmetry of being, it was me besotted and beguiled and content simply to be witness to her existence.

I was Tea Set Barbie the entire time.

God, I've been such a fool. For so long I've thought of love as a lie, as a sequence of compatibility and chemicals, or I've thought of it like I think of kudzu—a sneaking, snaking weed, reaching and grasping and choking all the life around it. I haven't wanted love because all I've known of it has been from my parents, and honestly, they've been very bad at it with each other. And sometimes bad at it with me. But how long am I going to use that as an excuse?

"I'm glad to hear it," Ma says, and her voice is careful but earnest. "I can't wait to meet her."

"That would make me quite happy," I say, and I mean it. "And I want you to be happy too, Ma. If you want to move up here with Ima, we'll find a way to make it happen, and if you want to start dating again, you know I'll support you. But it has to start with what you want. It can't depend on anyone else."

For the first time in a very long time, my mother gives me a genuine smile. "My daughter is very wise."

A low battery charge notification comes up on my screen and I tap it away—and when I do, I see the time in the corner. It's past nine now, unbearably late, and Delphine's probably already eaten supper without me—

Oh no.

Oh fuck.

The exhibition. It was supposed to start at seven. *That's* why she was texting and calling.

Oh fuck.

"Ma, I have to go," I say, jumping to my feet and scrambling for my things. "I forgot—I'm supposed to be somewhere with Delphine. It's important."

"I suppose I've kept you long enough," she says, but she says it lightly and not in the sighing way she might have done just an hour earlier. "Thank you for your honesty. I'm sorry for…a lot of things. But I want you to know I love you."

"I love you too, Ma," I say. It's the truth, and I think she's finally willing to believe it.

I do love her, even when I can't be the only reason for her happiness. We hang up and then I race downstairs as I call for my car.

When I get to Justine's, Delphine isn't there. I ask the concierge if she checked in—and she had—but he'd also seen her leaving about fifteen minutes prior. To the loft, surely, I think with some relief. I need to apologize to her—I need to *grovel*—and that will be much easier in private.

I try texting and calling her the whole way home from the club. It's galling to see how many times she tried to contact me tonight. I didn't see any of the notifications since they'd presumably come in while I had my head on the desk and wasn't looking at the screen, but I still should have remembered our date at the exhibition. How could I have forgotten?

I'll explain.

I'll finally come clean about everything—how much I've been keeping back.

I'll tell her I love her and she'll be so happy, and everything will be good, so good.

I just have to get to her. That's all.

But when I get to my loft, it's empty. There's no Delphine. I stand in the middle of it, my hands at my sides, my heart thumping in slow, heavy beats. I feel like I'm in the middle of a bomb blast, like I am the center of an invisible crater.

Delphine is gone.

I text.

I call.

I apologize.

Jesus, how I apologize.

I don't confess that I love her, because it feels manipulative to play that card when I've let her down, as if I'm using a declaration to leverage forgiveness, and I refuse to cheapen it by doing so. It's the sort of thing that should be said in person anyway, when I can kiss her afterwards, when I can look into her eyes and hold her hand and then eventually pull her to bed.

Delph, please, I finally write in a perverse echo of what she sent me earlier. **Tell me you're okay.**

I'm okay, the response comes finally. **Decided to go up and stay at my parents' for a bit while they're gone. I missed home.**

Here is your home! I desperately want to text back. But I stop myself.

Will you come back soon?

Those vexatious three dots appear, then disappear, then come back again.

I don't know.

I'm trying not to panic. I'm trying not to read too much into her abrupt trip to her parents' house, into the lack of kisses at the end of her texts.

How could everything have gone so wrong so quickly?

Lammas, I remember. She'll have to be at Thornchapel for Lammas, and I can tell her then.

Auden's birthday is next week. Will you still be there?

A pause.

Yes.

Can I see you there?

Another pause.

Yes.

It's my turn to pause. I have to ask this next question, because I don't think I can stand waiting the next seven days to learn the answer.

Are you still mine?

There's no pause this time, as if she expected this question.

For as long as you want me to be.

So yes?

Yes, Rebecca.

And I suppose that will have to do. Until Lammas at least.

29

St. Sebastian

"Do you suppose they're okay?" I ask Auden, looking across the walled garden to where Poe and Becket sit close, their heads bent together. Poe looks like she's about to cry.

Auden looks up from where he's been resting his feet in the fountain. He's rolled his trousers up to near his knees, exposing the strong bones of his ankles and the crisp, masculine hair covering his calves. The sun catches on his eyelashes and in his hazel eyes as he looks over to the others.

"I don't know," Auden finally replies. His voice is heavy. "Did she tell you about what happened up on the path?"

"Yeah."

Auden frowns down at his feet in the water. "I worry about it."

"Do you think the parishioner will tell someone?"

"I don't know. They should." Auden bends down to pluck a stray leaf from the fountain. He smooths it between his fingers as he talks. "No one should stay quiet about priestly sexual misconduct, no matter how consensual. But it's unfortunate because Becket is a good priest—he's a good pastor to his people. And he didn't choose his vocation lightly. He needs to live his life close to God."

I take the leaf from him. Not because I particularly want a small wet leaf, but because I want to touch his fingers, I want to feel his skin against mine, even if only for a second. "You think that he might not be able to after this?"

"If it gets reported? If he gets investigated? Then I don't know. His uncle is a cardinal, and I imagine he could pull enough strings to keep Becket in the priesthood if he wants. He'd probably be asked to repent and then he'd be moved to some parish where he can't cause any more damage. Or…"

"Or?" I ask. Across the waving lavender and heady, bee-visited blossoms of the garden, I see Poe pull Becket into a hug.

"Or Becket's uncle is a better priest than I give him credit for and will refuse to do that. Placing one's nephew in the parish he wants is a very different kind of nepotism than covering up sex with a member of the congregation."

I hand the leaf back to Auden. His fingertips drag over the Guest family ring circling my thumb. "Becket might not want to stay a priest either," I point out. "If they make him move away from Devon—or even just demand his full repentance—he might decide the price is too high. He loves it here."

Auden twirls the leaf by the stem, and his gaze is on where Becket's head rests against Poe's chest, where her fingers run through his golden hair. "He does."

"And so if he's not a priest anymore, by choice or by punishment…"

"Then I don't know," says Auden softly. He drops the leaf back in the water. "I really don't."

We don't say anything for several minutes. The garden is peaceful in the early evening—glowing with sun and redolent with life. Flowers, herbs, birds, bees, butterflies. The watery jabber of the fountain. Everything is informally jumbled and tastefully patinated—the overgrown beds and ivy-covered walls like something out of a dream.

It's all by design, and yet it's easy to forget that right now. It's easy to believe that Thornchapel somehow grew itself, that it slipped into existence from elsewhere—from a book or a half-remembered movie or a dream.

"Where is Rebecca?" I ask. Digging has stalled on the final stages of maze removal until they can get bigger equipment in, but I still expected her to come stay for the week.

"She's had a catastrophe on one of her sites. Flooding coupled with some kind of permissions conflict. She said she couldn't get away."

"And Delphine?"

Auden lifts his feet out of the water and props them in my lap as he leans back on his hands. Water starts soaking through my jeans and his legs are heavy enough that his heels dig into my thigh. It's just enough discomfort to be provoking, just enough humiliation to make me breathe faster.

Auden, for his part, doesn't seem to notice, although I know him well enough not to be fooled. He clocked the moment my pulse sped up; I'm certain he sees how hard it is for me to drag my eyes away from the sight of his bare feet in my lap.

It should be a casual touch. A fraternal liberty.

Instead, my body thuds with longing that's anything but fraternal.

"Delphine assures me she'll be here for Lammas tomorrow, but as I understand it, she's spent the last week watching her parents' dogs while they're on holiday."

"Without Rebecca?"

Auden presses down ever so slightly with his heels. It almost hurts, but not quite.

"Yes," he replies.

"Do you think they're doing okay?"

He presses down harder, and I instinctively grab at his ankles. Not to stop him, but to encourage him. To make him leave a small bruise on my thigh, one I can press on when I'm alone and remember—

No. *No.*

I push his feet off my lap and stand, needing away from him. Heat, sulky and lustful, flares in his face, but it's gone just as quickly as it came. And when he speaks, it's in his usual cool tones, as if he's completely unmoved by what just happened. "I don't know, actually. Delphine sounded rather anxious when I spoke to her on the phone, but she wouldn't tell me why."

I stretch. Poe and Becket are making for the door, Sir James at their heels, his snout bumping at Poe's dangling hand for pets even while they walk. "I hope they're not fighting."

Auden finally stands too. It's unfair that he should look so perfect when the rest of us occasionally fall victim to flushing and rumpling and dampening. Even with his hair tousled and the sun in his cheeks, he looks like a fairy-tale prince, like an archetype of polished male beauty and elegance. Like Mr. Darcy, if Mr. Darcy also had a half-brother he wanted to—

Okay, no. I have to stop thinking like this. I know it's wrong, I know it.

I *will* carve this hunger out of myself.

"I also hope they're not fighting," Auden responds. Unhappy thoughts knot between his brows again, and I think of how good it would feel to kiss him there. How that sun-warmed skin would feel against my lips. How he would taste if I licked him.

"They're both strong, but they're both also stubborn," he continues. "They'd rather suffer alone than inconvenience someone else with the reality that they have human feelings."

"And I suppose you're not stubborn at all," I say. It's a joke, I mean it as a joke, but his eyes darken as he looks back to me.

I realize that I'm tugging on my piercing with my teeth, using it to worry rhythmically at my bottom lip.

Auden's eyes darken even further as he watches.

"Not at all," he finally says. "It's only that I have no alternative but to be stubborn when my choices are so few."

Somewhere outside the garden, Sir James barks, and then Auden sighs. "Inside, St. Sebastian. Let's tend to our wayward priest."

30

St. Sebastian

I wake early Lammas morning.

It's a Sunday, and normally we'd all be getting up to go to Mass, but we went yesterday evening instead, and so the house is utterly still. I don't even hear Sir James Frazer pacing around, waiting to be let out. Poe is very asleep next to me, but it's a restless sleep, with flickering eyelids and quick, stuttering breaths.

She's dreaming.

I wonder if it's about the door.

Normally I'd be tempted to wake her up. She's naked and flushed from the simmering canicular heat that never seems to abate, even at night. We've all been so worked up lately, so tense and irritable and horny, and I don't think a day's gone by without my mouth between her legs or her plush thighs wrapped around my hips. I'll never know why the heat makes me want to be hotter, but even now, with my skin warm and clammy, I long to press myself against her.

To draw a nipple into my mouth and suck until she moans herself awake, to toy with her pussy until she's wet and pushing me on my back to mount me.

But I don't do any of that. Not this morning.

I slide out of bed and walk to the window, looking out over the slope of the estate, down to the trees lining the rocky seam of the river. It's well past dawn, but what's outside could hardly be called morning; thunderheads are hovering above, frowning and heavy and flickering every so often with lightning. Through the cracked window, Thornchapel is a hushed world, with only a faint stirring in the trees and the occasional growl of thunder to give it life.

I'm grabbing my clothes before I even know I've made the decision.

A few minutes later and I'm outside, striding across the terrace and down the shallow steps to the soft grass, still dewy enough to hiss against the sides of my boots. I make my way down to the secret path that leads out from the ruined maze and follow it to the thorn chapel.

The woods aren't dark and they're not light either. They're steeped in a strange stormlight, a fraught, electric gloom that makes it feel like anything could happen, like nothing is real. Like this one handful of hours belongs to another time, another world, and I am a guest in it, I am privy to a moment meant not for ordinary things, but for whispers and auguries and secrets.

It's the kind of morning that could make me believe in something, make me believe in almost anything. If you told me ghosts were real, fairies were real, that saints could be shot full of arrows and still live, I'd believe it all, I'd believe every word you spoke when the light was like this. When the air itself was laden with strange knowledge.

Snatches of thunder—muffled and distant—roll through the trees, and the branches and leaves stir intermittently with the petulant wind. It tugs at my T-shirt as I emerge into the clearing, it tugs on the roses and leaves and branches covering the thorn chapel. The tall grass waves against the standing stones, like a restless sea of green, and far above Reavy Hill, lightning crackles in the sunless sky.

Why am I here?

I don't have a good answer to that. Auden doesn't want anyone out here on Lammas or any other holiday, and it's not like there's anything out here for me today anyway. No fire, no magic, no Poe.

No wild god.

But here I am, roaming around the grounds like I used to do, long before I knew I had any kind of genetic claim to this place, stepping through sloe-laden branches and over stray rose petals to the cloistral area inside. I have no plan, I have no agenda. I just feel like here is where I need to be right now. Like if the world itself is going to thrum with possibility, then I should be in the one place where I know anything is possible.

Anything.

The breeze stirs again, and there's a quick flash of light from over the hills. The shadowy stormlight is even stranger here, inside the chapel, curling in the corners and in the hearts of the roses and limning the broken outlines of windows.

The exposed altar stands at the far end, cryptic and forbidding.

There's no door behind it. I don't know why that relieves me.

I don't know why that disappoints me either.

But even before I see the big dog jump to its feet and bound over to me, I think I know why I came, why I knew I needed to come.

As I dutifully scratch behind Sir James Frazer's ears, I search the chapel and finally see him sitting against one of the few bare stretches of wall, a sketch pad in his lap and his leather bag propped open next to him, spilling out pencils and erasers and other types of artistic detritus I can't even begin to identify.

Of course he's here. Of course he's waiting for me.

"Ah, St. Sebastian," says Auden, looking up at me. His eyes are magnificent in this light. As otherworldly as the forest around him. "I knew you'd come."

"Happy birthday, dickhead," I say, sitting down next to him. Sir James spins in circles and then does the same, huffing like it's some kind of unbearable dog burden to have to nap at a moment's notice. "I thought you told us not to come to the thorn chapel today."

Auden selects a pencil from his bag and then bends over his pad, his hair falling over his forehead. "Are you accusing me of hypocrisy on my own birthday, St. Sebastian?"

"You deserve it."

His eyes don't stray from his work, but a small smile tugs at his mouth. "Maybe."

"Why are you out here?"

"Because I knew you'd come out here," he says mildly, reaching for another pencil. "And because I was up early. I had trouble sleeping."

Because Poe stayed with me last night. I wonder if he misses her as much as I do when she's sleeping with him. It's nonsensical to miss her when she's only a wall away, but there it is.

We should have been a three. Not two variable sets of two.

I look down at what he's sketching. It's the thorn chapel, of course, but only the far end. The altar, the crumbling, rose-decked wall behind it, the dark clouds pressing against the trees behind all of that. And set in the wall, surrounded by roses that Auden's currently coloring a red so deep it's nearly black—

"That's the door."

Auden nods. I look up at the wall, which in real life is a bank of stone and untidy blackthorn studded with bright blue berries. And then I look down at the sketch. There, the penciled door rises above it all. Its top arch is pointed, its planks fitted with dark metal. It looks like a door that would belong in a medieval chapel.

"Is that what you think it looks like?" I ask.

"It's what I know it looks like."

"But shouldn't it look older?" I gesture at the altar. "Dr. Davidson's book said that the altar predates the chapel, predates even the standing stones."

Auden follows my gaze over to the altar. "You think the door and the altar are the same age?"

"Or the door came first. And the altar was built in front of it."

I get another smile. "I thought you didn't believe in the door, St. Sebastian."

I shrug, looking away from him and into the storm-shadowed forest. It's so hard to be close to him sometimes. So hard to see his smile and not think of what it felt like to have his foot on my chest, his drawings on my skin, his footsteps chasing after mine as we ran through the trees.

"It's the kind of morning where I don't care what I normally believe."

I'm not worried about whether he understands what I mean or not—I know he will. And he does.

"Yes," he says. "It is that kind of morning."

And then he lifts his hand over his sketch and starts working again.

"They didn't have doors in the Neolithic," I say after a long minute. I stretch out my legs and lean against the wall too, tangling my hand in the grass next to me. "It would have looked different then."

"I would suppose so," Auden says, a bit distractedly. He's filling in more details around the altar, using a few different shades of gray to capture the look of the weathered stone. "Maybe it would have been a breach in the air itself. A gateway without the gate."

"But to where?"

"I don't know. Poe says in her dreams of Estamond, even Estamond herself doesn't know. Although Estamond did believe that local stories of being abducted into fairyland came from the door."

"There're stories like that all over the world, though. Do you think that means there're doors all over the world?"

Auden contemplates this. "It certainly seems possible."

"So maybe this door isn't special."

I don't know why I say that. I of all people think that Thornchapel is the best and most interesting place in the world, for no other reason than I love it. Just by being associated with Thornchapel, the door is important to me.

"It's undoubtedly special," Auden disagrees, flicking a glance up at me from underneath his lashes. "Because it's ours."

And he's right.

He continues his work, and I watch him, feeling strangely restless as I do. It should be soothing, reassuring, doing this thing we did when we were sixteen. Him drawing, me watching, the summer heat settling in my bones as I lounge next to him.

But instead I feel like I did when I was sixteen, which is gashed and ragged with wanting him. Wanting his mouth on mine, his body against mine, his fingers wrapped around the part of me that aches for him so, so much. I watch him while he draws like I'll be allowed to have him if only I look hard enough. If only I memorize perfectly the fine cut of his jaw and the graceful, aristocratic swoop of his nose. If only I can recreate in my mind the faint lines on his forehead as he works, the infrequent blinks, the impatient flicks of hair out of his face. The firm, almost sensual wrap of his fingers around his pencils, the balance of abandon and precision in his movements as he draws. The sound of his breathing against the breathing of the hovering storm, as if they were one and the same.

I'm playing with the ring on my thumb as I watch, spinning it in slow circles, wishing it was him playing with it instead. Wishing it was another kind of ring on a different finger. Wishing that I wasn't so painfully, excruciatingly aware of how it will never, ever be a different kind of ring.

"If you don't stop looking at me," says Auden after a while, "I'm going to do something about it."

"You don't like being looked at?"

Auden sets down his pencil and puts his hand over where I've been fiddling with my ring. "I like being looked at too much," he says.

Our eyes meet, and I think the weight of his hand over both of mine is enough to press me right into the earth. Like I'll be pushed through the grass and the dirt and the rocks and right into the molten heart of the planet just by the gravity of his touch.

"I like looking at you too much," I admit in a whisper.

His eyes drop to my mouth, then to my throat, then down to where his hand covers mine. The thing between us is like a storm all on its own, a storm that won't break, that can't break. It can't ever, ever break, and yet if it doesn't, I think I might die from it.

Auden's voice is soft when he speaks. "We've been good, St. Sebastian. Haven't we?"

Those words are like brands on my heart, like silk sliding over my cock. My entire body erupts in goosebumps.

"Yeah," I say, the word coming out like gravel. "We've been good."

The tip of his finger finds the family crest stamped onto my ring and rubs over it slowly, slowly. I think of the mercies and cruelties that fingertip has given me. Caresses that curled my toes and bruises that made me thrash.

I never understood the phrase *ignorance is bliss* until now, I always thought it better to know, it should be better to know…

I wish I didn't know now. I wish I knew nothing about it. I wish he would thread his fingers through my hair and kiss me like I was his, because I *would* still be his if I didn't know the truth. We'd be in paradise together instead of in hell alone.

If you're already in hell, why not be there together?

You could trade longing for guilt and loneliness for shame.

But then at least you wouldn't be apart.

I know it's for my sake that he forbears. I know it's because he loves me that he keeps his love hidden away.

But what about me? For whose sake am I doing this?

Mine?

My mother's?

I don't know anymore. And I still know it's wrong to want him so much, but I can't stop, and maybe if I gave in—just once—just a little—just enough to feel better—

Auden's eyes lift back up to my mouth, and I know he's looking at my lip piercing, I know he's imagining taking it between his teeth and tugging.

I know he's remembering what it feels like on his cock.

"This is hard," he says. "It's always hard, of course, but right now, all I want is to—"

He stops before he can speak aloud whatever it is that's tormenting him.

Do it, I want to say. *Whatever it is, just do it to me, please, please, please.*

And for a moment, I think he might. His eyes are hot on my mouth and his hand curls tight over mine, and I see the Thorn King in his face, I see the god who runs through the trees, and I wish he would kiss me, grab me, fuck me. Make it so I have no choice. Make me feel his love, make it inevitable, and then I can have it both ways. I can be made to have him and I can have the hating him for making me.

But Auden is too wise or too cruel for that.

He pulls away, his hand lifting off mine, fitful lightning flickering through the clouds as he does.

My entire body mourns the loss of his touch, and not for the first time or even for the millionth, I hope hell is real and I hope Ralph Guest is there. Not just for what he did here in the thorn chapel, for what he did to my mother and Poe's mother, but for what he's done to me and Auden now. For the future he stole from us, for the love we can't share because we never had a choice about sharing his blood.

Auden drags his hands over his face. "Everything I want is wrong," he says, sounding unhappy.

Maybe it is.

But…

"I want it too," I whisper.

"That's what makes it so hard."

"Yeah," I say. I almost want to add *I'm sorry*, to let him know that I appreciate what he's given up for the sake of my soul. That I appreciate the gesture even more because everyone knows I don't even really believe in souls at all.

But I do know that the St. Sebastian who was my mother's son is slipping away bit by bit, day by day. And I'm terrified of waking up one morning and seeing a man she'd be ashamed of, a man roistering and carousing inside her greatest fears.

Don't see him again.

Don't see him again.

How could she have known, though, what she was asking? How could she have known that my heart was already curved and notched to fit perfectly against his?

The wind kicks up a little, fluttering the pages of Auden's sketchpad. He watches it dispassionately, staring down at the sketched depiction of the altar and the door as the paper rustles and flaps in the breeze.

"Do you think we're cursed?" he asks. "That the Guests are cursed for what they've done here?"

I suppose he's thinking of us. He's thinking of his father and his neglected mother, who lived and died in her unhappiness. He's thinking of Randolph, who according to Poe, watched Estamond die here and who later watched all his children die.

But I look around at the ruins—lush and carpeted with roses and berries and thorns—I think of the majestic house, the river, the hills, the everything else.

"I don't know. There is a lot to being a Guest that isn't cursed. Maybe Becket would say that they're—or we're, I suppose—blessed."

"I don't care what Becket says," Auden replies sharply. "I want to know what you think."

"Why?" I ask. "Why does it matter what I think? Curses aren't real."

"But what the Guests have done here might be real. And if that's real, then wouldn't it leave some kind of…imprint? Some sort of stain?"

He's looking at the real altar now, and I follow his gaze, thinking about it too. What people might have done here for centuries and longer.

Here and there, Poe's father had said. *King and door.*

"What do you think it was like?" asks Auden quietly. And I know he doesn't mean watching something like that, I know he doesn't mean witnessing it. I know he means doing it. He means being it—being the Thorn King. Striding up to the altar with the torc around your neck, knowing death was only moments away.

I hate the look on Auden's face just now, like he's already walking up to the altar himself, like he's already preparing to be slain. His eyes are wet and bright, and there's color high on his cheeks, and his breathing is fast, so fast.

Every curve and line of him has gone completely taut, like he's rigid with anticipation and fear.

"Auden," I whisper. "It's not going to happen again. It's never going to happen again."

"But what if it does?"

"It's not," I repeat firmly. "I won't let it."

"What if it's supposed to?" His hands twist into the grass, like if he holds himself hard enough to the ground, he'll be safe. Safe from the ghosts of his ancestors' sins. "What if it's the only way?"

I stare at him. "Are you listening to yourself? Killing someone is never the only way, especially not for a fucking door."

"Right," he says.

"A magic, invisible door," I clarify, to highlight exactly how ridiculous this is. But also to shake him out of this, because it sends shivers of unease dancing down my spine. I suddenly hate him looking at the altar, I hate him looking at the empty space where a door could be.

It can't have him, I think. *It's not allowed to have him too.*

I won't allow it.

And it doesn't matter what I actually believe about doors and sacrifices and kings; it's the kind of morning when I'll believe anything anyway.

What matters is that I do think people have died on that altar.

What matters is that I will never let Auden Guest be one of them.

I get to my knees and crawl over his legs, meaning only to come between him and the altar, to break his view and block the uncanny tableau behind me, but once I'm there, once I'm straddling his thighs, every thought and intention in my mind slowly fizzes away, like fireworks on a pond.

"Hi," I say, stupidly.

He peers up at me, the wind ruffling his hair and his ivory T-shirt. Because he's Auden Guest, he can't even wear T-shirts like the rest of us, and he's wearing some wide-necked linen blend that probably costs as much as ten normal shirts. His shorts too—lemon yellow things made for boats and picnics and private lunches in Lake Como.

And all of it is fitted and draped to perfection, hugging the strong curves of his shoulders and the firm swells of his pectoral muscles. Between my knees, the shorts are pulled tight around his thighs, and when I look down, I can see exactly where his thighs curve into his hips. I see exactly where he bulges behind his zipper, and how much he does. Through the thin, expensive blend of his shirt, I can make out the shadow of his navel, the dark pink circles of his nipples. If I wanted to lick him through his shirt, I would know exactly where to.

"What are you doing?" he asks curiously.

"I don't know," I say. Neither of us moves.

"I think you wanted to help me," he says, still looking up at me. It's so strange to be above him like this, to be the one trapping him, caging him. I feel like I can't catch my breath. "You wanted to distract me," he goes on, "from my morbid imaginings."

That's right, I remember. I remember how he looked when he was staring at the altar. And now he's looking up at me with something similar and yet so different—color in his cheeks and his breathing fast, and now it's because of me, it's all for me.

"Well?" I ask, and when I ask it, I realize I'm breathing fast too. "Is it working?"

His eyes are intense; I think they could burn holes in the air. But his mouth is pure laziness as he pulls his bottom lip between his teeth and slowly releases it. "Yes."

"Good."

For a moment, it's just this. Only this.

A successful distraction.

And then I brush the hair out of his beautiful eyes.

He catches my hand as I do it, as if to stop me, and I tear my hand away and do it again, deliberately running my fingertips over his forehead and letting all that tousled silk kiss against the backs of my knuckles.

"St. Sebastian," he warns.

"It's in your eyes."

"It's always in my eyes."

I do it again, wishing I could watch the flutter of those dramatic eyelashes forever. "I want to see your face."

"St. S—"

I put my hand over his mouth, and he goes completely still underneath me. Never, not in twelve years, have I done something like this. Never have I taken charge of his body, never have I taken what I wanted from him. And never has he let me. Never has he let me straddle him, silence him, slide a hand into his hair and twist, as I'm doing right now. Just enough to make him grunt against my palm. Just enough to make him swell even more in those Lake Como shorts of his.

The sensation of topping him is almost as forbidden, almost as reckless, as the knowledge that it's my brother I'm touching like this. It thrums through me like scotch, like the storm, like a thousand thousand sins, like nature itself.

I can't stop it. I won't stop it.

All storms must break, after all.

31

St. Sebastian

With a twist and a shove, I have him angled away from the wall and flat on his back in the grass. Pencils spill everywhere and thunder pounds through the air, and we both ignore it all, our eyes only on each other.

"What are you doing?" he asks again, this time in a voice that's rough. Almost angry. "We don't do this. We don't do it because this is how you wanted it to be. We haven't been—it's been for *you*, St. Sebastian."

He's right and I don't care. I don't care right now.

I swing my leg back over his hips, bracing my hands on either side of his head. It feels strange to be over him, and wrong too, but it's the kind of wrong that makes me hard—and it's that kind of morning, anyway. The kind of morning when anything can happen. So why not this?

"You wanted to imagine it," I say, dipping my face to run the tip of my nose along his jaw. "So let's imagine it."

"W-what?"

I'm gratified by the quaver in his voice. By the flush in his cheeks and the relentless bar in his pants, which even now strains against his zipper. "You wanted to know what the Thorn King felt? I can help you."

"St. Sebastian…" It might have been a dismissal or a protest, I don't know. But whatever it was going to be dies on his lips when I collar his throat with my hand.

His slow swallow against my palm might be the single sexiest thing I've ever felt in my entire life. The squeeze of the muscles in his neck. The graceful roll of his Adam's apple.

"A torc," I say, tightening my hand the tiniest bit. "He would have worn a torc."

Auden's lips part. He draws in a shuddering breath.

And then he nods, closing his eyes.

I've never felt Auden's neck like this. There were times—brief, stolen interludes—when I was permitted to caress him, allowed to explore his body, but it was never like this. Never me with power over him.

I sit up so I can circle his neck with both hands, with thumbs on either side of his throat. I can trace the knob of his larynx and the curved ridge of his windpipe. I can settle my touch in the sickle-shaped notch of his collarbone. Everything that keeps him alive—all the air, all the blood—all of it can be spanned by my fingers alone.

It's a humbling, terrifying realization. To know he's nothing but oxygen and carbon and hydrogen like the rest of us. It feels like a lie. Because how could it be true?

How could a wild god be this vulnerable?

I lift my fingers away and run them down his chest, down the tight furrows of his stomach to the waistband of his shorts.

"He'd be naked too," I say, "or mostly naked."

Auden raises an eyebrow at me. Even flat in the grass, he manages to look haughtily amused. "Oh, is that so?"

"It is," I confirm, even though I actually have no idea and why would I? All my information about human sacrifices and kings come from novels and low-budget fantasy movies. But it makes a kind of sense to me—if the point was to sacrifice the king while he was still hale and strong, then wouldn't all that health and strength be on display?

And anyway, I just really, really want to take his shirt off.

He gives me a look like he knows what I'm up to, but he doesn't stop me, he doesn't say anything else. He doesn't point out that this is a very, very dangerous game for us to play. He simply arches his back when I push the hem of his shirt up to his chest, he curls his shoulders off the ground when I tug it over his head.

I toss it to the side when I'm done, and then it's my turn to be distracted. By the firm lines of his chest, by the etched muscles of his stomach. By the flat coins of his nipples, which I run my fingers over.

"This is hardly fair," he rasps. "You can see me and I can't see you."

There's no hesitation in pulling off my own shirt. I ball it up and throw it next to his in the grass.

His eyes sear over my exposed skin so hotly I almost forget *I* am on top of *him*, that I'm the one in control. If looks alone could bind—if they could bite and bruise and fuck—then I'd be thoroughly used by now, I'd be transparently and indelibly his possession and belonging.

But as it is, looks can't do that. And even so, he keeps his cravings confined to his stare and to the restless roll of his hips between my thighs. He doesn't issue any orders, he doesn't take control. And when I circle his wrists with my fingers and pin them on either side of his head, he lets me. He allows it, even though there's a fierce tension thrumming through his body as he does.

I dip my face to his, close enough that we can feel each other's breathing. "You're being very obedient."

"A Thorn King would be right now," he whispers. But there's a small line between his brows, a small frown on his lips—and I realize that there's another reason he's being so amenable.

He's worried I'll stop.

I think I'm worried I'll stop too. Because I know we shouldn't, I know I should get up, I know there's only one way this can end...

I brush my lips over his.

We both freeze at the feeling of it, at the dazzling, sizzling thrill. It's been so long, it's been forever—ten weeks of raw, undiluted hell—and I can feel the firm warmth of his mouth everywhere, not just my lips, but on the insides of my thighs and along the column of my throat and on the arches of my feet.

With one kiss, he's kissed me everywhere, he's owned me everywhere. Just as he did when we were teenagers in his garden. One kiss and I was forever his.

"St. Sebastian," he whispers against my mouth, but I don't let him finish, I can't. He'll try to be sensible. He'll point out once again that I was the reason we haven't kissed in ten weeks, he'll tell me to stop and think about what we're doing. He'll tell me to remember what I said in that wheat and barley tomb, that I'd hate myself for loving him.

I don't care. I don't care right now.

It's Lammas and the thunder is growling over the hills and Auden Guest is underneath me, his wrists in my hands, and I want it too much. I want *him* too much.

Everything else be damned, however literally that may be.

I slot my lips against his and then slowly, torturously drag my mouth along them, letting him feel the piercing running along his lower lip.

He is all quivering tension underneath me; all rolling hips and jerky breaths. Above the place where my fingers cuff his wrists, his hands clench and flex and clench, like a big cat sheathing and unsheathing its claws.

"They might have drugged him," I say. When I speak, my lips graze and rub against his—the very act of speaking creating the kiss itself.

"Drugged whom?" Auden asks dazedly.

"The king. Sacrifices were often drugged."

"And this…are you drugging me right now?"

I let my tongue flicker against the arched underside of his upper lip. He moans up into our kiss, his pelvis seeking friction against me.

"You tell me," I whisper. And then I open my mouth to his.

It's impossible to separate the parts from the whole—the heat, the silky wetness of it, the demanding strokes of his tongue, which is the one part of him that can't pretend submission even for a game.

The taste of him, like mint and tea, and the feeling of his groans against my mouth.

His body arching up to meet mine, and the agonizingly carnal sensation of our bare chests and stomachs meeting, and the inevitable moment the angles all match up and our clothed erections slide against each other.

I can't stop kissing him, I can't ever stop. How have I ever stopped? How have I ever torn away from a mouth like this—commanding, sophisticated, filthy?

So filthy. This mouth that can speak Latin, that can discern the balance in a good Burgundy, can effortlessly rattle off the names of obscure philosophers, this same mouth is now predatory against mine. His tongue plunders every corner of me, his teeth catch on my piercing and pull, his lips seal over one of my lips and suck until I whimper.

He's mating with my mouth, and my body responds like it's being mounted. Like his cock is already pushing inside me and seeking out my tightest, hottest places. Like his fist is already shuttling up and down my dick. My testicles are pulled tight, and my erection throbs against my zipper.

And all because of those firm lips, that seeking tongue. Those needy, greedy strokes and nips.

I manage to pull away long enough to look down at him, and he does look like a man drugged now, like someone dosed well past sobriety. His eyes are glassy and unfocused, and his lips swollen and wet. The high contours of his cheekbones are dusted with pink.

Underneath me, his chest heaves and heaves and heaves.

"What next?" he asks, blinking up at me, and his eyes are so bright, his pupils so blown, that I know I could say anything to him, I could do anything I wanted.

Anything anything.

"They'd need your blood," I say, and then I bend my head and bite him over the heart, just as he once did to me. "There'd be knives."

I soothe the spot I just bit with my tongue and then bite him again. He jolts underneath me, and then trembles. I do it again, and again, moving my mouth to bite him everywhere I please—his collarbone, under his nipple, the juicy muscle between his neck and his shoulder. I let go of his wrists so that I can work my way down his stomach, nipping and licking, and he gasps.

Oh, how he gasps.

"These—are magnificent—knives—" he manages to say as my tongue dances around his navel.

I find the trail of silky hair leading down, and I lick through it, I bite my way down it until I get to the waistband of his shorts.

We both go still.

This is the moment, this is the choice. After this, there's no pretending, because brothers *don't* do this. They don't slowly pop the button on their brother's shorts, as I'm doing now. They don't unzip the zipper and groan when they see there's no underpants underneath, not even the poncy designer briefs Auden normally likes. They don't drag their lip piercing up and down the velvet skin of their brother's bare erection.

They don't.

They don't.

"St. Sebastian," says Auden, lifting his head to look down at me over his stomach.

I look up at him from between his legs, my mouth hovering over his thickness. "Yes?"

He blinks at me. "Why?" he asks, and he doesn't have to elaborate, I know what he's asking.

Why am I doing this?

Why now? Why this way?

I tell him the truth. "I don't know."

He stares at me for a long moment, his pupils still blown, his lips still parted. A man deeply drugged. "I should need a better answer," he murmurs. But then his head drops back into the grass, and he doesn't speak again—not until I suck the tip of him into my mouth and I hear him grunt my name.

He is, as he is in all other ways, perfect here. Eight and a half straight inches, thick and proud and crowned with a deliciously flared tip. The hair here is darker than the hair on his head, the color of chocolate rather than cinnamon, and it's short and silky and curled in perfect waves, as if he was painted or sculpted and not grown all messy and crooked like the rest of us.

I nuzzle the curls at his base and breathe him in—clean skin and the lingering smell of his soap—and then I tease my tongue along the soft underside of him. I let him between my lips and seal my mouth around his length.

He obeys the unspoken rules of our game, and he doesn't grab my head and fuck my mouth deeper, he doesn't search for my throat to hold as his cock nudges in and out of it. He keeps his hands to his sides—although they're hardly passive in their obedience. He rips at the grass next to him, clutches and yanks at it as I take him deep in my mouth for the first time since Beltane.

He's mine, like this, mine in a way that's so potent I'm nearly giddy with it. He quivers for me, he gasps for me. He grabs at grass and clenches his jaw for me. And when I crawl back up over him, there's nothing but wild desperation in his face. A king at his final battle. A god at the burning of his temple.

"Don't stop," he begs. "Don't leave."

"I won't," I promise, kissing him again. "I won't. I'm not done yet."

"Yours," he says, still begging. "Let me feel yours."

Lust punches me right in the stomach. I'm fumbling at my zipper almost before he even finishes speaking, shoving my jeans down far enough to expose myself. The minute I lower my hips and rub against his slick erection, we both grunt. His cock is so hard, so slippery, and I have to press all the way against him to keep us together the way we need. Press so that our stomachs and chest are flush, our legs a tangle of denim and yellow cotton-silk blend. When I grind against him, I feel the hot bar of him beneath me; each thrust of my hips has us both exhaling in sharp, short bursts. Mating, but cock to cock.

I won't last like this, it's too hot. Too, too hot.

"You would be tied up," I say softly, determined to finish this little game of ours. I find his wrists with my hands again. "Tied up and bound."

I pin him to the ground by his wrists, by his hips, and continue rutting against him. His eyelashes flutter up at me in the headiest way; he's beyond himself, beyond his normal restraint and sophistication, he's nothing but a horny, pleading boy underneath me. No longer the Thorn King.

Just a man needing the most essential release men need.

"You wore your torc, you were drugged and bound," I say low in his ear, still thrusting against him. "And now all that's left is to give it up. All that's left is to let go."

"Yes," he murmurs, his eyes closing. "Yes, St. Sebastian."

And with a long, hard shudder, he releases against me, spending onto both our stomachs and cocks.

And then it happens. The inevitable. What was inevitable from the kiss, from before the kiss, from when I saw him sitting against the wall while thunder rolled around us.

Pleasure scissors deep in my gut, knifing me with delirium, with jabs of euphoric and primal sensation. My spirit is huge, expansive, as big as the storm, and my body is nothing but heat and flesh and need, rutting in primal, biological drive. Something shears free at the base of my spine, like a strung wire being cut, and the whiplash nearly kills me. I growl wildly into Auden's neck as my hips pump and pump against his, as I ejaculate all over us both, spurting heavily over and over and over again.

It's not an orgasm, it's a death. It's a draining, an emptying. Ten weeks of longing, two and a half months of denial, all of it pumping out of me like blood from a vein, hot and life-giving. Spilling and spilling and spilling.

I don't even realize I'm crying until it's over and I'm slumped against him. The tears run down to my nose and drip onto his throat, where they slide in clear tracks down to the grass.

"I'm sorry," Auden whispers underneath me, and for a moment, I think he means about what we've just done, about the Thorn King game and what I used it for. But as he rolls me to my back and reaches for his bag, I realize he's not apologizing for what we just did, but for what he's about to do. "I'm sorry," he says again, moving me to my stomach and then crawling over me. "I need it too much from you. Just one more time."

"Do it," I tell him. *Fuck.* "Do it. Do it before we stop ourselves."

Something cool and slick rubs against my opening. Hand lotion, I think. Not that I care. He could tell me all he has is spit and a prayer, and I'd tell him to go ahead.

He pushes a finger inside of me and my cock swells anew, filling and throbbing back to life for him. "Auden, please, I can't wait any lo—"

I don't finish, because in one vicious move, he's replaced his finger with his cock. A brutal thrust that has me crying out into the grass.

"That's right, stubborn boy," he says, grabbing me by the hips and hauling me up to all fours. He enters me again, blazing a path so tight and hot that I think I might combust from the inside out. "That's right. I know you missed it. You missed me taking my pleasure inside you."

Gone is the pleading Auden from just minutes ago, gone is whatever docility he'd adopted for my sake. He is all wild god once again, cruel and victorious, with only one goal, one drive and one need.

To fuck.

It doesn't take long. It's been too much time apart, there's been too much space between us. It's too forbidden, too filthy, it feels too good. I don't even have to touch my own erection and it goes off, simply from Auden behind me and the silky drag of him against my prostate.

I explode and writhe back against him, my cock jerking and spilling onto the grass. He bands an arm across the front of my hips, and after a breathlessly mendacious series of thrusts, he gives a pleased grunt and fills me with his heat.

A hand, dispassionate and businesslike, reaches down and checks my erection to see if it's wet at the tip. To see if I came.

When he finds that I did, he lets out another satisfied grunt, and then slides free. He pulls up his shorts and then stretches out sideways on the grass, yanking me down next to him and crushing me into his chest.

"Not yet," he whispers into my hair. "I'm not ready to stop yet."

And neither am I.

I doze for a while like this, and then I'm awakened to be fucked again. I don't know if it's Lammas or merely the pent-up need between us, but Auden is insatiable this time around, like he can't settle for just one dish, he needs the entire menu.

And I encourage it.

When he kisses me, I find his hands and guide them to my throat. When he hauls me up against his chest, I twist over his lap and bait him into spanking me.

When he pushes me into the grass and wraps strong fingers around me, I wriggle out of my jeans and cover the hand curled around my hip, making it squeeze hard enough to send me squirming.

And when he crawls over me with swollen lips and tousled hair, his eyes once again like windows to the forest, I press my palm against his heart and say, "Say it and it's yours," just as I said that Beltane afternoon by the river.

Those forest eyes flash. "Is this the truth, St. Sebastian? Because you know what I want you to give me."

Forever, stubborn boy. Only that.

"Right here it's the truth. Right now."

His eyes glitter in the gloomy light of the storm. "Only for right here? Only for right now?"

"I don't know," I whisper. "Probably."

He sucks in a breath like I've just hit him, but when I reach up to touch his face, when I start to speak, try to explain that I really don't *know,* that I don't know what's supposed to happen when we want each other this much but we're also bound by a tie so strong it will never loosen, it will never set us free—he catches my hand and shoves it down by my head. And when he finally enters me, he does it with an angry, possessive thrust that has me crying out. He fucks me like I'm his worst enemy, like I'm prey that dared to run, and I love it so much that I can't even regret the anger, because I'm angry too. Does he think that I'm any less furious at fate than he is?

Does he think he's alone in wanting this always?

I meet him with all my fury, all my primal, uncontrollable need. My body doesn't care that he's my brother, neither does my spirit, and out here in the thorn chapel, we give each other everything despite it all. Vicious rolling in the grass, and bruising kisses, and slow, writhing grapples that always end with him winning, just like I want them to.

It's like Beltane, but *more*—more honest, maybe, more raw. There's more than love here, there's pain too, there's frustration and anguish and a marrow-deep knowledge that wonderful things can't last, they never last.

Even here.

I come first, my entire body clenching in one giant fist of pleasure, and then all of it, every bit of it rushing down and out my swollen, jerking length. Hot pearls of seed fly out of me, painting my stomach and my chest, one of them landing at the top of my sternum and then slowly rolling down to the hollow of my throat.

Auden watches its progress with avaricious thirst, and then he curls his lean frame over me to touch it with his mouth, to kiss it away. I moan at the soft press of his lips, and at the ticklish tease of his tongue, and my cock surrenders even more fluid, pulsing once or twice more and leaving me utterly, utterly limp.

Which is just how Auden likes to use me, and use me he does, like I'm his own personal plaything, his sex doll. An offering sent to a king as tribute. He's wedged so tight, even with me sated and loose-muscled, and sweat mists along his forehead as he has to use his strength to work himself in and out of me. To seek more friction, more heat, more St. Sebastian.

Lightning sparks up the sky above him, and for a moment I can't breathe.

With his eyes like the trees and his face set in an expression of elemental dominion, and with the sky dark and electric behind him, he barely seems human at all.

And when his stomach seizes and his hips slam forward and Auden finally roars his conquering triumph, the sky roars right back at him, a thunderclap so loud that I feel it in the ground against my back. He fills me endlessly, just as the thunder seems to roll on endlessly, both me and the earth trembling as we receive it.

His eyes burn into mine the entire time, and I know what he's thinking, even if he doesn't say it aloud.

Mine.

The thunder eventually rolls off, his cock goes still inside me. He lowers his mouth and wordlessly fits it against mine. We kiss I don't know how long like that. Softly, silently. Because what is there to say?

Nothing's changed. That's the thing about being brothers.

It can't be changed.

I hear it before I feel it. It's a slow hiss in the trees. A heavy, sporadic patter on the altar and the wooden platform I built for Imbolc. Drops in the grass.

Auden tears away from my mouth with a curse.

"Auden—"

"I know."

But he doesn't move right away, and part of me knows it's because moving will break the spell. When we pull apart, when we put on our clothes and leave the thorn chapel, reality will come back. The things we pretend to forget here we'll have to remember. The sins we've committed we'll have to answer for.

But the rain gives us no choice. It splashes onto Auden's naked back and shoulders, onto his hands planted in the grass. I think he would stay even then, but when the rain starts falling into my eyes and I have to blink it away, something in his face softens.

"Come on, stubborn boy," he says, getting to his knees and helping me up. "Back to the house."

The rain drops insistently on his open sketch pad, and I shove my T-shirt over it until I can find his bag and slide the sketches inside. It's been so long since I've seen him draw like this—for fun, for color and light and all the things he used to care about until architecture school ironed it out of him—and I can't bear to see his work ruined, not even a little bit.

Auden steps next to me, holding out his hand. He's dressed now, but his hair is hopeless. "Thank you," he says softly, slinging the bag over his shoulder. "Here."

He takes my T-shirt from my hands, and I shouldn't let him, I shouldn't indulge in this one last thing, but I do. He guides the shirt over my head and helps me into it, smoothing the faded jersey over my stomach and shoulders as if it were imported silk, oblivious to the rain falling around us, and the thunder pushing through the air more ominously than ever. It's no longer a magic sky, it's a *get inside* sky, but Auden doesn't seem to care. He takes his time, fussing with the frayed hem of my shirt like it's the last time he'll ever touch me.

I don't know. Maybe it is.

His eyes meet mine. "What happens next?" he asks me. The rain is falling between us. "What happens when we get back to the house?"

I know he's sick of this answer, but it's the only one I have. "I don't know, Auden."

Impatience flits across his face. His lips are wet with rain. "Then can you make a guess?"

I flick damp hair out of my face, feeling impatient too. "I don't know what you want me to say right now. Do you want me to admit that I'm miserable? Confused? Hurting and lonely like hell? That I could let you fuck me for a thousand years and still not be satisfied because it's never enough with you, it's never enough until it's everything and forever? Because all of it's true, you know, every bit of it, but it doesn't fix anything. It doesn't *change* anything."

His voice blends with the hissing sighs of the rain when he speaks. "It could be everything and forever, you know."

"I don't need reminded."

"Maybe you do."

We're both soaked now, fully wet. Our eyelashes spiky, our hair going slick and clinging to our cheeks.

"We can't solve us," I tell him through the rain. "We can't force our way to some different truth. There's no place we can go where we can hide from our DNA, no imaginary time we can wait for when we'll magically have different fathers." I close my eyes for a minute, just so that I don't have to see him so wet and tragic-looking standing there in the rain. "We can't run from this."

"So don't run," he whispers. "Don't run away again."

"And what happens if I stay? We suffer? Forever?"

"It's better than suffering apart. Forever."

I wish I knew he was right. I wish I could say this experiment—this *all the parts of love save for one*—could work with enough practice, could work in the right conditions, if only we tried hard enough. I wish I could say with certainty that what happened this morning won't happen again.

But I can't. And he can't either.

When I don't answer him, Auden drags in a deep, rainy breath and scrubs his hands over his face and hair. "Okay," he says, resigned. "Okay. Inside."

And so inside we go, jogging through the trees and up the path to the lawn and then to the house. The rain is so thick now that we can barely see what's in front of us; by the time we burst through the south door into the mudroom with Sir James, we're sopping and breathless, our clothes sticking to our bodies. Auden's thin shirt and pale shorts are practically indecent now, and he catches me staring at the corrugations of his stomach, at the visible curve of his cock through the wet fabric.

I expect him to look defiant or maybe even vindicated. I expect smugness, arrogance, maybe even reserve.

I don't expect sadness. And when I meet his gaze and see that he's about to cry, that his chin is quivering, that he's swallowing over and over again—

"Auden," I say, not really sure what I could possibly say next.

Don't be sad? It'll be okay? It'll get better?

No. None of those things are right, none of them are true.

"I fucked up," he says, looking away. It puts his face in profile and I can see the magnificent cut of his jaw, the working of his throat as he fights to keep his emotions at bay. "I broke my word. I said no more, and that was a promise to you, and I've failed to keep it."

"No, Auden. I was there too."

He shakes his head. "It's not enough. I know you, Saint, I heard you when you said you'd hate yourself for loving me. And still I let it happen. I really am no better than our father. Selfish to the last—"

My mouth is open to argue—regrets and sins aside, the responsibility is *mine*—but then a massive thud reverberates through the house, the sound of something huge slamming against stone.

Auden and I exchange instantaneous, wide-eyed glances, and then we're both darting out of the mudroom and down to corridor to the main hall, where the noise seemed to come from. Sir James bounds ahead, barking wildly, and between the three of us, I know we're leaving water everywhere.

"What in the bloody he—"

The storm has blown the front doors—both of them—wide open, and wind and rain are howling into the gap, wetting the flags and sending gusts of damp air through the massive room. But that's not what has Auden staggering to a halt and staring.

It's Father Becket Hess, kneeling in the doorway, dripping wet and framed by silver sheets of rain. The blowing wind lashes at him like a heaven-sized whip.

"I'm so sorry," he says. "I didn't know where else to go."

32

St. Sebastian

At some point Delphine must have arrived, although she's nowhere to be seen as we urge Becket into the library.

But her handiwork is everywhere—the room is filled with sprays of lavender and hung with garlands of fresh-smelling greenery. The tables are laden with all sorts of bready treats: rolls and pastries and homemade loaves with an artisanal butter bar—I suppose in keeping with the Lammas theme of harvest and grain.

There's small cakes and finger sandwiches and petit fours and piles and piles of fresh fruit. There's neat rows of cocktails that even I can acknowledge are very pretty—fizzing flutes of champagne, coupe glasses filled with drinks the color of violets, highballs garnished with tiny heads of lavender. And at the center of it all, a naked tier cake with frosting the color of cream and heaped with blackberries and more lavender sprigs.

Even Becket, in the state he's in, pauses to stare.

"Delphine really outdid herself," I marvel as Auden tugs Becket over to a battered leather chair.

"You," Auden says to him, "sit." Then to me, he says, "I'm going up for dry clothes. Get him a drink, will you?"

It's not even noon, but if ever a man looked like he needed a drink, it's Becket in his priest's collar and shirt, soaked to the bone and looking shell-shocked. I glance at the clock as I walk over to the sideboard and pour out a scotch. He would have only just finished Mass an hour ago, and St. Petroc's is at least fifteen minutes away—more in a downpour like this. I wonder what could have sent him running here so quick after the service when normally he likes to chat with his parishioners.

And from the look of him, it wasn't because he was excited for lavender cake.

"I saw Rebecca's car outside too, next to Delphine's," Becket murmurs as he accepts the scotch I hand him. "Do you think they're trapped outside in the rain?"

I shook my head. "They must be upstairs. Auden and I were just outside and we didn't see anyone."

Becket's eyes flicker with the first sign of interest I've seen from him yet today. "Were you in the thorn chapel?"

I suddenly decide I'd very much like a drink of my own. "Yes," I say, walking back over to the drinks. "We were. Hypocritical of us, I know."

"It's only hypocritical of Auden, and I suspected he'd end up there today anyway," Becket says. His voice is more wooden than usual, and it's hollow like an empty room. Or an empty church. "I wish he'd accept the inevitable."

I uncap the bottle as I look at him. The rain keeps the room dark, and despite Delphine's efforts with glass lanterns full of flickering candles and strings of lights hung over the tables, the room is full of storm-shadows. It's hard to get a good look at his face from here—save for his eyes. That radiant, unearthly blue.

"What's the inevitable?" I ask.

"That Thornchapel has already chosen him, even if he hasn't chosen it back."

I want to tell him he's wrong, but I can't.

"And," Becket continues, "we all must accept our inevitable too."

"Which is?"

Lightning flashes outside as he answers, in an empty voice. "That Thornchapel has chosen all of us along with him."

All of us.

The truth of it is colder than the clothes sticking to my skin, and I finish pouring my drink so I can take a few much-needed swallows. And as I do, I think of the storm sparking above Auden's head as he fucked me, I think of his voice thick with tears back in the mudroom.

If this is what it feels like for us to be chosen, I don't think I like it very much.

I take another drink and then walk back over to the circle of sofas and chairs and sit across from the pale-lipped priest. I've never seen him like this. Never shaken, never silent and haunted.

Worry nestles in my gut.

"What happened?" I ask. "Did something happen during Mass?"

He stares at the rain-streaked windows. "After Mass. It was after."

But he doesn't elaborate and so I don't push. I've always hated it when people pushed me for answers—except for Poe, but not all of us can be adorably curious librarians.

Some librarians are just sulky boys with good taste in music who never finished their degree.

And anyway, Auden is coming in with an armful of dry clothes and a still-sleepy Poe trailing behind him. She's pulled on a thin tank top and pajama shorts, and she's not wearing a bra, a fact that Becket and I become aware of at the same moment. My sore cock gives a kick at the sight of those hard nipples pressed against the fabric of her shirt.

Becket just gives a small shiver and bows his head.

Poe pads over to me as Auden distributes clothes. They both decamp to different nooks in the shelves to change, but I don't move, determined to finish my drink first.

"Where did you go this morning?" Poe asks me quietly. "You and Auden were both wet."

I don't answer—or rather, I don't answer with words. I pull up the hem of my shirt to show my stomach, which is currently inscribed with reddened bites the exact shape of Auden's mouth. His calling card.

Hope flits through Poe's bright green eyes.

I hate to extinguish it, but I won't lie to her. "It can't happen again, sweetheart. It won't."

"Oh," she says. Just that. Her plush mouth is in the shape of unhappiness.

I finish my drink and kiss the top of her head before I go to a corner to change. I wish I could tell her differently; I wish I could tell her we'd be a real three once again, just like she wants. Just like Auden wants. Just like I want.

I peel off my clothes in the same place where I once fucked Poe against the bookshelves with Auden right behind me, his arms a cage around me and Poe both.

This is the hurt I choose, Poe said that night.

But what about the hurts we don't choose? The ones that come for us anyway, the ones that chase us through time and through sins and secrets so old that they now belong more to the dead than to the living?

And if Thornchapel has chosen us, then does that mean it's chosen *this* too?

Auden brought me his clothes instead of mine, and as I walk back over to where everyone is settling on chairs and sofas, I have to fight off the urge to go to him. To curl at his feet like a pet, to climb into his lap, to revel in the feel of his clothes kissing my skin. I feel like a girl in her boyfriend's too-big shirt, I feel like a beloved child wrapped in a warm blanket.

Even when I make him cry, even when I return his love with doubt and regret, he still tries to pull me into his heart. It's both terrible and wonderful at the same time.

"Becket," Auden is saying as I sit, "finish the drink. And tell us what happened."

Becket obeys—four long gulps of liquor—and then he holds the empty glass like it's a relic he's been charged with safekeeping. His voice is still mechanical and vacant when he finally says, "I've been formally warned by my bishop that I'm in danger of being suspended."

"*Becket*," Poe whispers. She reaches for his hand, and for her and only her, he offers up a weak smile.

"He's also recommending that I take a leave of absence to spend time in counseling and prayer. And I've agreed to."

"Oh." Poe slides off her chair and moves to his feet, where she presses her face into the side of his knee. "This is my fault," she mumbles. "All my fault."

"It's not, darling," Becket says. "I was there too. I chose it too."

My eyes meet Auden's across the table. While most traces of the tearfulness I saw in the mudroom are gone, I still see a bone-aching sadness in his eyes. A sadness that I know must be reflected in mine.

"A leave of absence," Auden says, breaking our stare to look over at Becket. "What does that mean?"

"Two months away. I'll split my time between being mentored in Plymouth and going on a spiritual retreat in Argyll. Afterwards, I will be asked to demonstrate to the Bishop my renewed commitment to the church, and it was suggested to me that even if I do so successfully, I'll be moved to a different parish, lest I be tempted by Proserpina again." He says this last part with a smile, but his voice is blank.

"Is that what you want?" Auden asks. "To renew your commitment to the church?"

Becket stares down at his empty glass.

"I feel like there's two of me," he says after a minute. "One for the church and one for Thornchapel. In my eyes, both versions of myself serve God. But here, that service truly only benefits myself. At St. Petroc's, I help over two hundred parishioners. Wouldn't it be selfish not to choose the church?"

"Don't priests and monks lock themselves away from the world all the time?" I ask. "How would choosing Thornchapel be any different from being cloistered away like them?"

"A fair question," he concedes. He lets go of his glass with one hand and strokes the silky crown of Poe's head where it rests against his knee. "But there are other reasons why Thornchapel would be a selfish choice."

And I have nothing to say to that, not this morning. Not when I'm still sore and bite-marked from my own selfish choices.

The rain dashes against the windows while we sit, filling the silence.

"When will you go?" Auden finally asks, sounding very unhappy. He'll miss his friend, and I realize I will too. Becket was the priest who said my mother's funeral Mass, the priest who let me inside his church not to pray but to hurl accusations at God's feet. I trust him with my soul, and more importantly, with the curvy librarian tucked into a miserable ball by his feet.

I don't want him to go.

"Tonight," he says. "Well, this afternoon, actually. I'll need to be in Plymouth tonight so I can meet with my counselor in the morning."

"Are you okay?" Poe asks, and it's the most important question, the one we should have asked from the beginning. "Are you doing okay with this?"

"No," he says bluntly, his hand still on her head. "I'm not okay. And yet I know I've been straddling two paths for too long, praying a single foot on each would be enough—but it's not enough, not even close. Wherever I choose to serve God, I must do it with my whole heart, and the time has come for me to choose."

Poe nuzzles his hand. "You've always given everything your whole heart. You surrender to yourself better than anyone I know."

Pain carves itself into his expression. "Sometimes," he says in a ragged voice, "that has been to my detriment."

For a moment, I think he's talking about loving Poe, but the look on his face…

Horror. Like he's remembering horror.

But the expression fades and then he glances up at the clock on the mantel, his shoulders slumping in resignation. He cups Poe's head and then leans down to kiss her forehead. "It's time for me to go. Goodbye, Poe. Goodbye, you two," he says to me and Auden. "If you see Delphine and Rebecca, you'll let them know everything? Give them my goodbyes? I'm not sure how much internet access I'll have while I'm gone, so I don't want them to think I've ghosted Thornchapel altogether."

"They wouldn't think that," Auden assures him. "And we'll give them your goodbyes. Here, hand that to me." He holds out his hand for Becket's empty glass, and then Becket stands up. Poe does too.

Auden gives her a subtle nod, and then her eyes flick over to me, seeking approval. I nod too, knowing she wants to give Becket a more private goodbye.

"I'll walk you out," she says, and with a final look at Auden and me—and the library too—Father Becket Hess leaves us to face his future.

I immediately get up and get another drink, and without a word, Auden joins me, extending his glass for me to fill it.

"Table full of fancy drinks and we're drinking the same shit as always," I mumble, looking back at Delphine's hard work.

"I daren't touch them unless the hostess allows it," Auden says, a bit dryly, although his eyes are still somber. "And mind your tongue. This is a single malt scotch from a rare cask. It's hardly *shit*."

"What Becket said," I say, after taking a drink. "About straddling two paths. About choosing where to put his heart."

I stop, not sure where I'm going with this, or how to continue. But Auden must sense it before I do; he somehow knows where this is going.

"St. Sebastian," he says. "Don't. Don't do this."

"I thought I couldn't trust you. After you lied to me, after you kissed me in my mother's office, I thought you'd stop at nothing to have me, I thought you'd wage war on the space between us until there was none left and I was yours again."

"Don't," he says. "Please."

I can't stop myself. I won't. It needs to be said. Like Becket's reckoning, this sword has been dangling over us for months, and it's time to look up and name it.

"Don't you see? Don't you understand what happened this morning? That was me—all me. I thought I couldn't trust you, but the truth is that I can't trust myself."

He steps forward. He's close enough to touch me, but he doesn't. "Don't say it," he pleads.

But it has to be said. "I need to leave."

I hear the glass shatter before I realize he's flung it against the wall. "God*dammit*," he roars. "How many times will you run away from me? How many fucking times, St. Sebastian?"

I don't step back, I don't cower in the face of his rage, even though it burns like a fire, even though rivulets of whisky trickle past and the floor is a spray of shattered glass.

"This time is different," I say. "Because this time I'm telling you. This time you know why."

I'm backed suddenly into the bookshelf next to the sideboard; hard wood edges and leather spines dig into my back as Auden braces his hands on either side of me.

"You are *mine*," he snarls wildly. "And I'm sick to death of us pretending otherwise. Fucking or no fucking, you belong with me, you belong here, and there will be no talk of leaving, no talk of *choices*. If you want to be utterly celibate, if that makes you feel better about being in love with me, then so be it. But we will be *together*."

"We can't be together, Auden! We can't even make it three months without breaking down and fucking each other, how on earth do you think we can do this for the rest of our lives?"

He leans in closer, all muscle and potent, furious man. "I. Don't. Fucking. Care. We're doing it anyway."

"Let me go."

"Never."

"Auden."

"*Never.*"

"Do you think I want this? Do you think I wouldn't rather this be any other way? Jesus Christ, Auden, stop acting like I'm throwing some kind of pointless toddler tantrum and *think*. You know me. You know you. And you know Poe. If things stay as they are, then we'll end up where we started, and that's not permitted to us now."

"Who permits things?" he asks angrily. "Who?"

"It doesn't matter. The government, the church, the people in the village—they all know it's wrong because it *is* wrong. Brothers don't do what we do."

He glares at me. "Then let's make our own rules about what brothers do."

"I won't do that. Even for you."

He's trembling against me now, his every muscle tense and vibrating with possession. "What can I do, St. Sebastian? Tell me. Tell me and I'll fucking do it. Because I am at my wit's end here. I'd give you everything you wanted, I'd cut the beating heart out of my chest for you, and still it never seems to be enough."

"Don't you understand?" I say pleadingly. "There will never be anything that can be enough. Because there's nothing that can be done."

"No," he says in a fierce voice. "No, I don't accept that."

"It doesn't matter what you accept. It's like a law of physics—it's true no matter what you believe or think. Now please step back so I can go."

His nostrils flare and his hands tighten on the shelf on either side of me. "Absolutely not."

I try to push forward, and he only shoves me against the bookshelf harder, his chest and hips flush against me now. "Auden, you can't keep me here."

"Like hell, I can't," he mutters darkly, and I know this is pointless. I can argue with him about our future for another ten years, and he will never accept anything that isn't me by his side forever. I have to tell him the one thing I know that will make him back off. And the terrible part? This thing is actually true.

I take a deep breath. "You're acting like him right now," I say. I say it carefully, knowing the words are incendiary. That they'll scorch whatever they touch. "You're acting like our father."

The effect on him is immediate, devastating. He flinches away from me as if I've hit him, staggering back a few steps and curling in on himself. He shakes his head. "No."

"You're being selfish and you're trying to keep people who don't want to be kept. That's not how kink works, it's not how family works, and it's definitely not how love works." I set my glass down. "You said it yourself in the mudroom: you're no better than him. You're choosing the same things he would have in your shoes. Unless…"

"Unless I let you go," he says numbly. "So that's the equation you're proposing. I'm not our father if I let you leave me."

Pain lances through my chest, and I try to ignore it. The hurt and shame in his face—it's gutting to see. Excruciating. I want so badly to take it away, and yet I can't, because I need him wounded, I need him weak. Not because I want to hurt him, but because I don't stand a chance against him when he's strong.

"I'm going," I say. "And you have to let me."

He blinks those big hazel eyes at me. He looks so young all of a sudden, almost like he did when he was sixteen. Elegant and arrogant and vulnerable all at once. "We fell in love when you were in Thorncombe too," he reminds me. "Twice, in fact. You don't have to be living here for us to be in love."

"I won't stop loving you," I say, and it's the truth. But I don't say the other true thing, which is that I won't be in Thorncombe.

If I'm going to leave, then I need to leave for real. Someplace where the temptation of Auden Guest can't reach me ever again. What that means for me and Poe, I don't know yet, but I'll figure it out.

I hope.

"Is this goodbye then?" he whispers. "Is this our goodbye?"

I step closer, close enough to kiss his cheek, which I do. "Let's pretend this morning was our goodbye."

"We have to say goodbye precisely because of this morning," he says in a surly tone, but when he turns to kiss me, his gaze is raw and sweet. I let him kiss me—soft, chaste kisses. Kisses for beginnings. Or for endings.

"This morning was inevitable," I tell him. "We both know that. It was always going to be this way. A choice."

"A choice," he echoes brokenly.

"I love you," I tell him again, because he needs to know it, because I don't know if I'll ever be able to say it to him again. "I love you, Auden Guest."

And then it's my turn to walk out of the library and prepare to leave. I go upstairs to my room to pack and to think about how I'll explain all this to Poe, and my phone rings as I walk into my bedroom. I don't recognize the number, so I let it ring and go to voicemail while I find a bag and start throwing essentials into it. When my phone alerts me I have a new voicemail, I hit the button to listen to it.

"Hello, St. Sebastian," says a warm, polished voice that I can't quite place. "My daughter gave me your number, and I hope that's quite all right, I didn't know of any other way to contact you with some degree of privacy. And Delphine says you don't have Facebook or WhatsApp or any of the other places where I could message you…"

Delphine—*ah*. This must be her father, Freddie Dansey.

Strange for him to be calling me.

"I was hoping you could call me back and we could speak sometime. I debated reaching out, you know, but I think this is too important to go undiscussed."

And then he gives his phone number and asks me again to call.

When the message ends, I'm so completely baffled by it that I don't even delete it. But neither do I call him back—I hate the phone and I hate talking to people I barely know and combining the two is a special kind of hell.

And it's not like I don't have more important things to do right now. Like upend my entire life and walk away from the man I love in order to preserve what's left of my soul.

"Sorry, Freddie," I mutter and toss the phone on the bed so I can use both hands to shove clothes in my bag. "Maybe another time."

Besides, if it's really important, he'll call back, I'm sure.

But what could Freddie Dansey, of all people, want to discuss with *me*?

33

Rebecca

The Long Gallery is on the upper story of the Jacobean section of the house—a pointless space, I've always felt, built for some long-dead Guest ancestors to show off how many paintings they owned, built for promenades and for amusing bored house guests in between their extramarital trysts and amateur theatricals.

The only good thing about the gallery is its absurd number of windows. Huge, diamond-paned things lining the wide space on both sides. It would have cost Auden's ancestors a fortune to buy them all four hundred years ago, and it cost him a *second* fortune to restore them this year, but it was money well spent. They afford a view that's like something out of a movie, something out of a magazine about period homes in the countryside. The green and ancient forest with the stark, foggy hills rising up above it, glimpses of the pretty village to the east, a teasing glint of river to the south. The Thorne Valley in all its secretive perfection.

But I'm not up here for the views right now. I'm here for the blond standing alone in a window-lined alcove.

"Delphine," I say, my voice soft.

I'm surprised she can hear me over the rain lashing against the glass, but she does. She turns, silhouetted by the silver world behind her, and my heart flips over in my chest.

Beautiful.

She's so fucking beautiful.

The entire room is the color of rain—the windows to the storm, the gray wood paneling the walls and planking the floor, all of it pale and argent—and it makes her silvery too. She's made out of pearls today: her hair, her skin, even her perfect, rosy lips are the shade and sheen of unspoiled nacre.

My pearl.

God, I've been stupid.

For more than a week I've been denied her, and if I needed any more proof that I'd fallen in love, I certainly had it after ten sleepless nights and just as many miserable days—unable to work, eat, or even think without her sunny smiles and breathless kisses. My bed, my arms, my days, they all bore the burning imprint of her absence. I felt like she'd gone to the Cotswolds with one of my lungs, or maybe my liver, or maybe all my nerves and nerve endings since I couldn't seem to feel a damn thing without her. Since I felt half dead.

I am walking toward her now, my strides turning into a run, and then she's in my arms, all warm, ripe curves and berry-sweet scent.

She's letting me hold her.

She's pressing her face into my neck, she's letting me kiss her hair, and I'm shaking, I'm shaking like the leaves in the storm outside, as if it's all I can do to hang on. And I realize I'm talking too, talking like I never do, in a nervous, quavery chatter.

"I just arrived and I saw your car and the things for the party and Abby said you'd disappeared and I was searching for you everywhere, and I was about to go outside, but I thought I'd look up here—"

I break off as she pulls back and I see the smudges under her eyes, like she hasn't been sleeping either. Her mouth—though painted perfectly in something pale pink and scrumptious—is pressed together in some kind of struggle. And her eyes, those honey eyes normally so clear and open, are shuttered.

I'm shaking harder now, but even fear and guilt can't stop my Domme instincts; I reach up and brush a thumb along the apple of her cheek, right where the skin goes thin and delicate under her eye. She's wearing some makeup, but not enough to hide this.

"You haven't been sleeping."

"I missed you," she says simply. My heart lifts at this, floats right into my throat, because maybe this means she'll forgive me for missing the exhibition, maybe she'll forgive me for being such a bastard about love.

But her eyes don't open up for me, and strain still pulls at that plush, pink mouth.

Guardedly, I ask, "Is that all?"

She steps away from my touch and my hand hangs there in the air for a moment before I can make myself drop it back to my side. "I started a new kind of therapy this week with Dr. Joy," she says. "Exposure therapy, a type of CBT. It's, um. Intense."

I'm relieved that the answer isn't *because I've been pondering how to break up with you*, but this is a fresh cut on my heart.

New therapy? Something intense enough to give her trouble sleeping? I should know about this, I should have been there to help her. Are things really that fucked between us? That she didn't feel like she could tell me about this and ask me for support?

"Delph, you should have told me. Even if we're apart, I'm always here to help you with anything like that."

She hugs herself again, chafing her arms. She's in a tight, off-the-shoulder white top and a swishy lavender skirt with a pretty silk bow in the back. She looks like she's ready to be fucked over a tea table.

"It's hard," she says after a moment, "because no one can help me. Isn't that just silly? Laughably uneconomical? I'm surrounded with people who want to help me with anything I ask them to, but this is the one thing no one can do on my behalf. No one else can untangle the knots in my mind, no one else can forge new neural links in my brain. It will always and forever be my cross to bear."

I hate this. I hate anything that I can't point to and immediately solve, and I just want to *fix* it for her, I wish I could heal whatever wound this is myself. "I can still be there for you," I point out. "If you're having trouble sleeping, I can hold you, and if being inside your own mind is too hard to bear alone, then I'll bear it with you. I'll stay next to you, I'll keep you safe from everything else."

She takes her lip into her mouth—white edges cutting into soft pink flesh—and a familiar bolt of lust sizzles behind my clit. But I ignore it, still feeling uncertain and now very worried about my Delphine.

"Is this from…is it about what happened?"

It's funny, how we're all so euphemistic about it, when Delphine can be so matter-of-fact and blunt. "The rape?" she clarifies. "Yes, it *is* about that, except it's—it sounds so silly to say out loud, but here it goes, I suppose. I was wearing a lipstick that night. It was called Cherry Tree." Her voice goes a little wobbly when she says the words *Cherry Tree* out loud, but she keeps going. "It was smeared on the mouth of one of my rapists after he kissed me, and the memory of it…" Her voice does falter here, and she blinks back tears.

"It's like it's happening all over again. I can be in a car or watching a movie or in a restaurant, I can be in bright daylight and surrounded by people, but it's like my body doesn't *know* that, it's like I'm still not safe, like I'm—"

I can't listen to this without touching her. I can't. I slide my hands over the dip in her waist and pull her close, like I can prove to her adrenal system that she's safe if only I hold her tight enough.

"It started with the lipstick itself. I couldn't wear it again. I ended up throwing it away. But then I found myself not wearing anything by that brand anymore, and then I started avoiding the lipstick section in stores in case I'd see the brand's logo. Then I started avoiding the *stores* altogether. And then the word *cherry* itself began to bother me, and then the fruit, and then even pictures of the fruit. And it's so silly, you know? So strange and so stupid when I say it out loud, and so I couldn't bear to tell anybody. Not my parents, not Auden. Not even Dr. Joy until just last week."

I remember her red-eyed and forcing smiles in the shower. "That day, the day of your photoshoot—it wasn't a makeup allergy, was it?"

She shakes her head.

"No."

"Fuck, Delph. I'm sorry, if I'd known—"

"You couldn't have known," she interrupts softly. "I didn't want anyone to know. I didn't want to be a bother, and let's face it, I'm already silly enough as it is, without all that bosh about cherries."

I cup her face between my hands. "You," I say firmly, "are not silly at all."

Something flickers in her eyes—something fragile, followed immediately by pain. She flinches and twists out of my touch, her arms going back around herself.

And all along my heart, fresh lacerations gape open.

"Pet," I say beseechingly. "Please."

"We need to talk," she says hollowly. "Before we do anything else, I have to talk to you."

I try to take confidence from the fact that she missed me, that she told me ten days ago she was still mine as long as I wanted her to be. And then I say what I know she needs to hear—what she deserves to hear.

"Delph, about that night, about missing the exhibition. I won't make excuses about the day I'd been having or how much my mother needed me then, because you still deserved better. And I am so, so sorry, you'll never know how sorry, because the last thing I've ever wanted was to hurt you, and my most important job as a Domme is not to let you down and I failed. And I also realized—"

I reach for her hand and press it against my heart. I wait until she drags those big, soft eyes up to mine. "I realized I love you, Delphine Dansey. I was a fool to think I didn't, and when I think of how dismissive I was, how cruel I was when you tried to tell me how you felt, I could tear myself apart with my bare hands."

My heart is hammering against her palm, and it looks like her heart is hammering too—underneath the sleek golden waves, her bare shoulders heave up and down, like she's struggling to breathe.

"I love you," I say, staring into those Old Hollywood eyes, "and I think maybe I've loved you for a long time. Maybe even since you came to stay with me. And I want everything with you—not just kink, not just dates and fun—but love. And even more if you want it—marriage and kids and a second home so the kids can go to some pretentious school I'll hate—anything for you, Delphine. Everything you want, I'll give you."

A welling tear spills out of one of her eyes, followed by another, and then another, streaking so prettily across her cheeks. I lean forward and kiss them.

"I love you," I say again. "Do you think you can forgive me for that night? Do you think you can love me still?"

The salt taste of her tears is still blooming on my lips when she tears herself away.

"Delph—" I say, but she cuts me off.

"I was with someone else," she blurts. "That night. You didn't come and so I played with someone else instead."

And.

And I'm finally cut to death.

All those gashes on my heart, all those shallow wounds, it's nothing compared to this, it's nothing compared to having her words bayonet their way into valves and chambers, feeling her tear off the whole mangled organ from my aorta like fruit from a tree. Every place where I'm soft, where I'm vulnerable—every wall that I've let down for her—everything is mutilated, butchered. Hacked into bruised, pulpy nothing.

She cheated on me.

I've been in agony for days, loving her, pining after her; I only missed the exhibition because I was trying to help someone else—

And she cheated on me.

"Who?" I manage to ask, although what does it matter? It doesn't matter.

"Emily Genovese," she answers, meeting my gaze with one of defiant misery. "She was in town, so I invited her to Justine's. When you didn't show, she offered to take me up on the stage."

Emily Genovese.

Grief—frantic, jealous, painful grief—threatens to swallow me whole.

"What did you let her do to you?" I ask, suddenly and morbidly desperate to know. "Did you go to your parents' to hide yourself from me? To hide marks I didn't give you?"

She's already shaking her head. "She spanked me, Rebecca. Only that. Until the kiss."

I don't want to know. I need to know. "Did you fuck?"

"No." Her voice is thick with tears, but she meets my eyes so I'll know she's telling the truth. "We didn't fuck. No one came. No one even tried to come."

"But you kissed," I say.

"In the lobby, afterwards. She started it, but I—" Delphine looks away now, sucking in a deep breath as if to steel herself into giving me every piece of the horrid puzzle. "I kissed her back, Rebecca. There was a moment when

I knew what was happening, and I chose it anyway. For another few seconds, at least."

I don't think I can breathe. My eyes are hot, my heart is gone, my veins are dry. I'm nothing and I'm dead.

"Why?" I whisper. "For the sin of standing you up? For not saying *I love you*? Why did you get on that stage with her? Let her taste the mouth you knew belonged to me?"

Delphine winces, and she turns away so she's in profile again. "I didn't think you wanted me," she says miserably. "I thought you were embarrassed of me—too embarrassed to show me off to your friends at the club."

This is the literal last thing I would have ever guessed she would say. My mouth is open in shock. "You didn't think *I wanted you*?"

With her profile contrasted against the rain, I can easily see the defensive workings of her jaw, the quivering of her chin. "No, Rebecca. I didn't."

I'm almost sputtering, that's how utterly gobsmacked I am. "You're a fucking *model*, Delphine. You're famous, wealthy, brilliant, beautiful—and you thought *I* didn't want *you*?"

She swallows, looking down at her feet in their ballet flats. "I'm not a model like most people use the word, Rebecca. I have the body I have."

"Yes, a body I've been insatiable for! A body you've made an entire brand about being proud of!"

"It's not like—" She's crying now, tears sliding over her cheeks like rain on the windows. "—It's not like I was completely at peace with my body and then I made the brand. I made the brand because I *wasn't* at peace and I was tired of feeling alone about it all. And it still didn't get any easier—I have to have an assistant moderate my comments on an hourly basis, because people tell me horrible things about myself *every day*. Every day, Rebecca, someone reminds me that the world doesn't think I'm worth anything. Not desire, not respect, not the ability to travel, not decent medical care. So yes, I'm still insecure; so yes, I didn't think you wanted me, or if you did, you were embarrassed by your own attraction."

I don't even have the words for this, that's how nonsensical it is. "We were together publicly, Delphine. Photographed, Instagrammed, Tatlered—everything. I hardly hid you."

"Because you don't care about those things. But it felt like you did care what the people at Justine's thought."

"Delphine, the only reason I hadn't played with you publicly was because I hated the idea of sharing you so soon. I was—" I don't relish admitting this "—jealous. Possessively so. The idea of other people getting to see what was mine made me want to lock you in a tower and breathe fire at anyone who came near. Always, my time and my work and my energy have been at the disposal of someone else—even my mind, *especially* my mind—and I've always been expected to give it all without complaint or reserve. You were the first person who was just for me, the only thing I'd ever had that didn't belong to anyone else. So no, I wasn't eager to share you, but it wasn't because I was ashamed, Delphine. It was because I was so fucking proud to call you mine that I could have died."

And now I am dead. Not of pride, but of pain. Pain she sowed and watered and nurtured into torment. Her and Emily Fucking Genovese.

I press my fingers against my eyelids, trying to press the heat out of my eyes. I feel worse than dead, I feel like I'm *dying*. Because death would be a relief and there's no relief for me here. I'm shredded pulp and jagged bones.

"Rebecca," Delphine says, still not looking at me. "I'm sorry. I know—I know that's not enough, that it could never be enough, but you should know all the same. I'm so sorry it hurts."

Yeah. It hurts me too.

"Do you think…" She stops and then starts again. "I meant what I told you in that text. I'm still yours. If you want me to be."

I could almost laugh. In fact, I do laugh, a short bark that grates its way past my lips.

She finally lifts her eyes to mine. The hurt there—the pain—it almost matches my own.

But I've fallen for those eyes before, and I know where it gets me. I know now what happens when I offer her my love, when I show her where I'm softest, rawest, tenderest—I know what happens when I believe even for a second that I could have something good in my life. Something wonderful. Too wonderful to be true.

I can't be broken. I won't be. She doesn't deserve that, she doesn't deserve my pain, my sadness, my anguish. Those I'll have to save until I'm alone.

So for now: "I don't want you to be mine."

And even that's not enough, so I add emphatically, "In fact, I would like to never see you again."

Her face crumples, but she nods, as if she was expecting it.

"Yes, Rebecca." And she hugs herself once more, crying while the rain cries behind her. A pearl girl in a pearl world.

I don't watch. I turn around and I leave.

I leave her behind.

I walk down the stairs, find my bag, and then go to my car and get in. I'm wet, the world is wet, my face is covered in rain and tears, and yet there's no doubt, no hesitation in what I have to do. I'll call Auden later and explain. Apologize for missing his birthday. But I have to get away from here. I have to get away from *her*.

I put the car into drive and start back toward London.

34

Rebecca

That night, I dream of Göbekli Tepe.

I dream of walking there alone, because it's mine, because it's mine to tend to, except when I step between two stones, I find that I'm not at Göbekli Tepe at all, I'm in the thorn chapel, staring at the altar. And behind the altar is a door.

I'm back at Thornchapel the next morning.

The storm has gone, and with it, the heat, and when I get out of the car, I'm not immediately oppressed by the summer sun. But I barely notice, surprised as I am to see that mine is the only car in the drive. St. Sebastian's junker is gone, as is Delphine's baby blue Aston Martin. And when I get inside, there's no Poe humming to herself in the library, no Becket milling around, no Auden in his office. I don't even see the dog.

I go outside.

My feet know where to take me before my mind does, and I'm on the path to the thorn chapel, picking my way through the mud. I rub at my chest as I walk, my mangled heart giving me trouble.

I was Tea Set Barbie all along.

God, how I loved her.

And this is the worst part of it, the hardest part—even now, I still love her. Even now I want to curl around her, to kiss her, to stare worshipfully at her. To make sure her therapy is going okay and that she feels safe. To give her spanks and pets and orgasms and spoil her until I die.

What a miserable fool I am.

When I get to the thorn chapel, the whole place feels new-washed and vital. Lusty trees rustle their leaves, birds flit everywhere, and the storm has torn off a veritable carpet of roses and berries to walk on. Auden Guest stands in the middle of it, facing the back wall of the chapel while Sir James sits and pants next to him.

I come to stand beside him, and he looks over to me.

"You came back," he says.

"I had a dream," I respond. To which he nods, as if no further explanation is needed. Perhaps it's not.

"Where are the others?" I ask him.

Auden recites a litany of heartache. "Becket has to leave St. Petroc's. Delphine went back to her parents'. St. Sebastian left me, and Proserpina went with him."

"Poe left you too?"

He lifts a shoulder in a shrug, his eyes going back to the altar. "There was a promise. I'm making her keep it. It's complicated."

Doubtless. "So you're alone here."

He bumps my shoulder with his. "No, Quartey. Not alone."

I almost smile at that.

"Did you know," he says, "that in the Celtic calendar, a day starts at dusk? So Lammas started yesterday evening and doesn't end until dusk tonight."

"You're saying it's still Lammas."

"Fitting, isn't it? I told everyone to stay away, and yet here I am, breaking my own edicts."

"Some Thorn King you are," I say.

I feel the moment his mood darkens. "Indeed."

"You tried," I tell him, staring past the altar. "We all know you tried to stop it."

"It didn't matter, did it? It was like Poe said it would be. It was going to do what it was going to do. It wasn't enough."

It wasn't enough. How strange that we could both be standing here, looking at something so terrifying and impossible, and still sound this calm.

"So what do we do now?" I ask him.

He shakes his head. The wind pushes through the trees and tugs at his hair. "I wish I knew."

I wish I did too.

Because behind the altar, there is a door. It's the same door from my dream, and it's undoubtedly the same door Poe and Auden saw.

The same door our parents saw long ago.

The same door Estamond Guest died to close.

And it's open.

**The Thornchapel Quartet concludes in *Door of Bruises*,
coming Halloween 2020.**

Don't miss the conclusion to the Thornchapel Quartet,

DOOR OF BRUISES

coming Halloween 2020!

Acknowledgments

Firstly, this book would not have been possible without the infinite patience of Erica Russikoff, my editor. She cheered me, consoled me, corrected me—and all with her characteristic insight and humor.

I owe a huge debt to Julie Murphy and Nana Malone, for talking me through the rough patches, and another huge debt to Ashley Lindemann for her encouragement and wisdom whenever I decided to tantrum about the rough patches in the book instead.

I also owe a profound debt to Nana, Julie, Vanessa Reyes, and Karen Cundy for helping me make this book as accurate and authentic as it could be.

Writing is never possible alone, and I am extremely grateful to Tessa Gratton, Natalie C. Parker, Sarah MacLean, Kennedy Ryan, Kyla Linde, Nikki Sloane, Becca Mysoor, Kayti McGee, Robin Murphy, and Jean Siska, along with the RITA Writer's Room, for support, advice, and laughter.

I'd be helpless without Serena McDonald, Candi Kane and Melissa Gaston, and also without my wonderful agent team: Rebecca Friedman and the kickass women at Bookcase Literary. And a huge thank you to Nancy Smay of Evident Ink and Michele Ficht for making this book as polished as possible!

And finally, I have to thank you, readers. I know this series is quite the ride, and I am humbled by your willingness to go on it with me.

About the Author

Sierra Simone is a USA Today bestselling former librarian who spent too much time reading romance novels at the information desk. She lives with her husband and family in Kansas City.

Sign up for her newsletter to be notified of releases, books going on sale, events, and other news!

www.thesierrasimone.com
thesierrasimone@gmail.com

Also by Sierra Simone

Thornchapel:

A Lesson in Thorns

Feast of Sparks

Harvest of Sighs

Door of Bruises (coming Halloween 2020)

Misadventures:

Misadventures with a Professor

Misadventures of a Curvy Girl

Misadventures in Blue

The New Camelot Trilogy:

American Queen

American Prince

American King

The Moon (Merlin's Novella)

The Priest Series:

Priest

Midnight Mass: A Priest Novella

Sinner

Co-Written with Laurelin Paige

Porn Star

Hot Cop

The Markham Hall Series:

The Awakening of Ivy Leavold

The Education of Ivy Leavold

The Punishment of Ivy Leavold

The Reclaiming of Ivy Leavold

The London Lovers:

The Seduction of Molly O'Flaherty

The Persuasion of Molly O'Flaherty

The Wedding of Molly O'Flaherty